Dedication

Raymond T. Robinson

Acknowledgements

Special thanks to the following people for their invaluable help in the preparation of this book: Sarah Cypher, Dan Janik, Helen Babalis, and especially Katrina Robinson. I would also like to thank my family for the undying support they give to all my writing endeavors.

Charlie No Face

1

Everything in my life changed, just like that. I mean everything. This summer was supposed to be the best time of my short little life. And up until the middle of July, the summer of '59 was. But then everything changed. My dad started acting, well, different. He wasn't completely "there" some of the time, and I didn't know what to think of it. And on top of that, there was the whole thing with Charlie No Face.

Back in May, my life looked pretty good. It was spring. Baseball was in the air. And the season smelled great. Dad and I have always had baseball in common. He was a first baseman in high school—a pretty good one, I'm told. When he was a senior, he even got to play in the Western Pennsylvania High School Championship game at Forbes Field, home of our beloved Bucs.

"It was pretty amazing," said Dad. We sat together on the front steps, watching the cars go by. It was one of those warm nights in late spring when the days are so long, you think they might go on forever. "I was pretty overwhelmed when I stepped out of the dugout, knowing that I was standing on the same field where the best players in the National League played. But when I saw your mother in the stands, I calmed right down. Of course," he explained, "she wasn't your mother at the time; she was only my girlfriend. But I knew that someday we'd get married; I just knew it."

It seemed odd to hear him talk about my mother like she was a young girl, but she actually was. And he was just a boy. That was pretty hard to believe since Dad was so old now. Not sure how old exactly, but let's just say that when we celebrated his birthday, we didn't fill the cake with candles anymore. There are just three: one for the past, one for the present, and one for the future. That should tell you something.

"It was a game for the ages," he said with a laugh. "I got the first hit for our team, a sharp line drive right up the middle. I scored when my friend Bobby—you know, Mr. Turner—hit a fly ball that the right fielder misplayed into a triple." Dad stopped talking, just to let the scene settle into my mind.

"Then what happened?"

"I don't recall exactly."

I laughed and said, "Oh, yes you do."

"I guess so. We lost the game 7-1. My run was our only score."

"I'll bet Mom was disappointed."

Dad looked at me and a smile crossed his face. "No, your mom wasn't disappointed at all. When I came out of the ballpark, there she was. She gave me a big hug, which I didn't expect at all, and told me how proud she was of me. When I got on the bus with the other guys, she was still standing there, smiling and waving."

I loved that part. I imagined this pretty girl in a white dress squinting slightly into the sun, a broad warm smile on her face, her auburn hair blowing gently in the late afternoon breeze, waving and cheering for my dad, her future husband.

"Cool, Dad."

"Yes, it was cool," he said.

Dad didn't talk about Mom very often, so when he was in the mood to talk about his baseball career, it was a chance for me to hear old stories about her, too.

"Yeah, after the game we went to Jine's down on Route 18 to celebrate, even though we lost. Me and your mom, Mr. Turner and his girlfriend, Cookie, and some of the other guys. Your mom was a great dancer. We'd get the jukebox going with some Sinatra, and she'd be out on the floor in no time. I couldn't really dance a lick, but she'd take me by the hand and drag me out there anyway. I'd stand in one place while she floated around me, just like a butterfly, gentle and light and beautiful."

Dad stopped and stared.

"What would happen after that?" I asked.

"I shouldn't tell you this, but we'd go down to River Road and race our cars. Your mom would tie her scarf around my neck, kiss me on the cheek, tell me to be careful, and away I'd go."

"Did you win?"

"I don't even remember," he said with a faraway look, as if some other

2

memory had taken over while I was still enjoying this one.

Looking at Dad's face—especially his eyes—how he'd brightened, how the lines in his forehead had softened and the corners of his mouth relaxed. Seeing his face was as close as I could get to seeing her myself. If she could make him look like that, she must have really been something.

One time, he dug his old mitt—the one he used in that big game—out for me, but on my hand, it hung to my knees, making me look like a lobster boy. So much for being a first baseman. So he bought me my own glove. I was seven. It was a Duke Snider model. I didn't know who Duke Snider was, but Dad assured me he was a great Dodger player. It took almost two years of playing catch before the leather softened and I could fold my hand around the ball; by then I could catch almost anything. Dad would throw the ball as high as he could, and I would circle around under it, catching it almost every time. Other times, he'd bounce it along the ground, and I would go down on one knee, making sure it didn't squirt between my legs. If it was coming fast and furious, though, I'd turn my head and close my eyes; I didn't want it to hit me in the face like my friend Donnie, whose nose bled so much, he had to hold his head back for about an hour.

"Now, Jackie, just keep your eye on it; it won't hurt you." Easy for him to say: it wasn't his nose in the bull's eye. After a while, it got easier and instead of throwing the ball along the ground, Dad got out one of his old baseball bats and started hitting the ball to me in the backyard. That scared me to death at first, but then it didn't seem so worrisome. I wasn't afraid of getting hit in the face anymore.

He wanted me to learn how to field the ball first because he thought kids didn't pay enough attention to what he called "the fundamentals." I just wanted to swing the bat, hit the ball, and watch it fly, but he taught me to be patient about hitting and to take my turn in the field first.

My hands were still small when I was nine, and I needed to throw with four fingers, but even so, I threw the ball straight and hard. When it popped into my dad's glove, he smiled and said, "Atta boy." I smiled, too, and slugged my glove with my fist, just like the big leaguers.

We lived in Ewing Park, a part of Ellwood City, Pennsylvania, that had a bunch of baseball fields, a community swimming pool and a giant wooded picnic area. In our big backyard we had a gnarled sycamore tree that threw shade across the whole lawn.

When Dad and I weren't playing catch, my friend Brian came by to play whiffle-ball home-run-derby. To get a home run, you had to hit the ball on the fly across our yard and over Mrs. Sanders' yard to the next driveway. We weren't supposed to hit the ball across Mrs. Sanders' yard because it might hit the electric wire that ran from her house to the garage. But we didn't care about that. Every time we hit the wire, we hid behind our garage so she couldn't find us when she'd come stomping to the back door. Sometimes we hit the wire on purpose just because she would get so upset. It was usually pretty funny, except for the time she told my dad what we had done, and he lowered the boom on us. In no time, though, we were back at it again: playing ball, hitting the wire, hiding from old lady Sanders, and having a blast.

Of course, whenever I wanted to *really* practice hitting, Dad would pitch hard ball at the Triangle, a field across the street where there was an old, abandoned firehouse. I didn't have to worry about old lady Sanders there.

By the time I was nine, Dad had stopped pitching underhand to me. By that time, I had my own bat. It was a Willie Mays, and I tried as best I could to stand like the "Say Hey Kid." I crouched and leaned back a little on my right foot, cocked my knee, and turned my left leg just a little so that it was almost pointing at my dad. I held my bat straight up, my fists close to my chest, and wagged the bat head just a little. I looked great, but I couldn't hit anything when I stood like that. Dad finally convinced me to just stand comfortably.

"Relax. Don't swing at the first pitch. Get a feel for what the pitcher's throwing." This was hard for me to do when he served up a pitch that, as the ball seemed to grow as big as a pumpkin. I knew I could hit it, and hit it a mile, so I'd swing my whole body around in a corkscrew, but all I hit was air.

"Okay, let's get serious," Dad said. Then I'd start hitting. I loved the crack of the bat when I made solid contact with the ball. It felt solid and convincing. Sometimes he threw the ball harder just to see what I would do with it. Usually, I'd miss it completely, but every once in a while, I'd connect and send a line drive soaring right past his head.

"Good going, J!" I knew he was impressed; otherwise, he wouldn't have called me J.

The following year, when I was ten, I went out for Little League. I'll never forget those tryouts. There must have been a million kids with numbers on their backs. All the coaches were lined up along the first base benches, and everyone had three cuts at the ball before going out into the field with all the others. Brian came with me.

When it was my turn at the plate, I heard Dad's voice telling me to relax my hands, get settled, keep my front foot back a little, and lean into the plate. Although my heart was pounding, I felt ready, and when the first pitch came, I swung hard and hit a high fly ball down the left field line. I hit a sharp grounder up the middle on the second pitch and a soft liner to right on the third. I felt pretty good when I went out into the field.

Brian wasn't as lucky. The first pitch hit him, so he got to start again, but he became nervous. He missed the next one, then hit a grounder to the pitcher, and finally popped the ball up to the shortstop on his final swing.

"That's okay, buddy," I said, but he didn't even answer when he came out to left field. "That's okay," I said again, "you had some good cuts. They'll know you can do better. Don't worry about it." I patted him on the butt just like the big leaguers.

"Geez-o-man," said Brian. "I can't believe it. I been practicing for weeks." He kicked the grass, and just as he did, a line drive came his way; he held out his glove and snagged it.

"There you go, Brian! I know they saw that."

"Do you think that'll matter?" he asked.

"Sure it will. They need kids who can catch just as much as they need kids who can hit."

"I sure hope so," said Brian, punching his glove with his fist and looking sort of nervous.

Good old Brian. Brian and I had been friends since kindergarten. I remember his first day in school. His parents had moved to Ellwood from New Castle, and there he stood, clutching his mother's leg at the door to Miss Leslie's class. When Miss Leslie knelt down to greet him, Brian buried his head in his mother's dress and cried. Nancy Franklin, one of the girls in the class, said, "What a fraidy cat!" and a few other kids pointed and laughed.

Miss Leslie turned and gave us all her sternest look. I stopped immediately. I didn't want to be put in the corner for recess again. Anyway, I felt kind of bad for the new kid. Nancy was right, though; he was a fraidy cat.

During recess, headed for the jungle gym, assuming Miss Leslie would eventually straighten things out.

Next thing I knew, she was calling my name. "Jackie! Could you please come here for a moment?" I went to her, my eyes bugging out for fear I was in trouble. "Jackie," she said, "this is Brian. He's the new boy in our class that I've been telling you about." I guess she had told us some new kid was coming, but I hadn't paid any attention.

"Oh," I said. Miss Leslie just looked at me.

"Well, Jackie, can you say 'hi' to Brian?"

"Hi," I said, head down. Brian wasn't doing much better. I could barely see his face through the folds of his mother's dress.

"C'mon now, Brian," his mother said. "This nice little boy is talking to you." Brian wasn't at all impressed.

"Brian just moved here all the way from New Castle," said Miss Leslie. I'd heard of New Castle and thought I might have gone there once with my dad, but it could just as easily have been the moon, for all I cared.

"Oh," I said. Miss Leslie looked a more than a little discouraged.

Then Miss Leslie smiled at me the way she smiled when she knew she wasn't getting through. "Brian is moving into your neighborhood, Jackie." I still didn't say anything. "I thought you could help him out today since he's new and all. I thought maybe you could walk with him to school tomorrow, since he will be living right by you," she said. This was not something I wanted to do, but Miss Leslie's smile made me say I would. "Great!" said Miss Leslie, and Brian's mother became very excited. "Did you hear that, Brian? This little boy is going to be your friend." Now they had definitely gone too far. Why would I want to be friends with a kid who wore his mother's dress for a hat?

"Why don't you show him around, Jackie," Miss Leslie encouraged. I took Brian by the arm and pulled, but he just cried louder and held onto his mother's leg. I looked at Miss Leslie as if to say, 'You can't really be serious.' Miss Leslie finally took pity on me and helped remove Brian from his mother's leg. Together, we walked him around the room.

Brian's head was all sweaty and his face was fire engine red. He was actually kind of scary-looking, like he was a mutant tomato.

"Here's the story rug," I said.

"Good, Jackie," said Miss Leslie, "let's keep going."

"And here's where we talk about the weather and what day it is and other stuff. And this is the cloak room where you can stick your boots and stuff, but you can't touch anyone else's stuff when you're in there. And here's the potty. Got to remember: One at a time, and wash your hands."

I was on a roll and Brian had actually stopped crying, although he still had that thing going on in his throat that sounded like exploding hiccups. "These are the puzzles and coloring books, and over there's letters that you can stick on the cloth board." I could tell that Brian wasn't really listening. He was looking everywhere for his mother, who had snuck out like a thief in the night.

Poor Brian. I didn't think Miss Leslie would cotton to him grabbing onto her leg like he did his mother's. Brian tried, and I was right.

"Brian," she said, firmly but calmly, "we don't do that in class; we all look after ourselves, and if we need help, we turn to one of our neighbors, like Jackie here." I thought for a moment that Brian was going to grab onto my leg and I would have to drag him around the room all morning until his mother came back, but, thankfully, Brian had pulled his sorry little self together and was breathing almost normally.

He looked at me. "Hi, I'm Brian," he said, as if he noticed me for the very first time.

"I know," I said, "I'm Jackie."

I didn't give the idea of being friends much of a chance that first day. He seemed like such a baby, but actually Brian was okay, especially when he invited me to his house and I saw all the baseball cards he had. He even had a couple of Willie Mays. That's when I figured Brian might really be okay, since he was hooked into the national pastime.

He had a full-sized ball glove, too. We tried playing catch, but neither of us was big enough to manage the baseball mitt. Mostly we threw the ball in the general direction of each other and used our gloves to protect our heads. I was impressed by how hard Brian tried. He wasn't really a baby after all. He was just having one of those days. I guess you just never know about people.

Brian and I were both glad when tryouts were over, and we nearly went crazy when the *Ledger* arrived the next day. We tore open the newspaper to the sports page where the draft results were listed. Brian was picked by the Lions, the worst team in the league.

"That's why they picked you, Brian; they need some good players."

"You think so," he said.

"I know so." On the other hand, I was picked by the mighty Kiwanis, winners of the league championship for two consecutive years.

"Man, you got picked by Kiwanis!" said Brian. "That's fantastic!"

"Just lucky," I said. But when Dad came home, I almost jumped out of my skin running to his car.

"Dad, Dad, guess what? I got picked by Kiwanis!"

"You're kidding me, J boy!"

"No, I'm not."

"That is great! I told you they'd be looking for you."

It was great being drafted by Kiwanis, but I still had to make the team. Team tryouts lasted about a week, and every day the coach took a couple of kids aside, put his arm around them, talked with them in low tones, patted them on their backs, and away they'd go in tears. The "cuts" were awful; I had a stomach ache every day, wondering if I would be the next to go. Coach said he planned on keeping only two ten-year-olds this year. I hoped some of the other kids would mess up so I'd have a better chance. It came down to the last day, and my friend Richie and me were the only ones left for the final ten-year-old spot on the team.

Coach took Richie and me aside just like all the others. I thought for sure Richie would get picked. He was bigger than me, for one, and in a practice game the other day, he got a hit. I didn't, although I made two good catches in the outfield.

"Boys," said Coach, "this is a very tough decision; I like both of you and I think both of you are going to be good ball players, but I've got a decision to make, and I have to do it today." He looked at Richie. "Son," he said, "I'm gonna go with Jackie this year, but I don't want you to give up on yourself." Coach said some other stuff, but Richie was crying by then, and I don't think he heard a word. I was feeling light as a feather, knowing I would be a member of the team. I was so glad it was me and not Richie.

"Welcome aboard, young man," said Coach. All the guys cheered and pushed me around and knocked my ball cap off. When I turned to look, I saw Richie walking off the field alone.

"Good luck!" I called, but I don't think he heard me.

Ten-year-olds didn't get to play much, so I rode the bench most of that summer, but I did get to wear my baseball cap everywhere I went. Bright red brim that I bent into a perfect arc, light grey cap on top, big red "K". When I went to the playground or the swimming pool, kids would ask, "You play for Kiwanis?" I'd say, "Yeah," and they'd shake their heads, impressed. They'd offer to carry my swim towel or baseball bat for me. And sometimes, if they didn't offer, well, I'd make them, just for the heck of it.

The summer of '59, Brian and I were eleven, and both of us were starters. Brian played third base for the Lions, and I played centerfield for Kiwanis. We were loaded with great players, and I was by no means one of them. Our twelve-year-olds were unbelievable. Ray at shortstop hit everything you threw at him; Zeke on the mound was impossible to hit; Biff behind the plate swatted a home run almost every time he came up to bat. Believe me, I was just glad to be in the starting lineup. I practiced hard, ran hard, made all the catches, hit the ball (from time to time), and tried not to make "mental errors," as Coach liked to call them. When I was ten, Billy Macintosh didn't even see a fly ball hit right at him because he was picking his nose. Coach took him out of the game because he had made a mental error, although I wondered if Coach took Billy out mainly because he was being so disgusting. Anyway, I didn't want to make any mental errors. I always tried to stay alert, and I rarely picked my nose.

We were a "force to be reckoned with," as Dad would say. I didn't know exactly what that meant, but it sounded impressive.

Wouldn't you know that our first game of the year was against the Lions. Brian and I walked to the field together, although we didn't say much. It felt weird being on opposite sides. I mean, we fought a lot and argued about baseball cards, but we never wished the other one would lose at anything.

"Where are you in the lineup?" I asked. He barely raised his head.

"Ninth," he said. Everyone knew that the ninth batter was the worst hitter in the lineup. "How 'bout you?" he asked.

"Sixth," I said, which actually wasn't much better.

"Is Zeke pitching today?" said Brian.

"Yep."

"Geez-o-man," said Brian. There was a long pause.

"Look, Brian," I said, "don't even try to hit his fastball. There's no point. But I'll tell you one thing if you promise not to tell anyone else."

"What's that?" said Brian.

"You gotta promise," I said. "I mean it. This is important. If I get caught telling you this, they'll kick me off the team for sure."

"Okay, okay!" said Brian. "So what is it?"

"When Zeke throws his fastball, he always throws it right over the top, you know what I mean?"

"Yeah," said Brian.

"But when he throws his curve, his arm comes down a little, like a three-quarters angle. Watch for it. That's gonna be your only chance of hitting him."

When I ran out to centerfield at the beginning of the game, I felt like I was running across the top of the world. I leaned down into my crouch, the rickety old snow fence behind me, hands on my knees, eyes forward, as Zeke got ready to throw the first pitch. I snuck a peek at the stands, and there was Dad smiling. He pumped his fist once and clapped his hands. I raised my hand to the brim of my cap.

Zeke was so psyched up that he threw the first pitch right past Biff into the backstop netting. After that, though, it was a thing of beauty. Bang, bang, bang, he struck them all out. Ray got us started in the bottom of the first, launching a dinger over the left field fence with one on, and just like that we were ahead.

When I ran out into the field again, I tipped my hat to Brian and he nodded. It was funny how we couldn't really be friends during the game. We had to pretend, at least, that we were enemies. I had to admit it was much easier for me to tip my hat to him, knowing we were winning. Zeke took them apart again in the second inning, and before I knew it, I was up to start us off in the bottom of the second.

I stepped into the batter's box, looked down to Coach at third base to see if he had any signs; he swiped his cap and left arm and then leaned forward and clapped twice. I looked at him for a long time. I couldn't tell what all that meant, and I tried to remember what he told us before the game. I thought he had to be standing outside the coach's box and leaning with his hands on his knees to signal a bunt, but I never expected him to do all that other stuff. I stepped out of the batter's box, swung the bat a few times, and looked at him again. He cupped his hands over his mouth and called, "Swing away, Jackie!"

Okay then, I thought. How dumb can I be? I swung my bat a couple more times, looked down at Brian hunched over at third, calling to his pitcher, "Hum, baby, hum, no batter, no batter," and then I looked at Dad who called, "You can do it, J!" That's when my legs started to feel like mush and butterflies started circling my stomach. Which would it be? No batter? Or, I can do it? What would Dad think if I struck out? Did Brian really mean what he was saying? I was always a better hitter than him; that's why he batted ninth and I batted sixth, right? That's when I also noticed that my batting helmet was a size too small. My ears felt like someone was smashing them into my skull. My hands were sweaty, so I stepped out of the batter's box again.

"Time!" called the umpire. "You okay?" he asked in a low voice so no one could hear.

But the Lion's catcher, Angel, heard him. "You gonna cry, little Jackie boy? Gonna poop your pants?"

"Okay, okay," said the umpire. "Ready to go?"

I shook my head and stepped back in. The pitcher, Granger Popoff, looked like he was standing two feet away. He wound up, and I wasn't even set before the ball whizzed past my chest. "Steeerike!" called the umpire.

"Hang tough, Jackie, hang tough!" called Coach.

I stepped back in again and took a deep breath. Remember to bend your legs a little; wag your bat a little, too, so you're ready to swing; step towards the pitcher: everything Dad had told me. The next pitch was in my eyes, and I fell back in the dirt. Pretend you're down in the Triangle and Dad is pitching; just let it happen. Stop thinking! I thought. By then the next pitch was past me. "Steerike two!" Doggone it! I pounded my bat on the plate and took a couple more practice swings, then I rocked the bat back into place and settled my gaze on Popoff. He wound up again; I crouched another inch before he delivered the ball. This one was right over the plate. I lunged at it and got just a piece, fouling it into the backstop. Wow, I almost hit it! I almost hit it in the first game of the season! My first game ever, I almost hit the ball!

I leaned in again and took my stance. My legs weren't wobbly anymore, and my hands had stopped sweating. My breathing was even and calm. Popoff wound up again, and this time he served up a slow sweeping curveball out over the corner of the plate. Swing at it! I thought. I stepped into the pitch, leaning out over the plate to get it. I felt the bat hit the ball, and out of the corner of my eye I could see it heading towards right field. A pop fly! I started running to first as hard as I could just in case the right fielder dropped the ball, but when I rounded first and looked up, the right fielder was standing at the fence with his back to the infield. The ball was gone! As in over-the-fence gone! I couldn't believe it. I was jumping out of my skin, but I knew not to show it. I just continued my stride, head down like the Mick, hitting all the bases; when I rounded third, I heard Brian say, "Way to go." I looked up, and there was Dad standing and applauding me as I headed for home. Wow. If my life ended right then, I would have been satisfied, because I would have accomplished everything I had ever wanted to accomplish.

We won 7-0. Zeke threw a one-hitter. A one-hitter. Brian came to bat for the fourth time in the top half of the last inning. Zeke had thrown him nothing but heat the first three times he came to the plate, and poor Brian hadn't touched him yet. This time wasn't much different. Zeke got two quick strikes on Brian. Then I saw Biff, our catcher, put down two fingers, and I knew he was calling for the curveball. I stood straight up and called as loud as I could, "Let's go, let's go!" I got Brian's attention. And then before I went back down in my crouch I pretended I was stretching my arm and brought it down in a three-quarters motion. Brian got it. Zeke went into his wind-up and the pitch was on its way. Brian waited, and when he saw it break, he started to swing. He hit a little nubber between Zeke and Al, our first basemen. Both of them ran to the ball. When Al reached it and turned to throw, no one was covering first base. Brian had beaten it out. He got a hit off of Zeke and broke up the no-hitter. Brian looked at me in centerfield and touched the brim of his cap. I looked at him and then turned away. My father was watching all of this. He smiled at me. Zeke struck out the next three batters and the game was over.

Brian and I felt pretty good. I shook his hand after the game and said, "Way to go."

Brian said, "I'd been setting Zeke up the whole game; I was just waiting for the right moment."

I knocked his hat off his head.

"I could have sworn you had your eyes closed when you hit the dinger," said Brian.

"Just shows you I can hit better with my eyes closed than you can with them open." He laughed. Actually, I wasn't kidding.

Charlie No Face

2

Baseball season was under way! It was a perfect time. Memorial Day was coming, and school would soon be over for the summer. Even neater than that, my dad was on vacation. "I've decided to take a little time off," he said when I found him home one day after school.

"That's great, Dad, is someone else gonna do your job while you're on vacation?"

"No, J, it doesn't really work that way. Your job is your job; no one else can do it for you. I'm just, well, let's say I'm taking a much-deserved break."

He was a "sales rep" for a bunch of different companies, which meant he sold things. Lately he was selling new gas-powered lawnmowers. He even had some electric ones that were really cool because they didn't make a sound when they ran. Of course, you had to be careful not to run over the cord or you could fry yourself just as quick as anything. Our basement was usually full of lawnmowers. He could fit two in the back of the Rambler station wagon. "You have to show them how it works," he said, "that's the best way to sell something; show them that anyone can do it." He tried out the newest models on our own backyard, sometimes on Mrs. Sanders' yard, too.

"I must say, that is a fine cut," Mrs. Sanders would say.

"They're the best!" Dad said, always excited about anything he was selling.

For a long time he sold bleachers for football fields, but he had to travel too much so he gave that up. Then he sold refrigerators, but he didn't like working in a store.

"I don't like answering to someone else all the time," he said. "I want to call my own shots."

"Don't you have a boss, Dad?" I asked.

"Yes, but not one that's looking over my shoulder all the time; mostly I'm my own boss." I liked the idea that my dad was his own boss. He was really important, like no one could tell him what to do.

"Whadaya mean, he's his own boss?" Brian asked, his face all scrunched up in confusion. His father sold cars at McElwain's Oldsmobile in town. "My dad has a sales manager he answers to. Everyone has a boss."

"Does the president have a boss?" I said.

"Your dad's not the president, is he, Jackie?"

"Don't be a jerk. You know what I mean. Not everyone has a boss; some people are above that sort of thing."

"Are you saying my dad's not important?" said Brian, his hackles up. "Huh?"

"No, that's not what I'm saying."

"You better not be, because my dad's job is a much bigger deal than your dad's! Cars are more important than lawnmowers!"

I just looked at Brian. What a moron, I thought. "Yes, Brian, cars are about the most important thing in the world."

"Told you," he said.

Anyway, Dad was a busy man, and he *was* his own boss. He traveled to stores as far away as Pittsburgh, trying to get the owners to order his mowers because, he explained, "That's what people want and need. They're running to the suburbs as fast as they can. Everyone wants a piece of land to call his own. It's the American dream. And what's he going to grow on that land? That's right, grass, and lots of it. And what's he need to keep that sacred ground in tip-top shape? Yes, a lawnmower. But not just any lawnmower. Not a push mower, that's for sure. Those days are over. He wants what every suburbanite wants—a power mower."

I could tell he was good at it because of how he talked to people. Not just some people, but everyone, whether he knew them or not. He always smiled, stuck out his hand, and had something friendly to say: "My, my, what about this weather," or, "Haven't seen you in a while, how are you doing?" or "Keep up the good work," even when it wasn't clear what work he meant. And, if he couldn't remember the man's name, he just called him "Mac" with a great big smile, which seemed to work just fine, because no one ever complained, and everyone smiled back. When I watched him, I thought that he could sell furnaces in the Sahara!

Sometimes in the morning, because Dad had to hit the road early, I went to Mrs. Keeley's across the street and waited about a half hour or so before walking the four blocks to Ewing Park Elementary School. I liked Mrs. Keeley, but I hated going to her house. She had three daughters. The place was a zoo. Take yesterday, for example.

"Good morning, Jackie!" Mrs. Keeley said as she opened the front door. "Pancakes are on the table." Mmmm, that was the good part. Mrs. Keeley sure knew how to make tasty pancakes. Sometimes I got there a little early and sat in the kitchen just watching her get things ready, just watching her move around, I guess. In the last few months I noticed that Mrs. Keeley was, well, pretty in an old sort of way. Her hair was pulled up in a bun and her lips were all red and her eyes kind of sparkled when she looked at me. And sometimes when she still had her PJs on, I could swear that nothing was holding things together underneath, if you get what I mean. Unfortunately, Mrs. Keeley's three daughters, Kim, who was eight, and the twins, Nancy and Gail, who were a whole year younger than me, just drove me nuts.

"MOM! Nancy's still in the bathroom and she won't give me my hairbrush!" bellowed Kim, almost every day.

"Oh, shut up, you little baby!" snarled Nancy.

"MOM! Nancy's being mean!"

"Gail, take that top off right this minute," screeched Nancy.

"It's a free country. I can wear anything I want," Gail said with her nose turned up.

"MOM! Nancy pinched me!" yelled Gail.

"Girls, girls! Stop it! Jackie's here; what's he going to think with you acting like this? Be nice to each other!" Mrs. Keeley pleaded and then smiled at me. "Would you like some more bacon, Jackie?"

"Sure, that would be..." But then it started again.

"MOM!"

It was even worse when they came downstairs.

"Hi Jackie, how are you today!" Gail said in her sing-song voice. I didn't answer, but she still tried. "Is that a new shirt?"

"No."

"I've never seen it before."

"So."

"Ooooooo, Gail likes Jackie! Gail likes Jackie!" cried Kim and Nancy, making smooching noises.

With that, Gail burst into tears. "MOM!"

"Gail and Jackie sittin' in a tree..."

"MOM!"

"...k-i-s-s-i-n-g..."

"MOM!

"...first comes love, then comes marriage..."

"MOM! Please make them stop!"

"...then comes little Jackie in a baby carriage!" Gail stomped up the stairs, ran into her room, and slammed the door behind her. WHAM!

"Girls, girls!" Mrs. Keeley said. "I'm so sorry, Jackie. They're just a little wound-up today. Girls!"

When Mrs. Keeley turned away, I made a fist at Nancy and Kim and mouthed, I'm going to kill you.

See what I mean? A total zoo.

If Dad was going to be late, I had to stay at Mrs. Keeley's after school, too. Every day her daughters complained about their piano lessons with Mrs. Mok. Actually, I could see their point about Mrs. Mok.

"Pay attention! Read the music! Follow my lead!"

She was mean. She made them play the same notes over and over again for no apparent reason. They went up and down the piano from one end to the other; it didn't sound like any song I'd ever heard, and almost every time she came the girls were crying before she left. What was the point? Worse, she tried to get me to take lessons with the girls.

"Jackie, you have wonderful hands," said Mrs. Mok. "Why don't you try a few lessons? I'm sure you'd enjoy it, right, girls?" The girls just stared at her, deep frowns creasing their faces.

"No thank you, Mrs. Mok. My father won't let me."

"He won't!" exclaimed Mrs. Mok, her eyebrows raised, glasses slipping down on her nose and her mouth drawn up in a perfect oval. "For heaven's sake, why not?"

"Well, you see, my father's a very religious man, and he says there's no mention of the piano in the Bible, so I'm not allowed to play. Wish I could, but, you understand." She never asked me again.

Dad's vacation meant a welcome vacation for me as well: no Keeley girls to deal with.

All of this made me pretty happy.

At the end of Dad's first week of vacation, he woke me up bright and early. He told me to get dressed quickly and eat my Cheerios, because we had work to do. So, I did what he told me, and then we headed out in his car.

"What's up?" I asked.

"You'll see," he said, but I already had a hunch. When we crossed the railroad tracks, I could see the lumberyard just up the way.

"Hi, Judd," he said to the man at the counter.

"Hi, Bill," Judd said back, and then they talked for a bit while I looked in all the nail bins and checked out the hammers hanging on the wall. Pretty soon we headed out the door and across the lot to the warehouse stacked to the sky with all kinds of wood.

"Take a deep breath, J," and together we breathed in the sweet smell. "There're a lot of houses piled up in there just waiting to be built," he said.

Dad always bought pine when he was making a stool or a table for the house. "Easy to work with," he explained. Sometimes he bought long boards of knotty pine that he used to panel the walls in our house, then he'd paint the whole thing with this clear varnish stuff that made all the knots and grain stand out like they were in 3-D. He said he loved that natural look.

Mostly I stood around and handed tools to him. He'd say things to me like, "Measure twice and cut once," and I'd say, "Okay," wondering what that meant exactly, and why it was so important. He stuck pencils behind his ear, something I tried but couldn't do, and his hair was always full of sawdust from the table saw he used to cut things. God, it was loud! Like a hornets nest inside your head. I had to plug my ears after he told me to stand back just before turning it on. "Don't want you to lose a finger," he'd say, which made sense to me.

But today he was looking for something a little different.

"Couple of eight-by-ten sheets of plywood, Gus," he said. I didn't have any idea what he was going to do with plywood. Gus helped us lash the sheets to the top of our Rambler. I held the rope tight, just like Dad said, while we drove slowly home.

He immediately disappeared into the cellar with his plywood, all secretive, and said, "Fine enough," when I asked if I could go to Brian's. "Take your time," he added. I headed to Brian's with my shoebox full of baseball cards. I'd been collecting cards for over a year. Dad gave me a nickel every couple of days, and Brian would get one from his dad; then we'd go to Nick's Snack Bar on the corner and buy a pack of cards each.

"What're you hoping for?" Nick asked as we leaned on the front counter. "Mantle, Mays, Musial, Williams?"

Both Brian and I answered, "Yep!" and laughed.

Beyond the counter, we could see our friend Tommy inside playing pinball. Tommy was there all the time. We took our places beside him, trying not to bump the machine. The silver pinball was shooting every which way and bells were going off like crazy. Tommy flicked his wrist with ease and the flipper sent the ball back up to the top, racking up even more points.

"Hey, man," Tommy said, his skinny body hunched over the pinball machine. Tommy looked like a paper straw with a beak. He had great big brown eyes that bugged out of his head when he got excited and a horsey-looking mouth with way too many teeth. His belt always had a few extra holes in it because his pants never fit. All his weight was in his feet, which looked like miniature barges you might see on the Ohio River. Tommy was a pinball fanatic. He spent more time at Nick's than he did at home. And if he ran out of nickels for the machines, he'd go home and steal money out of his mother's purse. Sometimes he brought a whole quarter back, enough for Tommy to play all afternoon. Once he came back with a dollar bill. "I got paper!" he hollered. "I got paper!" I told him he was going to H-E-double-hockey-sticks for all his stealing. "Okay with me if they've got pinball down there," he said. He had the touch, and he knew how to shake that machine without ever tilting it.

I had to give it to Tommy, he stunk at every outdoor sport I could name. He couldn't throw a ball straight to save his life, but he was great at pinball, and he made the most of it. He was there so often that sometimes Nick had to send him home at the end of the day.

"Tommy!" Nick called. "Your mother wants you home! Pronto!"

"One more game," said Tommy.

"It's your funeral," Nick replied.

"Hey, Tommy, how's it going?" I asked.

"Look for yourself, I'm up five games already and I've only been on the machine for twenty minutes!"

"Way to go," said Brian.

Brian and I were minor leaguers compared to Tommy when it came to pinball. We played, but we weren't all that good. And Tommy made sure we knew it. "Man, you guys stink," he'd say if we didn't win every time. Sometimes I wanted to tilt Tommy with one good shot to the nose. When he was away from pinball, though, he was mostly okay.

Tommy was leaning hard to one side, trying to save the ball; he double-flipped it back to the top again, but it shot right back down the middle and he missed it. Tommy stepped back from the machine before pulling the trigger on the next ball.

"Hey, guess what?" he said.

"What?" I said.

"I've got to talk to you about something."

"What's that?" asked Brian.

Tommy looked around to make sure no one was listening. He started to laugh.

"What is it, Tommy?" I asked.

"You guys are gonna die when I tell you this."

"So tell us already," said Brian.

Tommy scanned the snack bar again. Two old guys were sitting in a booth playing chess, and Nick was waiting on some kid who wanted a root beer popsicle.

"How would you guys like to go see Charlie No Face?"

"Yeah, you're kiddin', right?" said Brian.

Charlie No Face was the local boogeyman, monster man, or whatever you want to call it. His face got burned off somehow when he was a little boy, and it turned him into a madman who hunted children and ate dead animals along the road. No one looked right at his face, because it was so ugly, that sometimes people, mostly girls, I suppose, would faint. And if they fainted, who knew what old Charlie would do to them.

Charlie lived way out in the country somewhere. All the high school kids went out by the carload looking for Charlie, like hunters might look for a bear. Never during the day, though, because Charlie couldn't go out in the sunlight. He turned vampirish in the daylight and foamed at the mouth. The sun made his skin peel right off, too, so he didn't go out for fear of leaving a bloody trail that people could follow back to the cave where he lived. That's why he only went out at night.

And he showed up in the oddest places. Tommy told us that once his mother found him eating out of their garbage can. When he saw her, she said he raised a long machete over his head and, just when he was about to cut her head off, she screamed and he hurried off, dragging his bad leg.

Tommy's eyes always bugged out when he told us that story. "I swear," he said, "I swear!" Brian's father told Brian that they found his cave once when they were boys. Charlie wasn't there, but there were three goats slaughtered on the ground and a ton of bones piled in a pyramid shape; they figured it was some kind of devil worship, so they ran like the dickens before Charlie could came back and sacrifice *them*.

Mostly, Charlie creeped around country roads and tried to stop cars so he could kill the people who were in them. I heard that once he strangled this kid and his girlfriend who were parking near the railroad tracks down by the river. He hid the bodies, so no one ever found out. He was sneaky that way. Everyone knew he was the devil, but no one could do anything about it. Nobody knew for sure how many people he'd killed over the years, but from what everyone said, it had to be more than ten, though.

Even the police wouldn't mess with Charlie. Not after he terrorized a police chief so bad that the officer went crazy and ended up in Dicksmont and his family had to move away. It just didn't make sense to get Charlie riled up. If you did, you paid a price, that's for sure.

"What are you talking about?" I asked.

"Like I said, would you guys like to go see Charlie No Face?"

"Yeah, sure. Then maybe we could fly to the moon," I said. Tommy had a way of talking like he had a big fish on the line when actually it was just a minnow.

"Listen to me. You know Kelso, my sister's boyfriend?"

"Do we know Kelso?" said Brian. "Everybody knows Kelso. I mean, he's the coolest kid there is, like, in the whole world."

"What about him?" I asked.

Tommy tilted his head back and raised his eyebrows like he was a king. "Well, boys, Kelso's gonna take us out huntin' for Charlie."

"No way," said Brian.

"Yeah, why would Kelso do that?" I said.

"Man, that's a story for another time," laughed Tommy. "Look, day after tomorrow, get the okay to sleep over at my house. That's all you need to do. I'll handle the rest. Are you in?"

"Yeah, I'm in." I didn't really think Tommy could deliver on this, but if he could, I definitely wanted to be a part of it.

"Brian?" said Tommy.

"Geez, I don't know," said Brian.

"Whadaya mean, 'I don't know'?" I said. "I thought seeing Charlie was all you lived for. You don't want to miss this. No way."

"I just don't want to get killed, you know?" said Brian.

"Well, that's always a risk," said Tommy. "Kelso said Charlie loves to torture little kids. He has a special cave where he takes them. He ties them up and then lets ants and bugs climb all over them. Sometimes snakes, too. He sits there and laughs while the kids scream. 'Scream all you want,' he says, 'no one's gonna hear you.'"

"How do you know what he said in some cave?" I asked.

"It's true, I'm tellin' ya; you can ask anyone! I wouldn't lie about something like that! I wouldn't!"

"Okay, okay, Tommy, don't get your bowels in an uproar. I believe you." Kind of.

I looked at Brian. His eyes were wide as saucers now. "I'm still in," I said. "Brian, whadaya think?"

"Me too, I guess," said Brian.

"You look all scared, man," said Tommy.

"I ain't scared!" he protested.

"Well, if you aren't scared, are you gonna come with us, or are you gonna come up with some excuse?"

"I'll be there!" he said, all defensive.

I wasn't sure. Brian had a way of not following through on things when there was danger involved. I remembered the time that Natty Pappagalo was pushing Brian around during recess, and Brian told him to meet him after school and they'd settle things. I couldn't believe he told Natty to meet him since Natty was a total nutcase and beat kids up all the time. "Lookin' forward to it, punk," said Natty, and he meant it.

"Me too," said Brian, but I knew he didn't mean it at all. Well, Brian spent the rest of the day in and out of the nurse's office. He threw up and got diarrhea and basically came undone.

"Maybe you could poop on Natty," I joked, but Brian didn't see the humor.

When the last bell rang, a bunch of us went to the parking lot. Natty came stomping out, taking his jacket off and throwing it on the ground. It appeared that Natty had been thinking of nothing else all day long, and now he had a full head of steam up. I could almost see it coming out of his ears. I thought, Oh my God, Brian's a dead man. But Brian was nowhere to be found. Instead he had left a note under a stone that said: *Dear Natty* (a big mistake already), *my mother* (second mistake) *told me to come home right after school to watch my sister* (third mistake), *so I can't fight you today.* Then he signed it, *Your Friend* (fourth mistake), *Brian.*

Natty was furious. Everyone else fell on the ground laughing. It was up to me to defend Brian's honor, what little there was.

"Hey," I said, "stop laughing; if he could have been here, he would. I heard his mother tell him to come home," I lied, "so back off."

Natty thought I was talking to him and he, well, took offense. "Wha'd you say?"

"Nothing, I didn't say nothin,'" I lied again.

Natty, in the meantime, decided I was a reasonable substitute for Brian. "So, Jackie's here to stick up for his little girlfriend, Bri-Bri."

I wanted to say, oh my God, you jerk, is that the best you can do, but instead, I said, "I'm not here to stick up for anyone. Yeah, Brian's my friend, but I don't have any quarrel with you, Natty."

Natty, unable to understand this concept, pushed me and said, "You wanna fight?"

To which I replied, "Now, how totally stupid do you think I am? We both know that you can beat me up. Actually you can beat up everyone in the school. We know that, right?" Natty didn't know exactly what to say, so I continued. "Rather than messing up your knuckles, why don't we just all agree that you are the toughest kid in school and leave it at that?" Natty was still thinking about this as I walked away. Quickly.

This whole thing about Charlie No Face was too important to have Brian chicken out, so I had to ask. "Look, Brian, if you don't think you can..."

"Shut up! I said I'd do it, so I'll do it," said Brian.

"Okay, boys, see you then," said Tommy.

Brian and I headed back to my house, cards in hand, ready to check out our luck. If Tommy was a little nutty about pinball, then that's the way Brian and I were about Topps baseball cards. I mean, at the end of a day of pinball, you've got nothing to show for it, nothing to take home. But baseball cards, they were an entirely different thing.

Brian and I didn't open them right there at Nick's. We came the whole way home so we could take our time. First we slid the flat square of bubble gum into our mouths, and then we checked out the Bazooka comic, which was never funny.

"Why does Bazooka Joe wear his collar up around his face like that?" Brian asked me this every single time we bought cards. I'd look at him, wondering if maybe he had a screw loose.

There were five cards in a pack, and we looked at them one card at a time.

"You go first," Brian said, so I looked at my top card and then he looked at his and we went back and forth like that until we were done. Today we got off to a bad start—Bill Tuttle and Pumpsie Green.

"Oh, man, who are those guys?" said Brian.

"I know, what the heck is going on?" I pulled another card out and it was the great Eddie Mathews. "Wow, how 'bout that!"

"Stupid luck," said Brian as he pulled out another card. "Ernie Banks!" And that was it. We both got one good player, which actually wasn't too bad.

Brian was still grounded to his room for having set a garbage can on fire (I'm telling you, he's a little nutty), but that was fine because we had some trade talk to do. I had two Mantles and Brian wanted one in the worst kind of way. All I needed was Dick Groat, the Bucs' shortstop, and Frank Robinson, a bona fide star in his own right; then I'd have my complete all-star team.

"Whadaya think, I'm stupid?" said Brian, when I suggested the trade. "Two for one isn't a good deal."

"But it's Mantle," I reminded him. "The Mick; big number 7. All I want is a little old Groat and one Robinson. Geez, I should get more than that! You should throw in Clem Labine or Gino Cimoli or even Vada Pinson just for good measure. Two for that particular one is a great deal. I'll bet you've got a mess of them in your box anyway."

Brian slid his box behind his back so I couldn't get a good look, but I knew he had what I wanted, and I knew that if I stuck to my guns, just like

Dad, I'd get it. And I did.

Brian went a little cuckoo when I gave him Mantle.

"My God, Mickey Mantle! You know what you just did? You gave me the greatest player of all time, you fool, you dummy!"

"I don't think so," I said, calm as could be. "I don't think he's as good as Mays, and he's sure not as good as Ruth."

"Your Aunt Ruth," Brian said.

"Yeah, Brian, my aunt, Ruth, that's what I meant."

Brian asked me to sleep over and Dad said, "Good idea." I didn't tell him we were planning to sleep outside on the porch because he gets a little weird about things like that. "Don't ask me that, Jackie. Don't ask me if you can sleep outside," he'd say. And when I'd ask why, he'd tell me that you never know what can happen in the middle of the night; it's just not safe. This made no sense to me. I hated it when he acted like a father. I knew for a fact that the only people who were out in the middle of the night were Brian and me. Maybe Charlie, too, but nowhere near us.

Once we laid out our sleeping bags on Brian's porch and his parents turned the lights out, we took a walk to the Fifth Street bridge, which was a big no-no because it was so high and adults thought it dangerous.

"Man, Jackie, you can't even see the bottom. Isn't that creepy?"

"I'll say," and then I pushed him from behind.

"Geez-o-man! What are you trying to do, kill me?" I just laughed. "You should know better than to do that! Geez, didn't your dad tell you about the kid from a bunch of years ago?"

"I know, I know."

"He was just about our age is what my dad said."

"Yeah, I know."

"And he fell off the bridge and got smashed to smithereens."

"Is that how your dad explained it?"

"Yeah, why?"

"That's not how I heard it. I heard the kid jumped off the bridge. Like, on purpose."

"But why would he do such a stupid thing?" asked Brian. "Didn't he know he'd get killed?"

"I think that was the point."

"What?"

"I guess he wanted to kill himself." About then we both decided to step away from the rail and head back to Brian's house.

"I wouldn't have to jump if my dad knew I was here in the middle of the night. He'd kill me himself!"

Brian laughed, saying,"I don't get why someone would want to die. I mean, then you miss out on everything."

"I know," I said.

"How dumb is that?" said Brian.

"Pretty dumb, I guess."

On the way back, we stopped at the Triangle and stared at the starry sky. Something about the darkness and quiet and the feeling that we were the only two people in the whole world, brought to the surface all the questions we had each been harboring over the years.

"My dad told me that the stars are so far away that their light could still be heading to the earth long after the star has died," said Brian.

"Geez, Brian, that doesn't make any sense. If the star is dead, where would the light come from?"

"That's the point, numbskull. The star is so far away that it could stop shining before all of its light reaches us," Brian explained in his best teacher voice.

"Are you trying to tell me that that big star right up there might not even be there; it's just the light from some star that doesn't even exist anymore?"

"Yeah. It's like turning a flashlight off and the light still goes on. Isn't that creepy," Brian said.

"I think you're the one that's creepy."

This kind of stuff always puzzled me. Like trying to figure out how the universe could go on forever. No matter how hard Brian and I tried, we couldn't get a picture of it. The universe had to end, didn't it? I mean, could anything go on and on and on? It gave me the willies thinking that we were surrounded by this great big universe, so big that big didn't even come close to describing it, so big that light could go on and on across the universe even after a star had died, so big that it made me feel like I was nothing at all, like I was less than a pinprick. Is that how the boy that jumped off the bridge felt?

"You know," said Brian, "if there's a heaven where all the dead people throughout history go, then it's got to be really big, right? I mean, if people have been dying from the beginning of time, they'd have to have someplace really big to go to, right? How else could they fit, right? Maybe that's why the universe is, like, infinity, so everyone has a place to go once they die. My dad told me the cemetery was closing because it had run out of space. Well, you'd never run out of space out there," he said, pointing towards the moon. "You'd have all the space you'd ever need. And I don't think people take up much space once they, you know, leave their bodies, so you could put as many dead people out there as there are stars in the sky. And you'd never run out of space."

That made sense to me. Of course there had to be someplace where everyone could go after they died. They couldn't just stay in the ground. At least, that's what Dad told me. "That's just their shell left behind," he explained. So if the shell stays here, where does the rest of the person go? That made looking at stars in the middle of the night, even stars that weren't really there, special. Surely they were so far away for a reason. Like, they were far away to make room for everyone, so that no one would be lost in the end.

That helped when I thought about that kid. And it helped when I thought about my mother. When I looked up at the stars, I thought, Maybe that's where she went. Maybe some things do go on forever, just like the light from a dead star goes on and on; maybe that's what happened to my mother, too. When I thought about it that way, the universe didn't seem so far away, and I didn't feel quite so small.

About two o'clock in the morning Brian dared me to take off my shirt and lie down in the middle of the street. He said he'd give me a nickel.

"It's so cold," he said, "your skin's gonna stick right on the pavement and you won't be able to get up, ever."

"What kind of moron are you, Brian?" The air *was* pretty cold, but I thought it worth a nickel, which would buy me another pack of cards. I was also sure that not much of my skin would stick to the pavement, so I said, "Sure," and he started to laugh. "Be quiet," I said, gesturing above me that his parents may still be awake.

"I don't think so," said Brian. "It's awful late." So we sat for a minute and listened hard and, when we didn't hear a thing, we decided it was all clear.

I took my shirt off and walked slowly out into the middle of the street. It seemed odd to be standing right in the middle of the street where cars zoomed by constantly during the day. It was so late that the corner light was on the blink, making the pavement look yellow. I heard a car start a few blocks away, but the sound faded as the car headed the opposite direction, probably trying to make the third shift at the tube mill. Brian stood on the curb.

"I can't believe you're gonna do something so stupid."

"Yeah, and I can't believe you're gonna pay me to do it," I said.

I sat down on the cold pavement, my shorts on and my shirt off; then, still sitting, I stretched my legs out on the street. God, it was cold. A dog barked the next block over and I nearly crapped my drawers. But then it was quiet again. I slowly laid back, inching down on my elbows until my back was on the pavement. Holy mackerel, it was cold. I felt goose bumps popping out on my back, and my toes started curling without me even moving them. I pulled my shoulders up just a little as my teeth started chattering.

"Jesus, that's cold!"

"I can't believe you did it," said Brian. "What a dope!"

"Maybe so, but you're the one who's gonna be a nickel poorer when I get up." I was shaking by then.

We both started laughing, when suddenly out of nowhere we heard the roar of a car engine and the screeching of tires. I looked up and there was a souped-up Chevy peeling through the intersection and shooting down our street like a bolt of lightning. "Get up!" Brian yelled. I rolled over on one side and started getting up, but my foot slipped on the dewy pavement, and I fell down again. The car was coming like a bat out of hell now, and its lights were nearly blinding me. The driver leaned on the horn and ten dogs in the neighborhood started barking. "Jackie!" Brian yelled, and I got up again. I dove for the yard just as the car zoomed past, the driver and his friends laughing. "Punk!" they called as they disappeared in the distance.

The dogs were raising a ruckus and lights were going on in houses all up and down the street. Brian's parents' bedroom light came on just as we ran up the steps to the porch. By the time Brian's father got to the front door, we were safely in our sleeping bags.

"What was that all about?" he asked. We looked at him bleary-eyed, like we had just woken up.

"What?"

"Didn't you hear all that?" he asked.

"All what?" Brian said, stretching his arms and rubbing his eyes.

His father laughed. "Wish I could sleep as soundly as you two. Goodnight," he said.

We smiled at each other. "Where's that nickel?" I whispered.

"I'd rather owe it to you than cheat you out of it," said Brian.

We tried to keep from laughing, but we couldn't. Brian laughed so hard he got the hiccups and I had to scare them out of him. "BOO!" I yelled, and he exploded with laughter again, but his hiccups stopped. We laughed some more, but pretty soon our laughter ran its course. We were quiet for a long time, listening to the crickets and the sound of the wind through the trees. The dogs had stopped barking, and all the neighbors' lights were out again. Puffy white clouds crossed the full moon. The air smelled like fresh mown grass and earthworms. My Kiwanis hat lay beside me on the porch floor, its brim curved perfectly. I slugged my pillow a couple of times and pulled up the zipper on my sleeping bag. My face felt cold, but the rest of me was warm as toast.

Sleep was coming on in a hurry now; my eyes were heavy. My muscles were going limp when Brian turned on his side and nudged me.

"Hey," he said. I ignored him, but he knew I wasn't asleep yet. "Hey!"

"What is it, Brian? I'm trying to sleep here."

"You don't think Charlie was in that car, do you?" he asked, his voice a little shaky.

"What?" I said, confused.

"I said—Charlie. You don't think that was him, do you?"

I hadn't even given this a thought. "No way, he never comes in town."

"Doesn't matter. I'll bet it was," Brian said.

"You think so, really? But he doesn't drive, does he?" I said.

Brian thought about this. "Maybe he was a passenger. Maybe he kidnapped those guys and made them drive around looking for people to run over. They sure seemed like they were trying hard to hit you." Brian was right about that.

"You know the stories, Jackie." Brian's eyebrows were raised in a convincing manner. "Just the other night my dad told me about another attack by Charlie. It was down River Road again, this time by that new golf course, the one with a big barn; you know where I mean?"

"Yeah, I know that place. I think my dad's golfed there before."

"Well," said Brian, "he might want to think twice before he golfs there again."

"Why, what happened?" I asked.

"It was in the early evening, just before the sun went down, and two guys were still way out on the thirteenth hole—the *thirteenth*," he repeated with emphasis. "The one that's by the railroad tracks. I guess one of the guys sliced his ball into the woods and when he went looking for it, Charlie came up on him out of nowhere. The guy was so scared that he started crying and begging Charlie to let him go, but Charlie just laughed at him. Then he cut him up in pieces with his machete. When the other guy came looking for the first guy and when he saw what happened, he ran away. Of course, Charlie couldn't run after him 'cause he's deformed and all, but the guy was so scared he didn't tell anyone what happened. In fact, he hasn't talked to anyone since; he just sits in his house rolled up in a little ball. When the groundskeeper came looking for the two guys, he found an arm on the thirteenth tee, then a leg halfway down the fairway, then a head on the green. And get this, when he looked in the cup, he found the man's eyeballs."

"You're kidding me," I said.

"I swear it's true," Brian said.

"What in the world!" I said.

"I know; it's unbelievable."

Man, it really shook me up. I wondered if Charlie might have been in the car. Whoever it was, he sure had it out for me. That's no lie.

The only person I knew who wasn't afraid of Charlie No Face was Dad. In fact, he said the whole thing about Charlie was made up by people with nothing better to do. He said he bet that Charlie was just a guy who had bad luck. I didn't want to argue with my father, but bad luck doesn't make you eat children and raccoons and God knows what else. I mean, there were just too many stories from too many people not to believe that Charlie No Face was real. And that maybe I had just escaped being his next victim.

I decided to keep one eye open while we slept. In the end, I didn't know which was worse, staying awake watching for Charlie or listening to Brian grind his teeth all night.

3

When I woke up in the morning, Brian had already gone into his house to get some more shuteye. I rolled up my sleeping bag, grabbed my pillow, and staggered down the street to my house. It was still cold. I could almost see my breath in the early morning light. Crows on the telephone wire outside cawed like crazy. A robin dragged a poor little worm from the yard in front of my house. Our front door was wide open. I pulled the screen door and walked in. I could hear my dad humming a tune in the kitchen.

"Hey!" I called.

"Hey, Jackie, how are you this morning?"

"Great, I'm great."

"So, did you and Brian stay in his house all night?" Dad always asked me this question, and I was never completely honest.

"Dad, you always tell me to stay in Brian's house…"

"Okay, J," said Dad.

There was a long pause. I wasn't sure what was up. Dad just stood there in the middle of the kitchen with a big, goofy smile on his face. He shifted back and forth and looked like he was about to explode.

"What's up, Dad?"

"I've got something for you, J. Come here for second," he said, and I walked over to the door. Then he stepped aside and I looked out the window to the patio. But I still couldn't figure out what I was looking at. There was a big green table sitting right smack dab in the middle of the patio.

"What the heck?" I said, still a little confused. I looked harder and my eyes bugged right out of my head when I realized what it was. "Geez-o-man, Dad, it's a ping-pong table! Where did you get it?"

"Where did I get it?" Dad said with a laugh. "I didn't get it anywhere. I made it. I made it just for you."

"You what? You made it?"

"What did you think we were doing at the lumberyard the other day? I thought for sure you'd figure it out," he said with a laugh.

"I didn't know why you wanted those big sheets of plywood, but I never would have guessed," I said.

"Well, this is why I wanted you to go to Brian's yesterday. I had a lot of work to do. I wanted this to be perfect."

I looked at my dad. He was staring at his handiwork, smiling his big, old smile, looking like a boy. For a moment I felt like I was *his* dad, and he had just come home to tell me he'd won the big game. He had painted the whole table green, and put white lines around the edges and down the middle where you served.

"I wanted to do something extra special for you this summer, J. I just wanted to make this time the best time ever. I know how much you like ping-pong and I thought, well, this would be the right thing to do. I thought it would be great for both of us. You know, it kind of kicks off the summer."

Now I was grinning ear-to-ear.

"Looks like I hit the jackpot with this," said Dad, pleased with himself.

"Gee, Dad, you sure did."

Dad put his arms around me. "That's great, son. I'm so happy that you like it." He gave me a big hug. "So, whadaya say, are you ready to play a little ping-pong?"

"Sure!"

I checked out the table while Dad rolled out the net. It stood on sawhorses and was clamped together in the middle so it wouldn't give. Dad even bought four paddles, two with sandpaper and two with rubber surfaces, along with a sleeve of ping-pong balls so white they glowed in the morning sun.

"Ready?" He twirled the paddle in his hand.

"Yep!" I said. Man, was this great. School was almost out, birds were singing, I had laid on the street last night and escaped Charlie No Face, and Dad was on vacation and he had built me a ping-pong table. I hit the first couple of serves right off the table, but soon enough I got the hang of it. We kept it going back and forth exactly 147 times.

Dad enjoyed it as much as me. "Oh, oh!" he'd say, stretching for the ball just as it was about to hit the patio. "Whoa, that was close! Keep it up, keep it up!" and that's just what we did.

Nick stopped by to check things out. "Heard there was a new contraption in the backyard," he said with a smile. He picked up a paddle and pretty soon we were playing three-man round-table. Each time you hit the ball you moved to the other side of the table. I was fastest, of course, but Nick and Dad hung in there pretty good. "Stop, stop," said Nick, "before I die!" He was huffing and puffing and my dad was making fun of him.

"Some war hero you turned out to be," Dad said, laughing.

That night Dad and I slept outside on the patio together. Dad bought two chaise lounges where we put our sleeping bags. He made a fire in the trash barrel at the end of the yard while I gathered a few long sticks. He whittled the ends to a point, perfect for cooking hot dogs and roasting marshmallows. Dad burned the trash and added some rotted wood from the cellar and soon the flames were shooting high above our heads, crackling, sparks filling the air like a squadron of fireflies. We liked our dogs black on the outside, and we never added mustard or ketchup because we wanted to taste the fire and the soot while we gazed at our red-hot bed of coals glowing across the yard.

Later I lay beside my dad on the patio as he pointed out the dippers and Orion's Belt.

"Look quick; did you see that?"

"What?" I said.

"A shooting star." We watched one corner of the sky for the longest time, and when another streak of light split the darkness, we both said, "Wow," low and soft.

"This is the best," I said.

"Yes it is, J, the best."

Did you ever have a moment when you felt all was right with the world and nothing could change it? Well, that's what it was like as Dad and I laid side-by-side on the patio, a shooting star overhead and our brand new ping-pong table beside us.

Charlie No Face

4

We were four games into our baseball season and had won three. Tonight we played our arch rivals, Moose, who were also three and one. Zeke was away at summer camp so Stevie Cook would have to pitch; another lefty, but not as tough as Zeke. Stevie had a tendency to walk batters. I felt really good in batting practice, even hitting two balls over the snow fence in left field. Usually I got butterflies right before the game, but tonight I felt loose and comfortable. I got two hits last game against Wampum and Coach said I was starting to hit my stride at the plate. Brian and Tommy showed up to cheer me on, but when I looked around for my dad, I didn't see him anywhere. Must have got hung up, I figured, or maybe he stopped to talk to Nick on the way to the field. "You see my dad?" I called to Brian.

"Huh uh."

Coach called the team out to the right field fence where he huddled us up and went over signals. The take sign was a left hand across the right elbow; bunt was two hand claps while standing in the front of the coach's box at third; that was about it. "Remember, boys," he said, looking each of us in the eye, "play hard and have fun." Then he gave each of us a stick of Juicy Fruit.

I don't know what got into Stevie, but he had his control and was mowing the Moose down like nobody's business. They didn't even get a hit until the third inning. Unfortunately, we didn't do much better. I hit a dribbler to third my first time up. I was coming to bat again in the bottom of third when I noticed Dad standing by the bleachers along the first base side. He had made it. He shook a fist in the air to encourage me, and I stepped into the batter's box. Milroy had looped a double down the right field line. We had a man in scoring position. Now it was up to me to bring him in.

The first pitch hit the dirt in front of the plate, and the catcher barely kept it from skipping through to the backstop. The second came in high and fast. Coach always told us to lay off the high ones because we'd never be able to catch up to them, but it came in so big and clear, I thought I could see the seams. I swung with all my might...and missed it completely!

I stepped out of the batter's box and looked at Coach down at third base. He stared at me as if to say, What did I tell you? He clapped, "Hang in there, Jackie. Keep your eye on it. Be patient." What did he mean, be patient? Was I supposed to take the next pitch? I looked at him again. He was holding his right wrist with his left hand. What did that mean? Was that the take sign? I didn't think so, but I wasn't sure anymore. What was he trying to tell me? I swung the bat a couple of times, spit on my hands, rubbed them together and stepped back into the box. I'll take this one. "Steerike!" called the ump. A perfect pitch to hit. Man! I stepped out again and banged the bat against my helmet. Two strikes. I always got nervous with two strikes and tended to swing at whatever was thrown next.

"Hang in there, J," my dad called.

The next pitch came in high and tight, putting me flat on my back in the dirt. "Hey, watch that!" someone called.

"Geez," I said, "what the heck was that?"

"Watch out, baby face," the catcher said. "He's after you now." The next pitch came in tight again and I chopped at it out of self-defense, hitting a nubber foul down the third base line that Coach fielded with one hand. He examined the ball and then threw it back to the pitcher, hard, like he was trying to tell the pitcher, Don't kill my ballplayer!

I spit on my hands again. I choked up a couple inches on my bat and stepped back into the box, this time tapping the plate twice with the bat. I looked at the pitcher, but he didn't look at me at all.

"Now he's pissed," said the catcher. "Better watch out."

"He's going to be even more upset after I swing this bat again," I said. With that, I settled into my stance, knees bent, bat up, eyes steady. The pitcher went into his wind-up and let loose with another fastball, but this time it was out over the plate. I wasn't sure if it was a strike or a ball, but I figured I'd better swing. At the last second I reached out and swatted at the ball, hoping I could at least foul it off. I caught the ball down on the end of the bat, but I caught it solid and hit it on a rope towards first base. The first baseman's mouth flew open and his eyes bugged out. He leaped for the ball, stretching as far as he could, the ball catching the tip of his glove and shooting down the right field line. I was rounding first and heading for second by the time the right fielder threw to third. Milroy slid across home plate and the whole team leaped from the bench, caps in the air, yelling like crazy.

I held up my hand to the ump. "Time out!" he called. I got up and dusted myself off.

Coach stepped in close and smiled, "Excellent, Jackie." My dad was yelling his head off while Brian and Tommy danced a little jig in the grass near third. The pitcher was circling the mound, his head down, his face red. He looked at me and I winked. He threw the rosin bag to the ground as his coach came out to calm him down.

We took a one-run lead into the last inning. But Stevie was running out of gas. He got two batters out but then walked the bases full. Then he ran the count full to the next batter and we were all shivering in our sneakers. Stevie sent a fastball down the pipe and the batter hit it square. As soon as I heard it, I took off to my left, the ball screaming over the infield just above our second baseman's glove. It was rising now and if I didn't get to it, it would reach the fence, clearing the bases. I looked up and suddenly the ball was on me; I stretched out with my glove hand, my eyes closed, and felt a sharp sting as the ball hit the center of my mitt. But when I hit the ground, my glove was empty; the ball was gone. Lying on my back I could see it floating out of reach when Milroy slid into view, catching it just before the ball hit the ground. Another roar went up from the bleachers and the whole team spilled out across the field, carrying Milroy and me off on their shoulders.

For a brief moment in the fading light of a summer evening in a small western Pennsylvania mill town, I experienced something I might never experience again, for all I knew. Many of those in attendance might not have even recognized what had happened; they might have missed it completely, like you miss a shooting star because you turned your head at the wrong moment, so fleeting is perfection. And that's what it was, or at least that's what it felt like to me. Perfection. When everything you hope might happen, happens; when you are called on to do what you must, and you do it; when everything that has to be aligned is aligned and the outcome is right from every possible angle.

Except, of course, if you were playing for Moose. I'm sure they didn't experience the perfection at all.

Coach treated us to hot dogs at the refreshment stand and Dad chipped in for popsicles. Everyone stood around rehashing the game, laughing and joking and boasting that we'd never lose again. Brian and Tommy tried to hoist me onto their shoulders, but we fell in a crumpled mass on the ground, not caring at all, just enjoying ourselves. Soon the noise and chatter died down, and kids started leaving with their parents.

"I'm very proud of you, J. I want you to know that," Dad said, crouched on one knee, his arms on my shoulders.

"Thanks, Dad," I said. "I played pretty good."

"Yes, J, you played pretty good, but it's more than that; I want you to know how proud I am that you're my son, okay?"

"Sure," I said.

"Never forget that," he said, his eyebrows raised, his eyes unblinking.

"Sure, Dad, I'll remember."

"C'mon, Jackie, let's blow this pop stand!" called Tommy, giving me a knowing nod. "Time to hit the road!"

"Okay, I'm coming," I said.

Dad still had his hands on my shoulders. "Go," he said, "have fun." Little did Dad know what he was telling me to do. This was The Night. We were going out hunting for Charlie. I felt bad that I wasn't telling Dad everything about sleeping over at Tommy's, but it would have been worse if I didn't get to go. This was a chance in a lifetime. I just hoped we lived to tell about it.

As Dad walked away, even though he was walking toward our house, he didn't look like he knew where he was headed at all. He looked lost. I watched as he disappeared around the corner.

"C'mon, Jackie!" yelled Tommy.

"I'm comin', I'm comin' already."

5

"So, Tommy, how'd you get Kelso to do this? I mean, what's going on?" I asked. Tommy, Brian and I were sitting together in his crabapple tree in his backyard picking crabapples while we waited for Kelso to arrive. We jumped out of the tree onto his garage roof and started eating.

"Let me tell you a little story," said Tommy with a sly grin. He looked around to make sure no adults were within earshot. "Okay, boys, this is where it all took place."

"This is where what took place?" asked Brian, getting a little impatient.

"This is where I was when I saw them," said Tommy in a whisper pointing at the tree limb where we'd been sitting a moment ago. "They couldn't see me because of the leaves, but I saw it plain as day."

"You saw what, Tommy?" I said.

"I don't know if you're old enough to understand what I saw," he said with a laugh.

"Tommy, I'm old enough to knock your block off. C'mon!"

"Yeah, c'mon!" said Brian.

"Okay, okay," said Tommy. "I was sittin' here mindin' my own business. No one was home, and then here comes Kelso, pulling in the driveway with my sister. Didn't think anything of it until they didn't get out of the car. So I shimmied over behind that limb to get a better look and..." He stopped.

"And what?" I said.

"I don't know if I should tell you this," he said, but his eyes were smiling.

"Maybe, if I smashed you in the face with my fist, it would help you decide," I said. Sometimes Tommy was so annoying. He was like bad-tasting medicine. I could only take him in small doses.

"C'mon," coaxed Brian.

"Okay, boys, okay," said Tommy, like he was suddenly ten years older than us. "So, I was sittin' there, and at first I didn't see anything but the two of them talking. But pretty soon, Kelso slides over and puts his arm around Patty and they start, you know, they start kissing like."

"Yeah, what else?" said Brian and me. Tommy went on to tell us that Kelso didn't stop with a kiss; before he knew it, Kelso was rubbing Patty's chest, and she didn't bother to stop him; in fact, she seemed to like it. So he unbuttoned her blouse and reached in. Tommy thought for sure Patty would smack him because once, when Tommy went into her room without knocking, she was in her underpants, and she almost killed him. But now it didn't seem to matter at all. Tommy said his eyes almost popped out of his head when Kelso put his hand under his sister's skirt. That was just too much, and Tommy yelled, "Hey, stop that!"

At first they couldn't tell where the voice was coming from, but Tommy yelled again and they saw him. Tommy said his sister turned about forty shades of red and Kelso threatened to strangle him if he ever did that again. Tommy told Kelso that their father might be interested in what was going on in his driveway. Kelso grabbed Tommy and put a fist to his face, but Patty told him to stop. She talked to Kelso for a minute in the car, and then everything changed.

"They took me to the drive-in to see *Old Yeller*, and another time they took me miniature golfing out at Stop 'n Sock," said Tommy. "I mean, they've been treating me like I'm a king or something. All because of what I saw." Tommy smiled. "I told Kelso the only other thing I wanted to see was Charlie. My dad wouldn't take me. He says it's stupid. 'Why would I want to go looking for some monster?' he says to me. I told him, 'because,' but that wasn't good enough for my dad. It was plenty good enough for Kelso, though —that and the fact that I saw him feeling my sister up and down. Best thing that ever happened to me," said Tommy. "Too bad you guys don't have sisters."

I wasn't so sure I wanted to see anyone doing something like that to my sister, but later Brian and I both agreed we'd like to see it done to Patty. "She's really stacked," said Brian.

Kelso was the coolest kid I'd ever seen. He wore pegged pants so tight I had no idea how he ever got them on or off. He had a perfect flattop and fenders and his car, well, what can I say.

"My God, it's a Caddy!" said Brian.

"No, it's not, dimwit." said Kelso. "It's better than that; it's a '57 Chevy, convertible no less; it's got four on the floor and you don't even want to know how many horses are under the hood."

"Wow," I said, once again, not having any idea what he was talking about. The sides of the car had flame decals, all red and orange, and there was a bald eagle on the hood head down, wings extended like it had spotted its prey. I bent over and looked at my face in the chrome hubcaps; the white walls didn't have a single spot on them.

"Don't touch anything; I mean don't even think about it."

"But I thought you said I could start the car," said Tommy.

"Yes, I guess I did, didn't I," said Kelso.

"You promised, actually," said Tommy.

"I know I did, kid," said Kelso, a little tense. "I remember exactly."

"You said I could do anything I wanted just so I kept my mouth shut," said Tommy. Tommy looked at Kelso and smiled, but Kelso didn't smile back.

Kelso said we had to wait until after dark or there would be no point in going at all. He said Charlie never went out during the day because it would cause a riot if people saw him in daylight. He said Charlie had been banned from coming into town for that very reason. He said that was because once Charlie had been seen during the daytime by two guys driving in a pickup, and they were so shocked by what they saw that they ran into a tree and both got killed.

Of course it was fine with Tommy, Brian, and me to wait until after dark. It just meant we got to stay up later. Tommy even got Kelso to promise to leave his convertible top down.

"Wow," I said, "I wonder what he'd do for you if you'd seen your sister naked." Brian and I laughed, but Tommy didn't think it was so funny.

"Hey, she's my sister!"

When the time was right, we all piled into Kelso's car. Tommy got to ride shotgun, and Brian and I were in the back. "Gotta make one stop before we go," said Kelso.

"What for?" asked Tommy.

"You'll see."

The night was warm, and the stars were just beginning to poke through the deep purple eastern sky. I laid my head back and watched the tree limbs rushing by, long arms waving at me in the summer breeze. I held my hand up flat and arm-wrestled the wind. Wow, this is so cool, I thought.

"Uh, Mr. Kelso," said Brian, "are all the stories true?"

"You don't have to call Kelso, Mr. Kelso, dimwit," said Tommy.

"Let him call me what he wants," said Kelso. "What was your question, Master Brian?"

"The stories," said Brian, "are they all true?"

"What stories are you talking about?" said Kelso with a fox-like grin.

"You know," said Brian, "The stories. The stories about Charlie."

"First off, kid, don't call him Charlie. It sounds like you know him, and he doesn't like people who pretend they are his friends. He's killed people for less."

"Okay, okay," said Brian. "What should I call him, Mr. No Face?"

With that, I burst out laughing. "That's rich, Brian. Hey, Mr. No Face, how ya' doin'? Uh, Mr. No Face, let me introduce myself; I'm Brian No Brains."

"C'mon," said Brian, edgy and still a little worried about how to address Charlie. "I don't wanna make any mistakes, y'know? I don't want him to get all riled up and, you know, do something."

We all knew what Brian meant by "do something." We had heard the stories, so Brain did have a point. One misstep and we could all be goners.

"Mr. Kelso, sir, could I ask a question, sir?" I said.

"Sure, jack-off, shoot."

"Following up on Master Brian's question—*are* the stories about Mr. Charles No Face true, sir?"

"Of course they're true," said Kelso, so quick and sure that we had to believe him. I mean, Kelso was older: He could drive; he'd gotten to second, maybe even third base with Tommy's sister; he'd been around.

"All of 'em are true," he continued. "Do you know anyone who hasn't heard of Charlie? Do you know anyone who hasn't heard the stories?" None of us knew what to say. "Of course you haven't! Everyone knows about Charlie, and everyone knows the stories. If they weren't true, do you think people would be talking about him so much? I mean, my old man says he knew about Charlie when he was my age, back when Charlie was not much more than a kid. I mean, the guy's a legend. And how do you think he stays a legend?" We just looked at him. "My God, I've got morons on my team," said Kelso. "He stays a legend by doing all the stuff people say he does. A little killing here, a little torture there. If he didn't do stuff like that, everyone would forget about him and then where would old Charlie be?"

Man, Kelso really knew what he was talking about. I could tell.

"My dad told me that when the commies sent up the Sputnik and the whole world went crazy watching the skies and worrying when the Russians were gonna attack, Charlie went out and killed all the chickens in some guy's barn, and then he ate the guy's dog. Then he scared a woman down on the River Road so bad one night that she fainted into a coma and hasn't talked since. She just sits and stares." With that, Kelso let his head drop to one side with his tongue hanging out. "Why do you think he did that?"

"'Cause he's crazy?" suggested Tommy.

"Crazy?" said Kelso. "Hell, I wish I was that crazy. He did it so everyone would stop thinking about the damn Sputnik and start worrying about him again."

"Wow," said Brian, his eyes bugged out, "he is smart."

Up till now, I was doing fine with the whole "let's go hunting for Charlie No Face" thing, but all of a sudden I was getting jumpy. I mean, it sounded like Charlie would stop at nothing to keep his legend alive. What if this was one of those nights when he thought that he'd better do something so people wouldn't forget about him? Then we come along in a car, just a bunch of kids, except for Kelso, of course, and Charlie says to himself, "This is perfect; if I kill them, no one will forget me ever again." If he actually talks, that is. I don't know if he talks or if he just grunts, like, "Uh, uh, uhhh, uh, uh."

"Okay, we're here," said Kelso as he pulled into a vacant parking lot.

"We're here!" said Brian, his voice sounding like Minnie Mouse's.

"Jesus, boy," said Kelso. "This ain't where Charlie is, you idiot. Like I already told you, he never comes into town, just like a vampire never goes out during the day. I just gotta do a little business."

There was a pickup truck parked in the corner of the lot. At first I didn't see anyone in it, but then a head leaned forward on the driver's side. opened the door, got out and walked with the man. They laughed and talked for a minute. Then the man handed Kelso a bag and Kelso gave him something in return. Finally, Kelso sauntered back to the car, cool as could be.

"What's that?" said Tommy.

"It's a six-pack of protection, Tommy boy," said Kelso.

"Whadaya mean?" I asked.

With that, Kelso pulled something out of the bag. "This is what I mean: a six-pack of Iron City beer."

"Wow," said Brian. "What are you gonna do with that?"

"I'm gonna stop by my grandmother's house and see if she'd like to get hammered. Whadaya think I'm gonna do with it?"

Brian just looked at him. "Your grandma drinks beer?"

"Oh my God," said Kelso.

"Is that for Charlie?" I asked.

"Go to the head of the class, Jackie. Yes, it's for Charlie. Seems this is the only thing that tames Charlie's appetite for children and small animals. Once he's had a few of these, he's as docile as my old granny."

This worried Brian. "Ain't it against the law to have beer if you're not, like, someone's father or something? Couldn't we get in trouble?"

"Which would be worse," Kelso sneered, "a little trouble with the fuzz or a lot of trouble with a raging maniac?" Brian sat back in his seat, looking even more worried.

"Everyone knows that Charlie likes his beer, and once he's good and drunk, he's easy to deal with," said Kelso. "We just can't open it for him."

"Why's that?" asked Tommy.

"Once some guys peed in a can of beer and gave it to him. He almost drank the whole thing before he realized something was wrong. By then the guys were speeding down the road. One said Charlie chased their car for almost a half-hour."

"How could he chase the car?" I asked. "I thought he had a hard time walking."

Kelso looked at me like I had twelve heads. "Because, dip squat, as anyone knows, when someone gets into a rage, they get super human powers. That's why you don't want to make Charlie mad."

We were all pretty quiet by now. This wasn't going the way I thought it would. I figured we'd go for a nice ride in the country and if we were lucky we'd see Charlie running through the woods or something, just a glimpse so we could say we'd actually spotted him. Like my dad and I spot deer on the old Wurtemburg Cutoff. We never get so close to any deer that they could stab us with their antlers, and we sure as heck don't bring beer along to coax them up to the car. So, why in the world would we do that with someone who has a tendency to kill people and eat wild animals? I mean, why would anybody invite a monster up to his car to share an Iron City?

I was just about to raise this question when I was pushed back in my seat as Kelso screeched out of the parking lot, laying rubber for about a mile. There was no turning back now.

He flew out of town toward River Road and then across the Koppel Bridge. Soon, we were at the traffic light on Route 18. All of this was familiar. This was the way Dad and I went when we wanted steak subs in Beaver Falls.

The light changed and we crossed 18, continuing on 351. Kelso said this was Charlie's road. This was where most people saw him walking late at night. The lights of town were behind us now, and the road weaved and curved through woods and knee-high cornfields. The wind had picked up and the trees were making a hushing sound. The moon was full, and if I hadn't known any better, I would have sworn it was following our car, peeking at us through every tree, watching our every move.

"Look at that," I said to Brian.

"What?" I pointed at the moon. "Yeah, so?" said Brian.

"It's gigantic," I said.

"It's just an octagonal transfusion," said Brian. "My dad told me about it. Looks real big, but it's not." I looked at the moon again, the grey features of its face as distinct as my own, the large round disfigured mouth warning us not to keep going.

"When will we see him?" asked Tommy.

"Never can tell," said Kelso. "Sometimes, Charlie doesn't show up at all; other times he just appears like a ghost: suddenly, when you least expect it."

"I hope this isn't a waste of time; I really want to see him," I lied.

"The only time that's being wasted is mine," said Kelso. "Right, punk?" He swatted at Tommy.

"LOOK!" Brian yelled so loud that Kelso swerved off the road and almost hit a tree. I somersaulted across the seat and ended up in Brian's lap.

"Did you see him! Did you see Charlie?"

"I…I don't know what I saw," said Brian, his voice wavering. "Looked like a bear."

"A what?" I asked, back on my side again.

"I'm telling you it looked like a bear. Right by the side of the road. I didn't know there would be bears. Maybe we should go back now. Bears—that's not good."

Tommy turned around in his seat and smiled at Brian. "Did the bear look like he was wearing a mask?" asked Tommy.

"Yeah, yeah, he was wearing a mask!"

"Are you nuts," I said. "A bear wearing a mask? That doesn't make any sense at all. What was he going to do, rob us?"

"I'm not crazy!" insisted Brian. "I don't know why it was wearing a mask, but it was. You gotta believe me."

"Maybe he was wearing a mask because he was really a raccoon," said Tommy.

Brian thought for a minute. "Why would a bear want to look like a raccoon?"

"Geez, Brian," said Tommy. "It couldn't have been a bear. It had to be a big raccoon."

"Jesus, Brian," Kelso said, "what's wrong with you?"

"Nothing, I tell ya, maybe it was just a little bear," said Brian.

"Yeah," I said, "a little bear dressed up like a raccoon. Maybe he was one of those undercover bears."

"Yeah," said Tommy, "checking out some delinquent squirrels that stole some nuts from his favorite tree."

"You mean the squirrels that were dressed up like chipmunks," I added.

"Yeah," said Tommy, "I saw Walter Cronkite talking about it on the news the other night."

"Will you all shut up!" said Kelso.

"Wait a minute. Did you see that?" I said.

"What?" said Kelso.

"Back there. I saw something."

"Another bear?" asked Brian.

"Jesus, Brian, would you stop with the bears?" said Kelso.

"Didn't anyone else see it?" I asked. "Down that other road, I think I saw someone; I think I saw someone sitting by the side of the road, just sitting there." This was no bear; no raccoon. If it was what I thought it was, I

48

didn't know what we should do.

"Must have been Charlie," said Tommy, his eyes as big as the moon.

"No, it wouldn't be Charlie," said Kelso. "He doesn't ever leave this road."

"How do you know that?" I asked.

"Because I know!" said Kelso, emphatically. I leaned forward and looked at him. His eyes were darting back and forth, and his hair was getting stringy with sweat.

"Have you ever actually seen Charlie?" I asked.

"What do you mean, have I ever seen Charlie? What kind of question is that? I brung you all the way out here and now you're asking *me* questions? I oughta just dump you all here and go on home!"

We all looked at Kelso. "But, have you ever actually seen him?" I asked again.

Kelso punched the steering wheel. "I don't have to answer any question from you punks! You understand?"

With that we all sat back in our seats. Kelso was wringing the steering wheel with both hands. My God, he's scared, I thought. What are we going to do? "Okay, okay," I said. "I'm sorry I asked. Just wanted to know…"

Kelso paused, thinking about what to say next. "Apology accepted."

"Good," I said, "so what do we do next?"

"What do you mean?" said Kelso.

"Well, I figured that since you got experience with this, you must have some sort of plan about what to do when you think you've seen Charlie."

"A plan," said Kelso, vaguely.

"Yeah, you know, I didn't know if you always just stayed on this road, or if, when you saw something suspicious, you would check it out. You know, go back and check it out."

"Well, yeah, I guess we could go check it out," said Kelso hesitantly.

"It's up to you, Kelso; I mean, we're just kids and you've done this stuff before." I looked at Brian and Tommy. "Right, guys?"

"Yeah, that's right," said Tommy.

"I don't know about going down…" I smacked Brian before he finished his sentence. "I mean, yeah, it's up to you, Kelso," said Brian. "Whatever you think."

Kelso was breathing hard. He pulled over to the side of the road. At first he didn't say a thing, just sat there with his hands on the wheel. "Okay, here's what we're gonna do. I don't think it was anything, but since you guys are all hopped up about it, I'll turn around and go back so we can take a look. Don't be surprised if it's a waste of time." He looked at his watch. "It's getting late. Your old man will kill me if we're gone much longer. So here's the deal. We'll go back to the crossroads and I'll slow down. You look," he said to me, "and if you see anything, maybe we'll check it out. Then we're going home. Got it."

"Great, thanks," I said, patting Kelso on the back.

"Don't touch me, punk."

He tooled back to the crossroads where he slowed to a crawl. There weren't any streetlights, but the moon was out again, and I could see everything clearly. I stood up on the back seat and looked as far down the road as I could. The right side was lined with ash trees while on the left side the road kind of fell away and was hidden in tall grass, a pasture just beyond, wire fencing along its border. The road was crumbling at the edges, and the faded white line disappeared over a rise. I could see boulders in the grass along the pasture side, some of them big. Crickets and peepers filled the air with constant cheeping.

"You don't see nothing, do you?" asked Brian.

"Shut up," I said, the sound of his voice making it harder for me to concentrate.

"Jackie?" said Tommy.

"Shut up, I tell you; I'm trying to see." Kelso didn't say a word for a long minute. I studied the road as sharp as I could. He revved the engine.

"C'mom punks, let's go; Charlie ain't showing up tonight."

Just then one of the boulders moved.

"Wait a minute. I think I see something."

"Yeah, right," said Kelso. "You're joshin' now, I know it. Let's go."

"No, wait!" I said. The boulder moved again and then began to get up. "Oh my God, it's him," I said. "Gotta be." No one said a word. I turned and looked at three sets of eyes bugging out of their heads.

"How do you know it's him?" said Brian. "It could be anyone."

"It's him," I said.

"What made you the expert?" said Kelso.

"I don't know," I said, staring at a figure struggling to stand. I knew I was right even though I wished I was wrong. It was him. I was sure of it. What had we gotten ourselves into? Were we going to end up part of another gruesome story about Charlie, just a bunch of stupid kids that other kids would talk about?

"I think he's right," said Tommy. "Now what?"

"Yeah, now what?" said Brian. "It's awful late and my mom's gonna be worried sick if she finds out I'm not in bed. Anyway, we all agree it's probably him, right? So we can go back. We can tell everyone we saw Charlie."

The figure finally stood, though still slightly bent over, and began to walk. But then he faltered and fell to his knees and sat back on his heels.

"What's he doing?" asked Tommy.

"Probably drunk," said Kelso.

"You still got the beer, right?" asked Tommy.

"Yeah, I got it, but he don't look like he needs it."

"Who knows?" said Tommy. "Maybe he'd like some more."

I looked at Kelso. "Well, we came all this way. Do we keep going?"

Kelso mistook my question as a suggestion. He turned the wheel, and we idled slowly down the road. "Don't say a thing," said Kelso. "I'll do the talking." He turned off his headlights as we inched closer and closer. Charlie's head was bowed, his hands were on his knees, and he was rocking slightly back and forth. He didn't seem to realize we were there. Unless he was trying to fool us. Unless he was setting a trap.

"Be careful," said Brian.

Charlie was making sounds I'd never heard before: moaning with a high-pitched but faint whimper. Sounds I might expect from an animal but not from a human being. My God, I thought, what the heck are we doing out here in the middle of nowhere with this crazy monster?

"Geez-o-man," said Brian, "let's get out of here. He's gonna attack, I know it!"

"Are you kiddin'?" said Tommy. "He doesn't look like he could hurt anything." Charlie rocked back and forth and made no effort to stand.

"Don't kid yourself," said Kelso. "He's as smart as a fox."

I figured Kelso was more right than Tommy; we might be in danger, big time. Charlie moaned again.

"What should we do?" asked Brian.

"Shut up," said Kelso, but it came out squeaky. He cleared his throat.

"I'll do the talking. Hey?" he called rather plaintively. Charlie continued to rock and moan.

"I don't think he heard you, Kelso," I said.

"What did I just tell you?" Kelso was jumpy now. "I'm talkin' here!"

"Okay, okay," I said, "so talk!"

"Hey! Charlie!"

This time Charlie heard Kelso. He stopped rocking and didn't make a sound. "Oh my God," said Brian, "he's gonna kill us. I just know it. He's gonna kill us, and then eat us, and then scatter our bones where no one can find them, and my mother's gonna wonder why I didn't just stay at Tommy's, and why I was so stupid, and she's...ouch!"

I smacked Brian on the head.

"Call again," I said to Kelso.

"Hey, Charlie! We got some beer for you!"

Charlie sat back on his haunches and raised his head. I had never seen a head like that before. It was as big as the globe that sat on Miss Loss' desk in social studies, but not exactly round, more ballooned out in spots, like something went terribly wrong at the factory when they made it. Like the whole continent of Asia stuck out as if it were as high as Everest, while South America was just one big indent. Like it was a reject globe, one that no teacher would ever want to put on her desk. Then he turned away.

Tommy jumped into the back seat with Brian and me.

"My God, look at that," he said.

"I know, I know," I said. Kelso was silent. Brian was wimpering.

"Jesus, Brian, c'mon, maybe that's what he wants us to do, cry like little babies; maybe it gets him all excited," said Tommy.

"Shut up!" said Kelso, angry now for no apparent reason. He got out of the car. "Come here, punk," he said to me, "and bring the beer." I slipped out of the back seat and tiptoed toward Kelso, six-pack under my arm. I gave it to him and he took a couple of steps towards Charlie.

I wondered what we would do if Kelso got himself killed. A couple more steps forward, and Charlie was right in front of us, looking away, a dark lump swaying back and forth.

"Kelso," I said in a whisper, "let's just leave the beer on the ground here and go. Really. You found him. We saw him. You did great. Now let's go home. Okay? I don't want anything to happen." But Kelso wasn't listening.

"Hey, Charlie!" he screamed. "Here I am, man! Come and get me, you freak!"

"We're all going to die," wailed Brian.

"C'mon, Charlie boy, let's you and me throw back some brew, whadaya say, huh?" Charlie didn't move.

"C'mon, Kelso, give it a rest. Just leave him alone."

"'Just weave him awone,' says the little baby." Kelso was out of his mind. He turned and looked directly at Charlie's back. "Hey, melon-head, why don't you say somethin' when I talk to you? I thought you were a tough guy, killin' people and all." Charlie didn't move. "Huh!" called Kelso back towards me. "Look at him!" Kelso laughed, "Just look at him there sittin' on the ground in the middle of the night, rockin' back and forth like some nutcase. C'mon, Charlie, give us a thrill!"

"Let's get the heck out of here before he really does something," I said, but Kelso wouldn't have it.

"Char-lie! Char-lie! Char-lie!" he yelled, dancing around like he was an Indian. "Hey, Charlie! I'm talkin' to you, man!"

The stiller Charlie remained, the more furious Kelso got. He looked around at the grass beside the road and saw a long, smooth stick that looked like it had been carved out of a tree branch.

"Go get that stick, Jackie boy, and bring it here."

"What are you gonna do?"

"Just shut up and get it!"

I walked over to where the stick was and picked it up. It wasn't just any old stick. It was smooth as silk, like it was made in a factory rather than grown in the woods. It was the kind of stick that hikers might use when walking in the woods. I held it tight, walked back to Kelso, and gave it to him.

"Whoa!" said Kelso, waving it around like it was a sword. He put one hand on his hip, stretched the stick out in front of him, and lunged at Charlie.

I moved towards Kelso. "C'mon, man, cut it out!" I yelled. I was so close to Charlie now, that I could hear him breathe, although it didn't sound like any breathing I'd ever heard before. It was a nasty, gravelly, wheezing sound, like he was gasping for every single breath. His shoulders traveled up and down, and I could see sweat on the back of his neck.

"Kelso!"

"Shut up, Jackie, you wanted to see him; now he's here right in front of you. I want to see this *thing*, too. I want to see what all the talk is about. He don't seem so scary to me." With that he stepped forward and lunged with the stick again, this time almost hitting Charlie.

"Kelso, stop it! Can't you see he's sick or something? He can hardly breathe!" I yelled.

But Kelso wouldn't stop. He waved the stick, whooped like a maniac, and lunged again, this time jabbing Charlie in the middle of the back. Charlie's back seemed to wince, and Kelso did it again. "Hey, Charlie, got no face? Poor Charlie!" he mocked, jabbing him again and again.

Then he lunged, and Charlie turned his face towards us. It shone brilliantly in the light of the full moon.

"Oh my God!" cried Kelso, throwing the stick at Charlie and leaping into the car.

There I stood, face-to-face with Charlie. Now *I* couldn't breathe. And I couldn't move. I was frozen in my tracks. He stood slowly, shaky on his feet, but close enough to reach out and grab me if he wanted. And his face, my God, his face. My mouth fell open.

"Jackie, let's get out of here!" cried Brian.

Suddenly I found my legs and dove back into the car. Tommy screamed, and Brian curled up in a ball on the floor. By now, I'd stopped breathing all together. I lay on the floor behind the front seat. Kelso threw the car into gear and peeled out as fast as he could, leaving Charlie and the six-pack in a cloud of dust.

I got back up on the seat and looked back at Charlie standing in the middle of the settling haze. He leaned over, picked up the long stick and the beer. He stood still for a few seconds as if examining the two objects, then started walking very slowly, stick in hand, tapping the road before each step.

Kelso sped back down 351 and across 18, the RPM needle on yellow, nearly hitting a car coming in the other direction. "What the hell!" yelled the man, but Kelso's foot never left the floorboard. The Chevy whined like an angry wasp as we flew across the steel grate surface of the Koppel Bridge. When we leaned into the turn for Ellwood, I swear we were balancing on just two wheels.

The lights of the West End in view, Brian looked around at each of us.

"Did you see his face?"

I looked back at Brian, but didn't answer. No one did.

The street lights on Lawrence Avenue were blinking. A few people were coming out of the Sons of Italy Hall and the usual suspects were standing outside the Oasis, a row of Harleys lined up at the curb. PeeWee's was still open, and, to my surprise, Kelso suggested we stop for some hot dogs, on him. His anger gone, he climbed out of the car, looking more like one of us than a tough-as-nails teenager. In fact, he looked small and a little unsure in his body, like he didn't know for certain which way his arms and legs would go when he moved them.

We grabbed some stools at the counter and watched Lydia, the owner, line our hot dogs along her ample arm. She slathered mustard and then ketchup on each one with a stick, the kind my dad used to stir paint. Then she ran her dipper round the chili pot a few times before topping off each dog with some meaty sauce. "Here you go," she said, sliding our plates along the countertop.

Lydia took her one and only spatula and scraped the grill. Little rolls of grease fell into a metal pan at the edge of the grill. Then she threw some burgers on for some guys at the end of the counter. We listened to the meat sizzle and watched the steam rise as she opened the bun drawer under the cash register and threw a few on the griddle. The drawer was always full, always warm, always ready. I watched appreciatively as Lydia worked her magic with mindless repetition. I breathed a sigh of relief, knowing that there were some things you could still count on, some things that didn't shock or surprise, some things that were what they were and nothing more.

On the way home, Brian fell asleep just like that, as if every ounce of energy had suddenly abandoned him. Tommy fiddled with the radio, trying to find KQV until Kelso told him to stop, and then Tommy just leaned back and stared at the sky. None of us knew what to say. None of us knew how to explain what we had seen.

Kelso turned his lights off as we turned onto Pershing Street. Then he pulled the car over to the curb just a few houses away from Tommy's. He looked hard at each one of us.

"Remember: None of this ever happened. Got it?" His jaw was locked and he clearly meant business.

"Got it," I said. Brian started to ask a question, but I nudged him and he shut up.

"Now hit the road, punks," said Kelso, and we crawled out of the car, our adventure over. I took a couple of steps and then turned again to face Kelso. "Hey..." I said, and then I couldn't find the words. I just looked at him.

"Sure," said Kelso. He pulled away, and by the time he reached the corner, his lights were on and his radio was blaring.

Our sleeping bags were lined up on the porch, and all the lights were out. Tommy peered through the front window to see if his father had fallen asleep on the recliner.

"We're in luck," said Tommy. "He's gone up to bed. They left the fans going, so they won't hear us."

I looked over at Brian and he was already asleep, his mouth wide open, cheek already resting on a little puddle of drool.

Tommy punched his pillow. "What a night, huh?" he said.

"Yeah, what a night."

"I never seen nothing like that before," said Tommy. "I mean, did he have a face?"

"I don't know," I said.

"What a freak," said Tommy as he zipped his sleeping bag.

"Man," I said.

I zipped up my bag, too, and closed my eyes, the events of the evening racing through my head. I'd never seen anything like him. Nothing even came close, not even the bearded lady that worked in the grocery store on the North Side. She was unusual, but you could look right at her and not even blink; she was funny-looking, but that was it. Even the unicorn man that we saw at the Wayne Township Firemen's Carnival couldn't hold up before Charlie No Face. I mean, I don't even think that the horn was real. I think it was just stuck on, but we wanted to believe it was real, because it added to the fun and made for great stories later. "He tried to stab me! Did he try to stab you?" I mean, we all figured it was fake.

But there was nothing fake about Charlie, nothing at all. He had no eyes, for God's sake. None. Just two indents, like thumbprints in soft clay. And no eyebrows that I could see. Just two flaps and a creased or dented forehead that looked like someone had gone at it with a knife or maybe a screwdriver. And he had a burned-out crater where his nose should have been, blackened like the bottom of the barrel after Dad and I have finished burning the trash. His upper lip was a big fleshy overhang that covered up whatever mouth he might have had. I assumed he had a mouth. I mean, I heard him, but I never saw where the noise actually came from. His voice had been high and distant, like the sound of a train whistle in the middle of the night, lonesome and piercing at the same time.

Charlie was so ugly that I didn't know what to make of him. I mean, was he a mad killer who liked to terrorize kids and animals and anyone else who got in his path? Or was he just a freak of nature, someone who turned out all wrong for reasons that never make any sense? Like, was it his fault? Did he decide to be evil? Maybe he couldn't help himself. I mean, that's the way things go sometimes. Sometimes awful things happen and there's no accounting for them, and if you stop to think about why they happen, you get stuck; you can't come up with any answer that makes sense.

If you think about it too long, you get a chill up your spine, because life suddenly doesn't quite look right—it doesn't add up the way it should. For instance, I must have asked my dad a million times why my mother died, and in the beginning he tried to explain. He'd say, "J, I guess she was too good for this world," or "God had a bigger job for her to do," or "God felt it was time to call her home," and I would say, "But *this* is her home, isn't it, Dad?" Then he would smile and hug me. As time wore on, he took to saying, "I don't have an answer, Jackie."

When your dad doesn't have an answer, you're in real trouble. I mean, if he doesn't know, maybe there's no knowing at all. And if there's no knowing at all, then everything is just one great big crap shoot, as Nick would say. "You roll the dice and wait." Whatever comes up, comes up. Might be a home run or it might be a man with no face or maybe a boy with no mother.

In the last year or so, I stopped asking altogether, at least asking out loud, but I never stopped asking inside. When I'd say my prayers at night —"Now I lay me down to sleep, I pray the Lord my soul to keep"—I'd never make it to the end. I just had too many questions about how God ran things. I'd keep praying, but it was just pretend praying, kind of like the way you say the Pledge every day in school until it doesn't mean a thing anymore.

I wondered if it was like that for Charlie. I wondered if he had questions, too. Why in the world did this happen to me? What in the world was God thinking? If Charlie could think at all, that must have been his number one question. Had to be. What in the world was God thinking by making me look like this, making me the scariest, meanest man ever to walk the face of the earth?

I kept trying to go to sleep, but it was no use. My mind just wasn't ready. I unzipped the bag and got up. I sat on the porch steps enjoying the night air, so cool and damp that it felt like I could pour it in a glass and drink it. All the houses across the street were quiet and settled and relaxed like so many faces waiting for dawn, waiting for the people inside to breathe them back to life.

I stretched my foot out and could see its shadow on the grass. I turned to look for the moon, but it was behind a telephone pole. I stepped down into the dewy grass and walked to the street, where I could see the moon sitting on the Morrows' roof, part of its face hidden behind their chimney. "Show's over," I said, "you can come out; nothing to be afraid of. Monster man is gone."

I sat down on the curb and thumbed the soft tar until I had a small ball, and then I popped it into my mouth and chewed it slowly against my cheek, just like the major leaguers chewed their tobacco. Dad told me that once during a game he wanted a chaw of tobacco but didn't have his pouch, so one of his teammates took some right out his mouth and gave it to him. He didn't think anything of it, just popped it in and headed out onto the field. I hocked some black juice onto the cement.

I wondered if Charlie ever made it home.

6

I tossed and turned all night trying to get Charlie No Face out of my mind. But every time I closed my eyes, there he was, reaching out to grab me, his dead sockets burning a hole right through me. The morning light helped, but even then it was hard to get him out of my head.

It didn't help that, when I reached home, my sleeping bag dragging behind me, my dad was standing at the screen door, as if he'd been waiting for me since dawn. He had an odd look on his face. Through the screen, I couldn't tell if it was a grin or a grimace. Oh my God, had he found out about last night? He'd kill me for sure, since he warned me against roaming around at night, and—let's face it—we did a lot more than roam around. Getting in a car with someone was a definite no-no. As for hunting Charlie, well, he would be worse than furious; he'd be disappointed in me.

"Hey, Dad!" I called with my friendliest wave.

"How you doing, J?" called my dad. Whew, I was home free. He wouldn't call me J if he suspected something. As I walked up the steps, I could tell he was smiling, but I didn't know why.

"Wait right there for a moment," he said. Dad disappeared into the house while I stood on the porch with my sleeping bag, which looked like a giant tootsie-roll. When Dad came back, he was whistling "Take Me Out to the Ballgame."

"Close your eyes and stick out your hands," he said.

"What's going on..."

"No questions; just do what I say."

So I closed my eyes and stuck out my hands. He put something in my hands, and I immediately knew what it was—a baseball card. But why the heck would he make such a big deal out of a measly ball card?

"Okay, J, open your eyes."

I decided I would be excited no matter what ballplayer it was. I didn't want to hurt his feelings. So I opened my eyes and took a look. At first I was totally confused. It wasn't a card at all. It was a ticket, but not like the tickets we got at the Majestic or the Manos. It was thick and it had numbers on it and a picture of a Pirate. I looked at it hard.

"Are you kiddin' me?" I said. Dad started to laugh. "You didn't, did you?"

"Yes, I did," he said.

"Really?"

"Really."

"C'mon, really really?"

"Yes, really really," he said, laughing so hard now that he was snorting.

"My God!"

Dad had bought us tickets for the Pittsburgh Pirates' big Memorial Day doubleheader against the mighty Braves of Milwaukee. I got so excited that I ran around the house waving my ticket in the air, and then, for no particular reason at all, I fell on the entryway floor and rolled myself up in the rug. I had never been to a big league game. Who cared about Charlie now? This was going to be the best day of my life.

Cars, cars, and more cars; horns blaring and cops trying to direct traffic; waves of people on each street corner, banners in their hands, Pirate caps on their heads; and kids with ball gloves, just like me. A man waved us into a parking space beside his house, and Dad paid him a whole dollar. I couldn't see Forbes Field, so we followed the river of people, all moving in the same direction. My dad held my hand, which usually would have been a big no-no, but not this time. The buildings crowded the street, forming a canopy over our heads. Never seen so many people, never seen so many buildings. How in the world did everyone get around? Trolley cars clanged down the avenue, people hanging off the sides. Taxi drivers leaned out their windows, yelling at each other. Kids played stickball in the alleys. Everything was cement and brick and glass with wires crisscrossing the sky above me.

All I could see were the backs of people in front of me as we flowed along, some people jostling for better positions and others shooting past us, like they were late for a fire. I felt hypnotized by the sounds and the colors and the movement, when all of a sudden I saw the sign—Forbes Field—and below it a series of archways with fans racing through them like streams converging on a mighty river.

We walked up to a chubby man, his shirtsleeves rolled up, cigar smoke surrounding his head. Dad handed him our tickets. "Welcome!" he said. My dad told him this was my first game ever.

"Well," the man said, "then before you can enter, you have to tell me who was the greatest Pirate of all."

I looked at my dad, who smiled and winked. "I think you know this, J."

I thought for a minute and said, "Honus Wagner," and the man said, "Fantastic," and patted me so hard on the back that I nearly fell down.

"Did you hear that, Yancy?" he called to another man. "This boy is a Pirate through and through." With a flourish he waved me on and bowed halfway at the waist.

"Thank you," I said.

"Enjoy the game!" he called, disappearing in the enveloping crowd.

There was red, white, and blue bunting everywhere, and American flags were being sold by the bunch. Men stood on boxes calling, "Get your scorecards here! Scorecards here! Get your Pirate yearbooks here!" Vendors came and went, the smell of hot dogs, peanuts, and popcorn trailing behind. One man had a mountain of Cracker Jack boxes. "Wow," I said to my dad, "look at all that." The lines at the concessions snaked through the runway. People craned their necks to see how long the wait would be. Everyone had smiles of anticipation on their faces. It was like going to a carnival.

We walked up a long ramp, like we were winding our way up the side of a mountain. The crowd was so thick I didn't even have to pay attention while I walked. We moved as one, all in the same direction, all with the same goal. One man mooed and everyone laughed, even my dad. I tugged his shirt, "Where's the ball field?" I asked, and he smiled and said, "You'll see." Finally we reached the top of the ramp and started towards the open runway. "Popcorn heeere, popcorn!" one man shouted. "Get your peanuts heeere, peanuts!" another called.

"Here's our section," said Dad, and as I turned, there it was. Green grass as far as the eye could see, like wall-to-wall carpeting, only real. There were vines covering the outfield walls in left and center, waving in the afternoon breeze. Men carrying long hoses sprayed the infield dirt and then raked it smooth; two men buckled each base into place. The foul lines were as white as a man's shirt collar on Sunday morning, and they seemed to run on forever.

The outfield was full of ballplayers. They looked like thoroughbred horses, galloping and trotting, tossing their heads and strutting their stuff, preparing for the race ahead. When they played catch, each player rocked back and forth in the same effortless motion I'd seen the older boys in the neighborhood use. And when the ball left their hands, it rose like a missile off a launch pad, riding the breeze and finally smacking a teammate's glove with an echoing pop. Players took turns at the batting cage. Balls flew off their bats like Sputniks heading into orbit. When I saw one disappear over the wall, it took my breath away. How could they hit it so far, these gods of baseball?

My dad smiled at me as he gave our tickets to the man who was going to seat us. "What do you think?" he asked, and I smiled back and punched the pocket of my baseball mitt again, showing that I was ready for the game, too.

"Here we are," the man said as he wiped off our seats. I looked up, and the great roof soared above us like the vaulted ceiling of a sacred cathedral, giant pillars holding it all in place.

My father pointed to the seats behind the right field fence. "See that first deck?" he said.

"Yes."

"See the second deck, how high it is?"

And I said, "Yes," again.

"Now look at that roof." So I leaned back to see the top. He said, "That roof is about ninety feet high." Then he pointed to home plate and said, "That's well over three hundred feet away. Babe Ruth hit his last homerun right over that roof. First one to do it."

"You're kiddin'," I said. "Babe Ruth played here?" He smiled. "Wow," I said. This was a place where history was made, where giants came to play while mere mortals watched and wondered. I sat back in my seat, waiting for the game to begin and thought, This is really something.

I looked at my father, and he was staring into space, his eyes small, his gaze narrow; I'd never noticed the lines on his forehead before, and the creases at the corners of his eyes. He took a deep breath and then another, still staring. "Dad?" I said, but he didn't hear me above the roar of the hometown crowd greeting their team as the Bucs ran onto the field. I stood up and yelled, "Go Bucs!"

Dad stood beside me. "Dad?" But he didn't answer again, this time because the National Anthem was being played. I took my hat off and held it over my heart, just like he'd taught me. I nudged him this time and he looked at me. I looked at my hat and gave him the eyeball. "Oh," he said, and put his hand over his heart.

Vernon Law, the Deacon, slow-motioned his final warm-up to Smokey Burgess. Burgess went to the mound and said a few words to the Deacon and then settled in behind the plate while Law rubbed up the ball. In stepped Billy Bruton of the Braves. Law threw high on the first pitch and then got him swinging on the second, but Bruton lofted a soft liner to center for a single on the third pitch of the game. A major league hit, I thought, just like it was nothing. Bruton rounded first and then skipped back to the bag.

"That's not a good way to start," I said, but my dad didn't say anything. "Dad? Hello, anybody home, anybody home?"

He looked at me and smiled. "Yes, somebody's home. Don't worry about the first batter," he said. "Watch and see what happens." The next batter hit a shot to the hole at short but Groat came from out of nowhere and snagged the ball, flipping it to Maz, who launched it to Stuart at first before it even settled into his mitt. Double play. The crowd erupted. "What did I tell you?" Dad said, patting my back.

In the bottom of the first, Dad pointed to the Brave in right field playing catch with the centerfielder. "There he is," Dad said.

"Henry Aaron," I said reverently. I couldn't believe he was just standing there in the grass a few hundred feet from me. "Hey, Hank!" I yelled, but he didn't even turn.

"I don't think he can hear you, J. If he could, though, he'd probably wave."

He hit a home run later in the game, and he robbed Clemente of a double, and he stole a base. But it was like you didn't even notice what he was doing. He just did it. My dad said Aaron was like an ice cold drink of water on a hot summer day, no carbonation, no fizz or sparkle, just plain and simple, but thirst-quenchingly good. He added that he thought one day our right fielder, Roberto Clemente, would be just as great.

"Wouldn't you love to be that good at something, J?" Dad said. "So good that you didn't even have to *try*; you just *do it*; you just do it and it goes the way it's supposed to every time."

I looked at him as he talked. It seemed like he was talking more to himself than to me. He looked down at me and his eyes were just a little wide and his brows were just a little pinched in the middle, and for a split second I could have sworn I saw fear.

"Yeah, that would be great, Dad." He smiled. "Dad, you okay?"

"Sure I'm okay, Jackie," and he put his arm around me and I put my arm around him.

"You gettin' hungry, son?"

"Starving."

By then the Bucs were up by two on a homer by Bob Skinner, so we took a break and went to the concessions. Dad ordered us a couple of hot dogs that were bobbing in a giant metal box full of hot water. Grey hot dogs. Not charcoally like Dad made them over the fire. Not split open and a little burnt here and there. But he assured me that boiled hot dogs and baseball went together like hamburgers and fries. I drowned mine in ketchup and mustard and even a little relish, and he was right. So we bought two more and some peanuts and two Cokes and headed back to our seats.

Law had things under control and by the time Elroy Face came on in relief, we knew it was a done deal. That little guy wasn't much bigger than me, but he had a jackhammer of an arm. No one could hit him, and he even picked a player off second. Our Buccos were victorious in the first game, 8-3. But in the ninth inning, clouds appeared over the left field wall and it began to rain. They rolled the tarp out over the infield and everyone waited, hoping the rain would stop so they could play another.

Spahn started warming up for the Braves and Friend went to the bullpen for the Pirates. After a while I could see the home plate umpire walking back and forth between the two managers, and finally the public address guy announced that the game was "called," which meant they weren't going to play. A great moaning "Aawwww!" rose up from the crowd. Most people sat for a few minutes, hoping they'd change their mind, but by then we were into some serious rain.

Dad finally looked at me, sort of mournful. "Well, whadaya think, J? Time to go?"

"I guess we'll have to," I said. "But that's okay; it was a great game."

Dad just looked down at me for a long moment. Then he took my hand and we started the slow trek out our row, down the steps, and up the tunnel. Of course, we hadn't brought any umbrellas, so we stood for a while inside the entrance, hoping it would slow down a little. When that didn't happen, we grabbed a copy of the *Pittsburgh Press* from the garbage, held it over our heads, and took off for the car.

By then we were laughing as we dashed and darted our way through the crowd. After a minute or so, the papers blew away and we were getting pretty drenched. I felt like a football player running for the end zone.

"You with me, Jackie?" Dad called, looking back over his shoulder.

"Yep!"

The cop at the corner was holding traffic for us. "Run, boys, run!" he said. And we did, Dad and me, we ran like the wind, side by side; I was surprised that I could keep up. Dad was breathing hard and my legs were getting a little tired, but we didn't slow down. Like Batman and Robin, nothing could stop us!

I raced ahead when I saw the car and was standing by the door when Dad held up short, a look of disbelief on his face. "What?" I asked. "What's wrong, Dad?" He didn't answer at first, just walked slowly to the front of the car, his hair plastered to his head, rain dripping off his nose. Then I saw it. Someone must have taken a baseball bat to the headlights. They were smashed to smithereens, the glass scattered everywhere. Dad shook his head but didn't speak. He just kept looking. I ran to the back of the car, still hunched over in the driving rain. "Dad?" He looked at me, and I pointed to the taillights that had also been bashed in. "Why would anyone do this?"

"I don't know, Jackie," Dad said.

"Should we go back and get that cop?"

"It's pouring rain, and I don't think that will do much good," said Dad. "Let's just get out of here."

"What? Some bad guys messed with our car. Maybe he could catch them," I said.

"I bet they're long gone by now, Jackie."

"But we gotta do something; I mean, we can't just let them get away with this. It's not fair! It's not right!"

"I don't know. I think we'll be wasting our time, J."

"C'mon, Dad."

"Jackie, sometimes life's not fair. Sometimes bad things happen and there's nothing we can do about them. We just have to keep going, is all."

I didn't say a word. I squinted up at him through the rain.

"Okay, okay, but let's hurry; you're gonna catch your death of cold," he said.

We ran back through the rain to the cop who called another cop who let us sit in his car while we told him what happened. He wrote a lot of things down and said he'd call if he found anything out. He frowned and added, "Don't count on it, though. This kind of thing happens all the time."

My dad looked at me. "Let's go," was all he said.

We were soaked to the bone by the time we got back to the car and pulled out into the thick traffic. Dad didn't say a word. He just looked straight ahead as we inched along.

I was surprised that Dad was so hesitant to talk to the cop. I mean, what's wrong is wrong and you have to do something about it, right? At least that's what he always told me.

"Isn't this a lot like Darlington Lake?" I finally asked. Dad looked at me and then looked back at the traffic. He let out a deep sigh and opened his mouth but didn't say anything.

We always went to Darlington Lake in the summer to swim. It was neater than the Municipal Swimming Pool and much bigger. One Saturday we were waiting in line under the hot July sun and there were three colored people waiting in front of us. When they got to the ticket window, the man inside asked if they had passes to get in. The colored people looked at each other and then said that no, they didn't. The man smiled and said, "Sorry, then, you can't enter; everyone needs a pass." He then asked them to step aside so my dad could get to the window.

When Dad got to the window, he said, "We don't have any passes either. Does that mean we can't get in?" I thought, What the heck is he doing? Of course we don't have passes; that's why we're standing at the window to buy some.

The man smiled. "No, you don't have to worry about that."

And then Dad said, "I guess I don't have to worry because I'm not going to swim here today. And I'm never coming back. I don't like the way you do business."

And the man just shrugged his shoulders. "That's up to you," he said.

All of sudden we were heading back to the car. I wondered what the heck happened and when I asked Dad, he said, "That man didn't want those colored people to swim in the lake." And I still didn't get it. I mean, the lake belonged to the man so he could do whatever he wanted.

But Dad said, "It's just not right, J. He wouldn't let them in because their skin is black. He wouldn't let them in because he believes that they would contaminate the water. He wouldn't let them in because he thinks they're not as good as us white people."

I still wasn't sure what that had to do with us. Then Dad said, "If we bought tickets and went swimming in his lake, we would be agreeing with him; we would be saying he's right. But he's not right. He's wrong. Just 'cause people are different doesn't mean they don't deserve to be respected and treated fair."

As I thought about this while Dad struggled through the Pittsburgh traffic, I couldn't help myself. I asked him again, "Why didn't you want to talk to the police? Isn't this like Darlington?"

"It's not really the same thing, Jackie. Whoever did this to our car didn't pick us out and decide to hurt us because of how we looked; they just saw a car and decided to wreck it up. They didn't do this because they hated us; they didn't care about who we were at all."

"Well," I argued, "isn't that just as bad? Treating us like we're just a couple of nobodies? I mean, doing bad things to people is wrong, isn't it, no matter what the reason?"

My dad sighed and patted my shoulder. "Maybe you're right, J." Then he looked back at the traffic and didn't say another word, his face stone stiff. Something about my father was different. I just couldn't tell what it was.

Charlie No Face

7

I wouldn't say that the whole mess with the car was the reason that everything else started going screwy, but things sure changed after that.

About a week later, Brian and I were at the Municipal Swimming Pool. We were paddling underwater, a whole new thing for us, and playing *Seahunt*, like the TV show. He'd throw a rock into the water and I'd go in after it. He'd count—one one-thousand, two two-thousand—until I came back up with the rock in my hand. We'd take turns, trying to beat our records. "Eight seconds, eight seconds, that's great! Okay, you go after it. I know you can beat ten." Just as I was about to jump in, the lifeguards started blowing their whistles and waving their arms for everyone to get out of the water. "What the heck is this?" said Brian. "We just had a rest period fifteen minutes ago." The lifeguards looked panicky and were pushing kids to hurry into the bathhouse.

"There's a storm coming; everyone out of the water right now! Hurry up, you can't waste time!"

"Big deal," I said to Brian. "What's a little water gonna do to us? I mean, we're up to our eyeballs in it anyway." Brian laughed.

One lifeguard looked right at us and yelled, "You two, move it!" And with that, a clap of thunder exploded so loud above us that I ducked and put my hands over my head for protection. A nasty-looking gash of lightning tore across the sky, and Brian and I were running like mad to the bathhouse. We were packed into the boy's locker room like Necco wafers. After about twenty minutes, it seemed like the rain was dying down, so Brian and I decided to head for home.

When we stepped outside, the wind was whipping like nobody's business; the trees were flopping back and forth with each gust, some looking like they were going to shatter into toothpicks. The sky looked wild-eyed, dark clouds running low and even darker ones swirling above them.

"Whadaya think?" said Brian.

"I think we can make it if we hurry. It's only sprinkling." He said something, but the wind was roaring now, and I didn't bother to ask him to say it again. I jumped on my bike and he jumped on his. We pedaled as hard as we could, hunched over against the wind. I had to squint because there was so much dust and dirt in the air, and I was afraid I might get blinded. I figured Brian was behind me, but I didn't turn around to check; I was too afraid I'd get blown right off my bike and onto the street.

Turning down Jefferson, we saw several small limbs in the street and leaves blowing loose everywhere. It was nighttime-dark now. "Man, this is crazy!" Brian yelled. I just kept pedaling for home. It started to rain harder, until each drop stung like a bee. Then we realized that it was bouncing off the pavement. I'd never seen hail before, and it was coming down like it was being shot from a machine gun high above us.

"Keep going, Brian, keep going!"

"What the heck else do you expect me to do!" he said.

Then the dam broke. Rain and hail came by the bucket, actually by the dump truck. We squinted into the rain; it was almost impossible to pedal. We ditched our bikes near Tommy's house and ran. When we hit the next corner we heard a loud POP! and a wrenching snap. The tree across the street was falling in slow motion onto the sidewalk. "Watch out!" I cried. We ran to the other corner, and that's when we heard it.

"Wait a minute," I said. "What's that?"

"Thunder," said Brian.

"That ain't like any thunder I ever heard before," I said. It started as a low, deep rumble and soon became a roar, like a locomotive was pounding through the neighborhood. *What the heck!* We turned and saw it: a dark snake-like funnel coiled and ready to strike. When it hit the ground, we could hear tree limbs snapping like twigs. We ran like hell then, our clothes drenched, our hair pasted to our heads, our eyes almost closed, just like we were swimming underwater.

The wind hit us broadside as we reached my front yard, and down we went. "Don't give up!" I called as I helped Brian to his feet. We grabbed hold of each other, knocked the front door open, and fell headfirst into the entryway.

"Close the door, close the door!"

"I can't!" said Brian. Together we pushed as hard as we could.

"Dad!" I yelled, but he didn't come. "Dad!" We kept pushing, and finally we did it. The door closed and we lay on the floor, afraid for our lives.

"Jackie! Jackie!" It was my dad. "Come down here quick!" His voice came from the cellar, so we ran down the steps, and there he was by the furnace.

"Come here! Are you okay?"

"Yeah, but we almost got killed," I said. Dad pulled both of us to him, and we huddled together as the storm rammed through our neighborhood.

And then—just like that—it was over. The rain that blew sideways was now coming straight down, steady and hard, but not angry. The sky looked like the inside of a mixing bowl filled with chocolate batter, but the funnel was gone.

"Is that it?" Brian asked.

My dad didn't say anything at first. He just listened. "Yes, I think it's over, boys."

Brian began to cry. When I looked at him, my eyes got all wet, too. I think it was because he was crying.

My dad hugged us both. "It's okay now, boys. You're fine. It's all gone. It won't come back."

"What the heck!" I said, trying to stifle my sniffles. Brian had moved on to that uncontrollable gasping that happens when you've cried so hard you can't cry regular anymore. "Was that what I thought it was?" I said.

"Well, boys, we got hit by a tornado. A small one, but a tornado nonetheless."

"Small!" I said. "Didn't seem so small to me. I thought we were gonna get sucked up like that girl in the movies."

"Like Dorothy?" said Dad.

"Yeah, her."

"Yeah, it was scary for sure," said Dad. "Haven't seen one of them around here since I was your age."

We went out the front door onto the porch. Mrs. Sanders was on hers inspecting a giant limb that had broken off her maple and lay across the yard like a slumbering dinosaur.

"That was really something, wasn't it, Ruth?" Dad called.

Mrs. Sanders shook her head. "Haven't seen anything like that in a long while. I don't know what to do with that," she said, gesturing to the limb.

"Don't worry," said Dad. "I'll get some help."

"I wouldn't have this worry if Frank was still alive."

"I know," said Dad. "Frank would be right on top of it, wouldn't he?"

"Yes, he would," said Mrs. Sanders. "It's just a shame," she sighed. "I guess we're in the same boat. We're both alone in the world."

A cloud crossed Dad's face. "Well, we'll get you fixed up as quick as we can."

"I appreciate it," said Mrs. Sanders.

She paused and took another deep breath. "You've sure been around a lot, Bill. That's not like you." She looked at him quizzically.

Dad took a step back. "Oh, yeah; just taking some time off so I can be with the boy during the summer. You know, time flies so fast, and before you know it—" Dad reached for the sky as if a rocket were blasting off, "—they're gone."

"What grade's he going to be in this year; what grade are you going into, Jackie?" asked Mrs. Sanders.

"Sixth," I said.

"Sixth what?" whispered Dad.

I sighed and frowned a little. "Sixth, Mrs. Sanders."

"My, my, you are growing up. Next year he'll be off to Lincoln High, won't he?"

"Yes, he will," said Dad.

"Your mother would surely be proud," she said to me.

"Say thanks," coached Dad.

"Thanks, Mrs. Sanders."

"You're welcome, dear," she replied.

There was a long, awkward silence. Other neighbors started coming outdoors to survey the wreckage. The rain had almost stopped by now. But the street was flooded.

"Can Brian and me go wade in the street, Dad?"

"You're gonna get even more soaked."

"It's just water, Dad."

"I guess you can; just roll up your pants."

"My dad told me that when it rains like this, and everything is clogged up with water, the snakes come out looking for dry land," said Brain. "He said they're everywhere. Especially where it's flooded."

"What are you talking about?" I said.

"Snakes in our street!"

"Don't be stupid. Come on."

"Okay," said Brian, "but if you get bit, I get to say, 'I told you so.'"

"Say it as much as you want, doofus; I won't hear you 'cause I'll be dead, right?"

"That's not funny," said Brian.

I was already up to my knees in the muddy water that had turned Pershing Street into an impressive river. The sewer drains swirled like whirlpools. "Stay away from there!" yelled Dad as I walked closer.

Dad was on Mrs. Sanders' porch now, and they were talking very serious. He was gesturing, and she was shaking her head. He raised both arms, and she crossed hers and placed one hand over her mouth. I wondered what he was talking about. Why did they both look so concerned?

"Help!" I turned around just in time to see Brian go under. He had fallen. I waddled to him as fast as I could, but by the time I reached him, he was on his feet laughing.

"Thought I was drowning, didn't you?" he said.

"Dumb dope."

"Gotcha, didn't I? Ha!"

"You got nothin'," I said lamely. Dad and Mrs. Sanders were still talking. Finally she placed a hand on his shoulder. Then he turned and left her porch, returning to ours.

"Hey, Dad! Look what happened to Brian!"

Dad looked and shook his head. "You two," was all he said. Then he went back into the house. A moment later he came out again and waved for me to come in.

I couldn't believe my eyes when I got to the back door. The sycamore tree that shaded our patio had toppled over like a giant bowling pin. I couldn't believe how much sky there was where it had stood. The yard looked like a massive jungle, with some limbs shooting up into the air while others covered the ground so thick that you couldn't even see the grass. "Cool," said Brian.

Dad didn't say a word. He opened the door. There, under the tree, was the ping-pong table, crushed. "Oh, no," I said. "Dad?" He didn't answer. He stepped slowly down onto the patio and carefully over some of the debris. He knelt beside the table, reached for the netting, but couldn't pull it free. He picked up one of the paddles and turned it several times in his hand. Then he slammed it on the cement, and it shattered into pieces. I held my breath.

"Dad?"

He didn't answer. He sat on the wet pavement, his head in his hands, and then I heard it. I'd never heard it before, but I was sure. He was crying. He was sitting in a puddle on the back patio, fallen tree and smashed table beside him. Crying.

"Dad?"

"It's nothing," was all he said. I put my hand on his shoulder. I didn't know what else to do. He blew his nose on a handkerchief, took a breath, and smiled slightly. "I'm fine, J, I'm fine."

8

Two weeks later, Mrs. Sanders' tree had been cut and hauled away. Everyone's yards looked pretty much the way they had before the big storm. Everyone's except ours. Two weeks later, the car still sat in the driveway, its headlights and taillights bashed in; and the maple tree still sprawled across the lawn, our ping-pong table slowly rotting under it. It was pretty amazing how long the leaves stayed green, living off whatever food was stored in those old limbs. But soon the leaves began to curl and turn brown, as if fall had arrived just in our backyard while everyone around us enjoyed summer.

It was the coolest thing having the tree all over the yard. At first I didn't see its potential. Mostly, I was upset that we couldn't play whiffle ball anymore, but soon enough I realized there were a lot of *other* things we *could* do. The longest limb stuck straight up like the mast of a ship. Brian and I stripped it and made a perch in the crook of three limbs near the top. We shimmied up the limb and sat in the crow's nest pretending we were pirates. "Arrr, matey," Brian said in his best Long John Silver voice.

"Arrr, 'tis, young bloke," I said. I took two handkerchiefs from my dad's dresser, and we put them on our heads and tied them in the back. We cut the tongues out of a pair of old shoes and used them as patches for our eyes, tying them with string from Brian's cellar. My dad would have killed me if he had found out, but I took our best carving knife from the kitchen and whittled a sword out of a limb we broke off the tree.

From our crow's nest we spied Nick's Snack Bar across the Triangle and Tommy's house just beyond it. "Look at those land lubbers," we growled.

"Let's go ashore and see what they're up to," Brian said. So we shimmied back down the tree and then, with our daggers in our mouths, we crawled across Mrs. Sanders' yard.

"Watch out," I said. "There's a witch about."

"Arrr," said Brian. "A hundred doubloons for her head, I tell ya."

We hid behind the cars across from Nick's and watched all the comings and goings, impressed that no one saw us. Except, of course, Nick.

"How you pirates doin' today?" he called from the counter window. "Are you gettin' hungry?"

"Whadaya think?" Brian asked. "Are we gettin' hungry?"

"Of course we're gettin' hungry!" I said, and we scurried across the street, my father's handkerchiefs on our heads and shoe tongues over our eyes, hoping no one would notice.

"Here you go," said Nick, putting a couple of cheeseburgers on the counter. "What'll you scurvy pirates have to drink? Cherry pop today?" We shook our heads. "So, if I give you this feast will you promise not to steal all the silver pieces I have hidden in the basement?"

"You've got silver in your basement?" Brian said, wide-eyed.

I poked him hard in the ribs. "Yeah, he's got a thousand silver pieces in the basement, doofus, and he's shakin' in his boots, 'cause we might rob him with these sticks."

"Well, could be," said Brian. By then Nick had slapped two cherry Fantas on the counter.

"Thanks, Nick. I mean, arrr, you lily-livered land lubber."

"Glad to keep the local marauders happy," Nick said.

Brian and I dove into our burgers, chomping away.

"So, Jackie," Nick said, "haven't seen your dad much lately. How's things going?"

"Fine, I guess," I said.

"Get that old jalopy fixed yet?" Nick asked.

"No," I said.

"I can see from here that you still got that tree in your yard. I'll bet that's a lot of fun, isn't it?"

"Yep."

"Any idea when your dad's planning to have it removed?"

"Nope."

"Probably been working a lot, huh?" Nick asked, eying me closely.

"Oh, no, he hasn't had to work at all this summer; he's on vacation."

"Hmm, vacation," Nick said. "That's great."

I said, "Yep." A few minutes later I saw Nick walking down the street towards my house.

By this time Brian's patch had fallen off, and he had poked Jimmy Bell, a high school kid and local tough guy, in the butt with his dagger. Jimmy just looked at him a long time, a toothpick dangling from the corner of his mouth. We apologized over and over and hoped Jimmy wouldn't smack us. "Twerps," was all he said.

Brian and I explored the parking lot and the Triangle field and snuck around the Dairy Queen down the street, but soon we got bored being pirates, especially when some lady told us we looked "cute as the dickens." So we ditched our pirate stuff and headed towards my house.

Brian headed home and I went into my house to get dressed for my game. It was very quiet. "Dad!" I called, but he didn't answer. I knew he was home because the car was in the driveway. The car hadn't moved in days. Found him sitting on the back steps drinking a can of Iron City.

"Hi, Dad," I said, and at first he didn't look up. "Dad, are you okay?"

"Oh, hi there, J; what you up to?" He smiled, but not his regular smile. It was crooked like he didn't have complete control of his face.

"Dad, you okay?"

"Yep, J-boy, I couldn't be better," he said, a little too loud. "Had a nice visit from Mr. Nick. Good guy, Mr. Nick." He gulped like he was swallowing a burp. "I'd ask you play some ping-pong, Jackie, but the table, well, the table seems to be broken." I thought he was going to cry again. I hated it when he cried; made me feel, I don't know, lost. "I'm sorry about all this, Jackie. I really am."

"That's okay, Dad, it doesn't matter. You can fix the table once we get the tree out of here, ya know?"

"Yeah, the tree," he said, and went all silent on me again.

"Look, Dad, I'm gonna get dressed for my game, okay?"

"Yeah, why don't you do that, J," he said.

"It'll be okay, Dad. You'll see." I patted him on the back. Then he stood up and gave me a big hug like he used to when I was just a little kid.

"I love you, J. You know that, don't you?"

"Yeah, Dad, sure I do." He held me for a moment and I didn't know what else to say.

It was a perfect summer for baseball. My team was playing great. We had won seven in a row, and I was starting to hit the way my coach had hoped. "Atta boy, Jackie," he'd yell whenever I swung my bat. "Keep your head in, keep your head in." And I'd keep my head in, watching the ball, not the pitcher. With each game the ball seemed to get bigger and move slower. I could almost see the seams coming at me. I got some wood on it almost every time I came to the plate. Three hits against the Elks, two against the Rotary, four against the Lions, and two more against the Moose in our rematch.

For some reason, baseball just kept getting easier. I stood in centerfield where I could see everything: the fence curving behind me, the foul lines limed white, the base paths and sacks, home plate and the mesh backstop. Everyone on the field had a position to play and a job to do, and if everyone did their job, things went well: I mean, you won. It all made sense. Things were in play or they weren't. You were safe or you were out. You scored or you didn't. You won or you lost. I liked baseball for its dependability. You always knew where you stood.

Of course, the coaches and parents got into arguments all the time about whether the umpire's call was right or wrong, or whether somebody's kid got enough playing time. Like Gino's dad. Poor Gino. I mean, the kid hated baseball. His knees banged against each other when he ran, and his elbows stuck out every which way so that he could never swing the bat all the way around before the ball was in the catcher's mitt. And when he struck out, which was most of the time, he cried. And yet, his father yelled at Gino's coach that Gino should get more playing time, that if he did, he'd play better, and on and on. Actually Gino just stunk at baseball. I'm sure Gino could do well at something, but it wasn't baseball. It was painful watching him cluttering up the batter's box with his crumminess, if that's a word.

I found that the game was simpler than the adults made it. If they'd just let the game play out the way it's supposed to, it would mostly go just fine. Baseball's pretty black and white that way. And in that sense, I guess it's fairer than most things in life.

Anyway, we were playing an away game in Wampum. That was always an easy win. My God, their field was a cow pasture; no, really, there were cows in centerfield. And their team was just awful. I mean, they could barely field nine kids, and some of them didn't have gloves. We had to let them use ours.

In the third inning I came to bat and the pitcher served up a low fastball that I golfed into left centerfield for a stand-up triple. "Way to go, Jackie," Coach said and patted me on the back at third. "Milroy will bring you in," he said. I shook my head. I stood on the base and cleaned off my uniform while Coach walked down the line to whisper instructions into Milroy's ear.

Through the trees beyond the left field line a train chugged into sight, and all of us turned as one, pumping our arms over and over until the engineer pulled his chain and the whistle blew. Whooooooo-whoo! I smiled and watched it disappear in a cloud of coal dust and smoke. I turned my attention back to the game, because I knew I was about to score. I had no doubt at all. On the very first pitch, Milroy squared to bunt and as soon as the ball nudged off his bat and trickled down the third base line, I was off, the third basemen running beside me. But I knew he'd never get to the ball before I got home. I knew I was safe before I ever reached the plate and knowing it was true, I relaxed. I relaxed and ran without effort. I ran so fast that my hat blew off and my hair streaked back across my ears. I was completely at ease, completely certain about what I was doing and what was gonna happen.

The third baseman reached the ball and shoveled it home, but I was already three strides past the plate, still leaning, knees kicking, elbows flying, feeling like I could run forever. Now that's the way things should go. Plain and simple.

Coach brought me home after the game since our car was still in the shop, nothing being done to it. Dad didn't like it when I asked about the car. "I'll take care of it," he'd say in a way that meant, "Don't ask again." He sure seemed edgy all the time, and he wasn't much interested in doing anything:

"Hey, Dad, you wanna play some catch?"

"Can't, J; I gotta get some things done in here."

Five minutes later I'd go in the house and there he'd be, fast asleep on the couch.

I thanked Coach for bringing me home and then called for my dad as I walked up the porch steps. No answer.

"Dad!" I called again as I walked into the kitchen. Nothing. "Hey, Dad, we won!" I called up the stairs and listened for a moment but didn't hear a thing. I figured maybe he was asleep again. Never knew him to sleep during the day, but since he'd been home so much, he'd been sleeping during the day, during the night, just about anytime you could think of. Asked him if he was sick, but he said, "No, just tired." Sometimes he'd say, "Just got a lot on my mind, J," and smile at me. Not a happy smile, but a smile that was supposed to keep me from seeing that he wasn't really smiling at all. It didn't work, of course; I could tell that something was wrong, I just couldn't tell what it was, and he wouldn't say.

I walked up the stairs and stood for a minute in the hallway listening for his snoring, but again I didn't hear a thing. The door to his bedroom was only partly closed, so I pushed it open and peeked in. Nothing. The bed looked like a plate of scrambled eggs; even his pillow had fallen on the floor. A pile of white shirts lay beside the hamper in the corner, two pairs of shoes beside them. A blue tie with yellow polka dots was folded on his dresser, his watch beside it. The alarm clock laying on the floor ticked and tocked, steady as could be.

I took a deep breath. I could smell my father, the perspiration of his shirts, his breath on the pillow, his scent gathering like dust in the corners and along the baseboards. It was a smell that usually made me feel good, made me feel like things were okay, but this time it was a tired smell, the smell of old coffee, the smell of someone who had come to a complete stop.

I sat on his bed. A picture of my dad and mom stood on the nightstand. It had been taken just a few blocks away in Ewing Park. I could see the Municipal Swimming Pool in the background where my friends and I often hung out. To the left of the pool was a pavilion with a dirt floor and picnic tables with bench seats attached. There was so much shade from the surrounding oaks and maples that there was hardly any grass on the ground. It looked like a hot, dusty day the way my dad's forehead shined. There were some other men and women looking busy with baskets of food and such; a few packages, tied with bows, rested on the corner of one picnic table.

Dad was looking down, his hand on my mother's stomach. Mother's hands were on top of his, and she had a smile on her face that was so broad it looked like her cheeks would burst. "Look at her," my dad would say when looking at the photo. "She's big as a house! Of course, I never said that to her face; she would have crowned me. Look how pretty she was, and happy, too." He'd always emphasize how happy my mother was, how she loved being pregnant, how she glowed all the time and couldn't wait for the baby to arrive. How she stenciled the room with clowns and trains and colorful horses, how she moved the crib from corner to corner trying to figure out the best place for her baby. How he'd find her when he came home sitting in the baby's room in a rocker, smiling and waiting.

"Yes, she was very happy," he'd say, messing my hair and smiling broadly like my mother, although his face never looked like it would burst. Instead it looked like it might crack from pretending so hard. "She sure loved you, J," he'd say, and I would try to appreciate it, but I never felt it, really. I never felt my mother's love. How could I? "She held you every minute," Dad would ramble on. "She held you and rocked you and gave you your bottle and changed your diapers and held you some more. She cooed and oohed and ahhed and was prouder of you than anything in the world. She loved you so much," he'd say, his smile beginning to crack slightly in the corners. I listened, feeling uncomfortable.

Brian's mother often told him in no uncertain terms how much she loved him, but it didn't sound gentle like I imagined it should. It seemed edgy, like she was reminding him of something to make him obey her. Brian always said, "I know, I know," not like it made him feel good, but more like he had heard it so many times that she might just as well have been asking him to take out the garbage or tuck in his shirttail.

I knew what it meant when Dad told me he loved me, because I could see it in the way he smiled, the way he patted my back or hugged me, when none of my friends were around. I didn't know exactly how to explain the feeling. You know at the beginning of the summer when you go to Edelman's to buy a new pair of tennis shoes and they're as white as can be? There's not a mark on them. The little plastic tips at the end of the laces are still perfect. Then, when you put them on, your feet have never felt better and you know you can run faster than the wind. You just feel good: taller, and more confident. Well, that's how my dad's love felt, like new Keds in June.

But I didn't know what my mother's love would feel like. Or had felt like. I was hardly even a person back then. All I did was eat, sleep, and poop; at least that's what my dad said. "That's all you were supposed to do," he would add. Didn't seem quite fair that my mother knew me but I barely had any sense of her at all. And then, in no time, she was gone.

Dad tried hard as he could to make it seem like she was part of the family. When I got an A+ on my South America project in Miss Loss' class, the first thing he said was, "Your mother would be so proud." As far as I could tell, according to him, my mother would have been proud of everything I did, no matter how small, no matter how stupid. She would have been proud or happy or in all ways pleased with everything about me. Yet, although this was nice to hear, it didn't make her any more real. Instead it made my dad seem more sad and lonely to me; these were his wishes, his dreams, his fantasies about the person he had loved most in the world, not mine. Nevertheless, I played along and smiled, just like I did long after I had stopped believing in Santa. You do some things just to make your parents feel okay.

Dad's closet was as big a mess as mine. I mean, he must stand across the room and throw his clothes, belts, ties and underwear into the closet like someone might throw darts at a dart board. You know, some hit the wall, others snagged on a hook or nail, and still others draped over whatever they landed on, and stayed for weeks on end. "We come from a long line of pigs," he'd say with a straight face.

On the right side of the closet, he had at least ten pairs of shoes, many of which had holes in the bottom or tears where the seams once held them together. All of them, no matter the original color, were grey with dust. Their waxed laces no longer stood straight out when I pulled on them.

Behind the shoes were two boxes: one full of old magazines, mostly *Life* and *Look* and *Mechanics Illustrated* and even a few *Mad Magazines* that I hadn't looked at in a while. It was a large blue box, wide and square and deep, worn at the corners and sealed shut with masking tape.

I slid the magazines onto the floor and dragged the other box into the middle of the room. I removed the lid, and under it was a large plastic bag. I took the bag out and unzipped it across the top. I pulled the insides out, and there it was: my mother's wedding dress. It was a little yellow in places, but it sure was beautiful. There was lacy stuff across the chest with pearls sewn right into the cloth. There weren't any straps, so I didn't know how it stayed up. My dad always said with a smile, "That wasn't a problem." It was all kind of layered from the waist on down; on top was a filmy-looking material that you might make doilies out of, and underneath was a smooth silky material, so soft that if I didn't have my eyes open, I might not even notice that I was touching it. There was lacy trim around the bottom, and in the back there was what my dad called a "train," which was just a bunch of dress that stretched out behind her when she walked. Dad told me that a little girl followed my mother around all day to make sure the train didn't get stuck on anything. Of course, there was also a veil, which looked like a little shower curtain that came down and covered her face. Not so sure what that was about, but my father said that seeing my mother in her veil was like looking at a dream.

I stretched the dress out on the carpet and put the veil where I thought my mother's head would be. I lay down right beside the dress, and for the first time, my head almost reached the veil. Dad always said my mother was a "bitty thing," meaning she was small. I wondered what she would think if she knew I was almost as tall as her.

"What are you doing?" my dad asked, his voice scaring me half to death. My head went up and so did my feet. And for a moment I was stuck there like a turtle. He was just a silhouette in the doorway; I couldn't tell from his voice if he meant "What in the world are you doing!" or just "Whatcha doin'?"

"I didn't know you were home," I said, finally getting to my feet.

"Well, I am," he said, his voice still hard to read. He stood beside me looking down at the dress, his hands at his side. He didn't say a thing for what seemed like forever.

"I just wanted to see it again," I said. He still didn't speak, but a sigh rose from his chest and filled the room.

"I was down at Scala's," he said, "checking on the car."

"Is it fixed?" I asked.

"Should be in a day or two."

"That's good," I said.

"Yeah, that's good," he said, as if it didn't really matter.

I looked up at him, but his gaze never left the dress. I wanted to ask if he was okay, but I stopped myself. It seemed like a foolish question.

The longer we stood there looking down at the dress in complete silence, the more I felt that I had done something wrong, like I had been caught stealing something, something that belonged to my father, not me.

"That's why I kept it," Dad said. I looked at him, unsure of what he meant. "I considered burying her in this dress. I wanted her to look the way she looked before she died. I wanted her to look like the beautiful woman I had married, before everything happened."

His voice was different. It wasn't a father's voice; it was just the voice of one person talking to another. I didn't know what to say.

"Must sound foolish," he said. "But that's what I wanted to do. In fact, I took the dress to Campbell's Funeral Home and everything. A lot of people thought it was a bad idea, that it was odd or maybe even a little crazy. They said she wouldn't have wanted it. But, in the end, what everyone else said didn't matter. I would have gone ahead with it except for one thing. I couldn't part with the dress. I couldn't let it go." His voice trailed off like he was remembering something he hadn't thought of in a long time. He sighed again.

"So I went to Edmin's and I bought your mother a new dress. At first I chose a black one, but then I decided, what the hell, and I bought her a bright yellow dress with daisies on it, the kind of dress she might have worn to the park."

I had never noticed how round my father's shoulders were, like they had been worn down slowly, slowly by the drip, drip, drip of time and memories. I reached for his hand and held it. He didn't hold mine, but he also didn't pull his away.

"And her favorite pearl necklace," he said.

He knelt down and took the hem of my mother's wedding dress in his hand and caressed it between his thumb and forefinger. He smiled. "Yeah, that's why I kept it. I couldn't stand the thought of never seeing it again."

Dad took the handkerchief from his back pocket and wiped the tears from my eyes.

"I'm sorry, J. I didn't mean to upset you."

"That's okay, Dad," I said.

"Sure is beautiful, isn't it?" he said.

"Sure is."

"And she made it even more beautiful." He looked at me for a long moment and smiled. "What made you get it out today?" he asked.

"I don't know. Just wanted to see it again, I guess."

I wanted to say more, but I couldn't find the words. I didn't know exactly why I had gotten the dress out again. It had been a long time. Even when I didn't see it for a while, I thought about it folded up in a box in my father's closet, just lying there in a dark corner under a bunch of my dad's junk. Just like my mother was lying in a box somewhere. Sometimes I got afraid, just plain scared that I never had a mother at all, that everything was just made up and I didn't really come from anywhere. That I was literally a motherless child, always the only kid in class who didn't have to make a card on Mother's Day.

On the other hand, I sometimes thought, would I have been better off not having a mother at all than having one and losing her? I hated myself when I thought this. I hated myself because I knew how much my father loved my mother. I knew how much he missed her. I knew he wanted me to love her and miss her just as much. And I wanted to, too. At least, I thought I did. It would have broken my father's heart if he knew how hard I had to try. That's why I was crying. That's what the tears were about.

"Are you okay?" he asked.

"Yeah, Dad, I'm okay. I'm sorry."

"What are you sorry for?" he asked.

"I don't know. For getting the dress out again. For making you feel bad."

"No, no, no," he said and put his arms around me. "Don't ever feel like that, J. You could never make me feel bad. Don't ever worry about that." He looked me straight in the eyes. "Okay?"

"Yeah," I said.

"Now, why don't you go wash up for dinner? Maybe we'll go to Nick's for burgers and milkshakes tonight. How's that sound?"

"Okay," I said.

"Good, go ahead, then. I'll put everything back."

When I came out of the bathroom, Dad was standing in the middle of his bedroom, my mother's dress in his arms. I could hear him crying, trying to be quiet about it so I wouldn't notice. I wanted to go to him. I even took a breath and was about to say something, but I didn't. He seemed too far away, even though he was right there. It was like he had gone to some place where I couldn't go. And then it hit me. For as close as we were, for as much as we loved each other and stood by each other, there were times when we were both alone and couldn't be reached by anyone else. All we could do was wait for the other one to came back. Coming back was everything.

Charlie No Face

9

"Okay, so what do you want to see?" Brian and I were walking across the Ewing Park Bridge on our way to town. We each had fifty cents in our pockets and life was good.

"Maybe we could see *Journey to the Center of the Earth*," I said. "It's on at the Majestic. I heard it's pretty good. This scientist finds a hole in the ground that leads to the middle of the earth. It's like a race. They even take a duck with them, and it gets killed, and there's lots of monsters and stuff."

Brian pulled a stone from his pocket, stepped back to the edge of the sidewalk, and took two quick steps forward before hurling it as far as he could. We both leaned against the railing and watched it disappear, finally seeing a tiny splash in the Conequenessing Creek, over two hundred feet below. "Tough luck," I said.

There was a tiny island in the creek that we tried repeatedly to hit, always unsuccessfully. I took a rock from my pocket and, instead of throwing it towards the island, I hurled it at the building on the shore, part of the local power plant. "Geez," said Brian, "don't do that!" But it was too late. Everyone knew that the guard inside the power plant had a rifle, and when anyone hit the metal roof from the bridge above, he would come out and fire back. But I wasn't worried. There wasn't any way he could run outside and get off a good shot before we were long gone. We watched the stone tumble over and over until it hit the metal roof with an echoing K-TWANG!

"Run, Jackie!" Brian yelled, laughing like a hyena. "Run, before he blows your brains out—not that it would be a big loss."

"At least I got some brains to blow out," I said, catching up to him just as he reached the other side. We fell on the grass, completely out of breath, more from laughing than anything else. Brian was still laughing when I clocked him on the head.

"Ow! Wha'd you do that for?"

"Because I wanted to," I said. "Is that a problem?"

"It is if you want to live to see tomorrow, monkey-boy," Brian said, rolling over on top of me, trying to give my head a dutch rub.

We wrestled long enough and got up off the ground just as the workers across the street at the tube mill broke for lunch. They were all sweaty and dirty-looking with their construction helmets, their t-shirt sleeves rolled up and their cumbersome metal-tipped boots, big as clown shoes. They sat on the grass outside the massive sliding doors where trains came and went, picking up miles and miles of tubing. Behind them we could see men in metal helmets bent over steel tubes with great flashes of lightning all around them. And loud, my God, it was always so loud at the mill! Loud enough that if I opened my window at night I could here it clear as could be, as if it were in my backyard. We waved to the men as they opened their lunch pails, and they waved back. "Whatcha got today?" we called, and they'd talk back to us like we were real people. "Ham and cheese!" or "Bologna!" or sometimes "Leftover fried chicken!" which made all the other guys howl with envy. We waved goodbye and continued our trek to town. "You young'ens take it easy," they called after us.

"So, Brian, you wanna journey to the center of the earth or not?" Brian looked at me with a sly grin on his face. "What?" I asked.

"Have you heard about *Operation Petticoat*? It's at the Manos."

"No, what about it?" I said.

"Well, I heard Kelso talking about it. He said there's a woman in the movie, and she has, well, she has..."

"She has what!" I said.

"Kelso said she had the biggest zoomers he'd ever seen."

"Zoomers, Brian?"

"You know what I mean, zoomers, coconuts, boobs!"

I admit that thinking about women's breasts had opened up a whole new world for Brian and me, especially since the whole thing with Kelso and Tommy's sister. Sometimes when we got together we didn't even get our baseball cards out because we wanted to talk about, well, other stuff.

But at the center of it all was the female breast, which to us was the most amazing thing God ever came up with.

"About the coolest invention I can think of," Brian said. "Have you ever noticed Nick's daughter, Bunny? I mean, she has 'em."

"Yeah, I know," I said. "One day I went to the counter to get a popsicle and she waited on me. When she brought me the banana-sicle, she bent over and I could see everything—I mean *everything*. And all she did was smile, like maybe she wanted me to see, you know, everything. It was the absolute best. Now I try to buy a popsicle everyday. But I have to watch for the right time, because sometimes Nick is at the counter, and I don't need to see anything of Nick's." We both laughed.

"That's for sure!" said Brian.

Then Brian started telling me about one of his dreams. He said he always had dreams about women, although I don't think they were dreams at all. I think saying it was a dream just made it easier for him to talk about boobs and stuff. Since he didn't have any control over what happened once he fell asleep, he could say just about anything.

"I'm tellin' ya," Brian insisted. "It's true! I dreamed it."

"That don't make it true," I said when he described a dream about a woman with three breasts. "I mean, inside your dream it may be true, but in the real world it's, well, just weird."

"Call it what you want," he said. "You're just jealous you didn't dream it."

"Why would I want to have a dream about a woman with three breasts? It doesn't sound all that appealing to me."

"Whadaya mean 'not appealing'? As if you've had any experience with this stuff!" Brian said, a little miffed.

"And you have?" I reminded him. "I mean, going through your mom's underwear drawer doesn't exactly make you an expert."

Let's face it, both of us wanted to know the score about girls and women more than anything else, but we didn't have any idea how to find out. I could never ask my father, "Hey, Dad, by the way, when you want to put your thing inside a girl, where do you put it?" I mean, it's not exactly dinner conversation.

Brian actually tried to talk with his father who just laughed, messed his hair, and said, "Oh, you don't need to know about that now." How would he know what we did and didn't need to know? When he was a kid, they probably didn't even have sex.

Tommy's father had magazines. Tommy called them girly magazines, and whenever we went to his house and his parents weren't home, we'd sneak into their bedroom and dig to the bottom of his dad's sock drawer for a *Playboy*. My God! I thought the first time I opened to the centerfold. "My God, look at that!"

"I know, I know," said Tommy. "Isn't it amazing!"

"My God," I said with the same reverence I had when I went to Forbes Field with my dad. "Is this for real? I mean, are these real women?"

Tommy laughed. "Are they ever!" he said.

"My God, look at them; I mean it, look at them." Of course, the "them" I was referring to were breasts. I couldn't believe their shape, like cantaloupes with Milk Duds on the end. I had never seen anything so beautiful in my whole life. Nothing compared. I made a vow right then and there to see as many of them as possible. Not in magazines, but in person. If someone would let me.

"And what about Rabbi Musselman's wife!" said Brian. "I'm telling you, sometimes when I go to bed at night my legs ache from thinking about Mrs. Musselman and her breasts." Rabbi Musselman's wife was a substitute teacher at our school. She had flaming red hair that she wore in a bun and dark red lips and, of course, the biggest, bounciest breasts we'd ever seen. When flu season came, we always knew Mrs. Mussleman would eventually substitute for Miss Loss who, as my father would say, had a "weak constitution." And when she did, I became the dumbest kid in the class, always raising my hand so she would come to my desk when I needed help. She always smiled and bent over. "How can I help you, Jackie?" And I'd say, "I can't seem to find Bolivia on this map, Mrs. Musselman." And she'd lean over to help me, her blouse slightly open and the top of her brassiere visible.

At recess Brian and I would compare notes. "My God, it was black!" Brian would exclaim. "And you could see her skin right through it; I mean, I thought I was gonna die."

"I know, I know," I'd say, punching him in the arm.

Sometimes Mrs. Musselman followed us right to bed.

"Yeah," said Brian, "I get this feeling like I'm gonna explode, and when I wake up, it's like I peed myself, except it isn't pee."

"I know exactly what you mean," I said. "It happens to me at least once a week."

"No, you're kiddin' me."

"No, I'm not kiddin'! And when Mrs. Musselman subs, I know for sure it's gonna happen."

"Wow, that is so cool," said Brian.

Mrs. Musselman, the rabbi's wife, was our centerfold, our dream girl. Made me wonder what it would be like to go to the Jewish church. When we looked around the classroom at Beatrice and Patty and Nancy and Betsy, we couldn't imagine that their flat chests would ever look like Mrs. Musselman's. Impossible!

Somehow, journeying to the center of the earth didn't seem nearly as exciting as seeing a beautiful actress with gigantic honkers. So we headed for the Manos Theater. The ticket window wasn't open yet, so we walked down the street to PeeWee's. Kelso was there with some of his crowd. When he was with his friends, he acted like he didn't know us. He even told us that if we spoke to him in front of his guys, he'd rip our faces off. A little discretion didn't seem much of a price to pay to protect our faces, so we honored Kelso's request and took a couple of stools at the end of the counter.

Lydia was working hard, dogs climbing up her arm, burgers sizzling on the grill, a Pirate game on the radio, Bob Prince's voice encouraging our hapless Buccos. "Put one in the pea patch!" Prince urged, but the next pitch was a called third strike. "God!" said Lydia, taking the paint sticks and whipping some mustard and ketchup on our puppies. "Couple of Cokes?"

"Yes," we said and spun around on our stools a few times until Lydia gave us a look. Richie Valens was moaning a tune on the juke box, "I had a girl, and Donna was her name..."

"This is gonna be great," said Brian, referring to our date with the monster-breasted movie star. "Can you imagine what they're gonna look like on the screen? My God, they'll be as big as Buicks!"

"Yeah," I said, watching Kelso and his boys talking and combing their ducktails. Kelso gave me a look like he was gonna nail me if I didn't stop staring.

"Two hot dogs with mustard and ketchup and two Cokes," said Lydia, sliding our meal down the counter. I took a long swig from my Coke bottle and a bite from my dog. Out of the corner of my eye, I could see Kelso and company leaving the scene. But a minute later he was back, standing right beside me. I didn't dare look up.

"How you doin', my little squirts?" he said.

"Hey, Kelso," said Brian, "we're gonna see *Operation Petticoat*. Should we sit in the first row?"

"I don't know, punk," said Kelso. "You may pass out from overexposure, if you get my meaning."

"Yeah," Brian said, laughing, but looking like he had no idea what Kelso meant.

"Hey you, punk number two," he said to me. "Guess who split the scene?"

"Split the scene?" I said.

"Yeah, split the scene, cut out, bit the bag." I stared at him. Kelso frowned. "Guess who's dead, you moron?"

"I don't know," I said.

"Well, guess," he said, his eyebrows raised as if he were giving me a hint. I still didn't get it, so then he started walking around bumping into things and acting like he couldn't tell where he was going.

"Charlie?" I said.

"Bingo," said Kelso. "Dead as a doornail, my little annoying friend."

"No," I said, "that can't be so. We just saw him a couple of weeks ago."

"Can be so," said Kelso, "and is so."

Brian put his hot dog down. "What?" he asked. "What happened?"

"Kelso said Charlie's dead."

"No way," said Brian. "How could Charlie be dead? I mean, after all he's been through, like he's been shot hundreds of times, for sure, and that never did nothin' to him. So how could he just up and die? He's never done that before."

"First time for everything, knucklehead," said Kelso.

"Wait a minute," I said. "How do you know this?"

"You doubting my word?" said Kelso in mock defense.

"No, I just need to know, that's all. Who told you?"

"Jimmy told me."

"Who's Jimmy?" said Brian.

"Jimmy is Jimmy, that's who he is."

"Jimmy Falzone?" I said. "One of the guys who was just in here?"

"The big ugly one?" said Brian.

"Hey!" said Kelso, pulling Brian up from the stool by his shirt. "Don't talk like that about my friend."

"Okay, okay," said Brian. "I was just kidding anyway, geez."

"So, Kelso, what did Jimmy Falzone tell you?" I asked.

"Well, it's like this, after I told him about beating Charlie up that night..."

"Beating him up," I said. "What do you mean, beating him up?"

"Don't interrupt me, punk," said Kelso. "You want me to tell you what happened or not?" It didn't seem like the time or place to explain to Kelso what a jerk he was.

"Yes, Kelso, I want you to tell me what he said."

"Okay, so shut up. Anyway, Jimmy and some guys from the valley started going out every night to find Charlie, but no matter how long they looked or where they looked, they couldn't find him. I mean, they slept out in the woods down on 351 waiting for him almost every night, and he never came out."

"So," I said, "that doesn't prove anything; maybe they just missed him. Maybe he went away for a while."

"Went away," said Kelso. "Where would he go and not be noticed? Anyway, that's not the whole story. So Jimmy goes down to the gas station to talk to Tony. Tony has seen Charlie more times than anyone anywhere. I mean, the guy has sat down and actually talked with Charlie, as much as Charlie can talk, mostly grunts and groans. Anyway, the guy's a genius for finding Charlie. Has been doing this since he was a kid. And you know what Tony said to Jimmy?"

"No, what?" I said.

"Tony said real matter-of-fact, he said, 'Charlie's gone.' Jimmy couldn't believe what he was hearing, so he asked again and Tony said, 'Yeah, Charlie's deader than dead.' They say he got hit by the B&O train that comes wailing through town all the time."

"He got hit by a train?" I said.

"Yeah, that's what the man said. You got trouble with that?"

"No, I just...when did he say it happened?"

"I don't know," said Kelso. "Who cares?"

"The train that comes through town?"

"Yeah, why?" said Kelso.

"Yeah, why?" said Brian.

"I don't know," I said. "It's just that the B&O track doesn't go anywhere near where Charlie usually walks. It's miles away. If he was dead, why wasn't it in the papers? I mean, the guy's a legend around here."

"What are you, Joe Friday? I'm tellin' you, Tony's got no reason to lie," said Kelso. "The monster-man's dead, that's it. Case closed. If you don't want to believe it, that's your problem." Kelso looked disappointed. "Just trying to be nice to you, you little twerp, because, in all likelihood, we were the last ones to see him. I guess I shouldn't'a bothered."

I was stunned. I couldn't believe my ears. I sat there while Brian finished his dogs and mine just sat on their plate.

When we left, Brian still wanted to see *Operation Petticoat*. "There's nothing we can do about it," he reasoned. But somehow, breasts, no matter how large, didn't seem that important. This was even bigger. I mean, it was like the president dying or something; Charlie was that much a part of things around there. Our fathers knew about Charlie; everyone knew about Charlie. The stories were legendary, and legends can't die, can they?

"No, man, I don't wanna go to the movie anymore," I said.

"But Jackie, c'mon, we may never get another chance like this."

"What are you talking about?" I said. "Charlie is dead, and all you can think about is a stupid movie. What's the matter with you?"

"Nothin's the matter with me," said Brian, all defensive. "I think you're the one that's got the problem. It's not like you knew him or something; he was just this freaky thing, and now we don't ever have to worry about him trying to run one of us over with a car. I'm tellin' ya, you gotta let it go of it."

This made me mad, because Brian was actually right. I didn't know Charlie. I mean, we went out one night like a bunch of hunters looking for Charlie, and we found him. It wasn't like we stopped by his house and had a nice talk or somethin'. It wasn't like he was a real person to us. So why did it bother me?

"So, man, you comin' or not?" said Brian.

"No, I'm not comin'. Let's get out of here."

"No way," said Brian. "I'm staying. I'm not missing this."

"You're kiddin' me, right?"

"No, I'm not," said Brian. "I been thinking about this for a week, and I'm not missing one minute of it."

"Okay, suit yourself," I said, adding, "I'm going home!" and with that, I walked away.

By the time I got to the end of the block, Brian was by my side. But we didn't say a thing the whole way home.

Charlie No Face

10

The dog days of August were just around the corner, and baseball season was winding down. All that was left was the Shaugnessy Playoffs, which would determine the season's champion. We had won the regular season with a record of 16-2, so we didn't have to play in the first round. We won the second round and then faced Moose again for all the marbles.

Brian's team didn't make the playoffs, which wasn't a surprise. Brian had had a good season, though, getting some hits and starting almost every game.

Since his season was over, Brian's family decided to leave for summer vacation a little early. His grandparents owned a cottage on Conneaut Lake where they stayed in August every year. Brian always got excited about vacation: "Man, it's so cool; we fish and swim, and you wouldn't believe the girls out on the beach. Some of them wear two-piece swimsuits! It's unbelievable!"

He left all his baseball cards with me. This was a big show of trust for Brian and I treated it that way.

"Don't worry, man; I'll take good care of them, I promise."

"You swear?" said Brian.

"I swear," I said solemnly.

Standing in their driveway, I didn't feel comfortable saying I would miss him. It was too, I don't know, mushy. So I shook his hand.

"Good luck with the playoffs," he said. "You guys are gonna win, I'm sure."

"Thanks," I said.

"Hey, don't forget; you and your dad are invited to the lake for a weekend whenever you can make it."

"I won't forget," I said, unsure if we would be able to go this year.

Our car was finally back on the road, and Bennie Stark had come by with his dump truck, the Blue Goose, to haul the tree away. But while things seemed to be getting back to normal, Dad still wasn't himself. When Bennie asked if he should take the ping-pong table too, Dad paused for the longest time and finally said, "No, I'll take care of it."

I really missed the ping-pong table, especially since Dad worked so hard on it. But I think he missed it twice as much as me. I don't know; it was like the ping-pong table was more than a ping-pong table to him. It seemed like the table measured him somehow, like it was a base hit in the bottom of the ninth that won the game. And when it got all busted, it was like my dad got thrown out at home. Whatever it was, he sure missed it. He hadn't been the same since the car and the storm and the table. He looked worried all the time, like he was waiting for the other shoe to fall. I asked him if anything was wrong, and he said, "Just big people stuff, J, nothing for you to be concerned about," which made me more concerned. What "big people" stuff? For someone who was on vacation, he sure wasn't having much fun.

Anyway, when all was said and done, "taking care of it" meant putting all the pieces in the cellar where it lay in a heap, the net still attached to a small chunk of plywood. He put the paddles on a shelf beside his tools, just in case we'd need them, which, of course, we wouldn't.

As Brian's car pulled away from the curb, he leaned out the back window and yelled, "Long live Charlie!"

I yelled it back, "Long live Charlie!" It just made sense; I mean, it was kind of a way to keep Charlie alive.

The final series against Moose was a major deal. I had never seen so many people at the ball field. I mean, usually there were lots of parents, but for the playoffs, people came who weren't parents at all. I mean, they came just because they were interested in who would win. Even the *Ledger* was on hand each night with Mr. Tucko reporting all the details the next day.

It was a best-of-three-games series. We won the first thanks to a masterful performance by Zeke, and it seemed like there was no way of stopping us. Though we felt confident about the second game, Moose was pesky, and even though they had a hard time hitting Stevie, Moose players bunted every chance they got. Then we made a few costly errors that led to three runs. Three runs was really nothing, but do you think we could score?

Not a run, not a single run. It was embarrassing, and by the sixth inning we were frustrated. Coach gathered us up and told us to calm down, it was only a game, have fun and everything would go the way it's supposed to. Well, I guess losing was the way it was supposed to go, because three of us went to bat in the sixth inning, including myself, and three of us struck out. When Biff was called out on a pitch that was clearly out of the strike zone, he threw his helmet so hard that it cracked. All of us yelled at the ump, and a few of my teammates threw their bats onto the infield. Biff's mother yelled at the umpire and told him he was a cheat. The ump looked at her and laughed, which didn't help matters at all. Some of our players sat on the bench and cried.

You might say we didn't handle losing very well at all.

After the game, Coach called a meeting under the bleachers in right field. He told us that if anyone lost his cool in the next game, Coach would take him out immediately. It didn't matter to Coach if we won or lost, but it did matter that we showed some "class." I'd never seen Coach so stern; I mean, he didn't get angry, but his point was clear. Biff was still upset about the final call, and when he started to complain, Coach didn't say a word; he just looked at Biff until he stopped, and then he looked at him a while longer until Biff finally said, "Okay, I get it."

It all came down to game three.

Usually I didn't get very nervous before a game, but this was so important that I barely slept the night before. I spent the whole afternoon lying on the couch holding my eyes shut in a desperate attempt to get some rest and calm down. My dad came in and saw me curled in a ball clenching my eyes.

"J, are you okay?"

"Yeah," I said, unconvincingly.

"If you're okay, then what's with the eyes?"

"Just trying to rest up for the game," I said.

"Rest up? You look like you're wound tighter than an Egyptian mummy."

He suggested that instead of lying on the couch, I get up, do some stretches, take a run around the block, and then come home to play a little catch in the backyard. So that's what I did. And he was right. We hadn't played catch in the yard since before the storm, mainly because there wasn't much yard to play in with the tree sprawled all over the place. So it felt good to be back in the rhythm with my dad, throwing and catching in turn. We'd come a long way since the days when Dad would throw the ball underhand to me, hoping, I'm sure, that I wouldn't miss it and get hit in the head. Now he didn't have to worry at all; I could do it just as well as him—well, almost as well.

"So, you think you're ready for the game?" Dad asked as he threw me a pop-up.

"Yeah, I think I'm as ready as I'll ever be," I said. "We should beat these guys, but I guess you never know."

"Suppose that's why they play the game," my dad said with a smile.

"Uh huh," I answered, trying to concentrate on the ground ball he had just thrown me. I went down on one knee just like Dad had taught me. I wasn't afraid of a bad bounce anymore. It seemed natural to scoop it up with my glove or play it off my chest.

"It's been quite a summer," said Dad, "with the storm and the car and everything."

"Sure has," I said.

"I've really enjoyed being home with you all this time, J. We got to do more things together this summer than ever before."

"Yeah, it's been great," I said, leaping for a ball that was over my head. "I wish you could be home like this all the time. I'm just glad your boss is letting you take such a long vacation."

Dad didn't say anything as he snatched the ball that I threw well to his left.

"Too bad about the ping-pong table," I said.

"Yeah, that was quite a disaster, wasn't it?" said Dad. "Maybe I can make us another one sometime."

The way he said "sometime" made me think he really meant never. Noticed this about my dad a lot lately. The words he said and the way he said them were often different, like part of him was trying to be happy or funny, while another part of him was feeling something else altogether, and the two parts couldn't decide who was in charge of what he was going to say. It had been confusing like this ever since the car got smashed at the Pirate game. Every once in a while he seemed like himself, but there still were lots of times when he didn't.

"J, do you remember your mother's aunt, Dorothy? She raised your mother after her parents split up. Do you remember visiting her a few years ago?"

I held the ball and thought for a minute. My dad tried to jog my memory. "She lives way out past Koppel near New Galilee, out in the country, almost to Ohio. It's kind of like a farm. You remember, don't you?"

"Was she the lady that smelled so bad that I almost threw up when I met her?"

"Well, yes, but it wasn't her that smelled; she had made a batch of anise cookies for us, if I remember correctly, and you didn't like the aroma," Dad said.

"Oh, yeah, now I remember; she had tables in her hallway with all these awful cookies cooling on them. She asked if I wanted one and that's when I thought I was gonna blow my breakfast all over her."

"Well, she's been living in Erie the last few years with her sister, but she moved back to New Galilee to help her nephew who has fallen on some hard times." Dad looked at me as if I was supposed to say something. "Anyway, she wrote me a letter and I called her the other day and I, we, thought it might be nice to get together."

"Uh huh," I said. It was getting late and I had to put on my uniform and head to the field. "Dad, I better get going."

"Okay, J, I just wanted to make sure it was okay about your mom's aunt; might be nice to have a little visit."

"Sure, okay," I said.

"Maybe stay for a few days."

"What?" I asked.

"Like a little vacation," said Dad. "We're not going to get away this summer, not even to Conneaut, so maybe...we'll see. Just a thought."

I didn't know what had gotten into Dad, but now I was really late and had to fly. I dashed into the house, put my baseball socks, pants, and jersey on. Got my cap out of the closet. Grabbed my glove, dangled it on the end of my bat, and then ran out the door. "Good luck!" called Dad.

For the life of me, I never thought we'd need luck to beat Moose. I mean, yeah, they were a good team, but we beat them twice during the regular season and, even though they beat us once in the playoffs, no one really considered them a threat. Even Nick said it was a fluky win. So imagine my surprise when I took the field in the fourth inning of our third and deciding game and we were losing 2-0.

Things came apart in the top of the first inning when our third baseman, Wayne, made two throwing errors on consecutive bunts, and Moose had two guys on with none out. No problem with Zeke on the mound, right? Well, would you believe that the next pitch got away from him and went to the backstop, advancing both runners? Then Boomer Blasingame hit a dinky pop to right field, but Skinny Thompson lost it in the sun; it rolled the whole way to the fence before I could reach it. I threw the ball home, but by then both Moose players had scored and half the crowd was going wild.

No problem, I thought. We would make it up.

But the game slowed to a crawl. We couldn't do anything to score. It was like we were totally jinxed. When I looked at my dad in the bleachers, he just shrugged, and Nick, beside him, turned his palms up as if to say, "What the heck is going on here!"

We hung tough, though, and finally broke through when Al Wilson hit a home run in the fourth, but Moose scored two more in the bottom of the inning and we were behind again, 3-1.

We came back in the fifth, though. I poked a soft liner up the middle for a single to get things started. Then Wicker hung a curve out over the plate and Biff launched it over the centerfield fence. Just like that, we were all tied up.

The crowd was into it now; my dad and Nick were hugging each other and jumping up and down. I skipped across home plate and waited for Biff as he rounded third. When he hit home we were both buried under a mountain of Kiwanis players. "C'mon, boys, the game ain't over yet," said the ump, but we were feeling pretty confident now.

Nothing much happened in the bottom of the fifth or the top of the sixth. We were still all tied when we started the bottom of the last inning.

Before we went back out onto the field, Coach called us together. "Remember," he said, "no matter what happens out there, you've had a great season. Each of you should be proud of how you've played; I know I am. Now go out there and give it your best!"

When I took my position in center field, I felt relaxed and confident. Zeke had mowed them down in the fifth; we were definitely getting to

Young. All we needed to do was get through this inning, and I felt sure we'd score.

The Moose Coach made a change to start the inning. He replaced Wicker Young with a pinch hitter, Richie Zinkman—yes, the same Richie that I had beaten out for the final spot on the Kiwanis team when we were ten. Richie wasn't crying anymore. In fact, Richie had grown almost six inches since then. He hadn't played much this summer because he'd broken his foot jumping into an empty swimming pool. Don't ask. Before he broke his foot, though, he was a very good player. But he still walked with a limp and looked pretty rusty at the plate.

Zeke went right after him with a fastball up under the chin. Richie barely got out of the way. The pitch worked, though, because when Richie got back into the batter's box, he was about six inches further from the plate. So Zeke hit the outside corner for a strike with his second pitch, and Richie never got the bat off his shoulder. Zeke went with a slow curve next, and Richie almost corkscrewed himself into the ground trying to hit it. Two strikes.

I leaned over a few times to stretch my legs and briefly practiced my batting stance in case I got to bat in the next inning. Coach told us that baseball was a team sport, and no team has individual heroes, but I couldn't help but think how cool it would be to knock in the winning run. If I knocked in the winning run, maybe it would put a real smile back on my dad's face again.

I leaned into my crouch, my hands on my knees, my cap shading my eyes from the setting sun. "C'mon, Zeke, c'mon kid, hum, baby, hum!" Richie leaned into the next pitch but didn't swing. The ump called a ball, and everyone groaned.

Maybe it would even be better if I could score the winning run. Just like the big leaguers, I'd run across home with my hands over my head; I'd toss my hat in the air and everyone would go wild. Yeah, maybe that would even be better.

Zeke went into his wind-up again, and I leaned into my stance. This time Richie swung at the ball and hit a high fly in my direction. I danced forward about five steps because it looked like a pop-up, but then I realized the ball was carrying. So I started to backpedal, but it kept going. I turned and ran, watching the ball over my left shoulder. I had it measured by then and patted my glove before I put it up to make the catch. But suddenly I ran into the centerfield fence; my hat flew off and I fell to the ground as Richie's ball sailed over the fence and landed three feet from where I lay.

Home run. Game over.

It was several days before I knew which end was up. My dad told me that I laid so still on the ground in centerfield that everyone thought I had been knocked out. Players and fans ran out onto the field to see. My dad and Nick pushed people aside to get to me. There was nothing wrong. I was just staring at the ball on the other side of the fence. It was like I was hypnotized or something. I didn't answer, even though I could hear my dad talking to me. "J? J, are you okay? J, answer me, are you okay? Does anything hurt?"

Zeke and Biff and the other guys stood around me. Al wondered aloud if I was dead, but someone said I couldn't be because my eyes were still open. Then someone else volunteered that they had a grandfather who died with his eyes open. I blinked just to shut them up, but I still didn't say a word.

I wasn't exactly sure why I didn't want to get up, or why I wouldn't speak. I knew I had to eventually. I knew I had to answer my dad. I had to walk off the field, go home, and try to forget about losing the game. For the moment, however, the ground seemed like the safest and best place to be. The grass was soft and cool, and the ground was firm; it felt like I was in the palm of someone's hand, someone who wouldn't drop me, who would just hold me for a little while.

Dad, Nick, and I walked home together, and both of them tried to cheer me up.

"That was one heck of a game, Jackie," Nick said.

"Don't think I've ever watched a better game," said Dad. "No one is going to forget that one, that's for sure. It was a classic. You played great, J." adding, "You got nothing to be ashamed of. You gave it your all."

"I'll say," said Nick. "I never seen a kid try as hard as you did. Man, when you went after that ball, I've never seen such determination. It was really something."

It was nice to hear all this, but it was like they were talking about someone else, not me. All I kept thinking was: *I can't believe we lost.* We were the best team in the league by far, but it didn't matter in the end. In the end, it came down to a few inches difference between winning and losing. If, instead of Richie, I had grown six inches, I could have reached over the fence and caught that ball without any difficulty. Just six inches, that's all. But it might just as well have been six feet or six miles because "what ifs" don't really count for anything in baseball. It's all just black and white. Geez.

Brian called all the way from Conneaut to tell me he couldn't believe we lost. He told me he was sorry about the way it ended and that he hoped I was okay. Then he told me about all the teenaged girls on the beach and their two-piece bathing suits. It seemed to me that Brian had developed a one-track mind, and it sure wasn't focused on baseball cards. I thanked him for calling and wished him luck in his never-ending quest for a glimpse of the female breast.

Tommy had also been away when the whole thing happened. His parents had a fishing cabin on one of the Finger Lakes in New York. Each year he came back smelling something awful with a portable refrigerator full of trout, all with their eyes and mouths frozen open. I never could get the thrill of fishing. I went with Tommy and his dad once over the hill to the Conequenessing. I even caught a fish, a little chub that we put in a can of water after ripping the poor thing's lip to shreds removing the hook. Once I got home, I didn't know what to do with him. Tommy wanted to gut him and look at his insides, but the miserable little fish was still gasping for air. I was sure glad we had grocery stores, because if I had to kill stuff so I could eat, I would be a goner in less than a week. Anyway, once the little guy died, I buried him. Tommy still laughs when he tells the story.

Tommy was shocked when I walked into Nick's. He was playing Hearts, running up the score, as usual.

"What the heck happened?" he said. "I couldn't believe it when I read the *Ledger*! Did you guys fall asleep or what?" Tommy was always the supportive type. His comments made me feel almost as bad as I felt lying on the centerfield grass.

"Yeah, Tommy, we thought it was our Christian duty to let the other guys win."

Tommy stopped flipping and looked at me, not sure if I was serious or not. "You kiddin'?" he asked.

I leaned against the pinball machine, tilting it. "Yeah, I'm kiddin'."

Nick called to me from behind the counter. "Hey, Jackie, my boy!"

"Hey, Nick," I said, looking kind of sorrowful.

"Whadaya say I treat you to a chocolate popsicle, huh?"

"I don't think so, Nick."

"C'mon, Jackie, worse things than this have happened." He paused for a long moment. My face must have convinced him not to contrast my loss with the plight of the poor starving Armenians or the ineptitude of the Washington Senators. I had already heard enough from my dad about "putting things into perspective," as he liked to say. "C'mon, J, it's not the end of the world." Of course he was right, but that didn't matter; I still felt awful.

What had happened to my summer?

Things couldn't have started any better. Dad was home and we got to hang out together all the time. Saw my Buccos play for the first time, and they won. I played the best baseball of my entire life. Got to see Charlie.

After that, it had all collapsed. I mean, Charlie died. And we lost to the stinking Moose because Richie grew six inches and I didn't.

"I don't know, Nick; it seems like much more than an eleven-year-old should have to endure."

"What do you mean, Jackie?" asked Nick as he pulled a chocolate popsicle from the freezer and handed it to me. I ripped off the paper and took a long draw on the 'sicle.

I wasn't sure how much to say, but Nick looked at me, his eyes begging me I to talk.

"It's like, well, we were the best team for sure, and we lost. It's like I needed a win; I mean, sometimes it's hard, just Dad and me. I don't have a mom, so stuff like winning the big game feels real important. I don't know."

Nick pursed his lips and attempted a smile.

"I don't know. I just feel like I deserve a little good luck."

When I finished, Nick got surprisingly quiet. He looked at me like he wanted to say something, but he couldn't. He even opened his mouth, but nothing came out, so he closed it again. He got down into a catcher's crouch and put his hands on my shoulders. He tried to smile, but it looked more like a grimace than anything else.

"You're right, Jackie. You're completely right," was all he finally said.

11

My dad thought that a visit to Great-Aunt Dorothy's might get my mind off things. "You'll really like her, J," he said over and over, like he was trying to sell me a new lawnmower or something. "You sure you don't remember her? She used to play Lincoln Logs with you when you were little." I must have been really little, because I didn't even remember the Lincoln Logs let alone Great-Aunt Dorothy.

My dad looked for pictures, but he didn't have any. He told me stories, but it didn't help. "Dad, what was I, like three or four? I'm telling you, I don't remember her!" That stopped him. For a few minutes.

"Now think hard, J."

"All I remember, Dad, is those awful-smelling cookies, and that doesn't exactly make me want to run off and meet her, unless you've got one of those gas masks we're gonna have to wear if the Russians drop the A-bomb."

Great-Aunt Dorothy lived way out in the country, west of New Galilee, almost to the Ohio line. Part of the road was familiar because that's where Kelso took us to see Charlie. That seemed like years ago. I looked down the road where I last saw Charlie struggling to find his way. It still seemed impossible that he was dead.

Route 351 wound through wooded hills and rolling farmland. Cows were grazing along the side of the road, some sticking their heads through the fences, reaching for some greener grass. Every once in a while I'd see a hawk perched on a telephone pole or a red-winged blackbird balanced precariously on the end of some tall grass. The sun flickered through the tree limbs, making me squint to see the oncoming dips and curves in the road. A B&O train chugged off in the opposite direction, the tracks parallel to the road, the rat-a-tat-tat of the trestles comforting in their rhythm, the men in the caboose waving their train caps at us as we passed. Ponds dotted the landscape, and a stream crossed under the road. The corn was coming on now, more than waist-high.

Kids were playing ball in their front yards or swinging on rusted swing sets, stopping to watch us as if they'd never seen a car before. A farmer was pitching hay into his loft, his young son beside him. A woman was hanging clothes on a line, clothespins dangling from her mouth. Everyone looked like they were wearing overalls. Their hands looked dirty, their boots looked muddy, and the air smelled so strong of manure that I had to hold my breath.

We turned a bend and there was New Galilee, the train track running through it, a few bars, several church steeples, a VFW, a stoplight, and then it was behind us.

I looked at my father, both his hands firmly on the steering wheel. "Where in the heck does she live?" I asked.

He smiled but didn't look at me. "You'll see," was all he said.

The land flattened out beyond New Galilee. More ponds. "Farmers use them for irrigation," Dad said.

"What?"

"The ponds. Farmers use them for irrigation," he repeated. "They pump water out of the ponds and into the fields when it gets dry in August. They've got to protect their crops. It's their living."

I guess I knew this; I mean, we saw a movie in social studies on America being the bread basket of the world, but I never gave it any thought. My dad would call in our grocery order on Saturday mornings, and then an hour or so later we'd go to Spoa's to pick it up. I mean, they had lettuce and corn and beans and nasty-looking cabbage and peppers and onions and all kinds of stuff. I never gave any thought to where it came from. I never gave any thought to the farmers, their kids playing in the front yard or helping in the barn or driving their father's tractor.

"Is Great-Aunt Dorothy a farmer?" I asked.

My dad looked at me and smiled again. "No, she's a little old for farming, although she may have a garden."

"Really?"

"Maybe," he said.

I thought about how neat it would be to have a garden. "Maybe I could get my own overalls. Could we have a garden?"

"Well, J, it's a little late in the year to start growing much of anything, but maybe next year if you'd like."

"Okay," I said, a little disappointed. It was quiet for a moment, and then Dad took a deep breath.

"Maybe if Great-Aunt Dorothy has a garden, she'd let you work in it, pulling weeds and stuff; how about that?" Dad asked.

"Okay, I guess." Seemed like an odd thing to say since Great-Aunt Dorothy lived almost in Ohio; the chances of seeing her on a regular basis were slim. I couldn't exactly take the train from Ellwood to Wampum and on to New Galilee and then walk the rest of the way to Great-Aunt Dorothy's, wherever the heck she lived.

"How much further, Dad?"

"Not much."

"How much is 'not much'?"

"Not much at all, 'cause I can see it from here."

Dad pointed through the windshield. I couldn't see anything except an old house with all the paint peeled off and the grass out front as high as a row of bushes.

"Right there," he said.

"What do you mean 'right there'? That thing?" I said, more than a little concerned.

"Yep!" said Dad with enthusiasm that was all out of proportion to what we were looking at.

"You've got to be kidding," I said. Dad pursed his lips. I could tell he was annoyed. "Dad, really, that doesn't look like any house I've ever seen before. I mean, look at it yourself. Some of the barns we passed along the way were nicer." His face was turning red, but I couldn't stop. I knew I was making sense. "Okay, the paint is all chipped off, and the shingles on the roof look like a mouth full of missing teeth. And look at the yard—hasn't been mowed in, like, forever! I mean it, Dad. How does she live like this?"

Now my dad's face looked worried. "Your great-aunt, Dorothy, is a wonderful person," he said. "Your mother loved her more than anyone. I think you will see that your mother was right."

I didn't know what my dad was talking about. This had nothing to do with whether Great-Aunt Dorothy was a nice person, and it definitely had nothing to do with whether my mother was right or wrong. That wasn't the point at all. The point was that she lived in what looked like a pig sty almost in Ohio, which might as well have been the other side of nowhere. And she didn't farm or, apparently, even take care of her house! What did she do was live like a hermit, or worse, a crazy person! Why in the heck was she living like that, I couldn't guess.

In a moment of rare good judgment, I didn't say any of this out loud.

Dad didn't speak again. His face was still red and moist, like he had just come out of a hot shower. I could tell this was very important to him, but I wasn't exactly sure why. Must be because of my mother. Must be because she liked Great-Aunt Dorothy so much. That made sense even to me. There wasn't much left of those days for my dad. Except Great-Aunt Dorothy and me, of course. But I was different. I reminded him of the end of those days. Maybe Great-Aunt Dorothy was like a time machine to Dad; maybe the thought of her took him back to the days before the end times, when he and my mother were young—when they didn't have any idea how things would turn out. I looked at my dad again.

"If Mom liked her, I'm sure she's nice."

Dad looked at me and smiled.

"I just can't figure out what the heck she's doing…"

"J, stop while you're ahead," said Dad. I considered this and thought it was good advice.

We turned into Great-Aunt Dorothy's raggedy-looking driveway—more of a a dirt path, really—and there was Great-Aunt Dorothy's house, hidden behind tall grass. It had, at some time in the distant past been painted white, although one side was almost entirely grey now. The chimney was missing some bricks at the top; what was left of the roof peaked over the front porch, and the windows were mostly shuttered. The covered porch stretched across the whole front of the house, making it the only appealing thing I'd seen so far.

Dad was right about one thing. There was a garden beside the house that was as big as our whole backyard. There was also a pond with a long board leveraged over a boulder, and beyond that, ten rows of overgrown Christmas trees that backed up to a thickly-wooded hillside. On the other side of the house was a barn or maybe garage. I wasn't sure which.

"Hello, William!" came the call from a tall, wiry woman standing on the front porch.

She wore a flowered dress and a bright yellow apron. Her face was pointed and sharp, her nose long, her ears large; in fact, everything about her seemed large. Her head was bigger than Dad's, which made her face stand out like she was on a movie screen. She had a broad, manly smile, and her grey hair was wound up in a bun, a stick of some sort pushed through it. She wore a pair of old white Keds and black socks to the middle of her calves. She had work gloves on, and her wire-rimmed glasses rested on the end of her nose. When she smiled, her teeth looked like a whitewashed fence row with a few crooked posts.

I felt drawn to her and yet unsure about her all at the same time. She stepped down off the porch. "Watch that one there," she said, pointing at the third step. "Almost break my darn leg on it every day; should do something about it. Should do something about a lot of things," she said, laughing.

She reached out to shake my father's hand, but then thought better of it and took him in her arms. "It is so damn good to see you, William!" she said.

"You, too, Aunt Dee," he said, and I looked quizzically at him. Aunt Dee? I hadn't heard that before. He said it like a little boy, all hesitant and excited at the same time.

"Let me look at you," she said, holding him out at arm's length. "My God, son, you've gotten fat."

"Well..." said my dad, but he didn't get a chance to finish.

"And who's this?" she said, looking at me. "This can't be Jack! My God, you've gone and growed up. You were just a little nothin' the last time I saw you, all spindly-looking with little noodly legs. Now look at you." I smiled, not knowing what to say. No one had called me Jack before. It sounded grown up. I wasn't sure what to expect from Great-Aunt Dorothy. By the looks of her, I thought she might just eat me up in one bite.

"Let me get a close look at you," she said, kneeling down in the grass and tipping her head forward so she could examine me over her glasses.

She laid a steady gaze upon my face and then looked into my eyes. I, in turn, stared into hers. Blue on blue. The lines on her face drew down at first, as she studied me closely. Then they turned up, and her mouth stretched into a grin. She put her hands on my shoulders, then looked back at my father.

"Yes, she's still in there, William. I see her twinkling in there. I see our Gretchen." And with that she hugged me so hard, I thought I'd burst. Just as quickly, she let go and stood up.

"You'uns have any trouble finding the place? It's been a few years,

William. How have you been?" She asked question after question, never waiting for an answer. "You must have wondered where the heck your father was taking you," she said to me with a high-pitched laugh. She couldn't have been more right.

"No trouble at all," my dad answered, several questions behind at this point.

"I just can't get over the size of him," she said again to my dad, this time as if I weren't there at all. "Did you ever think that he'd grow up so fast?"

"No..."

"Well, are you'uns thirsty or hungry? I made some lemonade. Some cookies, too." And she was gone, taking the porch steps by twos and calling over her shoulder, "You wait right here!" And we did.

Dad smiled at me. "What do you think?" he asked. I shrugged, unsure of the correct answer. I'd never met anyone like Great-Aunt Dorothy. She was like a cartoon character you'd see at the Majestic before the double feature started. Not quite Olive Oyl, but in the same ballpark. "She's somethin'," he said, and I agreed. That much was sure.

"Let me help you," my dad called as Great-Aunt Dorothy dragged three kitchen chairs onto the front porch. By the time Dad got to the front steps, she was gone again, returning with a pitcher of lemonade, some glasses, and a plate of cookies. Before the screen door closed, a little black dog scuttled out onto the porch, barking like mad and looking at Great-Aunt Dorothy all worried. "Hush, Abigail!" said Great-Aunt Dorothy. "Don't mind her. She's my old cocker pup, a little on the nervous side." By now, Abigail was squatting in the front yard taking care of business. Afterwards she scooted her butt on the grass like she was playing electric football.

"How old is she?" I asked, reaching to pet her.

"And he even talks!" she said, looking at my dad. "First words I've heard out of him. Wasn't sure if a cat had got hold of his tongue or what." She laughed again, this time her hands on her sides as if to hold her ribs in place. Abigail was inching closer, her ears perked like a baby elephant's.

"Old," was all Great-Aunt Dorothy said. "Don't know for sure. Found her layin' in a gutter after a storm when I was living up in Erie. Thought she was an old mop head just tossed aside until I heard a whimper. Oh my God, I thought, this poor thing is alive. Well, I took her in and figured I'd tend her until she died, but she didn't die after all. Ain't that right, Abigail? I'm tellin' you, she's a good listener; she looks at me when I talk, and I can tell she knows what I'm saying. She understands English, I swear, or maybe I'm just a little tetched in the head, you know." Then she looked at me with her eyes wide, and I thought for sure she was right about being tetched until she started laughing again.

"Got you thinkin', didn't I? I like this boy of yours, William. I can tell you've done a good job with him." She took my dad by the arm. "Come up here and sit. I'll pour you something cool."

Abigail was inching closer, but each time I reached out, she stepped back and barked at me. I sat in the grass and pulled my hand back. I looked at her and folded my hands in my lap. She was jet black, and you could barely see her eyes behind her pug nose. She was trimmed close along her back, but the fur on her legs and belly was a little longer. She had a tuft of curly hair on top of her head that made her look a little like one of those Marx brothers.

"C'mon, girl, you're okay," I said. I smiled and tried to sit still, hoping that would convince her I was safe. She sniffed my shoe and then tugged a little on the lace. She looked right at me, her tail wagging now. "What's a matter, girl?" I lay my hand on the grass below her chin and she sniffed it for a minute. Then she licked my hand, and I reached for her head, scratching behind her ears. "Atta girl." She leaned her head against my hand, her sad, brown eyes all relaxed. She lay down, her back legs stretching out behind her, her paws resting on my leg.

"Atta girl," I said soft and low and scratched behind both ears at once. "Hi there, Abigail; hi there, girl. How you doin'? Tell me, is Great-Aunt Dorothy crazy or just colorful? Huh? What do you think?" Abigail licked my hand.

"Jack! Come get some lemonade!" cried Great-Aunt Dorothy. Abigail trailed along behind me as I headed for the porch. She collapsed in the shade by the front door like a bag of bolts.

I had never tasted lemonade like this before. It had little bits of lemon in it, and it was tart and sweet at the same time, and if I closed my eyes I felt like I was right inside the lemon itself.

"Have some more," said Great-Aunt Dorothy, noticing I had downed the whole thing in one gulp. "Try a cookie, too," she said, sliding the plate in my direction.

Uh oh, the cookies. My throat started to close as I remembered the anise of old. "Thanks," I said, eying the plate and trying to sniff the cookies without putting my nose right on them. But they didn't smell so bad. I mean, there was a hint of anise, but basically they looked like sugar cookies, all soft and, to my surprise, warm. The first bite melted in my mouth. Best lemonade and cookies I think I'd ever had.

Once she noticed a cookie in my hand, Abigail rushed to my side, whimpering. She sat down on her butt and then sat up on her haunches, her front paws dangling.

"Look at that!" I said to my dad. "Look at Abigail sitting up."

"How about that."

"Yes," said Great-Aunt Dorothy. "That's her one trick, and I didn't teach her; she knew it when I found her. She'll sit like that forever if you keep eatin'." Abigail's eyes settled on the cookie in my hand, and she followed it back and forth to my mouth with every bite.

"You can give her a piece if you'd like," said Great-Aunt Dorothy. "She mostly eats people food anyway. Just toss it to her," which I did, and Abigail snatched it right out of the air and swallowed it whole.

I laughed. "She didn't even taste it."

"No. She eats, but she doesn't taste much," said Great-Aunt Dorothy.

"Dad, can I look around?"

"Ask your great-aunt," he said.

Before I could say another word, Great-Aunt Dorothy said, "Of course you can look around, Jack; you're family; you can look anywhere you'd like."

The notion that we were family caught me off-guard. I always thought of me and Dad as family, just the two of us; Mom, too, in a way. But the idea that there were others in our family had never occurred to me. I didn't even know Great-Aunt Dorothy, or at least I didn't remember her, and she called me family without the least hesitation. It felt kind of good to be thought of like that.

Great-Aunt Dorothy's garden was neat and tidy. There were about eight rows of corn, several rows of leaf lettuce, what looked like scrawny little green beans, some hills with long-stemmed broad leaves and yellow flowers —hadn't any idea what they were—and several rows of stuff that didn't appear to be anything. I couldn't see any fruits or vegetables attached to them at all. The rows were clean, no weeds that I could see, and the dirt was soft and damp. I walked up and down, in and out, Abigail on my heels. I knelt down to scratch her ears again, and she rolled over on her back in the dirt and lifted her leg, waiting for me to rub her belly. "Good girl," I said. "Is this your garden? Is it? Got some dog biscuits somewhere in all these rows? Huh?" I just kept talking, and she kept wagging her tail.

The pond looked brown, and there were millions of little bugs skittering across its surface. It was about forty feet across and maybe thirty wide. There were two rocks in the middle, one covered with several turtles sunning themselves. Every few minutes I heard something that sounded like my father's best belch ever, but I couldn't see where it was coming from. I walked around to the other side, and suddenly something leaped into the water. It was a monstrous frog; its legs looked a foot long.

I took a step onto the board, and it held me without any trouble, so I stepped out a little further. That's when I heard my dad's voice calling, "J, J! Stay off of that thing, you hear me?" I waved and backed off the board. At least for now. The pond was still and muddy, and I couldn't see an inch below the surface. I fiddled around at the edge until I found a stone. I threw the stone in a high arc, and it disappeared with a hollow g'looop when it hit. I knew that it must be deep water, maybe eight or ten feet.

As I turned back to the house, I noticed something move in the window on the second floor. I watched for a moment and didn't see a thing, so I figured I was mistaken. But as I turned my head away, I could have sworn that I saw something again, this time out of the corner of my eye. I looked back. Nothing.

Abigail was barking like crazy now. She was going nuts over the mailman who had just come up the drive. Great-Aunt Dorothy called to him from the porch and then hurried to his car with some cookies wrapped in a napkin. The mailman was smiling and gesturing. He reached out and shook my father's hand, who then pointed in my direction. I waved.

I threw another stone across the pond, just to test my arm. It landed with a dull thud on the opposite bank.

Before heading back to the porch, I looked at the second-floor window again. Something was different, but I couldn't tell what. I kept looking until it occurred to me that the Venetian blinds were lower than before. At least I thought they were. Or maybe they weren't. I watched for another minute. "Okay, J," I said to myself, "knock it off; it's just your imagination." Or the effect of the anise.

"Well, I don't know yet what the future will hold," said Dad as I reached the porch.

"How long do you think this will take?" asked Great-Aunt Dorothy. Abigail was back in her favorite spot by the screen door. I stopped and scratched her ear.

"I hope not too long," said Dad.

"Not too long what?" I asked.

"Oh, nothing," said Dad.

"How 'bout another cookie," said Great-Aunt Dorothy, "and maybe some lemonade." She held out the plate and I took a cookie.

"Thank you, Great-Aunt Dorothy," I said.

"Great-Aunt Dorothy!" she exclaimed. "That sure is a mouthful. Your mother always called me Aunt Dee. Know why?"

"No, I don't."

"Well, when she was just a little peanut, much smaller than you, she couldn't say my name. All that came out was 'D', so that's what she called me. I guess it stuck because that's what most everyone calls me. Even your dad. Even my neighbors!" she said with another thunderclap of laughter. "So why don't you call me Aunt Dee? How's that?"

"Okay," I said. "Aunt Dee it is."

She laughed at this and looked at my dad. "He'll be fine, William, I have no doubt. I'm sure he'll do well out here."

I didn't know what she meant by this, but my dad seemed relieved. She tilted her head forward again and looked at my dad, all serious.

"You know, there's worse things in life."

"I know," my dad said, sympathetic. Aunt Dee shook her head and leaned back in her chair. "How's he doing?" asked Dad.

"How's who doing?" I asked.

"J, it's not polite to interrupt," said Dad.

"He keeps keepin' on," said Aunt Dee. "That's the most I can say. Been awful sick lately, but won't go to the doctor no more. So mostly we wait things out. Might be the croup this time. Gets sick more often than most folks." She shook her head and looked at the ground. "I don't know what to tell you. He's planning on going back to his own place pretty soon." My dad looked at her and opened his mouth, but didn't say anything. Suddenly it was all quiet and uncomfortable.

Aunt Dee looked at me with tears in her eyes but with a smile on her face. "Jack," she said softly, "I'd love to have you come stay with us for a while."

I didn't know exactly what to say. "Okay." I looked at my dad; he reached out to me and squeezed the back of my neck. It was quiet again. I felt like I had missed something, but I didn't know what.

"Well," said Dad, "we better head back to civilization."

"Yes, I suppose you'uns better," said Aunt Dee. "You wouldn't want our country ways to rub you wrong."

They were talking all casual, but there was something un-casual about the whole thing; their faces didn't match their words. Their eyes looked like they were saying something else all together. It was like when Miss Loss talked to the class in her friendly voice when I could tell she felt bored or maybe even frustrated. Dad and Aunt Dee were talking one way, but they were feeling something else, and I couldn't tell what it was.

Dad backed down the dirt driveway and onto the road. Aunt Dee stood on her porch and waved, Abigail beside her, looking all confused and worried again. I rolled my window down and waved back. "So long, Abigail!" I called. Aunt Dee never moved from that spot as we headed down the road. I looked back when we hit the first curve, and the Venetian blinds were up.

We didn't talk much as we drove back through New Galilee. I watched the southern sky as storm clouds gathered and billowed; I could see the soft gray of rain below them even as we drove in sunshine. I looked at my father, his hands tight on the steering wheel, his lips pursed and his forehead creased. His face was white as sandstone, and for the first time I noticed that he had less hair than I remembered. He sighed.

"Aunt Dee was real nice," I said.

"What was that?"

"Aunt Dee. She's real nice. I liked her." With this, the creases in Dad's face faded, and his skin took on the pinkish shade of being alive again. He perched one arm on the open window and steered with the other arm in his lap.

"Yes, she's quite a lady. Like I said, she practically raised your mother."

"How's that?"

Dad looked at me as if he was deciding something. "You know, J, your mother's mother and father, your grandparents, well, they never got—how can I put this—let's just say they didn't stay together after your mother was born."

"Why not?" I asked.

"Well, all the details aren't that important. Your grandfather worked in the coal mines near Charleston, West Virginia, and your grandmother was, well, she was pretty young when she got pregnant." He looked at me as if this was supposed to make things clear.

Dad stopped talking and watched the road.

"I don't get it," I said. "What does that have to do with Aunt Dee?"

"Well, Aunt Dee was your grandmother's sister, and your grandmother, as I said, was kind of a young girl at the time; she didn't really know how to be a mother, even though she tried hard for a couple of years." He took a deep breath. "Well, turns out, J, that one day she just up and left."

"What do you mean, she up and left?" I asked. "Where did she go?"

"That's the sixty-four-thousand-dollar question," said Dad. "No one knows."

This was more than puzzling, I thought. "Well, how could that be? I mean, how could someone up and disappear like that? She must have been somewhere."

"That's certainly true; everyone is somewhere, but in the case of your grandmother, no one knew where her somewhere was."

"And no one ever found out?" I asked.

"Aunt Dee said she heard your grandmother was in California, and then she heard Alaska, but no one knew for sure, and after a while everyone gave up."

"What about Mom's dad?" I asked. "Didn't he do anything to help?"

"'Fraid not," said Dad. "'Fraid he wasn't such a good guy. At least he wasn't when it came to being a father. He didn't want any part of your mother. He wouldn't even come to see her. Said he had his own life to tend to."

This was unbelievable to me. "How could they be that mean?" I said.

"I think they just didn't have any idea what they were doing, and so they ran away from it," said Dad. "They didn't think about the person who was right in the middle of it all." He looked at me. "That's where Aunt Dee comes in.

"Aunt Dee had a hard life before your mother ever arrived on the scene. She never married, which just about broke her heart. She fell in love with a young man who couldn't let go of his mother's apron strings."

"What does that mean?" I asked.

"Well, his mother didn't care for Aunt Dee, and when it came down to proposing marriage, she told her son to make his choice. He could marry your aunt if he wanted, but he'd never see his mother again. Your mother told me that one night Aunt Dee got all dressed and perfumed because Duncan—that was his name—was coming over, and she knew he was planning to propose. A friend of Aunt Dee's had seen him at Kimpel's Jewelers buying a ring. So Aunt Dee was beside herself with excitement.

"But when Duncan came to the house, it wasn't to propose; it was to tell your aunt he needed more time. Your aunt tried to hide her disappointment. She said that was fine and asked how much time he needed. She said she was willing to wait, but Duncan couldn't say for sure how long it would take. She asked if it would be a few months or maybe even longer but, as your mother told it, Duncan just looked at his shoes. They didn't speak of it again. Your aunt went ahead with the dinner she had prepared. But neither of them ate much, and the apple pie she had cooling on the window sill stayed there for days, uneaten.

"Duncan didn't come around the house after that, and soon Aunt Dee fell into a very bad way. She took to her bed and didn't get up for weeks on end. Friends came and the doctor came, and no one could figure out what to do until one day she just got herself out of bed, packed all her things, and moved to Pittsburgh, where she got a factory job. Your mother told me that all Aunt Dee said was, 'Enough of this foolishness.' She never spoke of Duncan again. At least not until she told the story to your mother.

"You see, when Aunt Dee's little sister, your grandmother, abandoned your mother, Aunt Dee stepped in without a thought and said she would take your mother; she would raise her. And that was that. Aunt Dee always told me that was the happiest day of her life. She moved back to Ellwood City and made her way sewing and taking in laundry for other people—anything so she could be at home with your mother."

"So she was really my mother's mom, right?"

"Yes, that's true as can be," said Dad.

"I guess that makes her more my grandmother than my aunt, doesn't it?"

Dad looked at me. "Yes, I suppose that's true as well."

This was a lot to take in all at once. I mean, I had just met Great-Aunt Dorothy for the first time (no matter how much my dad insisted I remembered her), who then became Aunt Dee, and finally in the blink of an eye, she's my grandmother.

I wasn't sure how I felt about all of this. I liked Grandma Aunt Dee, or whoever she was. I liked visiting with her; I liked Abigail; I liked the idea that there was someone else in the world that was connected to us. To my mother. I mean. Dad was an only child. His dad had died of a heart attack before I was born, and his mother had died, too—of pneumonia, I think. Anyway, I never knew them. So, Dad and I were a lot alike. We didn't have anyone but each other. Now we had at least one other person in the world. It seemed right that we should have another person to call family.

At the same time, it all felt very weird. It was hard to imagine that so many odd things had happened before I was born: that Aunt Dee was young once, and her heart had been broken by a man who couldn't leave his mother. That Aunt Dee's sister, my real grandmother, who was just a girl herself, refused to be a mother. That Aunt Dee volunteered out of the goodness of her heart to be a mother—my mother's mother, to be exact—even though she was really my mother's aunt. It reminded me of Abbott and Costello. "Who's on first?" he asks, and the other guy says, "That's right, Who's on first," meaning the person on first was named Who. You see what I mean?

Brian's family was simple. There was a mother, a father, Brian and his little sister. His mother was his mother. His father was his father. His grandparents came to visit every summer. As far as I could tell, his grandparents were his grandparents. Everyone had one job to do. No one had to be something they weren't, like an aunt being a mother or a grandmother. It seemed that in my family you couldn't be sure of almost anything. Take Abigail. She looked like a little black cocker spaniel dog, but for all I knew, she could be a long lost cousin twice removed!

So while I liked the notion of having more family, I didn't like the idea that we needed a scorecard to tell who was who.

One thing for sure, Dad was mighty happy that I liked Aunt Dee. He kept talking about me going to visit her and staying for a while and how it would be fun to be out in the country and how Aunt Dee would love to have me there because I reminded her of my mother. He said it would probably be good for me to get close to the person who raised my mother, even though, as I have already pointed out, Aunt Dee wasn't really my mother's mother, though, actually, she was a mother to my mother in a more real way than my mother's real mother, who wasn't such a real mother after all. I'm telling you, it was impossibly confusing.

Anyway, I tried to act enthusiastic about this. I had to admit that with Brian gone and baseball over, there wasn't nearly as much to do. Tommy's parents were taking a "vacation" from each other, whatever that meant, so Tommy was shuffling back and forth between his real home and where his father was living. Tommy said the whole thing had put his pinball game into an absolute tailspin. He couldn't win at all. And I thought I was the only one with troubles and worries!

At last, the backyard was rounding into shape again. Dad patched the patio, which had gotten all busted up when our tree collapsed on it. We even planted a new tree right beside the old stump, an oak this time. I counted the rings of the tree stump—seventy-five in all. That meant the tree broke ground sometime in the 1880s. Dad said that was back when Ellwood City was just beginning, and, in all likelihood, Ewing Park wasn't much more than a big forest. When the tube mill came in, they started building houses so the factory workers had some place to live. To build the houses, they cleared a lot of trees, except the one that stood in our backyard for seventy-five years. It must have gone through a lot of storms along the way, though probably nothing like the one that hit this summer. Everyone, even Mrs. Sanders, who was as old as our tree, couldn't remember a storm like that. Dad said I would remember this summer for the rest of my life, because I may never see another storm like the "Tornado of '59."

Nothing more could be done with the ping-pong table pieces that Dad kept after Benny Stark came by. So we decided we'd burn what was left of it in the trash barrel. In fact, we tried to make a regular party out of it. At least I did. Dad bought some dogs at Spoa's and some Snyder's chips and some Verner's ginger ale, and we sharpened a few sticks left over from the tree, and we stuck the dogs on them, and there we stood in the twilight. Dad burned each piece of the table, one at a time. Soon the fire was crackling and the hot dogs were bulging and splitting.

I got to thinking. "Dad, who were you and Aunt Dee talking about?"

"What?" he said, like he didn't know what I was talking about.

"When I came up to the porch, the two of you were talking about someone, and I asked who, but you told me not to interrupt. Sounded like it was someone who was sick or something."

"Oh, that," said Dad. "It's nothing for you to worry about."

I turned my stick over so my dog wouldn't burn too much. "I'm not worried, just wondered."

Dad looked at me and smiled.

"Well?" I said.

"Your Aunt Dee was telling me about her nephew, that's all."

"What about him?"

"She kind of looks after him even though he lives by himself mostly. He's had a hard life, been unhealthy always, and she takes care of him when he'll let her."

"What do you mean, 'when he'll let her'?"

"Like most grown men, he'd like to take care of things by himself, even if sometimes he can't do the job. He doesn't want to be a bother. Your aunt is about the only person he lets in. He's just a little odd that way."

"Odd how?"

"Like I said, he doesn't like to be around other people much."

"Was he staying there at the house when we went visiting?"

Dad looked at me, his forehead creased again like he wondered where I got such an idea.

"No, I don't believe he was there. Why do you ask?"

"Well, I could have sworn I saw something moving by the upstairs window when I was out in the garden with Abigail."

"What did you see?" Dad asked, this time his voice flat and serious.

"I don't know exactly. All I know is that each time I looked at the window, something was different."

"What do you mean, different?"

"Well, the blinds seemed to be in a different position, like someone was raising them and letting them down."

"Oh, I bet that was just the wind and your imagination." He laughed. I laughed too, but I knew it wasn't the wind, because the wind was still as could be, waiting for the storm to arrive. He was right about my imagination. It's a good one. But not good enough to move blinds up and down.

"What's his name?" I asked.

"Henry, his name is Henry."

"Henry?"

"Uh huh, Henry." Then it dawned on me. If this Henry person was Aunt Dee's nephew, then he must be related to me, too. Another family member! If we kept adding people this fast, before long we'd be busting at the seams. "So, Dad, is Henry my uncle or cousin or something?"

Dad didn't answer right away. He got a faraway look, like he was trying to think this through. "Well, not exactly. Henry has always called Aunt Dee his aunt because she has looked after him for so many years. He's had a lot of problems along the way, and his family kind of disowned him."

"Why would they disown him?"

Dad ignored my question. "So, your aunt has always been there for him, and since everyone called her Aunt Dee, he did too, except he also referred to himself as her nephew. Made him feel like he had family, I suppose."

After the other stories my dad told me about our family, it wasn't too hard to accept this tale; it didn't seem so unusual the way he explained it. To my mind, though, since none of my family attachments were all that normal, Henry was just as related to me as anyone else; I mean, it didn't seem to take blood to make a family. In our case, for example, all it took was hardship.

I hate to say it, but summer was starting to drag a little. August was closing in, and the dog days were coming. The cicadas were buzzing already, a sure sign that we were way past the midway point. There wasn't that much to do. Brian wrote me a couple of letters: "*...man, I seen a lot of you-know-whats on the beach. You wouldn't believe it!!!*" Dad was a whole lot busier than before. He spent all his time hunting and pecking away at his typewriter. He'd stop and look at the page for a long time, and then he'd start again, and then he'd throw the whole thing away, and then he'd scroll in another page and start over.

"What are you doin', Dad?"

"Oh, just some work," he said, but I didn't understand why he was doing work when he was on vacation. Besides, typing sure wasn't the work he usually did.

I idled some days at Nick's. He always had something for me to do. Empty the bathroom trash or run an errand to the grocery store down the street. He even let me wait on kids if all they wanted was a popsicle, something simple.

"How's your dad doing?"

"Okay, I guess. He spends all his time typing something; then he throws it away and starts all over again." Nick didn't say much about this, but next thing I knew he was walking up the street toward our house. Didn't matter much to me because that meant I was left alone with the always-alluring Bunny and Sandy. We had never made it to the movie with the woman who had giant breasts, but Sandy and Bunny were no slouches. I bet if they were on a movie screen they'd be just as big.

Almost every day, either Sandy or Bunny caught me staring at, well, you know, their bosoms. I couldn't help it. They were so round, and they swayed just a little every time either one of them moved, but they were also all firm and, geez, pointy. They were the most fascinating things I'd ever seen.

"Hey, little boy," said Sandy. "I'm up here." She smiled, her eyes, deep pools of rich chocolate, looking right at me. I got that feeling—you know what I mean—just below my belly button, and pretty soon something started to happen, and I had to sit down so I wouldn't embarrass myself.

Sandy and Bunny laughed out loud, and they asked me to get a box of hot dogs from the back room, which meant I would have to stand up. They watched me and laughed some more while I remained sitting, undecided. I smiled sheepish-like and tried to stand up, but I had to stay half bent over.

"What's the matter Jackie?" asked Sandy, but I knew that they knew exactly what the matter was, which made me feel even more embarrassed. I sneaked off to the bathroom until things, well, returned to normal.

It was awful, and yet, I liked it. This summer I'd gotten more curious about my thing. I'd never given it much thought before except, of course, when I went to the bathroom.

But I'd been having those dreams that you have when, well, you know what I mean. Not the made-up dreams that Brian always talked about, but real dreams about grown-up women and stuff.

When it first happened, it worried me. I told my dad the next morning because I didn't want him to think I wet the bed, but he understood right off. He smiled while he took the sheets off my bed, and all he said was, "It's all part of growing up." This didn't really clarify anything. What's "all part of growing up"? Having the dreams? Messing the bed?

I didn't like the whole idea in the beginning, but lately I was eager to go to bed just in case I'd have another such dream. I even added it to my bedtime prayers, although I wasn't quite sure what God thought about this sort of thing. If I didn't have a dream before I went to sleep the next night, I would lay in bed trying to remember the last dream. I hoped that would help the dream part of my brain get the hint. Once I did that a few times, I found that I couldn't get the thoughts out of my mind even during the day. I mean, sometimes it was the only thing I could think of. And I didn't even have to try! I could be looking through my baseball card collection and studying the statistics on the back of Stan Musial's card, and all of a sudden, I'd get all hard and stiff.

I'm telling you—it was like I had two brains: One was in my head and was mostly in charge of what I was doing, but there was another brain down there that was working overtime trying to get my attention. And succeeding!

By the time August rolled around, I didn't need to dream at all. I had Mrs. Musselman, Bunny, Sandy, and the dancers from the *Lawrence Welk Show* on my mind all the time, and when I stiffened at night, I just rolled over and sort of rubbed myself hard against the mattress and, well, it would happen like clockwork.

At the same time, I felt awful about it. I mean, it was fine if it happened while I was asleep. I didn't have any say over that. But to make it happen on purpose seemed unnatural even to me. The good me was losing out to the bad me. I mean, it wasn't even a contest. With Brian gone and baseball season over and the ping-pong table burned up in the trash barrel, there wasn't much else to do.

I wished I could have told my dad about it, since he already knew it had happened. But I was afraid he would think I was a pervert if I told him I was making it happen, and besides, he was so busy every day I didn't want to bother him. "Sorry, J, I've got some paperwork to do," he'd say every time I asked him to play catch or even go for a walk to the park. I'd get up in the morning, and he'd be sitting at the kitchen table, and when I went to bed each night, he'd still be sitting there. Letter upon letter, stamp upon stamp, envelope upon envelope. "What are you doing?" I'd ask. "Oh, just some work," was all he'd ever say.

So what was I supposed to do? Between stuffing the envelopes and licking the stamps say, "Oh, by the way, Dad, I can't stop messing with myself"? It wasn't something I could easily slip into the conversation. It worried me, though. I looked at other kids my age and even older, and they didn't look like they were thinking about it at all. To me they looked like they were thinking regular everyday things, like what's for dinner and let's go swimming and who won the game and what's that stuck in my teeth, stuff like that. Certainly not women's bosoms and what to do with your thing when it acts up. I started to write a letter to Brian about it, but I was afraid his parents might intercept it and tell my dad.

Finally I realized I had to talk to my dad or I'd go crazy. I decided that when he came in to say goodnight, I'd bring it up. I just wasn't sure how to say it: "Dad, could I talk to you about something?" or "Dad, I've got something on my mind" or "Dad, have you ever looked real close at Mrs. Musselman and felt something just below your belly button?" Oh my God, what was I gonna do?

"Hey J, how's it going," he said. "About ready for bed?"

"Yeah," I said, working up the nerve to mention my dilemma. I took a deep breath, but before I could get a word out, he said, "J, I have to talk to you about something."

Oh my God, he knows! He knows what I'm thinking about and dreaming about and how I look down Bunny and Sandy's shirts and all about Mrs. Musselman's black brassiere and rubbing against the mattress! But how? How could he possibly know? I hadn't said a word. My eyes were bugging out of my head, and I was holding my breath.

He was all fidgety like he didn't know how to bring it up either. He cleared his throat and looked at the floor and wrung his hands. Finally he sat on the bed beside me. He took my pillow and plumped it up for me. "There, that's better," he said, even though there wasn't anything wrong with the pillow to begin with. My God, I thought, I must be in real trouble this time. My God, he's clearing his throat again, and it looks like there's perspiration on his forehead. Are they gonna have to put me away in some cracker factory for kids who can't leave their things alone?

"It's been a pretty wild summer," he said with a slight smile.

"Uh huh," I said.

"I mean, we've had some fun, haven't we?"

"Yeah, Dad," I said.

"Even with all the crazy things that have happened. The car and the storm and the tree and the ping-pong table." He laughed, or I should say, he made a sound like a laugh. This seemed like an odd way to bring up my problem, but I decided to let him take the lead, just in case he got cold feet and we didn't have to talk about it at all.

"You know how I've been home a lot this summer, right?"

"You mean your vacation?" I said.

"Yeah, my *vacation*." He said vacation in an odd way, like he was quoting someone else who had told a lie or had used the wrong word.

"Yeah, Dad, I know; it's been lots of fun doing stuff together." Although this was true, I also hoped this comment would throw him off the trail and he wouldn't pick up the scent again.

"Yes, it has been fun. All the nights cooking dogs over the trash barrel and all the baseball games, and even the ping-pong while it lasted." We both laughed this time. And meant it.

"Don't forget the Pirate game," I said.

"How could I forget that? Most fun I've had in the longest time," he said, as if he wasn't really speaking to me.

He looked so gloomy that finally I said, "Don't worry; we still have a whole month to go before I start back to school and you go back to work. We could go visit Aunt Dee again. We could do lots of stuff."

He didn't respond. Instead he looked at the floor and sighed. That's when I realized that while I thought he had come to talk to me about one thing, actually he had come to talk about something else entirely. Now I was the nervous one. "Dad? What is it?"

He looked at me with cloudy eyes. "J, I've got to tell you something. I should have told you weeks ago. But we were having such fun, and I never thought it would drag on so long."

"What is it?" I asked.

"Well, you see, I haven't really been on vacation all this time."

"What do you mean?" I asked, thoroughly confused. "Dad, what are you talking about? You said you were on vacation and you were all excited that we would have time to spend together. What do you mean you aren't on vacation? What's going on?"

"J, don't get upset." I didn't realize I was upset until Dad said so, but he was right. My voice had gotten higher, and I could tell that my face was red.

12

"Look, J," he said. "I haven't been home because of vacation." He paused and sighed again. "I've been home because, well, because I lost my job."

I heard the words "I lost my job," but they didn't register. I mean, those are words I never expected to hear from my father. They didn't make any sense. How could he lose his job? What did that really mean?

"What do you mean, you lost your job?" I was surprised at the sharpness of my voice.

"Well, J, Pittman decided to let me go."

"Let you go? I don't get it," I said.

"It's this way, J. They decided—my boss decided—to go in a different direction, to make some changes. And he decided that I didn't fit in with their plans."

I sat down on my bed; my head was spinning. How could I have not known this? How could Dad have kept this from me?

"This doesn't make any sense!"

"I know..."

So all summer while I thought everything was okay, this was going on? And I didn't know anything? It was just like one of those movies where the characters on the screen are happy, and then a voice comes in and says something like, "Little did they know that while they were having so much fun, one of them was dying from a terrible disease; soon everyone's lives would be turned upside down and ruined forever."

"I didn't want to worry you, Jackie. I didn't think it would last very long. I figured I would get another job in no time, and then I'd tell you once everything was in place."

"I can't believe this. What's going to happen now?"

Dad stood in the middle of my room, his shoulders curled and his hands clasped in front of him, his head slightly bowed. He could have been praying. His voice was just above a whisper. "I'm sorry, Jackie; believe me, I don't like this anymore than you."

"But you were so good, Dad. You were the best. You told me, remember? You said you had more sales last year than anyone in the company. You made more in commissions than anyone. Remember?"

Dad looked at me and smiled. "That was all true," he said. "I sold more than anyone."

"So are they stupid, or what?" I said. "It doesn't make any sense. I don't get it." Dad looked at me as if he was deciding whether to tell me more.

"It's this way, Jackie. They decided to hire someone new and pay him less to service my territory now that I've set up all the customers. They save some money on salary and make more money on sales. It's better for the company." He sighed and shrugged. "That's the story anyway."

"That's crazy! Can't you do something? Isn't there someone you can talk to?"

"No, Jackie, not really. It goes with the territory. It isn't fair, but it's just part of the deal. You're always out there on a limb trying to do your best, trying to sell the product, trying to satisfy the customer, trying to dazzle the boss. And when you're out there, you hope no one cuts the limb off behind you. Sometimes it doesn't work out, and suddenly you're on the ground." He tried to laugh, like he knew it was all a game, but it sure didn't sound like a game to me, not when your father could get hurt.

"Just like our old tree," I said.

"Yep, just like our old tree." All of a sudden it was quiet and awkward, and he didn't know what to say, and I didn't either.

"So what's gonna happen now?"

"I'll try to find a safer limb," said Dad. "I want you to know that you don't have to worry. I saved some money away just for something like this, but it's important that I get a job again soon."

"Can't just lay there on the ground," I said.

"That's right, J, can't lie on the ground."

"Is that why you've been working on the typewriter so much?"

"Yes. I've been sending out resumes to companies all over western Pennsylvania and eastern Ohio and even western New York. And I've gone visiting some places, too, just to introduce myself and tell them what I can do. But things are a little slow right now. Not a lot of hiring going on, so I'll just have to work a little harder at it."

I couldn't believe that while I had been thinking about stupid stuff like baseball cards and Mrs. Mussellman's breasts, my dad was keeping this secret and trying to figure out how to get a job before I found out he'd lost his old one. It made me feel all sad inside, like something deep down was melting.

I asked him if there was anything I could do. He said no, it wasn't my worry, but he felt I should know because he would be busier now looking for work. He might have to take some short trips to meet people who might be willing to hire him. He kept telling me not to worry. But when someone tells you over and over not to worry, it's the same as the doctor telling you a shot won't hurt; you know it's gonna hurt like crazy.

I was so angry at Pittman. How could they do this to my dad? I mean, he was a grown man with a son and a house, and he did good work. He wasn't some kid with a paper route who threw one in the gutter by mistake. I thought things were supposed to be fair, that when you grew up people treated each other right and didn't do stupid stuff to each other like kids do. But I guess I was wrong. To think that my dad was being beaten up on the big people's playground was almost unbearable.

Something else bothered me even more. I was angry at my dad. It was a crazy, unfair anger, but I couldn't help myself. How could he let this happen? How could he not know? How could he? He was the one and only thing I could count on in this world. He was like one of those big rocks down by the Conequenessing. You could stand on them, and they'd hold you, and they'd never move; they'd never crack; they'd never break, not even when it rained for days and the creek ran rough and high. The water wouldn't touch you; you were always safe.

I knew these thoughts were bad, but I couldn't help thinking them. I mean, I didn't have anyone else to fall back on, and if my father messed up, what was going to happen to me? There, I said it. May sound awful selfish, but I couldn't shake the thought.

I didn't dare tell my father any of this. It would have destroyed him. But the feelings were too strong to ignore, and since I was afraid they might slip out, I steered clear of him for a few days. Slept over at Tommy's, but I didn't dare tell Tommy what was going on. He had his own troubles, what with his parents fighting all the time. He cried himself to sleep one night.

Dad didn't notice that I was keeping my distance. He was working all the time on his resume and job applications and making phone calls to people. I wished Brian was home. I could tell him stuff, and even if he didn't really get it, at least he wouldn't say anything stupid, and he definitely wouldn't use it against me if he got angry later.

I was glad I had stayed away from Dad because soon enough the anger left. If I'd have said something, I would have hated myself forever. I mean, there he sat at the kitchen table, a cup of coffee beside the typewriter, a cigarette clutched between two fingers, the blue smoke circling, his face serious and always just a little damp like he was cooling down after a run, his mouth set low, lips parted, and his eyes narrow and focused and just a little unsure, like a kid who sees a multiplication problem for the first time and can't quite figure it out. Mostly I felt sad for him. And worried for me.

I was glad to see Dad working so hard, though. That helped. I knew he would solve this thing. Maybe he would go back to selling scaffolding. Maybe hardware. Maybe construction equipment again. He said that after he graduated from high school he got his first real job at B&W, a steel mill down in the valley; he cleaned the floors while other men drove cranes and forklifts and moved tons of steel. He hated his work and said he'd never be stuck in a mill job again, or any job where he was inside being told what to do. He liked the idea of being out on the road, relying on a smile, a slap on the back, and a special talent for persuading and convincing and, in the end, selling. The idea of selling something to someone who needed it, who was happy with the end product, who paid you well and thanked you when you left, was intoxicating. "It made me feel like I was somebody," he said to me at one point. I looked at him, not knowing what to say, and he looked at me, not knowing if he should have said it. He didn't try to explain further, and I didn't ask.

13

Have you ever heard that old saying about waiting for the other shoe to drop? Well, after Dad told me he had lost his job, I figured that was the whole shebang; in my view, not only had both shoes dropped, but so had the roof and a great big chunk of the sky. But I was wrong. There was another shoe hanging in the air waiting for just the right moment, and that moment came about three days after Dad broke the big news.

He reminded me about needing to go on some short trips so he could interview for jobs. I hadn't thought anything of it at first, because he was always going on "short trips." His territory had been several counties in western Pennsylvania including Allegheny County, which is where Pittsburgh is. But that wasn't what he meant at all by "short trips." His short trips were what I would call long trips—very long trips. Trips that would last more than one day. Trips where he would be gone overnight, and I would have to stay with someone. He would call me when he got to wherever he was going so I'd know he was safe, but I would have to sleep in someone else's bed and eat someone else's food, and if I had a problem I would have to wait until Dad called and then talk fast so we wouldn't go over three minutes. I wouldn't be able to look at him to see how he was responding, and he'd have to hang up shortly, which would remind me that he was far away. That was definitely not a "short trip."

I didn't know if the saying about shoes dropping allowed for this, but in my case there was a third shoe, and it made the biggest noise of all when it hit the floor.

"So, J, this is what I was thinking. I was thinking that it might be nice for you to stay with Aunt Dee while I go to New York—to Jamestown, Buffalo and Rochester. It wouldn't be for long. She really loved having you visit. She told me she'd love to have you come and stay for a little vacation."

He looked at me, and he could tell that I wasn't buying. Maybe he wasn't such a good salesman after all. "C'mon, J, it will be fun. You can help her in the garden and explore the woods behind her house. And you really liked Abigail, didn't you?"

I didn't answer. I liked Abigail for sure, but I knew that if I said yes, Dad would take that as me agreeing with the whole scheme, so I didn't answer.

"It wouldn't be for long, J. I have several interviews with different companies, and I can do them all in a few days. Then I'll be back."

"How long is a few days?" I asked.

"Three or four tops. Maybe a week."

I wished that Brian was back, because I knew Dad would let me stay with him. I decided to take a chance.

"Why can't I stay with Tommy?"

"I think you know why you can't stay with Tommy," said Dad. He was right. Things had gone from bad to worse at Tommy's. He told me that he had found his mother in the backyard burying his father's clothes.

"There's just too much turmoil at Tommy's right now," said Dad. "I don't think his mother could, uh, manage it right now." That was an understatement. Tommy told me his mother was going nuts. She felt so bad that she went to the doctor's, and he gave her some pep pills. She took them and spent the next three days cleaning the house. She didn't stop to eat. She didn't stop to sleep. She just cleaned and cleaned. Tommy got worried when she insisted on giving him a bath when she noticed some dirt on his hands.

"Well, what about Nick? I could stay with him." Okay, I guess you all can see right through this idea. I mean, I liked Nick a lot, but Sandy and Bunny were the real reason I came up with the suggestion. Just imagine spending every moment of every day with them. Maybe they could help me get over the awfulness of my dad's job loss.

Dad just smiled when he heard this idea. "You're kidding, right? Nick hardly has enough room over the Snack Bar for him and his daughters. Where would he put you? Besides, there're too many teenagers hangin' around there all the time. Like that kid, Kelso. I hear bad things about him. Not a good influence on an eleven-year-old boy." I couldn't believe my dad knew anything about Kelso. It was kind of cool actually; Kelso's reputation had reached the adult world. Man, if my dad only knew. I decided not to say anything more about Nick.

"What if I stay here by myself? Mrs. Sanders could check in on me." Even I knew this was a lame idea. Mrs. Sanders was too old to be checking in on me, and I wasn't so sure I even liked the idea of being in the house all by myself. But it was worth a shot.

"C'mon, J," was all Dad said.

So, the third shoe dropped. I was going to Aunt Dee's.

I stood on the front porch for a long time watching my dad back out of the driveway and then disappear down the road. A final honk of the horn and a wave from the car window would have to last me. I looked down, and there was Abigail sitting beside me, her paw on my sneaker as if to say, "Everything will be alright."

"Hi, girl," I said, scratching behind her ear. "How you doin'? Huh? How's old Abigail doin' today?" I sat on the step beside her and she looked at me, unsure of my next move. I put my arm around her and gave her a hug. She wasn't so sure about this and pulled away, even though her tail—actually it wasn't a tail; it was more like a thumb on her bum—wagged furiously. She picked up a soup bone that was lying on the porch and came to my side, but when I reached for it, she pulled away, teasing me. "Hey, you!" I said, reaching again; this time she let me take it.

"That's a good sign, Jack." Aunt Dee was right behind me, a peanut butter and jelly sandwich in one hand and a plate of chocolate chip macadamia nut cookies in the other. To Aunt Dee, food was the answer to everything. "I think that old mutt likes you," she said with a smile. I looked at her and smiled back, but didn't say anything.

All of a sudden I realized that Dad was gone and all I had was an old woman and her old dog. She must have read my mind.

"First time away from your dad, is it?" she asked.

"Yeah, first time like this, anyway."

"Here, eat your sandwich; I'll get you some lemonade. I know you like my lemonade." The screen door smacked shut behind her. Abigail was already sitting up, drool trickling from the corner of her mouth, a breathy whimper rising from her throat. I broke off a corner of the sandwich and tossed it to her. She caught it, and down it went.

"I'm glad this worked out," Aunt Dee had told Dad as he got ready to leave.

Dad cleared his throat. "It's great of you to do this on such short notice."

"Oh, yes, of course," she said. "Don't you worry one little bit about young Jack here. He's a big boy, and I'm sure we'll have a fine old time together."

I wasn't nearly as sure as Aunt Dee. As the time drew near for Dad to leave, I had felt downright sick to my stomach.

"Why can't I go with you?" I asked.

"There'd be nothing for you to do while I'm in meetings, and I couldn't possibly leave you in a strange hotel all day long in some big city." I didn't say anything. "I thought we'd been over this," he said, low and consoling. "You'll be fine. Better to stay with family, right?" At this point, I didn't know if I thought of Aunt Dee as family at all. She may have been family to my mother and then to my dad, and I know she was blood to me, but right then, more than anything, she seemed like some strange lady who lived out in the middle of nowhere in a ramshackle house with a ramshackle dog.

I looked at my dad and knew there was no point arguing any longer. He was going away for a "short trip," and I was staying with Aunt Dee. Case closed. Dad gave me a big hug and held me longer than usual.

"Be good for your aunt, okay?"

"Okay," I said. I didn't want to cry, but I couldn't help myself. Just a little, though. I wiped the tears away before they reached my cheeks. I hadn't wanted to blubber.

"Here's your lemonade, Jack," said Aunt Dee. "I'm goin' out back to hang the wash. You can come if you want or stay here and eat while Abigail keeps you company."

"Okay," I said and sat on the rocker, sandwich in hand. I tossed Abigail the last bite and reached for the cookies. What was I going to do now? I didn't see another living soul anywhere. There was a house down Aunt Dee's road and another one farther in the distance, and I thought we had passed one just before Dad and I turned in the driveway, kind of hidden up on the hillside. Didn't see a single kid anywhere. I figured I was learning firsthand what it must be like to live in Siberia. "C'mon, girl," I said, and we headed out to the garden.

The garden looked totally different. The corn stalks were over my head now and were starting to tassel. There were yellow flowers on the squash plants. The lettuce had just been cut. The beans were hanging low, and feathery carrot greens fluttered in the breeze. I could see the carrots' tops, now as thick as my big toe.

Aunt Dee was standing by the clothesline in the backyard, sheets flapping, clothespins dangling from her mouth like buck teeth. Her hair was up in a bun, and she was wearing her sneakers. She was humming something, but I couldn't make it out. Abigail rolled around in the dirt, sniffing, snorting, and finally sneezing several times from the dust.

The garden looked a little droopy so I called to Aunt Dee, "Do you want me to water the plants?"

She smiled and called back, "That would be great, Jack. The hose is there by the side of the house." And so it was, curled up like a snake. I unrolled it and turned on the faucet, Abigail jumping and biting at the water until she got a snoutful and started sneezing again.

I stood in the middle of the garden so I could water everything from one spot. The corn stalks crackled when the water hit. Good thing she had tied the tomatoes to stakes, or I might have knocked them right down. I noticed a few baby tomatoes and hoped they would be more impressive in time. I sprayed in a high arc, and Abigail nearly went nuts trying to figure out what was going on. Once she was completely drenched, I turned the nozzle shut tight and dropped the hose to the ground.

Next thing I knew, there was a rabbit in the carrots, chewing on the leaves, its nose twitching like mad. She was a baby bunny, actually, and I looked around for her mother but didn't see her. I watched her for a minute, and she gazed at me as if to say, "What are you looking at?" I knelt down and held out a leaf, but it didn't budge, so I just sat there cross-legged and watched. Abigail was busy licking herself and didn't notice the rabbit at all. The bunny didn't have to worry about Abigail; the only way she could have caught it was if I tossed the rabbit to Abigail while she was begging at the kitchen table.

Dad would have gotten a real kick out of this bunny. He told me once that when he was a boy he made a trap out of a box, a stick to prop it up, and some string. He put lettuce under the box and hid behind a tree in his backyard until one of the rabbits that lived under his garage came sniffing. To his amazement, the rabbit went under the box to eat the lettuce. He pulled the string, tripping the stick, and the box fell, trapping the rabbit. He carefully turned the box while folding the flaps over the open end. He could hear the rabbit scratching inside. When the rabbit stopped making any noise, Dad opened one flap and took a look. The rabbit was waiting and watching and suddenly leaped out of the box, almost hitting my dad in the face, and hopped away, just like that. Dad said he gave up hunting right then and there. It made me smile imagining my dad's face when the rabbit almost clocked him in the head. I wished he was here to tell me the story all over again.

Aunt Dee saw us and dropped her clothes in the basket and came running. But no sooner had she reached the garden than the bunny was gone.

I said, "What's the matter; did I do something?"

"No, not you," said Aunt Dee. "It's them pesky rabbits! They're eating me out of house and home!" I decided not to comment on his cute little button nose since I had just learned he was our mortal enemy.

"Can't you build a fence of some sort to keep them out?"

"I built one out of chicken wire, but they dug right under it. I planted marigolds all around because rabbits don't like the smell, but these ones must have defective noses, because they love the flowers. I tell you, I think their main purpose in life is to torment me."

This seemed like an exaggeration, but I didn't want to suggest otherwise since Aunt Dee was more than a little put out.

"What about a scarecrow?"

Aunt Dee broke into gales of laughter, and, I swear, crows from the tops of every tree headed for the hills, squawking all the way. "That is the best idea I've heard yet!" she said. I was glad I came up with a helpful idea until she suggested I make the scarecrow.

"I don't know anything about scarecrows."

"Sure you do," said Aunt Dee. "Everybody knows about scarecrows."

"But I've never even had a garden."

She looked at me serious. "You've never had a garden? You mean to tell me that William, I mean your father, has never taught you how to grow vegetables out of the dirt!"

"No, never," I said, feeling like I was tattling on him in some way.

"What in the world?"

"I don't know," I said. "He's awful busy. We do play baseball together and lots of other stuff." She just shook her head.

"You can't eat a baseball, now can you?" She paused. "Well, obviously, the garden's already planted; we can't re-plant it, can we? But I can teach you how to make a scarecrow and how to tend a garden. We'll give you a proper education starting tomorrow morning."

My bedroom wasn't a bedroom at all. It was a storage room in the back of the house that Aunt Dee had used for sewing. "I haven't sewn a thing in years," she said, "so I thought you could stay here instead of all the way upstairs." She had moved her sewing machine and her scraps of cloth and thimbles and pins and various needles to her bedroom, which was right across the hall. "There's even a little bathroom beside the kitchen," she said, "so you don't have to go upstairs at all. Why don't you unpack, and I'll start dinner."

I pulled the dresser drawer open. It was empty.

I laid my suitcase on the bed and unsnapped the buttons. It popped open, and from the amount of clothes Dad had packed, I could have stayed at Aunt Dee's until I entered high school. I threw the underwear and other junk into the drawers. My baseball mitt and a ball were at the bottom of my suitcase. In a separate cardboard box Dad had packed all my baseball cards. He had even thrown in three brand-new packs. I held them in my hands and started to cry. I didn't try to catch the tears this time. I just let them fall. How could things have gotten so messed up so fast? There's no accounting for life, no way to tell which way things are going to go, what will be around the next bend or over the next hill.

I opened the first pack of cards and slapped the stick of gum in my mouth. Smokey Burgess was the best of the lot. There was a Harmon Killebrew in the second pack, but I had five Killebrews already. I opened the third pack, and there he was, right on top, Mickey Mantle. I chuckled and thought of Brian. He would have flipped to know that I got Mantle back. "Geez-o-man," he would have said, "you have all the luck! Geez!" And I would have gloated just a little, well, a lot, to see him so envious.

I missed Brian. I missed Tommy. I missed my dad. And my house. And Nick's. I have all the luck? Sure didn't feel like it sitting on a lop-sided, squeaky bed with a strip of flypaper hanging by my window. I wondered how long my dad would be gone. And what in the world would I do, after I made the scarecrow, of course, until he returned.

"Jack! You ready for supper?"

"Yes, Aunt Dee!" I answered, controlling my voice and sniffling back the last of my snot. "I'm coming!" I looked around my room again and turned for the door when I heard something. At first I thought it was the wind. I waited a second and then heard it again. It wasn't the wind, unless the wind could stand in the room above you and make a noise like it was picking up a chair and setting it down; it wasn't the wind, unless the wind could make the sound of feet shuffling from one end of a room to the other. It sure wasn't any wind I had ever heard before.

"Jack! You comin'?"

"Yes, Aunt Dee, I'm coming!"

And the noise stopped.

Dinner was homemade macaroni and cheese with saltine cracker crumbs on top. It was so gooey that, when she served me, it looked like long yellow vines stretched from my plate to the casserole dish, strong enough for Tarzan to hitch a ride. The green beans weren't nearly as inviting. Homemade applesauce, though, was something new. I mean, it actually had chunks of mashed-up apple right in it. She gave me the cinnamon shaker, and I laid it on heavy. Homemade bread, too, that was still so warm I didn't even have to spread the butter. It just melted in without any help from me at all. Dad and I didn't eat this good very often. Not that he wasn't a good cook. Well, actually he wasn't a very good cook. For a long time, I thought food only had one flavor.

Abigail sat up beside me and started to whine. "Better give her a little corner of your bread," said Aunt Dee, "or you'll never hear the end of it." So I tossed it to her, and, sure enough, she settled down. I guess she was confident I wouldn't forget her.

"You all settled in?" asked Aunt Dee.

"Yes," I answered, trying to get some macaroni into my mouth without losing the cheese on my chest.

"Do you need anything?"

"I don't think so," I answered.

"There's a little cupboard in the bathroom with towels and washcloths. You can take whatever you want. I just have one rule."

"What's that?"

"You have to wash at least every other day." I almost laughed, but she wasn't kidding. Dad made me wash every single day, sometimes a couple of times a day depending on how many layers of dirt I had collected.

"That's fine with me," I said.

"You know," she continued, "in some countries, like Europe for instance, they barely ever wash at all—don't see a reason to—and nobody minds." She thought for a minute. "When this great country was first founded, I don't think people washed much at all. They didn't have time to. They had work to do, and they weren't afraid of a little dirt under their nails and a little sweat under their arms. Vanity is a dangerous thing, Jack."

"Vanity?" I asked.

"Yes, vanity. You should never pay so much attention to yourself that you end up thinking your sweat smells better than anyone else's. We all smell the same, if you know what I mean." Of course I had no clue what she meant, but I shook my head in agreement and then tried to erase the image of smelly pilgrims from my mind while gagging down a few green beans.

"Want some more?" asked Aunt Dee.

"Aunt Dee, can I ask you something?" I said, eager to change the subject.

"Sure, Jack, what is it?"

"Well, when I was in the bedroom..."

"*Your* bedroom," she interrupted.

"What?"

"It's not *the* bedroom, Jack, it's *your* bedroom."

"Oh, okay. When I was in my bedroom, I heard something."

She put her fork down and listened, her face pinched with a look of worry. "You heard something?"

"Yes," I said.

"Was it a scratching noise or a skittering noise?" she asked, the brow of one eye raised. "We've had some trouble with mice. I can put some traps in your room tonight before you go to bed."

Now I put my fork down, finding it hard to eat with the picture of a dead mouse in my head. "No, it wasn't a skittering sound. It was more like a bumping and a shuffling sound." She listened closely. "And it didn't come from my floor; it sounded like it came from the floor above me; it sounded like someone walking or moving a chair."

She smiled. "Oh, must have been Henry." With that she picked up her fork again and started eating, as if everything was clear. My face must have told her different. "Didn't your dad tell you about Henry? He said he would."

"Yes, he mentioned something about him—that sometimes he's sick and you take care of him."

"That's right," said Aunt Dee. "Mostly he lives alone, but when he's in a bad way I look after him. Sometimes he comes here to, well, rest."

I listened but didn't say anything. Dad specifically said that Henry wouldn't be here. I remembered that much. I didn't like the idea that some stranger was living in the house. I mean, I was still getting used to Aunt Dee. Who was this guy?

"Yeah, Henry will probably be here for a while," she said.

"Oh. What's wrong with him?"

"Well, that's a very twisted tale for another time. Let's just say he's not well."

I didn't want to ask, but I had to. "How sick is he? Is it something that's catching?" I didn't know if this was a "vain" question or not, but I didn't like the idea of living in a house with some stranger who might be very sick with some dreaded disease.

"Oh my goodness, Jack, of course not! It's not that kind of sickness at all."

She paused as if she wasn't sure what to say. "I suppose it's more the kind of sickness one gets from having a hard, hard life." Dad and I had lived a hard, hard summer, but neither one of us got sick from it.

"Will I get to meet him?"

Aunt Dee pushed the food around her plate with her fork and then put it down. She finished chewing and wiped her mouth with a napkin. She looked at me and smiled. "I like you, Jack, because you have lots of questions. You're what I call inquisitive. Am I right?"

"Well, I guess I am inquis...inquisi...I guess I do like to know things. Dad says I'm very curious."

"Curious, that's it; you're very curious," said Aunt Dee, still smiling. "You know, the Good Book says you must become as a child in order to understand some things, the really important things. And the Good Book doesn't lie, mostly. I think it's right about this. Most grown-ups don't really ask the right questions. And they don't want to hear the right answers. They don't care enough to look close at a thing in order to really see it. They lose their curiousness somewhere along the way, and they get satisfied looking just at the surface of things. But the important things aren't skittering around on the surface. They're way down deep, way down deep where you can't see unless you stop and really look. And I don't mean looking with your eyes. I mean looking with your heart. Sometimes your best eyes are in your heart. Sometimes you can only see something, really see it, if you feel in your heart what that person's life must be like. Then nothing else matters about them— how they look, what others say about them—nothing except what your heart sees."

I didn't know exactly what she was talking about, but I shook my head anyway, because again it seemed like the right thing to do.

"You agree?" said Aunt Dee.

"Yes, I do."

"Do you have that kind of heart?" asked Aunt Dee.

"I think I do, but I'm not sure. How do you know?"

"That's a question that can't be answered with words," she said.

Now I was totally lost. What kind of question couldn't be answered with words? How could you know something if you couldn't put some words on it? Maybe she was playing with me. Maybe she was just pulling my leg. But I looked at her face, with its wrinkles and faintly fuzzy cheeks, her face with its steady blues eyes framed by wisps of grey hair, the corners of her mouth turned so slightly, and her face told me that she was serious in the most gentle way.

"How do I find out what kind of heart I have?"

"Yes, that's the question, isn't it, Jack?" was all she said. Then she picked up her fork again and began to eat. "Maybe you'll find the answer while you're here."

My little conversation with Aunt Dee puzzled the heck out of me, but it stayed with me all evening. I mean, how do you know if you're seeing things the right way? I thought I was seeing things the right way all summer, and then I found out I wasn't seeing things correctly at all. How else could I have missed what was really going on with my dad? Is that because I was looking at things with my eyes and not my heart?

Lucky for me, I found a Penney's catalogue in the living room and took it to bed with me. Aunt Dee didn't notice. I had learned about catalogues from Brian. "You wouldn't believe what kind of pictures you'll find!" he told me, and he was right. I mean, there're pictures of women wearing bras and underpants and something called a girdle, which looks like a straightjacket for your hips. It wasn't a *Playboy*, but way out here in the middle of nowhere it was pretty good. I started leafing through the pages when I heard some scratching. But it was way too loud to be a mouse.

I opened the bedroom door and there stood Abigail, thumb wagging. She walked right past me, stood at the side of my bed shuffling her paws, as if she was measuring whether she could make the leap or not, and then jumped onto my bed, her back leg slipping off the edge. She pulled herself up and stretched out right on top of the catalogue. I rubbed her belly and scratched behind her ears. She stared at me with her soft brown eyes and then panted as if she was trying to smile. "Hey, girl," I said. Abigail stretched her legs out behind her. "You wanna go to sleep?" She sniffed my breath and licked her lips. I'm sure she was thinking of macaroni and cheese. "All gone, girl, all gone." She put her head down on my pillow, and I put my head down as well.

The window beside my bed was open halfway, and the night air felt cool and moist on my face. I looked out but couldn't see a thing in the tar-black night. But I could hear the trees on the hillside and, once my eyes got adjusted, I could see a sprinkling of stars. I wondered where my dad was sleeping tonight. Usually he'd tuck me in at bedtime. I didn't really need him to do it, since I was eleven. Sometimes I pretended I was asleep already, but if he forgot, I noticed.

Abigail was snoring now, and one leg was twitching. She must have been dreaming. Maybe she was a pup again chasing that rabbit. I nudged her over so that I had a little more room. Then I turned on my side and closed my eyes. That's when I heard it again. The sound was faint but clear. It was Henry. I could hear his bedsprings. I could hear the floorboards. I could hear the bathroom door close and then the toilet flush. Then I heard the staircase creaking. He must be coming down, I thought. I watched the crack below my bedroom door, but no lights went on. I went to my door and opened it slowly. I peeked down the hall and saw a shadow disappear around a corner. "Hello?" I called in a loud whisper. The sound stopped. I waited for another minute, deciding whether to call again. Then I remembered that Aunt Dee had never really answered my question about whether I could meet Henry, so I decided not to call out again. I waited another minute and, when I didn't hear him, I went back to bed. As soon as I pulled up the covers, I heard the footsteps again, this time going back up the stairs. It would be a while before I fell asleep.

Charlie No Face

14

I woke up the next morning to what sounded like gunshots. I ran to the front porch, Abigail trailing behind me, and found Aunt Dee leaning a board against the house and then kicking at it with her right foot, trying to break it. Crack! The board splintered and shattered, leaving two long flat sticks. "G'morning, Jack!" she said as her foot hit the floor. "Ready to make us a scarecrow?"

After breakfast, I sat on the porch, Abigail by my side, with two long sticks, a hammer, nails, and some old clothes. I asked Aunt Dee what it should look like and she said, "You're a bright young man, Jack; use your imagination." It was already hotter than blazes and the flies were swarming everywhere. Even Abigail couldn't stay awake in the morning heat. And I sure didn't feel very creative. In fact, I didn't even feel interested. But I went at it, nonetheless. I crossed the two sticks and tried to hammer them together with one of the nails Aunt Dee had left on the porch. I held the nail between my thumb and forefinger and took a whack at it. It was about five minutes before my thumb stopped throbbing. This didn't increase my interest in the project at all. I sucked my thumb and then put some cold water on it. The next time, I hit the nail square on the head and drove it right through the stick. Hit it again and the two sticks were snuggly together.

I felt pretty good about myself until I tried to pick up the scarecrow skeleton and realized I had nailed it right to the floor. Now not only was I not interested—I was angry and not interested. Using all my creative energies to figure out what to do, I kicked the sticks as hard as I could and, whadaya know, the nail popped right out of the porch. I was back in business.

I took the stepladder that was leaning on the porch rail and set it up in the middle of the garden. I put the hammer in my pocket and grabbed the skeleton with my left hand while I stepped gingerly up the wobbling ladder.

It started shaking like crazy. I dropped the skeleton and tried to get my balance. No sooner had the skeleton hit the ground than I hit the dirt as well. I looked up, and there was Aunt Dee standing in the backyard. She waved at me and then went back to whatever she was doing. I couldn't believe it! I mean, I fell off the doggone ladder! I could have broken my neck, and she just waved.

This time around, I used the heel of my sneaker to dig some small holes for the legs of the ladder; that way, it wouldn't tip over. I went back up, hammer in hand, and thumped that stick right into the ground. Bam, bam, bam! The sweat was pouring off my forehead as I whacked the top of the stick over and over again. Soon I was out of breath, and I let go of the stick, which, to my surprise, stood there steady as could be.

Abigail sat in the dirt by the tomato plants watching. "How 'bout that, girl? Whadaya say, huh? Pretty good, right?" Abigail seemed impressed. Either that or she was still thinking about the macaroni and cheese from the previous night. I know I was impressed. This was going to be a scarecrow to beat all scarecrows. I sucked my thumb a little more.

Next I took an old flowered raincoat that Aunt Dee had left on the porch and draped it over the arms of the skeleton. I cinched it up tight with some rope and then put one of Aunt Dee's old hats on top, peacock feather flying. I added a purple scarf around the neck and, just like that, I had a scarecrow. It looked just like Aunt Dee. In fact, the first car that passed after I finished blew the horn and waved. All that was missing was a pair of black socks and some Keds. Luckily, Aunt Dee didn't notice the resemblance.

"Land sakes alive, Jack, that is one terrific scarecrow! And you said you didn't know nothin' about scarecrows. Wouldn't surprise me if all the neighbors come knocking at our door asking you to make them one, too!" She looked at me. "See there, you did it. And you didn't think you could. Now you know that every time you think you can't do something, you probably can."

I was just about to speak when Aunt Dee said, "Okay, let's show you how to tend this garden." She wheeled out what looked to me like a unicycle. It had one big wheel and two long handles. Just behind the wheel were two knife-like blades.

"This'll do as a tiller. It's been on this property for as long as I can remember and maybe longer. When I moved in, I found it in the back shed there, and it's done just fine ever since." I looked at it.

"Okay," I said, not knowing what to do with it. She smiled.

"Here, let me show you." She took the tiller by the handles and pushed it. "See how the blades cut right into the dirt. Look at that clump of weeds there." She ran the tiller right over the weeds and up they popped, deader than doornails. "See, that's how it works. Try it." I gave it a push. My hand slid down one of the handles and my forehead hit the other one. "That's a start," was all she said. "Try again." This time I grabbed the handles and shoved the tiller with all my might, and the blades carved the cleanest-looking path I could imagine between the corn rows. "Okay, Jack, you're officially my tiller man!" she said with her cackling laugh.

I didn't mind pushing the tiller. Abigail walked beside me the whole time, and I went up and down each row with ease. It was a little trickier around the squash hills, where I had to go in a circle.

Next she wanted me to pick every little weed I could see between every little plant. She also wanted me to be on the lookout for bugs. Another mortal enemy. I had no idea that a garden was such a battlefield. I knew bugs. I mean, they were everywhere: houseflies and bees and dragonflies and stuff. I never gave them any thought. They didn't bother me much, except mosquitoes, and I didn't take that much interest in them except for the fireflies we caught in jars on summer nights.

"Looky here, Jack," she said, bent over a bean plant. It looked to me like a little ball of snot had gotten caught on the bottom of one of the leaves. But then it moved, and it was all I could do not to puke.

"See that? That's a slug," said Aunt Dee. "I want you to look at all the leaves that are about six inches off the ground and if you see one of these, I want you to smash it like this." She took the ball of snot and squeezed it between her thumb and forefinger. And that wasn't all. She didn't like the leafhoppers either. For the life of me I couldn't figure out why, because they weren't any bigger than the nail on my pinky finger. "They'll suck the life right out of any plant they crawl on." She flicked one with her finger. "If there are too many to flick, then you should get a bucket of soapy water and scrub these leaves until they're all gone.

"Oh my God, I can't believe we have them, too!" she said, marching toward the tomatoes as if she was leading an army into battle. "Beetles! Surely you know beetles," she said, and I shook my head. I had seen them on

Mrs. Sanders' rose bushes but had never given them a thought. "They are very tough little buggers," said Aunt Dee. "You really have to work at killing them. See there, they have a hard outside shell." She put one on a rock and crushed it with her thumbnail. I didn't expect to hear the beetle crackling as she smashed it. The combination of crunchiness and goo was more than I could handle first thing in the morning. "What's wrong?" she asked. "You look like you seen a ghost." I was sitting on the ground by then, sweating right through my shirt, my pants, my everything. "Jack, it's just nature," she said and walked on to another battle.

As I sat in the dirt with Abigail licking my arms and legs, I saw him again. At least I thought it was him. Something moved at the upstairs window, just like when I came with Dad the first time. I shielded my eyes from the sun so I could get a better look, but all I could see was a forearm. I waved anyway, but he gave no response.

"You okay, Jack?" called Aunt Dee.

"Yeah, I'm okay," I answered. I looked back, and the blinds were down. What the heck was going on? Henry was more difficult to track than the leafhoppers, and he was considerably bigger. Why was he hiding? Brian's mother always told him that anyone who wasn't willing to be seen in the light of day was up to no good. This was her way of telling us to stop sneaking around the basement or the garage or anywhere we were trying to do secret things. What was Henry doing that he didn't want anyone to see? What was the secret?

Dad finally called. He had been in Jamestown and was now staying in Buffalo, which he said reminded him a lot of Pittsburgh with its smokestacks and steel mills. He said things were going pretty good, that everyone was nice and some of the bosses seemed interested in him. I was happy to hear his voice all full of excitement. I told him about the scarecrow and the bugs and how dark it was at night.

"It's not the same as being at home," I said.

"I know, J, but it's only for a little while. Is Aunt Dee taking good care of you?"

Aunt Dee was sitting at the table, so it was hard to say anything except, "Yes."

"Are the two of you getting along so far?" I thought about this for a minute and realized that, yes, we were getting along. Aunt Dee was odd, but odd in a good way. She had an unreasonable amount of confidence in what I could do, but I was getting used to that. She acted like I was a little adult, which was different than Dad, who treated me, I don't know, softer. For instance, he would have gone nuts if he'd seen me fall off the ladder. But not Aunt Dee. To her, it was just something that happened. No sirens necessary. At first I thought she didn't care, but it wasn't that at all. She cared, but in her own way. Sometimes her caring meant she kept her hands off and let me figure things out.

"Yeah," I said to Dad, "we're getting along." Aunt Dee smiled.

"No problems?" he asked.

I figured this was my chance. "Uh huh," I said. "Henry's been laid up sick here."

"What's that?" asked Dad, sounding a little surprised.

"I said Henry's upstairs resting, trying to get better from his hard life."

With that, Aunt Dee asked if she could talk to my dad. "Jack, why don't you take Abigail outside? Looks like she's got some business to take care of." Abigail was just sitting there with her face hanging out, not doing much of anything, but I took her anyway. Maybe I wasn't supposed to say anything about Henry. I stood close to the window.

"Yes, he had to come back," Aunt Dee said. "Just the night before you came...I'm sorry I couldn't find a way to tell you when you...no, it's been fine...he's staying upstairs...yes, Jack knows he likes to stay to himself...no, he doesn't know..."

Doesn't know what? This was getting creepier by the minute. Aunt Dee called me back and handed me the phone.

"So, it sounds like things are going pretty good," said Dad, as if nothing had happened. Aunt Dee had left the room.

"Dad, what's going on? Why didn't you tell me this Henry guy was going to be here? It's giving me the willies. Are you coming home now?"

"Look, J, I didn't know Henry was sick again. He's got lung trouble. Aunt Dee said he just showed up the night before we came, and she didn't have a chance to tell me. I'm sorry this is so mysterious, but Henry's, well, let's just say Henry's an unusual man or just different, maybe that's a better way to put it. He's very shy, and he's not at ease around people. He mostly wants to be left to himself. I'll bet he's as uncomfortable being there as you are uncomfortable having him there."

I didn't care about this Henry talk anymore. "Dad, when are you coming home? That's all I want to know."

Dad sighed, and there was a long pause. "J, it's this way: Things are moving along, but it's going to take a little more time than I thought."

"What's that mean?"

"It means I need to stay here a few more days, maybe a week."

"A week! I thought this was going to be a short trip!"

"J, listen."

"I don't want to listen. I want to go home."

"J, I can't come home right now. Your father doesn't have a job. And he's got to get one. Period. I'm sorry that you have to go through this, but it can't be any other way. I can't come home without a job."

With that, either the phone connection or my dad's voice began to break up. It was quiet except for some static.

"Dad? Are you still there?"

"Yes, J, I'm still here. I just can't come home right now."

After I talked with Dad, Aunt Dee sat down with me and said that everything would be fine; that Dad would get a job, and I would go home soon, and we'd be back to normal in no time. I shook my head yes, even though I didn't feel that way inside.

"And don't you worry none about Henry," she added. "He wouldn't harm a flea." I know this was supposed to comfort me, but the possibility of Henry harming someone, me in particular, hadn't even crossed my mind. Until now. But I listened, said, "Okay," and went off to bed.

My room was quiet. Abigail was already lying on my pillow licking her paw. No noise from upstairs. Henry must have gone to sleep early. Fine with me. I took Aunt Dee's advice and didn't wash. I just threw my clothes on the floor, put on my pajamas, and flopped into bed. Once my dad used the phrase "bone-weary" to describe how tired he felt, and, although I wasn't completely sure what that meant, the sound of it fit exactly how I was feeling that night.

I closed my eyes and thought about my dad. I realized that he hadn't told me where he was staying. I guessed that was okay, although I didn't have his number if I wanted to call. I figured he would call me again soon. He was good about calling. Unless, of course, something happened to him. I turned over and looked out the window, hoping to erase that thought. I jumped when a car peeled out on the road in front of Aunt Dee's house—scared me to death, a bunch of kids yelling and screaming. I thought about Kelso and how crazy he had driven the night we went looking for Charlie. I wondered if my dad was driving that night or waiting until the morning. I couldn't remember where he was headed next. Buffalo? Rochester? Just names to me.

One thing I knew for sure—it was a long way to New York and back, and there were tons of people on the road, including those big semis that hog up the lanes. Didn't I hear a story this summer about a truck driver that fell asleep at the wheel down in West Virginia and completely demolished a car, killing a whole family? Was it West Virginia or New York? I turned over again and hugged Abigail. I bet that family was out driving around enjoying their lives, maybe going somewhere for vacation or maybe just driving to the Dairy Queen to get some dillies. Just like that, it was all over. Right out of the blue!

I lay on my back and stared at the ceiling. Our car wouldn't stand a chance against one of those great big road hogs! My God, maybe my dad was driving down the highway right that minute, and a trucker was coming in the other direction, and he had been driving for like a hundred hours and, who knows, maybe Dad was looking down at the cigarette lighter or he was winding his window down or he was yawning and—BAM!—just like that, the trucker was asleep and my dad was a goner.

I sat up in bed. My pajamas were all wet and I was breathing hard. Abigail licked my hand and looked at me. I thought, my dad is never gonna make it home again. No way! There're just too many cars and trucks and crazy drivers, and he probably didn't know about the family in West Virginia because if he did, he would be very careful, but since he didn't, he probably wasn't paying enough attention to what was going on around him. He probably thought the driver of the truck coming in the opposite direction was doing just fine, when actually the guy had just fallen asleep, and his head had just hit the steering wheel, and the truck was about to cross the line!

I was laying on the floor at this point. I could hardly catch my breath. I'm gonna have to live with Aunt Dee and Abigail, and Henry, for the rest of my life, and I don't even know for sure if Henry kills fleas. Even if he doesn't, I didn't know how he felt about eleven-year-old boys. Maybe to him they're worse than fleas!

Thank God I got up, reached for the string over my bed, and turned on the light. Abigail was sitting still as could be in the center of the bed, her eyes bugged right out of her head. "I'm okay, girl, I'm okay." She nudged her nose against my hand as if she was petting me. Somehow the naked light bulb and the two moths dive-bombing it made a difference. The darkness got smaller and moved outside again where it belonged.

I avoided thinking about my dad by trying to imagine Mrs. Mussellman's face on the bodies of the Penney's ladies. I lay across the bed, the night air drying the sweat on my back. Abigail lay beside me, her head up and her eyes wide open as if she was keeping watch, which was fine with me. I took each breath as slow as could be, remembering that my dad always told me to breathe slowly when I got nervous before a baseball game. It helped. I pulled myself up on my elbows, closed the catalogue, propped my chin on my fists, and looked out the window at the dark night, now safely at a distance.

I thought about my dad being far away, and it didn't seem quite so scary. Not that I didn't wish he was home. I did, but I knew he was probably fine, and I was, too. At least I hoped so. "Man, that was crazy, wasn't it, girl?" Abigail stared out the window, her ears perked, listening hard. I reached over and scratched her neck.

I looked at my alarm clock, and it was midnight. I was wide awake now, my bone-weariness scared right out of me. I was hungry, too, so I tiptoed to the kitchen with Abigail close on my heels. I looked for a box of Wheaties and, lucky for me, I found it. Filled up a bowl, poured on the milk, and loaded it up with sugar. Abigail was up on her haunches by now. I took a handful of dry Wheaties and dropped them on the floor, just a few at a time, making a trail. Abigail followed me to the front door, which I opened with great care, and then both of us went out on the porch where I sat with my cereal while Abigail finished the little pile of flakes I had left on the porch floor.

The full moon was back, just like that night at Tommy's. Light clouds floated across its face, making the moon look like it was rolling across the night sky. I watched the road for a few minutes until it dawned on me that not a single car had passed. The guys in that squealing hot rod were long gone. I knew I was somewhere, but it sure felt like I was nowhere. A breeze came up, and I could hear the cornstalks rustling in the garden and the willow tree at the base of the hillside swish into motion. I stepped off the porch and looked up. The Little Dipper was easy to find, but I always struggled to find the big one. There was good old Orion's Belt.

I was breathing pretty easy now. Abigail must have sensed that I was okay, because she was asleep again, her front paws twitching, as usual. I tested myself by thinking about Dad to see if I got upset again. It wasn't so bad; there was a small lump in my throat, but nothing I couldn't swallow. I guessed he was just doing what he had to do, and I would have to accept it no matter how much I didn't like it. Accepting things you didn't like seemed impossible just a couple of months ago, but now it was just "part of the deal," as Dad would say.

I sat down beside Abigail and listened to her snore. The wind was picking up, and the chill made my toes curl. "Abigail, wake up, girl." I hesitated to touch her, because she never knew where she was or what was going on when she woke up suddenly; she would leap to her feet and wander around in a circle as if she was lost. I put my hand on her back and she jumped, but I held her with both hands, and she calmed down quickly. "Atta girl," I said. "You're okay." She looked at me and snorted. "C'mon, girl, let's go in."

That's when I saw him.

At first I thought it was a shadow at the end of the drive right between a telephone pole and a tall ash tree—maybe a bush. But the bush was too tall and too straight, and it didn't bend at all in the breeze. It stood absolutely still. And so did I. God, I wished Dad was there. The bush moved, and I could see he had two legs. I couldn't tell if he was facing me or not. I couldn't see his face or make out his clothes. Then an arm went up as if he were scratching his head. Then down again. Then nothing. He just stood there. It was as creepy as the night I saw Charlie. I didn't know what to do, so I backed up to the front door and eased it open.

Abigail stood on the top porch step staring at whoever was at the end of the driveway, her thumb wagging hard. "Abigail!" I called in a loud whisper. She kept looking at the man at the end of the driveway. I didn't want to let go of the screen door, and I didn't want to leave Abigail behind. I held the door with the tip of one finger and stretched as far as I could with my right leg. I still couldn't reach her, so I pushed the door wide open, and before it swung back, I leaned out to Abigail and poked her with my foot, turning in time to grab the door. Abigail almost leaped out of her skin, she was so startled. She started barking. "Abigail, shhhh, c'mon girl, Abigail!" I reached her collar and yanked her into the house just in time to meet Aunt Dee, who had her robe on and a frightening display of curlers in her hair. She looked like one of those aluminum Christmas trees.

"What's going on?" she asked, her voice sounding scared. "Did something happen? Are you okay?"

"It's nothing, Aunt Dee. I thought I saw someone out there by the road, that's all."

"What are you doing up at this hour of the night? You know you're not supposed to go out alone at night. You'll catch your death of cold in this damp air." She put her hands on my shoulders and looked me over to see if all my parts were in place. "Come in here and close the door. Are you okay?" she asked again.

"Yes."

"Now what's this talk about someone in the road? What exactly did you see?"

"I thought I saw a shadow down by the telephone pole. I didn't think anything of it at first, but then the shadow moved, and I could see an arm. He just stood there."

"Where is he now?" asked Aunt Dee.

"I don't know. Abigail started barking, and then you came, and I don't know what happened to him."

Aunt Dee opened the door and looked down the drive. "I don't see anyone," she said. "Are you certain you saw something?" I could tell she wasn't sure if she believed me—not that she thought I was making the whole thing up, but maybe that my eyes weren't working right in the dark. That maybe since I wasn't from the country, I saw things that weren't exactly there. When I didn't answer, she said, "You're sure, aren't you?" I shook my head.

Her face softened, and she looked at me for a long time. "Well, Jack, my guess is that you saw Henry out there. Sometimes he likes to go for a walk at night when it's cool and there's no one around. It's relaxing for him, if you know what I mean."

"I guess so," I said. "It's kind of like what Charlie used to do."

"What do you mean—Charlie?" she asked.

"Charlie No Face, you know. The guy with the giant head and a face that's no face at all. He used to walk on the roads at night. Out in the country,

I'm told. Maybe you've seen him, Aunt Dee. Have you?"

"How do you know about such things?" Aunt Dee asked, her voice sounding worried.

I wasn't sure if I could tell her I'd seen Charlie because she might let my dad know.

"Well, I heard the stories, how he walked the roads and sometimes killed people and stuff."

"Killed people? Is that what you heard?" she asked, an edge in her voice now.

"Well, yeah, I guess. I mean, yes, I heard it from everyone, even adults."

Aunt Dee's face was all scrunched in a wrinkly knot. I thought, Oh no, now she's afraid; maybe she's thinking that was Charlie down by the telephone pole.

"You don't have to worry about it, though," I said, "'cause Charlie's, well, he's dead."

"He's what?" she asked, surprised.

"Well, I heard he's dead. No one's seen him for weeks. He never goes that long without being out on 351. So everyone figures he must have died."

"Oh," said Aunt Dee, "that's what everyone figures."

"Uh huh."

"And you believe 'everyone' about this so-called Charlie No Face, do you?" I didn't know if I was supposed to say yes or no, so I didn't say anything at all. I mean, I knew I was right; I'd seen him. But the way Aunt Dee looked, I didn't think being an eyewitness mattered at all.

"Let me tell you something, Jack. A lot of people say a lot of things. That don't mean you should believe them. If I believed every tall tale I've heard in my life, I'd be convinced of a lot of crazy things. And I'd be none the better for it. Gossip is an ignorant person's truth, Jack; don't forget that." She looked at me as stern as a statue.

"Okay," I said, even though I knew for a fact that all the stories were true. Gossip! It sure wasn't gossip when Kelso poked Charlie with that stick; it wasn't gossip out there on the road with no eyes or mouth or ears or anything to make him look like a human being; that wasn't gossip struggling to his feet, searching for his walking stick; that wasn't gossip I saw walking down the road that night. But what was the point? Why try to explain it to her? I could tell her mind was set, and nothing was going to change it.

Aunt Dee must have realized she had gone overboard because she took a deep breath and forced a smile on her face. She touched my shoulder gently. "Now, are you sure you're okay, Jack? Are you ready to go back to bed? Or would you like me to fix you something more to eat?"

"No, I'm okay," I said, a little less friendly than I intended. She must have noticed, because she gave me a hug.

"It's hard not having your dad here," she said. "But we'll do just fine, won't we?"

"Uh huh," I said.

"Has Abigail been sleeping with you?" Now she was trying to change the subject, and that was fine with me.

"Yes, she has. Every night."

Aunt Dee laughed, but not her loud, cackling laugh. "That's good. She's not always so friendly, you know. She must like you very much. And I think you like her, too."

"Yes, I do." I couldn't help but smile even though I didn't want to.

Abigail followed me to my room, and Aunt Dee stood in the hall until I disappeared behind the bedroom door. "G'night!" she called.

"'Night!" I called in return.

15

"You sure you'll be okay while I run to the store?" said Aunt Dee.

"Yes, I'll be fine."

"Just need to get a few things: pork chops and some chicken breasts, peanut butter and ice cream and, well, just a few things. I already called in my order. It should be bagged and ready to go when I get to the A&P, so I shouldn't be long." Aunt Dee looked more than a little unusual behind the wheel of her old, dilapidated Ford truck. She was grinding the gears as she talked.

"Anything wrong?" I said, watching her struggle.

"Lost first gear a couple of years ago, and some days I have a deuce of a time finding second. Got to let it roll down the drive a little, and then it should pop in." With a push from me, she drifted slowly down the drive until the gear popped into second. Then she disappeared in a cloud of blue smoke and several blasts so loud that you might have thought there was a cannon onboard.

It was quiet all around. Some of the maple trees on the hillside had started to turn. There were rabbits near the garden, but they were more hesitant with the scarecrow watching. I took a deep breath and could smell manure from the farm across the road and down the way. "Mmmm," I said to Abigail, "ain't that just about the sweetest thing." I yanked a tall blade of grass from the ground and stuck it in my mouth, farmer-like. Then I knelt down beside Abigail and scratched her ears. She stared up at me. "Ready to hit that garden, girl? Huh?" Although she didn't have a clue what I was saying, Abigail understood the meaning of a smile, and she wiggled like crazy. "Just you and me," I said, and then looked up at the second-floor window. It sure was strange to have someone living in the house but pretending like no one was home.

When I woke up earlier in the morning, I had heard Aunt Dee upstairs talking a mile a minute, and then an occasional low mumbling response. It must have gone on for a half-hour before I heard the stairs and knew that she was coming back down. I peeked out my door and saw Aunt Dee with an empty tray in her hand. Must have been delivering breakfast.

Anytime I brought up the topic of Henry, Aunt Dee answered like she had a mouth full of clouds. For instance:

"Aunt Dee, is Henry happy staying upstairs all the time? Don't you think he'd like to come down and eat with us sometime?"

"I'm not so sure I can answer for Henry. He's got his own mind."

Or:

"When will I get to meet him? I mean, I don't think it would do any harm if I went up and said hello, do you?"

"Well, Jack, harm is a difficult thing to measure; one person's inch might be another person's yard. See what I mean?"

She didn't make any sense at all. This morning, though, I almost got her:

"Aunt Dee, since I saw Henry last night, maybe it would be okay to officially meet."

Aunt Dee smiled at this. "Now, you're in charge while I go to the market. You and Abigail, okay? And remember, no going upstairs, you hear?" That was that.

I stood in the garden, watering hose in hand, and stared at the second-floor window. The blinds were down, but the window was open, and the wind rattled the blinds back and forth, giving me glimpses of Henry's room. I watched for several minutes, trying to figure out if I was looking at Henry's shoulder or just the corner of his dresser. Must have been a shoulder because after a minute or so it moved. But I kept watching, and a few minutes later I saw a belt buckle, the top of a pair of trousers, and two buttons on a shirt. Looked like Henry was standing at the window looking at me while I was looking at him. I waved, but the wind blew the blinds again and I couldn't see him. I kept watch for a while longer, but I didn't see anything. I was making a big mud hole from holding the hose in one place for so long, so I closed the nozzle and laid it on the ground. I walked up to the house to get an even closer look, but by then the window was shut and the blinds were still.

I walked to the garage on the other side of the house to drag out the tiller and a shovel. Maybe I could cover up the mud hole with some dirt before Aunt Dee came home. Abigail was ahead of me, standing in the garage and wagging her little nub. "Hey, girl, wait for me!" but she went inside.

I followed. Then she ran through the garage and out the back door.

Aunt Dee's garage was full of every rusted thing you could imagine. One wall had Pennsylvania license plates that dated back to the 1930s. Random planks and window frames and even an old wheelbarrow hung from the rafters. Across the back was a long table piled high with empty paint cans, oil cans, glass jars for canning tomatoes, wrenches, pliers, a half-dozen hammers, two buckets of screws and nails, several screwdrivers, paintbrushes as stiff as the tabletop they laid on, oil-stained paper bags, calendar upon calendar, and a stack of boxes all marked "fragile." I opened one box and there were plates with flower designs on them and several tea cups with curlicue handles. I closed the box and then noticed something leaning in the corner. I stepped closer. It was a walking stick. I reached for it and then almost jumped out of my skin when I heard the Ah-oooo-ga! of Aunt Dee's horn. She was rumbling up the driveway. I ran out to meet her as she pulled into the garage.

"They didn't have the chops I wanted," she said, as if I'd been in the truck with her the whole time, "but Milton had a great rump roast, so I took that instead. Do you like beef, Jack?"

"Yes," I answered.

"That's good, because that's what we're eatin' tonight," she said, her loud cackle filling the garage. "I'll make some mashed potatoes, too. Do you like mashed potatoes, Jack?"

"Yes, I do."

"That's great. You know why?"

"Why?"

"Because that's what we're having to eat tonight!" she said, laughing all the while. Aunt Dee looked at me and noticed I wasn't laughing.

"If you were listening, you should be laughing, Jack. Something wrong?" she said, her head cocked to one side. "Did something happen while I was gone? You look like you ate something that's not sittin' well, or you saw somethin' your eyes weren't ready for. What is it?"

"Nothin'," I said.

"Abigail run off again? You know she'll do that every once in a while. She'll run off up the hill and won't come back, and I'll go up in the woods calling after her, but she always comes back." She was grabbing the bags from the truck and heading to the house. "Grab that last bag, will you, Jack?"

"Okay," I said, and she started for the house.

She stopped and looked at me. "Sure you're okay?"

"Yeah, I'm fine." I took in the bag and then walked back outside.

I wanted to look over that walking stick in the garage again.

I looked closely at it. It was no ordinary stick. All the bark was gone, and it had been tapered from top to bottom, with a squared-off point at one end and a rounded knob at the other. I reached out and touched its smooth surface, so smooth that if you had your eyes closed you might mistake it for skin. About a third of the way down the handle, there was a lattice design carved into the wood so the walker could get a good grip. At the top, just below the knob, there were tiny shapes that didn't look like anything at first, but when I touched them and studied them, I could see that they were the outline of three small birds. I held the stick in my right hand. It was sturdy and unbending. The tip was dirty from use, but the rest of it was white and clean, a brown knot here and there. Someone had worked a long time on this stick.

It made me think of the night we went looking for Charlie and found him along the road. Kelso had found a long stick in the grass and poked Charlie with it over and over. It wasn't just any old stick, either. I remembered; it was the kind of stick someone would use to go on hikes and things. And as we left, I saw Charlie feeling around for that stick and, finding it, start off down the road, using the stick as his guide. I didn't think Charlie's walking stick was nearly as long as this one, and I didn't see any designs on it, for sure. But it made me wonder: Who the heck is this Henry person, anyway? Why did Aunt Dee make such a big deal about me not seeing him? Geez-o-man, Charlie and Henry both had long walking sticks; could there be some kind of connection between Charlie's death and Henry?

I walked around the garage, stick in hand, and even though it was too long for me, I liked the feel of it. It made me feel like an explorer or like that Moses guy in the movies. I walked slowly to the pond, taking long strides and looking as serious as possible. I stepped onto the outstretched board, waving the stick over my head, frogs belching in the late afternoon. Maybe I could part the pond enough for Aunt Dee to drive her Ford truck through it. I closed my eyes and wished as hard as I could, but when I opened them the pond was still there. There were tiny ripples from the water bugs, but no big gash dividing the waters. Still, I felt all-powerful standing at the end of the board, gazing out over the pond. I closed my eyes one more time and spread my legs like the movie-Moses and cried, "Let my people..." And with that my left foot slipped off the board, and I began to wobble, then shuffle, then tilt to one side. I wheeled my arms as fast as I could, but I was losing my balance in a hurry. The stick shot out of my hand and disappeared into the water. All that was left between me and the pond was air. Splash!

Aunt Dee must have heard the splash because she came running from the house, Abigail a few steps behind, barking like crazy. "Jack! Jack!" she called. She stopped short of the pond, a grin slowly crossing her face.

There I stood, my head covered in mud, my legs still ankle-deep in the stuff. The pond, lapping my armpits, was shallower than I had thought. I spit muddy water from my mouth and swatted at the mosquitoes circling their prey. I hocked again and spit some more and blew my nose and tried to lift my legs out of the goo.

"What in the world were you trying to do?" asked Aunt Dee, not angry, just curious, as she lay down on the end of the board, extending a hand, her legs wrapped around the plank so she wouldn't join me in the drink. "Give me your hand, Jack," she said, stretching as far as she could. I grabbed it and she pulled hard. I could feel the muddy bottom of the pond sucking me back, but finally I broke free, my sneakers left behind as a sacrifice.

I reached for the board with my other hand and hoisted myself up with a mighty twist of my right leg. I lay on the diving board, my chest heaving and my clothes dripping, Aunt Dee was sitting beside me now.

"That was pretty impressive, Jack. You know, son, even though this isn't much of a pond, you could have drowned; and then what would I have told your dad—'Hello, William, just wanted to say hi, and by the way, Jack jumped into the pond and drowned today.' How do you think your dad would have liked that?" she said, reaching out with one hand to wipe some mud off my left ear. "You okay?"

I was struggling to catch my breath, and between deep gulps of air I said, "Yes, I'm okay." I didn't want to tell her that it scared the crap out of me.

"Here, take my hand," she said, standing up. "Let's get you off this old piece of good-for-nothing wood." I followed her to the end of the plank and sat down in the grass. She ran to the house to get me some towels.

When she got back, Aunt Dee wrapped me in one towel and started rubbing my head dry with the other. By now, I felt just a little stupid. I hoped nobody saw me walking the plank and falling into the pond, pretending to be movie-Moses.

"Thanks," I said. "I'm really sorry. I didn't mean nothing."

"That's okay, Jack, I know. You'll be fine. And I won't have to call your dad with any bad news. I don't think he could take losing you on top of losing your mom."

In the short time I'd been with Aunt Dee, she had spoken of my mother more often than my dad and I did in a year. She spoke of her like she was still alive, like she was away on a trip and was expected back any day now. Whenever I said or did anything that struck Aunt Dee as funny or clever, she'd look to the sky and say, "Did you see that, Gretchen? I'm telling you, you got quite a boy." At first it made me feel uneasy. I'd look away or pretend I didn't hear what she said. But pretty soon, it felt normal, like my mother was somewhere in the house, and she could hear Aunt Dee talking to her, telling her about her son, about me. I liked it.

"No, I guess he couldn't take it," I said. I looked at Aunt Dee while she dried my arms. I tried to imagine what it was like to remember my mother. Aunt Dee's eyes had seen her, and here I was looking at those same eyes, the ones that had smiled on my mother so long ago, the ones that were smiling on me now. I didn't know how to explain it, but it was like my mother was just inches away.

"Aunt Dee, can I ask you something?"

"Sure, honey, whatever you want."

"What was my mother like?"

With that, she stopped drying me off and sat back on the ground, looking at me like she wasn't sure what I was asking.

"Hasn't William—I mean your dad—ever told you about your mother?"

"Yes, he's told me some of his favorite stories; he's told me about dating in high school and things like that, but you're, well, you're not my dad. You were kind of my mother's mother, and I figured maybe you saw her different since you knew her longer." She looked at me expressionless, and I felt self-conscious. "I don't know; maybe it's not important."

She took my arm in her hand. "Why don't you sit down, Jack." She held my hand and looked into my eyes, smiling the saddest smile I'd ever seen. "Let me tell you about your mom," said Aunt Dee. "I guess you know that her mother, my sister, wasn't any great shakes of a mother herself. I worried about your mother even before she was born because my sister, well, my sister was just a girl herself at the time, hardly ready to be a mother. She wanted big things out of life, and she thought your grandfather, your mom's dad, was going to be her ticket to something better in this world. But she was wrong by a country mile. I'll just say it—your grandfather was a big nobody that never amounted to nothing." With that she spit on the ground. "Sorry about that," said Aunt Dee, "but I can't even stand the taste that's left in my mouth when I talk about him.

"Your grandmother was crushed when he left. She was crushed, and there she was with a brand-new baby daughter, and she didn't like it, and she didn't think it was fair. And I worried about that baby girl, your mother. She was such a bitty thing. She barely made a noise, like she knew that she wasn't really wanted. I'm sorry to say that, Jack, but it was true. At least not wanted by my sister." She hissed the word "ssssister", like she was talking about a snake. "When your mother was born, she had the most delicate little hands, and she was bald as a cue ball, and she had great big blue eyes and chubby cheeks that folded over her rosebud mouth." Aunt Dee stopped and stared for a moment, like she was painting a picture in her mind and didn't want to miss a stroke.

"God, she was the sweetest thing. But my sister—I won't call her your grandmother anymore; it would be giving her too much credit—my sister couldn't see it. She couldn't see that she had the whole world right there in front of her. One day she just up and left. She walked away without telling a soul. All she left was a note. 'Please look after Gretchen' was all it said, as if she was going down to the market to buy a roast for Sunday dinner and would be back in no time. 'Please look after Gretchen.' And I thought to myself—that's exactly what I'll do. That very day I went to the dry goods store and bought a couple yards of flowered cotton cloth and made her two little dresses. And then I made her some rice cereal and started to put some weight on her, and soon enough, she was growing like she wouldn't stop.

"My God, Jack, I wish you could have seen her." Aunt Dee's broad smile erased all the lines and most of the years. She was young, if only for that single moment. "After that, I hoped to goodness that my sister would never come back. Every once in a while we'd get a card from her, and I'd think, 'Please don't come back this way, little sister.' And I got my wish. I heard she died somewhere in Alaska, God rest her soul. She'd taken up with a miner, of all things, who was panning for gold in the Yukon. How crazy is that?" She shook her head. "What a waste. She kept looking and looking for something that didn't exist. She desperately wanted life to be easy, but she made it so hard that she couldn't survive.

"Your mother, my Gretchen, never skipped a beat after my sister left. She blossomed like a flower. She was sweet but strong; once she got something in her mind, she stuck to it. I'll never forget the time I took her to Penney's to buy a winter coat. She must have been four, maybe five. I had picked out a perfectly respectable, brown, cloth coat that would have lasted all winter, but she had her eye on a blue checked coat that had a fur collar. She tried it on and hugged herself in front of the mirror. Well, it wasn't practical and my goodness it was three dollars more than the other coat. But, you know, she wouldn't take it off. And when I went to the counter to pay for the brown one, she threw herself right down on the floor, kicking and screaming like it was nobody's business."

"So, what did you do, Aunt Dee?" I said, laughing.

"Well, what could I do? I bought her the darn coat, that's what I did!" We both laughed. "She wore it to bed every night for a week! That was your mother. Once she set her mind to something, watch out! And that's the way she was with your father. Up until he came along, she wasn't much interested in boys. She had her girlfriends, and she studied and got good grades, and she joined the school newspaper staff; I mean, she wasn't no wallflower. She was popular and busy all the time, but she wasn't one to date. Until your father came along. It was like she saw another coat she just had to have.

"I remember she came home from school one day and said to me as casual as could be, 'Aunt Dee,' that's what she called me, she said, 'Aunt Dee, I met a boy in my English class today, and I think I'm gonna marry him.' Just like that. And you know what, I didn't doubt her.

"Your dad started coming around all the time, looking like a lovesick puppy." Aunt Dee laughed again and so did I. "I could see it in his eyes; I could tell that when he looked at your mother, he saw her the same way I did. I knew I didn't have to worry because your father would love her just as much as I did.

"They were so young. So young and in love. Good gracious, they were babies themselves on their wedding day." Aunt Dee looked at me. "Jack, I've never seen anything before or since that matched the beauty of your mother when she came down that aisle, her skin so soft and her hair so bright, her arms as delicate as a swan's neck, her eyes like warm embers, and her smile, well, I can't find words for her smile. I can almost hear the rustle of her dress, the swish of her train. I can almost see the sun on her veil.

"Your poor father didn't stand a chance! I could see his legs shaking in his sharp creased trousers, and I could read his lips when she appeared at the back of the church. 'Wow,' was all he said, just 'Wow.'"

I felt like I was falling into a trance as I listened to Aunt Dee, her voice so calm and low and peaceful. I closed my eyes for a second, trying to see my mother, trying to imagine being there, trying to find my place in this picture. I couldn't help but wonder why it all had to be lost before I had a chance to be a part of it.

"Aunt Dee, what happened?"

"What do you mean, Jack?"

"What happened to my mother?"

She looked at me, confused. "Why, Jack, you know. Your mother got very ill and died when you were just a baby."

"I know that, but what happened?"

Aunt Dee looked at me hard like she was sizing me up, like she wasn't sure what to say.

"Well, Jack, what did your father tell you?"

"Just what you said—she got sick and died when I was a baby."

"That's all he's ever told you about it?"

"Yes."

"Have you asked him more?"

"Yes, I have, and he always says something like, 'There will be time for that when you're a little older.' I feel like I've been a little older for quite a while now."

I looked straight into Aunt Dee's eyes, and I couldn't tell at all what she was thinking. She looked at me—no, she looked *through* me—and then her eyes refocused on me and she smiled.

"Well, Jack, I'll tell you what happened. See those front steps," she said, pointing at the porch.

"Yes."

"Well, I can still see your mother running up those steps, calling to me that March day, 'Aunt Dee, Aunt Dee!' She yelled so loud I almost jumped out of my skin. Your father was barely out of the car before she had her arms wrapped around my neck. 'Guess what! You won't believe the news!'

"You know, Jack, they hadn't been married much more than a couple of months. And, of course, I knew what the news was, because I could see the shine in her eyes and the glow all around her. She was gonna have a baby. She was gonna have you, Jack. But I said, 'Land sakes, honey, what's the matter? What's gotten into you?' Your dad was coming in the front door by then, grinning from ear to ear. 'She told you?' he asked, and I said, 'No, she hasn't done anything yet but pique my curiosity to the top of Everest.'

"'Sit down, Aunt Dee,' your mother said, and I did. 'The most wonderful thing has happened.' She was smiling so wide that her cheeks looked like they'd explode, and there were tears in her eyes. 'Come here, Billy,' she said, 'stand beside me.' Your dad put his arm around your mother and hugged her close. 'Aunt Dee, it's a miracle; that's what it is. Aunt Dee, I'm gonna have a baby!'

"And she just stood there with her hands over her mouth and her eyes wide and warm as fresh blueberry pie and your father kissed her cheek and looked at me, and I got up from my chair and said, 'Goodness, my sweet child!' and I placed my hands on her shoulders and I pulled her to me and by then she was crying hard and laughing loud and I told her, 'You are blessed, Gretchen, you are blessed.' And I said, 'This will be the luckiest baby in the history of babies because you will be its mother.'"

Aunt Dee looked at me. "Are you okay, Jack? Is something the matter?" Then I realized I hadn't taken a breath since she started the story. "You're red as a beet, son, are you okay?"

"Yes, yes, I'm fine," I said, trying to catch the breath I had left behind when my mother broke the news that she was going to have me. I was there, I thought. I was actually there when my mother ran up the front steps while my father was parking the car. I was there on the porch and in the sitting room when my mother got so excited that she laughed and cried all at the same time. I was there when she broke the news, and (this part was still hard to believe) I was the reason everyone was so excited, so happy. For the first time, I felt like I had a reason for being here. And I didn't just mean here at Aunt Dee's, but here in the world. Two people wanted it to happen, and because they loved each other so much, they made me happen.

"Before I tell you what happened to your mother, Jack, I want you to know that the happiest days of her life began when she learned she was going to have you. And you know what?" she asked.

"What's that?"

"She never stopped being happy. It's important that you understand that, Jack." I looked at her, not knowing what to say. "Do you understand, Jack?"

"Yes, I guess I do."

"Good," she said. Aunt Dee cleared her throat and started again. "Seemed like you were in a hurry to be born, because you grew and grew inside your mother so fast we could hardly believe our eyes. I remember when your father called me on the phone to say he felt you moving inside your mother's belly, and I can still hear your mother talking to you soft and low as she rubbed her tummy and tried to figure out if she was touching an elbow or a knee." Aunt Dee laughed at this. "Can you imagine such a thing, Jack? You were that small once."

Of course, I could not; I could not imagine being so small. Once upon a time, I was so tiny that my mother was my home. Actually, she was my everything. And I didn't even know it.

"Your father was so proud. And, my goodness, so protective of your mother. He wouldn't let her carry things; he would tell her to sit on the couch and put her feet up, which your mother, well, your mother just wasn't one to sit still for a minute, but I admired the protective streak in William. Made me know that he would be a good father when the time came."

Aunt Dee paused again and looked away. Abigail was curled beside me on the grass. I reached over and scratched her ears. She rolled over and lifted one leg so I could rub her belly again. When I did, she laid her head back on the ground and sighed. I looked at the pond, its brown water very still again, the old board slightly curled from the drama that had just concluded. I looked again at Aunt Dee, and she was smiling slightly, although her eyes looked drawn and sad.

"Your mother went to her doctor for a routine check-up. I think she was about five months pregnant by then. She put on her gown and sat on the exam table until the doctor came in. They talked for a few minutes, all friendly-like. He checked her out, and everything was going well. You were healthy and so was she.

"Turns out on that particular day she wore a pair of bobby socks that went just a little higher than her ankles. As she was sliding off the exam table and the doctor was about to step out of the room so she could dress, he noticed a dark stain rising slightly above the top of her right sock, the shape of a half moon. He stopped. Your mother didn't think anything of it at first. But then he asked her to sit back on the table again. He took her foot in his hand and pulled the sock off. And there it was: an unusual mark on your mother's leg, just below her calf. It was dark brown, maybe even black by then; I don't recall exactly."

Aunt Dee paused again and looked down at the grass she was fiddling with. She took a deep breath.

"The doctor asked how long your mother had had this mark on her leg and your mother said, 'I don't know,' but when he insisted that she try to remember, she said she had had the mark for a year or more, that it had started as a little bruise, a little nothing, really, that stayed longer than she expected, but she didn't think it was anything and decided to ignore it. 'Why do you ask?' she said. He took her hand and smiled. He told her it was probably nothing, but since he was the doctor, he'd better check to make sure. He even apologized for the inconvenience.

"She went to the hospital a few days later, and they gave her a shot and then took a tiny sample of the crescent moon on her leg. She left and didn't think anything more about it until her doctor called her a couple of weeks later. He asked her to come to his office. He asked her to bring your father, as well. Your mother was worried. She was afraid that something was wrong with her baby, with you.

"Your dad told me they were holding hands when they entered the doctor's office. The doctor tried to smile. 'First things first,' he said. 'There is nothing wrong with the baby. The baby is healthy as can be.' Your father said they both breathed a sigh of relief. They told the doctor that he had scared them half to death. They were laughing now and joking about how worried they had been.

"But your father said the doctor didn't smile, which worried him right away. Then he said, 'There is one thing, though. Gretchen, the test we did on that spot, you know, the one on your leg, well, it came back positive.' Your dad said neither of them knew what 'positive' meant. It sounded good, but the doctor didn't look like he was giving them good news. So your mother asked him, 'What does that mean?' Later, your mother told me she didn't remember much of anything that the doctor said after that, but your father did. He told me the doctor said there was a problem. He told them the spot was a skin cancer that didn't usually amount to much, but it had been growing for such a long time that it had gotten deep into your mother's skin, and he worried that it might have gotten into her blood and gone who knows where. There would need to be more tests. They would need to check her lymph nodes, and he said they had better act fast. He said she should not worry, the baby would be fine, but he just wanted to make sure she was fine, too."

Even I knew what the word "cancer" meant. Everyone did. When Brian's family found out that his grandmother had cancer, they cried and cried and asked how long it would take. "Not long" is what they were told. And it was true. Before they knew it, Brian's grandmother was dead. Her cancer ate her up; there's no other way to say it. She just disappeared right before their eyes. Yeah, even I knew what it meant. Cancer may be spelled differently, but it was really just another word for death.

"Well, Jack, none of the news was good after that. The doctor said the only thing they could do was operate. Not only would they take the spot, but they'd remove the nodes and God knows what else. He told her it was major surgery, but there was a good chance they could get it all. Your parents were ready to go. They were willing to do anything. But the doctor said there was something else to consider. He said that the length of the surgery and the anesthesia could put the baby—you, Jack—at risk."

I asked Aunt Dee what "at risk" meant, and she told me the doctor said there was a chance the baby could die.

I couldn't believe my ears. How could this be true? Aunt Dee must have seen it on my face. "I know, Jack," she said. "I know. We were all stunned. For several days, your mother refused to talk about it at all. The doctor started calling the house every day, and she wouldn't answer. She pretended that everything was okay. But your father finally stepped in. He told her that they had to make a decision, that if they didn't, he was afraid he would lose her and the baby.

"Now, Jack," said Aunt Dee, taking my chin in her hand and making me look in her eyes, "remember what I said: Your mother had never been happier than when she had you growing inside her. She wanted to have you more than anything else in the world. That was the thing that mattered most to her. Understand?" She let go of my chin and I shook my head.

"First she told your father, and then she told the doctor. No, she would not have the surgery, not if it meant any danger to her baby. She would gladly have the surgery after her baby was born, but not a minute sooner. It didn't matter to her when the doctor explained it might be too late by then. Your father said she acted like she didn't hear him at all, and maybe she didn't. She had made up her mind, Jack; she was going to have a baby, and no one and nothing was going to stop her."

With that, Aunt Dee smiled. But I didn't.

Aunt Dee told me that my mother did well for the next six weeks or so, but then she started getting weaker. She had to stay in bed until I was born. Dad didn't work much; Aunt Dee came by every day and a nurse did, too. And then it happened. I was born on a Friday night just after sundown. Aunt Dee said my mother went to the hospital on Friday morning and worked all day giving birth to me. My dad was on the road when he found out she was in the hospital. On the way home, he was stopped by the state police for speeding, but when he explained what was going on, they led him to the hospital, sirens blaring. Aunt Dee said it caused quite a commotion.

"And then you were here," said Aunt Dee, her voice soft as the fur under Abigail's chin. "You were here, and when I saw you, I almost gasped, because you looked just like your mother when she was born, exactly. And I thought, This is good."

Aunt Dee scooted over beside me and put her arm around my shoulder. My mother lived for three more months after I was born, she said. My mother stayed in bed, me by her side, the whole time. She held me everyday and cooed and talked and smiled and even laughed when I scrunched my face or yawned. The first time I followed her with my eyes, she screamed so loud that my father came running from downstairs, afraid that something had happened to her, but she was just screaming for joy. Aunt Dee said I watched my mother's face every moment of every day, that I curled into the crook of her arm to sleep, and that my mother slept folded over me like a blanket, both of us at peace. That is how my father found us that morning: one of us asleep, the other gone.

I tried to imagine my mother so close that her every breath was mine, and mine hers. I tried to feel what it must have felt like in those few months when she was my whole world and I was hers. I thought the memories might still be in my mind, piled up behind all the years that had come and gone since then.

Aunt Dee brushed the hair away from my eyes and gave me a Kleenex. She rested her hand on my shoulder and looked at me. Her mouth curled slightly at the corner, the faintest sad smile. She sighed. "It is the awfulest thing not to have your mother, I know. But at least, Jack, you have your mother's heart; I can tell. You have your mother's heart."

I didn't eat any dinner, and went to bed early that night. Aunt Dee was worried about me. She put a piece of apple pie with a slice of cheddar cheese on my dresser just in case I changed my mind. She asked if there was anything she could do, but there wasn't. She started to apologize for telling me the story, but then she stopped. She sat on the bed and rubbed my back for a long time until she thought I was asleep, and then she tiptoed out the door. I wasn't asleep, though. I was holding my eyes closed so she wouldn't talk anymore. My ears were full.

I heard her walk down the hall, the floorboards creaking, Abigail's nails clicking behind her. She went upstairs, and soon I heard low murmurs coming from Henry's room. Their talk sounded serious, although I couldn't make out a word.

I lay on my side looking out the window, Aunt Dee's lace curtains floating in the night breeze. The air felt soft as cotton on my shoulders and back. And there was that moon again, full, casting light across my face. Where was my father tonight? The last time he had called, he had insisted things were going well, but I could hear him using his best salesman's voice to get me to believe what he was saying. "It won't be too much longer" was all he had said when I asked if he was coming home soon.

What had it been like for my dad during those last three months of my mother's life, the first three months of mine? Those last three months when he watched his wife's life drift away, leaving nothing behind but me.

"Oh my God," I said right out loud even though there wasn't anyone there to hear me. Was it all my fault? Did he blame me?

Aunt Dee had told me that when he found us that morning, he kissed my mother and then picked me up and held me tight, crying like a baby himself. He picked me up and held me like he had nothing else to hold onto in this world. When Aunt Dee got to the house, my father was sitting in the bedroom with my mother; he was sitting in her rocking chair with me in his arms, and when Aunt Dee tried to speak, he shushed her because I was sleeping so soundly. Aunt Dee said, "It was like he took all the love he had for your mother and gave it all to you, just like that," and she snapped her fingers.

But still, I had to wonder. I got up one last time, opened my suitcase, and pulled out my baseball mitt. I put it on my hand, got back into bed, and went to sleep.

16

My sneakers were ruined, and I had nothing else to wear, so first thing the next day, Aunt Dee and I drove the whole way back to Ellwood so I could get a new pair of sneaks. There were two little kids riding a tiny merry-go-round at Edelman's shoe store when we arrived. Their mother watched, not sure whether to enjoy them or worry that they might fall. After a minute or two, she looked back at her magazine, never looking up again.

Edelman's was the store to visit in Ellwood if a kid needed to buy sneakers. Mr. Edelman was about ten feet tall, and he had a long, pointy nose; in fact, his whole face was kind of long and pointy. But he had a great, warm smile, and he greeted me like a long lost friend. "And how are you doing, Master Jackie? Haven't seen you since the beginning of the summer." He looked at my bare feet and scratched his chin. "I've seen worn-out shoes," he said, "but I never seen them worn down to nothing!" We all laughed.

My great-aunt introduced herself. She reached out her hand to shake his, and suddenly I noticed how different she looked compared to everyone else in the store. She had her sneakers on and socks, a flowered hat that she wore when she gardened, with a feather in the brim to boot, and she looked all, well, rumpled, like a well-worn, but comfortable, old overcoat. I smiled to myself while looking at her. Mr. Edelman didn't seem to notice. "How can I help you?" he asked, all cheery and interested.

I sat in the chair, and he pulled up his stool and put the measurer on the floor. "Okay, Jackie, stand up straight so I can see if you've grown over the summer." To my surprise, I had grown almost a full shoe size and didn't even realize it. He went to the back of the store and returned with four boxes—low white Keds, high white Keds, low black Keds and high black Keds. The low blacks were tempting, but when I looked at the shine on the rubber soles of the low whites, and the gleam of the bright canvas tops, I was hooked. Mr.

Edelman laughed, "Every year you look them all over and then choose those good old low whites."

When we left the store, Aunt Dee suggested we go across the street to the sporting goods store. I almost started drooling when I saw the new Al Kaline glove in the window. When I walked into the store, I could smell leather everywhere. I went to the rack of bats and pulled out a few thirty-inchers. They felt perfect. I thought by the next year I'd probably be swinging a thirty-one. Aunt Dee handed me a paper bag with three rubber baseballs.

"It's not the same as the baseballs you usually play with, I know, but I thought you could find some use for these." This was great. I missed baseball a lot. The season seemed like a distant memory, and with Dad gone, I didn't have anyone to play catch with. But now all I needed was a wall, and I could play catch all I wanted.

Aunt Dee surprised me when she stopped at Pee Wee Lunch. She'd never been there but had heard my father praise it up and down. "He told me I should come here at least once before I die," she said. When we went in and sat down, I could see her lip was up her nose, because it wasn't exactly the cleanest place in the world, what with the grease and all. "I hope this isn't the reason I die!" she said. I ordered a hot dog and a bowl of chili. She ordered the same. After her first bite of the dog and her first spoonful of the chili, she was smacking her lips and smiling. "I guess your father knew what he was talking about after all." It was a little odd being there with my great-aunt instead of Brian or Tommy or even my dad, but I liked it. She was in my world now.

Our stomachs full, we headed back to Aunt Dee's. I leaned back in my seat, stretching my legs out so I could get a good look at my new Keds. I knew I would run faster now. I took the balls out of the bag and tossed them back and forth from hand to hand. It was a sunny day, but the air had that early smell of autumn, like dry leaves. I looked at Aunt Dee. She was staring straight ahead, both hands on the wheel, and she was humming a song. I didn't know what it was, but I liked the sound of it, the sound of her throaty breathing turned into music.

The previous day seemed like a dream. I thought about all the stories Aunt Dee had told me, each one more surprising than the last. I thought about my mother and, for the first time, she seemed real to me. She was a real person who lived a real life with real feelings and dreams, and she loved me. That was real, too. It still made me sad if I thought about it too long. I had to look at it sideways in my mind. But at least I had my mother in a way I had never had her before.

I still worried about how Dad might have felt about everything that had happened, but the worry was a little more distant today, like the sound of a fire whistle the next town over—still real, but far enough away for the time being that you didn't have to cup your hands over your ears anymore.

I watched Aunt Dee's steady gaze and listened to her calming hum. I tried to imagine her as a younger woman, as the one who held my mother in her arms when she was little and sat with her when she was so ill. "Aunt Dee," I said, "thank you."

She looked over briefly and then back at the road ahead. "You're welcome, Jack." We were both quiet for a moment. "Jack," she finally said, "why don't you turn on the radio and see if you can find KDKA? I think your Pirates are playing today."

After dinner I went out to the barn with my mitt and my new rubber baseballs, Abigail on my heels. "C'mon, girl, I'll teach you how to play ball." She leaped at my glove, trying to take a bite out of its hide. I laid two balls in the dirt and stepped back a few more feet before I wound up and tossed the ball as hard as I could against the side of the barn. Thwomp! The ball shot back across the dirt and gravel. "It's a liner, Abigail! I got it!" I ran to my left and lunged for the ball just as Abigail reached my pant leg, which she grabbed tight in her jaws, growling and tugging her head back and forth. I started to laugh and fell to the ground. Abigail tugged on my pant leg, jerking me inch by inch across the driveway. "Okay girl, okay girl, okay girl!" Finally she stopped growling and jumped at my chest. I grabbed the ball and threw it across the yard and away she went, her stubby legs pumping hard. By the time she caught up with the ball, she was panting like crazy. She sniffed at it, picked it up, dropped it again, looked at me, then collapsed on the ground, legs straight out behind her. She was pooped.

I grabbed another ball, wound up and threw again. This time it hit a crack and shot in the opposite direction. I scampered to my right and short-hopped it just before it got past me. Okay, I thought, I still got it. I pounded the ball into my mitt a few times to soften it up and threw the ball towards the barn again; this time I missed the mark, and the ball scooted through the garage opening and disappeared into the darkness. "Geez!"

I wasn't a big fan of going into the barn once the sun started to set and the shadows took over. Mostly I didn't believe in vampires and ghosts and stuff like that, but you never know about these things. Tommy told Brian and me that the ghost of an old lady lived in their house, and sometimes she even showed up for breakfast. For obvious reasons, she couldn't eat anything, but they'd put a chair out for her so she wouldn't get upset and make noises when they went to bed. I always told him that was the dumbest thing I'd ever heard. Even his father told us it was all made up, but Tommy insisted it was true and that his father said it wasn't true so we wouldn't spread it around. He didn't want people coming to the house all the time looking for their ghost. On those nights, even though I was pretty sure Tommy was full of it, I called my dad to meet me halfway when I walked home.

At first, I thought I could get Aunt Dee to help me look for it, but I felt like she'd done enough for me and, anyway, I was old enough to go in a stupid barn by myself to look for a ball. Just in case, though: "Aunt Dee!" I called, but she didn't hear me. That's when I spotted what I thought was the ball, a round blob in the far corner behind some of Aunt Dee's gardening tools. I walked carefully but quickly, hoping to get it before someone or something strangled me to death. But when I got to the ball, it wasn't a ball at all: It was a rolled-up bag of grass seed. So I poked around and moved some rakes and a shovel or two. That's when I saw it. No, not the ball. The walking stick. I stood bolt upright, and my eyes about bugged out of my head. The hair on the back of my neck got all prickly and my knees started rattling. My God, the walking stick. How the heck did it get there? Last time I saw it, that stick was floating across the pond, finally disappearing under the skanky brown water. But sure enough, there it was. And you'd have never known it had sunk to the bottom of a muddy pond. It was clean as a whistle. I ran my hand across its surface, which was smooth as could be. It felt like the handle had been re-carved, just like new.

I leaned it back against the corner and turned to leave, figuring I didn't need that old rubber ball tonight after all, and then I heard a shuffling noise behind the barn. "Oh my God," I said as low as possible, a shiver running up my spine as quick as a mouse. Someone tugged on the back door, and with that I took off like a bat out of hell, knocking knees and all. In a flash, I was on the porch, bent over, panting like crazy, but safe and sound. Abigail met me at the door, her ears cocked as she looked back at the barn, her thumb wagging hard. She started down the steps. "Wait, Abigail, wait!" I called in my loudest whisper. But she trotted off to the barn without hesitation.

I went into the house and headed straight to my room, yelling goodnight to Aunt Dee over my shoulder. "Something wrong?" she called.

"Nope, just tired, that's all," I lied. I sat on my bed, and once I caught my breath and my senses, I realized that it must have been Henry. Who else? How in the world did he get that walking stick out of the pond, and why was it so important to him?

And why in the world wasn't I allowed to meet this guy? What was the big deal anyway? I mean, what was Aunt Dee protecting me from? It couldn't be any worse than what I'd learned about my mother in the last twenty-four hours. It just didn't make sense to be living under the same roof with someone and never meet him.

I could hear Abigail barking outside, but when I looked out the window, I couldn't see her. The sun was completely down, the moon was rising, but Abigail was still invisible. I tried to locate her by sound and heard a rustling beyond the pond, like something big shuffling through tall grass. Then I heard Abigail, not barking, but panting, and a soft voice. It sounded like someone was talking to her, but for the life of me I couldn't make out a word. I folded my hand over my forehead to cover the soft light of the half moon. And when I did, I could see a shadow at the base of the hill. I watched it closely, and then I saw another shadow. I lost track of the first shadow, but the second was much bigger. I could tell it was a person, a person who was walking slowly into the woods behind the house, a person who was carrying a long stick in one hand like a crutch. Henry, for sure.

Figuring this was as good a time as any to solve this mystery, I put my sneakers back on and tiptoed to my door. I listened for Aunt Dee but couldn't hear a thing. Then I heard the water running upstairs and knew she was getting her bath ready. She might talk a lot about the importance of *not* washing every single day, but, I mean to tell you, she sure loved her bath. Sometimes she was in the tub for almost an hour. I wouldn't hear a thing for the longest time, so long that I'd wonder if she'd fallen asleep or even drowned. Then she'd stir, and the hot water would go on again, and she'd start singing; sometimes it was some old hymn, "...he walks with me and he talks with me...," but other times it was something she called the "Boogie Woogie

Bugle Boy." When she really got going, Abigail would get into it and start howling. I didn't know if she was trying to accompany Aunt Dee or get her to stop. Neither worked, because she just kept on. I knew that since she'd just turned on the water, I had plenty of time to get out of the house and back again before she was done.

I closed the screen door behind me as gently as possible. The moon was just above the treetops now, which gave me a little light until I reached the base of the hill where the thick underbrush and tall trees made it harder to see where I was going. The breeze was gone now, and the air was heavy. Mist was collecting on the pond, and the woods ahead of me looked, well, like someplace I didn't really want to go. I stood still for a few more minutes, trying to get my heart to stop pounding, and then I heard Abigail bark in the distance. I turned to face the sound, and when I did, I noticed a shadowy opening into the trees. I thought it might be a path. I took several steps forward, and I was right. The trees were all around me now, like giants, their arms about to enfold me. I looked back, and Aunt Dee's bathroom light was still on. Then I took a few more steps into the darkness ahead. Looked back again. Several more steps and another glance over my shoulder. I figured that if I was quick, I could count on the bathroom light to guide me back home.

I took several more steps up the path and then tripped on the root of a tree. I fell flat on my face and lay there a moment, shaking like a leaf, trying to get my bearings. I could hear crickets and peepers but little else. I wondered if I had lost Henry altogether. I got up again and continued on my way, more careful than before. The path was covered with twigs and drying leaves and the occasional small branch that jumped up to bite me in the leg. All I could hear now was the crunch of my own footsteps and the sound of my own panting as the hillside got steeper. I stopped to catch my breath. I looked up and could see a shadowy figure ahead with one arm up, as if he was holding something. It had to be Henry—Henry and his walking stick. But then he disappeared. I kept going and kept watching and tried to keep my balance and tripped again. I didn't fall but, after several minutes, I realized why he had disappeared. He had reached the top of the hill and was heading down the other side.

I stood for a minute trying to see what was ahead. The half moon shined brightly now. I closed my eyes and listened. I could hear Abigail panting again, and even a shrill bark as a car came down the road at the bottom of the hill. I heard the voice again, the low tones, and Abigail stopped barking. I moved forward more quickly now, and soon I was at the bottom of the hill, walking across a stretch of grass that ran right up to the road.

When I reached the roadside, I looked back and realized Aunt Dee's bathroom light was clear out of sight. I gulped and stepped to the edge of the road and looked to the left, but there was nothing for at least a hundred yards or more, which was where the road began to bend. Then I looked to my right and there they were: two figures emerging from the shadows of a lazy willow.

I watched as they stepped into the moonlight. I could not believe my eyes. "Oh my God," I said out loud, "Oh my God." There was Abigail trotting beside Henry, who was using his stick to find his way. But it wasn't Henry at all. It couldn't be. I watched his every move as they walked several more steps and then disappeared into the shadows again. I was sure. I knew it had to be, but how could it? I had only seen a head like that once before. I looked up and down the road again. Was this the same place? Was this the road? I thought of Kelso and the guys and that ride and what we saw and how we didn't say a word the whole way back to Ellwood, how we sat in silence, how we didn't speak of it much after that night, and how stunned I was when I heard that he was dead. But now I knew the gossip was wrong. Now I knew the truth. I stepped out into the middle of the road, not a car in sight, and squinted to see if I could catch the shadow again, but I couldn't. Neverthless, I knew.

Charlie No Face

17

When I woke up the next morning, my bedroom door was open and Abigail was asleep on the pillow beside me. I patted her side, but she didn't move a muscle. I whispered to her— "Abigail, where did you come from?"— but she couldn't hear me through her own snoring. I sat on the side of my bed, trying to put everything I had seen the night before in proper order. I got up to close my door. I held the knob for a minute, thinking. I was sure I had closed it when I went to bed. I didn't know why it was open this morning, unless Abigail had nosed it open herself.

My trip back home to Aunt Dee's the previous night started coming into focus. It had taken me twice as long to find my way back, even though I ran the whole way. I was frantic, which was probably why I went down one wrong path after another, ending up in the middle of nowhere and then trying to retrace my steps to the main path. I didn't know how I ever made it, but eventually I was at the top of the hill again with the house in sight, although the bathroom light was out. I tripped and fell and hollered out, but no one heard. I rolled part way down the slope, and I was finally standing beside the pond. I almost jumped out of my skin when a frog started belching. I ran for the porch, and by the time I got to the front door, I was sweaty and barely able to catch my breath.

That's why I was sure I had closed my bedroom door. I hadn't wanted Aunt Dee to hear anything. All I needed was for her to wake up and find me sweating like a pig, unable to explain what I had been doing. Yes, I definitely closed it the whole way. Abigail couldn't have opened it unless she had grown a thumb on one of her paws. I had flopped on my bed and hadn't even taken off my clothes, including my Keds. I must have fallen asleep in a hurry because I was still in the same position when I woke up. The only thing that had changed overnight was that Abigail was lying on my pillow and my door was open.

I turned again to look at Abigail, still sound asleep, when I noticed something beside the bed. It looked like dried mud. I ran my toe across the mark. I knelt down and looked at it closely. And even though I had scrambled part of it with my toe, I could see that it was the perfect outline of a shoe.

I thought I was going to have my heart for breakfast because suddenly it was in my mouth. That sure wasn't Aunt Dee's shoeprint. Someone, namely Henry, really Charlie, had been in my room the night before, probably staring down at me wondering if he should kill me or not. Probably deciding it was too risky, what with Aunt Dee being in the house and all.

I closed my bedroom door, and that's when I noticed something else. Behind the door, leaning against my dresser, was a walking stick. It was smaller than the one I'd found in the barn, actually about as tall as me. It was smooth and white and there were knots in two places, and the bottom came to a point while the top was rounded into a knob.

"Hey, Jack!" Aunt Dee called, scaring me half to death. She was coming down the hall fast. I slid the stick under my bed just as she pushed my door open. "My goodness, boy, you are a mess," she said. And I was. My face was dirty; my shirt and my trousers were all wrinkled, and my hair stood out on one side like the ledge of a cliff.

"You slept in your shoes?" Aunt Dee asked.

"Yeah, I did, I was just so tired..."

"What about your face and hands? You look like you fell in the pond again."

"Well, Aunt Dee, like you said, in some countries I would be considered clean."

"I don't think anyone anywhere would consider you clean," she answered. "Now wash up good before you come for breakfast. I got something for you."

I told her I would take a bath if she wanted, and then she was gone. I closed the door behind her and pulled the walking stick out from under my bed. I ran my hand along its length and didn't feel a single splinter, not a single rough spot except the knots. I drew a deep breath. What in the heck was going on?

I ran the bath long and hot and eased down in the water, shivering from the heat. Abigail sat up beside the tub. I lathered my hand, dipped it in the water, and then rubbed it on the edge of the bathtub. Abigail got down off her haunches and licked the soapy water as it ran down the side of the tub. Then she rested her chin on the tub and waited for more. "You are one strange pup," I said. I looked at her as she whimpered and scratched the side of the bathtub, begging for more. I dripped some soapy water down the side again, and she licked away. I reached out with my wet hand and pulled the curly fur on her head up into a point, like Alfalfa on *The Little Rascals*. Abigail didn't think anything of it, so long as I kept the soapy water coming.

I knew for a fact that one of the things Charlie liked to do was eat animals. Everyone knew that. When he couldn't find kids, he ate almost any other two- or four-legged thing he could find. Yet Abigail had walked side-by-side with Charlie like she didn't know he was dangerous at all. She didn't even bark. I mean, she barked like crazy every time the mailman came up the drive, even though she'd seen him a million times before. But not at Charlie. She acted like there was nothing to be afraid of. She acted like he was normal as could be, even though it was obvious to anyone who looked at him, even a dog, that he wasn't. I'd never forget that face: little dark craters for eyes and barely a slit for a mouth and no nose at all. It scared me to death just thinking about it.

What in the world was Aunt Dee doing with Charlie No Face living under her roof? She sure didn't seem crazy to me, but what else could explain it? Or maybe he had some power over her. Maybe that's why she let him hide upstairs and come and go as he pleased. Maybe she didn't have any choice in the matter if she wanted to stay alive. Maybe she couldn't even tell my dad what was going on. Or maybe she made a deal with Charlie to stay away from me or she'd tell everyone where he was. Maybe that was the only reason I was still alive.

Abigail begged for more.

One thing, though. There was no explaining why he made me a walking stick, why he went into the woods to find a tree limb, why he shaved back the bark and then carved it smooth as could be, why he came into my room and left it there. I mean, it just didn't fit with everything I knew about Charlie. No one ever mentioned that he might be generous or thoughtful or anything like that at all. This made my head kind of ache, like when a giant chunk of popsicle got plastered to the roof of my mouth.

When I got to the kitchen, Aunt Dee was standing at the stove stirring some oatmeal. There was toast, buttered and everything, already on the table. A glass of juice and a glass of milk beside my bowl. Also beside my bowl was an envelope, a letter addressed to me. I recognized my father's printing right off the bat.

"Is this for me?"

"Yes it is, Jack. It came this morning. Your very own mail."

"What's it say?"

She turned and smiled. "Now, Jack, would I open mail that wasn't addressed to me? They could come and carry me off to the hoosegow!" She wiped her hands on her apron and looked at me. "This mail is just for you."

I tore it open. A postcard fell out. It was a picture of a beach with lots of people swimming in the water and laying on the sand, kids building castles and playing volleyball. Across the top it said, "Summer Fun for Everyone!" My dad had drawn an arrow to one of the people and had written, "This is me! (Ha! Ha!)." On the back, it said, "Charlotte Beach, Lake Ontario, Rochester, N.Y."

Aunt Dee said, "Can I see that?" I handed her the card and she said, "My goodness, it looks like the ocean. Can you imagine a lake as big as the ocean?" But by then I was unfolding Dad's letter. I read:

Dear J,

I thought you'd like to see this lake; it's one of the Great Lakes. I think you studied about them in school this year. I miss you very much and hope that you are having fun with Aunt Dee and Abigail.

He should have added "and Charlie." I continued reading:

I've got some good news. I have a new job. It's with Kodak, the people who make all the film for cameras. I will be selling their film to stores and companies in western Pennsylvania. I think it will be good for both of us. Steady work. I won't have to be gone overnight very often. They're a good company. People will always need film. There's just one catch: I have to stay a while longer, maybe a couple of weeks, to get trained. I need to learn everything there is to know about film. I hope you are not

disappointed. I will be home before school starts, that's for sure.
Be good to Aunt Dee. Scratch Abigail. I'll talk to you soon.

    Love,

    Dad

Aunt Dee came over to the table. She reached into her apron and pulled out a handkerchief. "Here," she said, "this is clean." I wiped my eyes and blew my nose. "Can I read it?" she asked. I shook my head. She looked at the letter, saying each word under her breath. "Why, Jackie, this is good news! You should be happy for your father. This is a happy day, for goodness' sakes!"

"I know, Aunt Dee," I said through tears, my voice sounding creaky.

She sat down beside me and held my chin in the palm of her hand. "Then what's the matter, Jack? What's bothering you? Don't you like staying here?" What was I supposed to say —"I like it alright, except for the fact that I'm living out in the middle of nowhere and Charlie No Face, who's supposed to be dead, is actually sleeping in the room above me, and my dad went off to some lake to learn about camera film, or something, and doesn't even know I could be dead by the time he gets back; other than that, I love it here"?

I blew my nose again.

"You know your father loves you very much, Jack. He'd do anything for you. That's why he's way off in Timbuktu trying to get a good job. He wants you to have a good life. He wants you to have everything he didn't have when he was growing up."

Aunt Dee kept explaining things in her most soothing voice, but soon her words stopped making sense; they just dribbled out of her mouth, collecting in a pile of mumbles on the floor. I knew that she cared. But I also knew that she didn't understand. And I didn't know how to explain things.

The last day of school seemed so long ago now. When I had walked out of school, my feet weren't even touching the ground. Brian and Tommy and I had run and run, not actually going anywhere—just running because that's what our insides told us to do. We had laughed and laughed, and Nick had treated us to popsicles, and we had slept out at Brian's that night, and I had laid on my back looking at the sky, watching billowy white clouds against the velvet, thinking life couldn't get any better. I had a home, Dad, friends, baseball. Everything I loved. And then the wheels fell off my summer. Each day seemed strange and unfamiliar, like I was wearing a pair of shoes that were a size too small one day and a size too large the next.

"That's better," Aunt Dee said. I had stopped crying. "Are you okay, Jack?"

"Yes."

"That's good, because everything will be quite alright. You'll see."

I looked into my Aunt's eyes. "How's Henry, Aunt Dee?"

She stammered at first and looked away. She stood up and, as she walked back to the kitchen to retrieve her potholder, said, "Yes, well, as a matter of fact, he is feeling much better and soon may go back to his own place."

"And where is that?" I asked.

"Not so far—just on the other side of the hill and back up in the woods across the road. It's just a small place, but it's his, and I think he'd prefer to be there. I can always drop in and check on him." She smiled, but it was a smile that must have strained the muscles in her cheeks.

"I'm glad he is feeling better," I said.

"I will let him know," said Aunt Dee.

"Maybe I could tell him," I said. "Since he's feeling better, maybe he'd like a visitor. I hear him upstairs all the time, walking in his room; maybe he's restless and would like to see someone new."

Aunt Dee turned to the sink and ran some hot water to wash the dishes. She answered in an airy voice. "That is so thoughtful of you, Jack. I'll ask him, but don't be surprised if he'd rather not have a new visitor. As I said, he is very shy around people."

I didn't question this. I left Aunt Dee to her dishes and got dressed. I spent that day pitching against the barn, throwing stones in the pond, and looking for tadpoles. I ran the tiller through the garden, though the dirt was dry and didn't need it. I crushed a few bugs. Abigail trailed along with me. By dusk, I had a plan.

18

Clouds had rolled in just as the sun began to set. The days were getting shorter. It wasn't so long ago that the sun's glow lingered in the west until 9:30 p.m. Now it was completely dark by 9:30, and without the moon, the night was black. I had hit the sack around 9:00. I had told Aunt Dee I was wiped out; that was why I was going to bed so early. I didn't like lying to Aunt Dee, especially because she acted all concerned about me. "Are you sure you're just tired?" she asked. "Is that letter from your father still bothering you?" She had walked me to my room and had patted my shoulders and had even given me a hug. I had told her I was fine, but I'm sure she hadn't believed me entirely.

That night I snuck out my window onto the back lawn. The crickets fell silent. I stood still for a long while until my eyes adjusted to the dark. Then I headed for the pond and hid behind a small bush. I watched the lights in the house go on and off, depending on what Aunt Dee was doing. First the kitchen, as she finished the dishes; then the front room, as she watched Lawrence Welk and all those terrific dancers and their terrific you-know-whats; then the stairway light, as she went up to bed; next the bathroom; finally her bedroom. As I watched Aunt Dee lighting her way through the house, I felt relieved that the light outside my door didn't go on. That meant she didn't check on me one last time. I had closed my door tight, and Aunt Dee wasn't one to barge in unannounced. "There comes a time when a boy needs his privacy," she had said, giving me a long stare, like she was trying to say something else to me as well. It made me wonder if she knew about stuff that I didn't want her to know about. Anyway, she was good about not opening doors.

I was glad I had worn a sweatshirt and jeans instead of my usual shorts and nothing on top at all. Once the sun went down, the nights, even in

August, got downright cold. The dew was heavy on the grass, soaking right through my Keds, and mist rose up again on the pond, making it perfect for ghosts and such stuff, which wasn't what I had hoped for at all. I was waiting for Charlie, and I didn't need anything else adding to the creepiness.

I figured it was time to take things into my own hands. It was clear that Aunt Dee wasn't going to help me out. Why wait any longer? I'd already seen Charlie once and had lived to tell about it. How awful could it be? He had his chance to kill me, and he hadn't taken it. Instead, he made me a walking stick, of all things. I didn't understand why he had done such a thing, but I had it right beside me in the grass, just in case I did some walking tonight. Who knew what the outcome would be. I just knew I had to do something to solve this mystery, and I had to do it now.

Finally, my eyes were adjusted, and I could make out the silhouette of the house, fast asleep against the cloudy sky. It was getting colder, and I hugged myself to fight off the shivers. My teeth were chattering away when I thought I heard something—something high-pitched and faraway, like a screechy old owl. I held my jaws tight and heard it again, this time clearly. I knew the sound well. It was the spring on the barn's screen door. I couldn't see anything, but I felt something; I felt something was near. Then I heard coughing and snorting and sneezing and rustling near the back window of the house. I knew immediately what it was. Poor Abigail must have just gotten up from a nap and found herself stuck outside. It happened every once in a while. I would be sleeping sound, and then something would wake me up. She wouldn't bark real loud, but she'd whimper so sharp that it was like a knife being plunged into my ear. I'd call out to her—"Wait a minute, girl, I'll be there" —and then I'd go to the back door and let her in. She'd wiggle the whole way down the hall, all appreciative, like she owed me her life.

I hated to leave my hiding place, but I couldn't bear the sound of her whining like some lost little black sheep, so I stood up and called, "Abigail!" But she must not have heard me, because she kept snorting and coughing and whimpering. I was all ready to call out again when she stopped. Now I could hear her panting, not the I'm-thirsty panting of mid-afternoon, but the panting that comes whenever she's excited.

I thought for sure she had spotted me, even though I couldn't see her. I waited and listened, but she didn't come any closer. I called again, "Abigail!" Nothing. So I walked toward the back of the house and, just as I was about to turn the corner, I heard something. And it wasn't Abigail. I heard a high voice that sounded like somebody scratching the wind. A shiver ran through me again, but it had nothing to do with being cold. Charlie was around that corner. I froze. I held my breath and closed my eyes. But nothing happened. I waited another few minutes. Not a sound. I inched toward the corner of the house and peeked around to see what was there. Nothing. He was gone, and Abigail was gone, too.

I didn't know what to do. I looked in the house. Nothing. I walked around to the screen door and peeked into the barn. Nothing. I came back out and thought I heard something again. I stopped and listened as hard as I could, eyes closed and everything. It was the crackling sound of sticks and twigs underfoot. I followed the sound across our back lawn and right up to the wooded hillside. There was an opening, and I stepped into the darkness ahead, listening all the while.

I wasn't nearly as scared as I had been the first time I walked up the hill. My feet must have remembered because I didn't wander off the path once. Occasionally, I could see Charlie's silhouette up ahead, and I could hear Abigail running crazy through the woods. I stepped hard on a dry branch, and it snapped. Charlie stopped dead in his tracks, and I held my breath. But then he started walking again, slowly but steadily.

So much for not feeling scared. It occurred to me that no one in the whole wide world knew where I was. Even though Charlie had passed on all the other chances he had to kill me, he could turn on me now and no one would be the wiser. I would lie out here in the woods all through the winter and into the spring before anyone found me. And what they'd find would be just a pile of dry bones.

I heard a loud snort that made the hair on my neck stand at attention. What the—?! Darting across the path no more than twenty feet in front of me was a doe—must have stood six feet at least—and then a little fawn came trailing behind. Gave me the absolute willies! I stood like a statue, not moving a muscle. What else was in these woods? We had made fun of Brian when he insisted he'd seen a bear, but it didn't seem so funny now. Maybe he hadn't seen a bear, but that didn't mean there weren't any bears out here. There could be a bear behind any one of these trees, or even up in a tree looking down on me, waiting for just the right moment.

I was running now and breathing hard. I was off the trail and ramming through the brush like a lunatic, heading absolutely nowhere fast. Finally I got a hold of myself and stopped. I bent over, hands on my knees, caught my breath, and listened to the night and the woods and the quiet all around. I couldn't hear anything. I couldn't find Charlie's silhouette. Not even the sound of Abigail. What was I going to do now? I looked all around, searching for a clue, but everything looked the same. Okay, calm down, I said to myself. Turn around and go straight back. Find the trail again. Just take your time, you moron.

I took a few steps and then heard something. It was a car engine in the distance. Then a spray of light whooshed through the trees as the car rounded the bend. I heard Abigail bark. I turned toward the sound and, in the gathering light of the oncoming car, I could see Charlie on the road. He stumbled to the side and stood behind a tree, hoping, I'm sure, that no one would see him. It seemed to work because the car zoomed right past him without hesitation. But then I heard the wheels screech and saw the car lurch to a halt. It turned around slowly in the middle of the road and came back. This time someone in the car was shining a flashlight at every tree, every bush, looking for Charlie. "I know I seen him, I seen him plain as anything," someone said. "Just go slow, I'll find him."

Charlie stood with his back against a large maple tree, but even I could tell that wasn't going to work. They'd find him as sure as anything. I wanted to yell for him to run, to get out of there as fast as he could. I opened my mouth, but nothing came out. I just stood there watching. Charlie flicked his walking stick, and I could see Abigail run off into the woods. He looked more like he was waiting than hiding, like he knew there was no sense in trying to get away. He was caught.

"I know I seen him, I know I did," said the kid with the flashlight. He was hanging out of the window now, and the car was easing down the road a few feet at a time. "I think you're nuts," said someone else. I could hear several others muttering in agreement. "Wait till you'uns see him; I'm tellin' you, you'uns won't believe your eyes! The guy looks like he escaped from a carnival freak show!"

The car was just a few yards away now. Charlie didn't turn one way or the other. He didn't look over his shoulder to see who was coming. It was like he expected this.

The light caught the side of his face. "There he is!" cried the kid in the car, falling back into his seat.

"Jesus!"

"Oh my God!"

"Stop the car! Stop the car!"

"Are you crazy? I ain't stopping; he might kill us all."

"Stop, I'm tellin' you; he's harmless. He's scary-lookin' but that's it. Let me show you."

The driver stopped the car, and the kid with the flashlight got out. "Where's the beer, man? He won't bother us if we give him some beer. It's like those gorillas in the circus, just give 'em a banana and they'll follow you home."

"Here you go," said another kid from the backseat, tossing a bottle out the window.

"Hey, hey, you're gonna spill the whole thing before Charlie-boy gets his drinky." The kid took several steps forward. "You better not try anything or so help me, I'll beat your ass!" Everyone in the car laughed. "Whoa, you bad ass!" called one of the guys in the back seat. Charlie didn't say a thing. He didn't even move.

"So, how's it hangin', man?" I could hear a faint murmur. I assumed Charlie had answered him.

"Is that right? Did you hear 'im, boys? I told you he could talk and everything. We brought you some Iron City, what do you say?" Another murmur. "Listen to that, boys, Charlie's picky. He doesn't want to drink my beer 'cause I already opened it. Hey, Louie, toss me another, the opener too." Out flew another bottle and the kid opened it. "Here, I'll put it on the tree stump; I don't want to get too close to you, Charlie. No offense, but you're a freak, y'know." He looked back at his friends and they all laughed again.

At first Charlie didn't move a muscle. Then he stepped forward, reaching with his walking stick until he found the bottle. "There you go," said the kid. "Pick it up." By now everyone in the car was whooping it up and beer bottles were flying out the windows, smashing on the pavement. Charlie leaned over to pick up the beer, and when he did, the kid reached out and pushed Charlie to the ground. Everyone howled. Then the kid took the beer and poured it on Charlie's head. He danced around Charlie with his arms in the air while his friends cheered.

I didn't know what to do. There were too many of them for me to fight.

I had my walking stick, but I wouldn't be able to do much damage by myself. I thought for a moment, and then I grabbed a bush and shook it as hard as I could. Then I reached for a tree limb nearby and shook it, too. Then I shuffled loudly through the leaves and made a low growling noise, the kind of noise that Aunt Dee makes when she's clearing her throat in the morning, and then I gave out a high-pitched howl. "AHHHOOOOOOO!!"

"What the hell?" said the kid who was standing over Charlie.

"Jesus!" said another kid. "What was that?"

"I don't know; let's get the hell out of here!" said a third kid from the backseat.

"C'mon, Otter, let's get going!" Otter dropped his bottle and dove into the front seat. They peeled out and were gone in no time.

It was quiet again. I felt something standing on my left foot. I looked down and it was Abigail, her ears pinned back in fear. "You're okay, girl," I said, kneeling down to scratch her. "C'mon, girl." We walked slowly out of the woods.

I stood in the road looking at Charlie, who was sitting by the old tree stump, struggling to get up. I called to him, "Hey! Are you alright?" He didn't answer. I took a few steps forward and tried again. "Hello! Are you okay? Did you get hurt?" He straightened up and turned around. Even though it was dark, I was close enough to see his face, the empty sockets, the slits for his eyes and mouth, the ridges and swollen parts of his head, like the surface of the moon. I wanted to look away.

"Are you okay?" I said again. "Did those jerks hurt you?" He took a deep breath and sighed, a whistling sound echoing from his mouth and nose. His mouth spread wide like a crack in an over ripe watermelon. Then I realized he was smiling. Abigail ran to him, wagging her mini-tail.

"Warm beer doesn't hurt all that much," he said, his voice thin and drawn as if every word was an effort. "Doesn't taste very good though," he said, breathing in and out rapidly, squealing. I didn't know what to make of this. Could he be laughing? Couldn't be, I thought. Charlie doesn't laugh. Does he?

"Thanks," he said.

"For what?" I said.

"For raising a ruckus."

"Oh. I didn't know what else to do."

"Scared me half to death, too," said Charlie. Then he started breathing fast and squealing again. This time I smiled. I couldn't believe I was standing there in the middle of the night on some old country road, talking to Charlie with nothing but trees and wind and darkness all around. What would Brian and Tommy say? And Kelso? Man, I would be the coolest kid around if they knew.

I looked back at Charlie, and he was trying to wipe the beer off his face with his sleeves, but he lost his balance a little every time he took a swipe. "Here, let me help you," I said, stepping forward and taking one of Aunt Dee's old hankies from my back pocket and giving it to Charlie. "Here, use this." I took his arm in my hand to help him stay straight. His arm felt thick and strong, just like a regular person's, no different than my dad's.

"Does your Aunt Dee, know you're out here in the middle of the night following me around?"

It was hard to imagine that someone as famous as Charlie knew anything about me—harder still to believe that we were connected in this weird way through Aunt Dee.

"I don't think so," I said.

"Good," said Charlie. "She'd be worried to death. You can't be too careful out here; a lot of strange people come this way." I almost laughed at this. Charlie didn't realize that he was the only reason that people were afraid to go out on this road alone at night. He took another deep breath and arched his back, the air whistling as he exhaled.

"You followed me before, didn't you?" he asked. I hesitated, wondering how in the world he could know this since he couldn't see a thing. "Right?" he asked again.

"Yes, I did, once."

"I wasn't sure, but I thought it must be you," said Charlie. "Guess I was right."

Charlie took another deep breath. He held his walking stick in is left hand. For the first time, I noticed that his other sleeve was empty. It hung loose at his side, cuff buttoned and everything.

"How did you know it was me?" I asked. Maybe Charlie had magic that no one knew about. Maybe he could smell things from miles away or hear a pin drop in a hurricane. Maybe he didn't need his eyes because he had powers no one else could even dream of.

"I didn't until you just told me," said Charlie. With that, he reached out with his walking stick until he found the grass on the side of the road. Then he began to walk slowly back down the road, tapping his stick first on the pavement and then on the grass, all the while counting. "One, two, three, four, five, six..." Then he stopped and turned his head to the side. "Did you bring your walking stick?" he asked.

"Yes, yes I did," I answered.

"How's it working for you?" he asked.

"Good," I said.

Charlie took another deep breath and the air whistled out again. "I'm glad. Come along; Aunt Dee will worry."

I watched him amble down the road, one foot on the pavement and one on the berm, his stick moving back and forth rhythmically, his sleeve dangling in the breeze. "Twenty-one, twenty-two, twenty-three."

"My God," I said under my breath. "This is unbelievable." I felt like I had crossed over into another world, a world that no one else had ever entered, the world of Charlie No Face, the most notorious man alive! And yet it seemed odd that Charlie was so, well, for lack of a better word...normal.

I don't mean normal in the normal sense. He was pretty hideous to look at, and the missing arm only made him more, well, Charlie-ish, but if I closed my eyes, or if I was blind like Charlie and had just run into him along the street and we started talking, I'd have no idea he was the same Charlie No Face who filled every child's sleep with nightmares. I'd just think he was somebody that was walking down the street like everyone else. Of course, he wasn't. But it sure seemed like he was.

Charlie was pretty far ahead of me by now, so I held my stick up like a sword and ran down the road, Abigail nipping at my heels.

19

When I woke up the next morning, I laid in bed for the longest time, trying to figure out whether the previous night was a dream or not. In the bright morning light, it didn't seem possible that I could have talked to Charlie No Face and lived to tell about it. It didn't seem possible that I could have walked the road with Charlie, Abigail at our side. But it was all true.

On our way back through the woods and over the hill to Aunt Dee's, two more cars had passed. Both times Charlie told me to get off the road. One of the cars didn't even slow down. But the other car stopped and then crawled up beside Charlie, its motor purring. Charlie just kept walking, his stick out ahead of him. Someone in the car had a flashlight and shined it on Charlie's face. Charlie kept walking. Two girls screamed, and their boyfriends laughed. After a few minutes of name calling—"Hey, Halloween head!"—away they went. And Charlie just kept walking.

"We're almost to the path," he said, as if nothing had happened. "Are you still there?

"Yes," I answered.

"Okay. Stick near me or you'll get lost on the hill." I realized then that we were going back a different way, and he was right; I would have gotten completely lost. How in the heck did he know where the path was? I mean, when he turned towards the woods, I didn't see anything that looked like a path. But he was dead right. He slipped through a crease in the brush and disappeared into the darkness. I hurried to catch up, walking more closely to Charlie than before.

He didn't talk much on the way back. I could hear him huffing and puffing, and he stopped once or twice to catch his breath. "Are you okay?" I asked, but he didn't answer. Instead, he kept going.

When we reached the top of the hill, he stopped again, took several deep breaths, and said, "We're almost there." But I couldn't see Aunt Dee's house anywhere. This made me a little nervous. I mean, Charlie was blind as a bat. Maybe he thought he knew where he was going but got mixed up. I didn't want to press him on this, even though he'd been nothing but nice so far. For all I knew, maybe he could change in a flash, like Dr. Jekyll and Mr. Hyde. Then what would I do? I could hear Brian: "So let me see if I understand. You were out in the middle of nowhere after midnight with the world's most dangerous monster, right? And he suggested you follow him, right? And, of course, he was blind and was taking you in a completely different direction, right? So, even though you knew how many kids he'd killed, you decided to go along with him, right? Okay, that makes complete sense!"

"Oh my God," I said right out loud.

Charlie, still catching his breath, turned in my direction. "What's the matter?" he asked.

"Nothing," I said, "nothing at all."

"Are you worried that I might eat you?" I froze. "Is that what's bothering you, Jack? That I might eat you right here in the middle of these woods?" I still couldn't speak; my voice had backed up in my throat like a five car pile-up on 351.

"You know, you really don't have to worry about that," he said. "I'm still full from the kid I ate for dinner." There was a long pause, and then I heard him squealing again, laughing at me. He was still laughing when he walked away. I watched him for a minute. What in the world is going on? I thought.

The moon had disappeared behind some clouds, and now I couldn't see beyond the end of my nose. I tripped over a tree stump. "Ouch!"

"Hold on to me," said Charlie. I grabbed for him and latched onto his belt. I couldn't believe I was actually touching Charlie No Face. An owl hooted in the distance and twigs crackled continuously under our feet. I tramped up the hill, an arm's length behind him. He smelled like my father's clothes closet after it had been closed up for hours on a hot summer day. But I didn't mind. Abigail barked at who knows what, and I about jumped out of my skin again.

"She sure is a nervous Nellie," said Charlie, laughing.

We got back to Aunt Dee's safe and sound, coming out of the woods about a hundred yards from where I had entered. "Don't make any noise," said Charlie. "Don't want to wake her up." He opened the garage door slow as could be so it wouldn't creak. He leaned his walking stick in the corner where I had found it.

"How did you get it back?" I asked.

"What?" he answered.

"How'd you get it back? I mean, I chucked it in the pond by accident. How'd you get it out of the water?"

"Very carefully," was all Charlie said. "Very carefully." He turned for the garage door, and I leaned my stick in the corner beside his and followed him to the house.

Once inside, he held a finger up to his mouth, shushing me so I wouldn't make any noise. Then he headed slowly up the stairs, holding onto the banister. I, on the other hand, couldn't see a thing and didn't dare turn on a light. I took a step, and Abigail yelped. I'd landed square on her paw. I leaned down to pet her. "You're okay, old girl, you're okay. C'mon, let's go." I felt like a pinball as I ricocheted through the living room and down the hall to my bedroom. I paused by Aunt Dee's, and it was pretty clear that I could have shot off a cannon and she wouldn't have heard it. That's how loud she was snoring.

As I lay in my bed enjoying the morning sunlight streaking across my ceiling, I listened hard for any movement in Charlie's room. But it was quiet as quiet could be. On the other hand, I heard Aunt Dee humming and water running in the kitchen and Rege Cordic on the radio, and I smelled coffee in the air. My legs were a little stiff as I sat on the edge of my bed. Abigail was waking up. I rubbed her side, and she stretched her legs in every direction and then rolled over on her back and wiggled like crazy, trying to reach an itch, no doubt. "Your legs stiff too, girl?" I stretched mine again and then stood up. What a night, I thought. How am I ever going to keep this a secret from Aunt Dee? She told me not to bother Charlie. She said he was sick. She said he liked his privacy. She'd spent the last few weeks trying to keep us apart and had done a darn good job of it. Then, just like that, I broke all of her rules. I had laid in wait and had followed Charlie in the middle of the night. Going out in the middle of the night was crime enough in Aunt Dee's eyes. "Don't go wandering off in these parts," she'd told me early on. "There aren't that many houses, and it's easy to get lost if you're a stranger to the area."

"Yes, Aunt Dee," I'd said. "I won't wander off." At the time, I thought her warning was completely unnecessary. I mean, I never went any farther than the garden and was hardly even interested in going that far. But as the days wore on and I got used to my surroundings, I did wander off sometimes when she'd go into town for groceries or to get her hair done. I'd been in the woods before, but never up the hill. And never late at night. Of course, I had never told her. And I sure wasn't about to tell her now.

"Morning, Aunt Dee," I said, sliding into a chair at the kitchen table.

"Mornin' Jack," she said without turning. "How'd you sleep?"

"Uh, fine, I slept fine."

"And Abigail, how'd she sleep last night?" I looked down and Abigail was already sitting up beside my chair in anticipation of whatever I might toss her way.

"She slept all night right beside me, sawing logs, snoring louder than my dad." Aunt Dee laughed at this. I relaxed. She didn't know a thing about last night. I was safe. Aunt Dee was stirring the oatmeal. Not exactly my favorite, but I'd eat it without any complaints today. There was a stack of toast on the counter as well, cherry preserves already on the table.

I was feeling pretty hungry as I thought about the previous night's adventures. I was the luckiest kid in the whole world. I'd be a hero to everyone in my class when school started again. Their jaws would drop right to the floor when it was my turn to talk about my summer vacation. We'd go through the usual trips to Conneaut Lake or Erie or to some relative's in Wildwood, New Jersey; maybe even a trip to the Grand Canyon. Gracie Timmerman always had a big story about how she went "abroad" and saw the Awful Tower or Uncle Ben's clock, things no one had ever heard of. A few kids would say they didn't do anything except go to the Municipal Swimming Pool every day.

And then it would be my turn. The teacher would ask, "What did you do this summer, Jackie?"

I'd started small. "Nothing much, ma'am. Played some baseball." Then I'd mention the tornado and the tree in my backyard. And then I'd say something like, "Oh, yeah, I almost forgot; I met Charlie No Face." Everyone would gasp. Some wouldn't believe me until I gave them all the details. "Did you know he is missing an arm? And he can't see a thing. And he carries a walking stick. And he's not all that creepy once you get to know him." I'd have to be careful about telling them that, because they'd call me a liar. Maybe I'd have to say something like, "I saw him eat a squirrel raw" or "He told me he'd taken the summer off from killing kids." Anyway, I'd figure out what to say.

Aunt Dee dumped a ladle full of Quaker oatmeal into a bowl—plop!— then sat it in front of me. The brown sugar bowl was right beside the cherry preserves. I got myself a glass of juice from the refrigerator, grabbed the plate of toast, and sat down again. Abigail whimpered, and I tossed her a corner of the toast. Dumped about a pound of brown sugar on the oatmeal and watched it melt for a moment before I stirred it in. Reached for the preserves and slathered it on my toast.

I was just about to take a bite when Aunt Dee said, "How was your walk?"

Oh no, I thought, what do I do now? Should I tell her the truth or should I make something up? If I told her the truth, maybe she'd take pity on me and not get too upset, because at least I was honest. If I lied, maybe it would work and I'd be off the hook entirely. But if it didn't work, not only would she be mad, she'd probably punish me twice as hard for lying. I was trapped! Wait a minute. Was I really sure she was referring to the walk I took last night? No, I wasn't. Maybe she was talking about some other walk. I mean, I walk somewhere just about every day. I walk down the road and out to the garden and around the pond. I'm walking all the time, now that I think about it. Before I answered, I'd better check it out a little more. I wouldn't want to confess to something that she wasn't even talking about.

"My walk?" I said with eyes wide open, like I didn't have any idea what she was talking about. I thought the expression on my face, part curious and part innocent, was done well.

"Yes, Jack, your walk. Didn't you go out for a walk last night? Late. Well after dark."

Okay, cleared that up. She was on to me, that's for sure.

"I don't think so," I answered. I still hoped I could play dumb enough that she would back off.

"Hmm," said Aunt Dee. "I got up to go to the bathroom last night and then peeked into your room to see if you were asleep, but no one was in your bed."

"Gee, Aunt Dee, I'm pretty sure I was there." Oh my God, "pretty sure I was there." What kind of answer was that? Now she would not only get angry because I went for the walk and then lied, but also because I'm stupid.

"Pretty sure, are you?" she asked, zeroing in like a hunter with a deer in her sights. She stared at me, one eyebrow raised, one hand on her hip.

"Oh, I remember now. Yeah, I did get up because, well, I couldn't sleep. Abigail was snoring too loud, and so I got up, yeah, I got up and I went out. I went out, but not for a walk; I just went out front and sat on the porch for a while; yeah, that was it. I completely forgot 'cause I've been asleep, and sometimes after I've been asleep I forget things."

Okay, I didn't exactly come clean. But I did admit to getting up and going outside. I should at least get points for that.

"Jack." Her eyes narrowed. "Jack, let me ask you again. Did you go out late last night for a walk in the woods? Something I've told you never to do."

I took a deep breath, and my eyes wandered.

"Before you answer," said Aunt Dee, "carefully consider what you are going to say."

I let my breath out in a huff, and my shoulders folded over in defeat. "Yes, Aunt Dee, I went out for a walk last night. But I didn't do nothing wrong, I swear. I just, well, I wanted to see..."

"What did you want to see, Jack?"

"I wanted to see where Charlie went at night." I barely got the words out of my mouth and Aunt Dee said, "Charlie?" Now I thought *she* was playing dumb. She had to know who I was talking about. What other Charlie was there? I mean, c'mon, I thought. But her look was serious and her eyes never left mine and she didn't blink. "Charlie?" she said again.

"Well, yeah, you know—Charlie No Face."

Aunt Dee's lips pursed and her eyebrows narrowed as if they were reaching across her forehead to join forces against me. "I don't know any Charlie No Face," she said, "and neither do you, Jack. You know why you don't know any Charlie No Face, Jack?" I wasn't sure what she wanted me to say. "Jack," she said again, "do you know why you don't know any Charlie No Face?"

"No, ma'am, I guess I don't 'cause I thought I did. I mean, I thought everybody did." She still didn't blink. "But, of course, I could be wrong, I mean I'm just a kid and all, maybe I got it wrong."

"You got it wrong, Jack, and so has everyone else. You know why?"

I wished she'd stop with the questions because they felt like quicksand. I knew that every time I opened my mouth I'd sink in a little deeper. "No, I don't know why," I answered.

"Nobody knows Charlie No Face because there ain't no one by that name. There ain't no Charlie No Face; there never was, and there never will be."

"Oh," was all I said in return. I didn't want to argue the point because Aunt Dee obviously had an ax to grind on the matter of Charlie No Face. She had her own beliefs and that was fine, but I knew for a fact that Charlie existed. For goodness sake, I spent the whole night with him; in fact, he was the reason I had gotten home safe and sound. If Aunt Dee didn't believe me, she could ask Abigail. Even Abigail knew Charlie existed. But this wasn't the time to quibble. She had a head of steam, and I had already got caught in a lie, so I didn't really have a leg to stand on. I would be better off keeping my mouth shut.

"But I seen him with my own eyes," I said.

Okay, I can't keep my mouth shut. I know that. But in my opinion, Aunt Dee was a little off her rocker about this. How could she say he didn't exist? No matter what you called him, he was for real. I mean, c'mon.

"Aunt Dee," I continued, "I spent last night with him. We talked to each other. Even Abigail knows I'm telling the truth. It was Charlie. I know it was!"

Aunt Dee came over to the table, pulled out a chair, and sat down. She took a deep breath that softened her face. "Jack, Charlie No Face is just a made up thing that kids and teenagers and mean-spirited adults want to believe exists. You wanna know what this Charlie No Face stuff is all about? It's about people who don't want to look any farther than the end of their noses when it comes to truly seeing someone."

Aunt Dee looked at me. I didn't know what she wanted me to say. I mean, I wasn't the one who started the whole thing about Charlie No Face.

"Do you want to be one of those people, Jack? Do you?"

Geez, I thought, why was she pinning my ears back like this? I didn't really do anything bad. But it didn't seem like the right time to mention this.

"Do you want to be like all the others?" she asked again.

"No," I said, my head bowed, my forehead creased.

"Then you better clear that Charlie No Face junk right out of your head, because there ain't nobody by that name living in my house. There's just you and me. And Mr. Henry Hopewell. That's all."

I had never heard Aunt Dee refer to Henry in that way: Mr. Henry Hopewell. I didn't even know he had a last name. She could call him whatever she wanted, but to everyone else in the world, including me, he was Charlie No Face. No way to get around that. It was a plain old fact.

"Where is he?" I asked.

"Who?" answered Aunt Dee.

My God, I thought, are we going to play this game? "Mr. Henry Hopewell," I answered, just a hint of smart-aleckness in my tone. She looked at me but decided to ignore it.

"He's where he always is, Jack. He's in his room. Got a cough this morning from all the shenanigans last night."

Hmm, sounded like I wasn't the only one in the doghouse. "Can I go up and see how he's doing?"

She opened her mouth like she was going to tell me he liked his privacy and he didn't want visitors and all the other excuses she'd been using. But instead, she said, "Sure."

When I tapped on Charlie's door, no one answered. It was partly open anyway, so I pushed it a little further and took a peek. Charlie was propped up in bed, his head lying over to one side. I took a step into his room. I'd never seen him in the daylight. His head wasn't nearly as big as it seemed when we were out on the road. It just looked swollen in places. He had a little bit of hair, but not really enough to comb or cut. His ears were all mangled like a dog had nearly chewed them off. If it wasn't for his heavy breathing, I wouldn't have been able to tell for sure that he was asleep. I mean, he didn't have eyes. His nose was just a crater with an opening. And I had never noticed that his skin was greenish, like a grass stain left over after your pants had come out of the washer. He didn't look like any human being you could imagine. But everything else about him seemed human enough, like how he talked and how he acted towards me. Actually, this just made things more confusing. I mean, how in the world do you account for someone like Charlie?

Charlie's breathing evened out, and he moved his head so it was straight up on his pillow. He pulled his legs up to his chest and then stretched them out again. But he didn't speak, so I didn't know if he was awake or just having one of those dreams where you think you're doing something and so you move your body every which way. Then he stretched his arms; actually, he stretched an arm and a half.

About then I felt a little uncomfortable and figured I should leave before he realized I was there. I turned and took one step. The floor creaked.

"Dee, is that you?" he asked. At first I didn't answer, thinking I could sneak out and he wouldn't be any the wiser. But I was wrong. "I know someone's here," he said, "and since I'm pretty sure it isn't Aunt Dee, it must be you, Jack. Right?"

Now I just felt foolish. How would I explain why I was standing in the middle of Charlie's room?

"Jack, is that you?"

"Uh, yes, uh, it's me, I mean it's Jack. I wasn't doing anything. I just wanted to see..."

"You just wanted to see Charlie, right?"

"Well, kind of, I guess, but not really. I mean, well, Aunt Dee said you were sick today after all the shenanigans last night, and I guess I wanted to see if you were okay. I wasn't, uh..."

"You weren't sightseeing?" said Charlie, wheezing a little as he spoke.

"No," I said, a little embarrassed.

"Okay, then you're on an errand of mercy to see how I'm doing." This time I couldn't tell if he was being sarcastic. It's very hard to understand someone who doesn't have a face. It's like talking to a wall, except the wall talks back, laughs, and can even be sarcastic.

"I'd be doing a lot better if I had my cup of coffee," he said.

At first I didn't know how to respond, but then I said, "Do you want me to get you some coffee?"

"I'd appreciate that."

"How do you like it?"

"Black as black can be."

"Okay, I'll be back." And away I went to the kitchen. Aunt Dee wasn't there, but the coffee was still on the stove. I got a good, solid-looking mug from the cupboard and carefully poured the coffee right to the rim, and then I walked heel to toe the whole walk back to Charlie's room.

When I walked in, Charlie was sitting on the side of the bed, pants and sleeveless t-shirt on. He was bent over, coughing up a storm. It sounded all loose and nasty, and he held a handkerchief over his mouth to catch whatever was coming out. Soon, though, he sounded more like he was choking than coughing, and I wasn't sure what to do. I went to the hall and called out for Aunt Dee, but she must have been outside. When I came back, Charlie was all sweaty and couldn't even speak.

"Are you okay?" I asked, even though it was obvious that Charlie wasn't okay at all.

Finally Charlie caught his breath and stopped coughing. He reached for the mug of coffee and said, "Much appreciated." He didn't seem upset at all by what had just happened. On the other hand, it gave me a bad case of the willies. How sick was Charlie?

"Are you okay?" I asked.

"I guess it depends," said Charlie as he slurped his coffee. He let out a sigh after the first sip. "If by 'okay' you mean, am I able to swallow without choking anymore, then I'd have to say, yes, I'm okay. But if you were asking me if I'm 'okay' in some bigger way, I don't think I could answer you, at least not until I've finished my first, maybe even my second, cup of coffee." He took a gulp, and I forced a laugh that sounded more like a groan than anything else.

"I guess I meant the swallowing; are you okay?"

He turned his head in my direction as if he was looking at me. His thin streak of a mouth stretched as if he was trying to smile. "Yes, Jack, I'm okay for swallowing. Thanks for asking. Now if you wouldn't mind fetching me another cup of coffee, I'd be much obliged."

He held the cup out, and I realized I was supposed to take it even though it wasn't pointed at me at all.

"Thanks," he said.

"That's okay; I'll be right back."

By the time I came back, Charlie was nearly dressed. He was buttoning his flannel shirt and pulling his suspenders up over his shoulders. He sat down on the side of his bed again and slipped his feet into his shoes. He crossed one leg and then the other as he tied his shoes in double knots with one hand, like he was picking a guitar.

"Double knots are the best, Jack. You never have to worry about losing your way so long as you got your shoes on right."

"Uh huh," I said, looking at my own shoes and noticing that one was untied, the laces dangling all over everywhere. I tied it and then tied it again.

"Good boy," said Charlie.

I don't know how he knew I was tying it because I didn't make a sound, at least not a sound that I could tell. Over the next couple of days, I learned that while Charlie couldn't smell much at all, he could hear better than anyone I'd ever met, and he could feel things with his hand and know exactly what they were. He could sense things, too, like the afternoon we were sitting on the porch and he said we'd better get ourselves sweaters 'cause the cold was coming. I thought he was crazy 'cause the sun was out, and I felt hot as a pancake on a griddle, but no sooner had he said it than dark clouds came in from the west, and the wind blew up, and the temperature must have dropped twenty degrees. He was sitting there, sweater buttoned up, warm as could be. I tried to sneak into the house to get a sweatshirt, but, of course, he heard me.

"Told you, my young friend," he said.

I watched him work on a walking stick in the garage. "I think I'll make me a back-up," he said. "Never can tell when mine might fall into a pond or something." He waited to see if I laughed before he started squealing. Then he sat on his stool, put a slender branch he'd pulled out of the woods under his half-arm, and shoved the top end into the crook of his neck. Then he took out what looked like a Bowie knife and ran the blade back and forth across a little rectangular stone-like gizmo, and then, turning the blade to the branch, he stripped the bark off just like nothing. The shavings covered his lap and pant legs and the floor all around the stool. He didn't speak as he worked. His head was steady, and his face was forward, like he wasn't paying attention to what he was doing at all. His breathing was as even as I had ever heard it—none of the wheezing that usually rode along on every breath, none of the deep sighs that seemed to help his lungs catch up. He seemed settled and calm as the wood shavings gathered around him. He ran his thumb along the stick from time to time, looking for rough spots and knots.

Once he'd trimmed the branch down, he put the big knife away and got out his pocketknife, ran the long blade back and forth on the stone, and shaved fine curlicues off the stick over and over again. His hand looked rough and odd-shaped, like someone had beaten it with a hammer, but he touched the stick so gentle that he could have been caressing a baby.

I sat and watched him, mesmerized. I mean, it just didn't come together clear in my head what Charlie was all about. I'd learned one fantastical story about him, a story that everyone knew and everyone believed, a story with lots of examples to support it, a story that had been around for a long time, but here I was face-to-face with a different story altogether. *This* Charlie No Face wasn't anything like the one I thought I knew. The whole thing just didn't add up. I started wondering if Aunt Dee might be right. Maybe there wasn't really a Charlie No Face after all. But if that was the case, who was this guy sitting in Aunt Dee's garage, 'cause, for all the world, he looked like the Charlie No Face I'd seen on the road just a month ago.

"How long you been making these sticks?" I asked.

He stopped whittling and leaned back, considering my question. "Well," he said, "let me see." Then he went back to shaving the stick without saying another word. I watched for several more minutes, and he stopped again.

"Twenty-eight years ago. I made my first walking stick twenty-eight years ago. Of course, I didn't know that that was what I was making at the time. I'd got a knife as a gift and a pile of sticks to go with it. The people at the children's home thought it might be something I could do, you know, sit in one place and carve sticks into sawdust. At least I'd be passing the time. They didn't figure I was much good for anything else. So I obliged them and carved up all the sticks they gave me; some I made into wooden knives, and a couple I carved into little dolls. And one was long enough for me to make a walking stick.

"'What in the world is this?' they said to each other, not believing I could have done such a thing. 'Look what he's up and done with this pile of sticks!' They didn't talk directly to me. They figured I couldn't speak, because I hadn't said a word in such a long time. Of course, they were wrong."

"Why didn't you speak?" I asked.

"While my momma was around, she taught me that you didn't speak unless you were spoken to. Well, nobody ever spoke to me. They kinda spoke around me, or over me, or through me, but never to me, at least not in a way that made me feel like they wanted to hear what I had to say. Don't get me wrong; they were nice enough. They just didn't think of me in the same way they thought of the other kids. Anyway, after that I had all the sticks I could ever want: short ones, long ones, crooked ones, straight ones. It gave me something to do. And it seemed to make them feel good about themselves."

"Where were your mother and your father?"

He stopped working again and leaned his head on his hand. "I never knew my papa, except what Momma told me. She said he went away to the war and never came back. She said he was a good man and that he loved me and that he kissed me before he left, but he never came back. I figured from what she said, and what she didn't say, that Papa got himself killed overseas, but we never talked about it. And Momma, well, that's a different story. She raised me for several years pretty much by herself, and she took good care of me after everything happened, but in time it just got to be too much. The doctor come by once and told my mother that I'd be much better off, 'much happier' is actually what he said—'The boy would be much happier somewhere where they could take care of him'—that's what the doctor said.

"My momma cried and cried when she took me to the children's home. And I cried and cried when she left me there. She visited me as much as she could, but after a while, it was less and less often. Then one day she came to visit with some man, and she explained that she was going to get married again, and she would be moving away, but she would write to me, and she would come back to see me, and she was sure I would be alright. I guess after that, I didn't have much to say for a long time."

He reached for the stone again, but it had fallen on the floor, and he couldn't find it. Finally, I picked it up and put it in his hand. "There you go," I said.

"Thanks," said Charlie. He ran the blade back and forth over and over again. I waited for him to say more, but he didn't. He went back to his walking stick. He shaved and shaved and shaved the stick, each time with a little more elbow grease.

That was Charlie. Sometimes he talked and talked, and then he'd just stop. He'd go as silent as Aunt Dee's barn in the early evening, and it didn't matter if I said a thing. He was in another world, a world where nothing else seemed to exist. When that happened, I would sit there with him, not saying a word, just sitting; it was calming in a way that's hard to explain. I mean, nothing seemed worrisome or troubling; instead, everything seemed to be the way it was supposed to be. Not that everything was right, but that in some larger sense, everything was at least okay. I don't know how else to say it. I guess Charlie, for how monstrous he looked, was a peaceful sort. And if you gave him a chance, you could feel it.

"Can I ask you something?" I said. Even a peaceful kind of quiet can get on your nerves.

"What's that?"

"Every time I'm around you, you're counting. I noticed it that first night on the road. What's all the counting about?"

Charlie laughed at this question, and then he coughed, and then he choked, and finally he caught his breath and answered me. "I been counting all my life, sometimes under my breath, sometimes right out loud. It's how I make my way. When I stop whittling this stick tonight, I know it will be two steps to the back door of the barn and then eight more to the house, and once I'm in the house, if I want to go upstairs, it will be seven steps to the staircase and then thirteen steps up and four steps right to my bedroom door. Pretty simple, actually, Jack. As long as I can count and remember, I can go anywhere; as long as I can count, I'm free.

"It's 567 paces to the log at the top of the hill, but only 483 to the bottom of the other side, and it's sixteen more to the road. If I keep one foot on the road and one foot on the gravel, I can go just about anywhere with my walking stick to guide me. And it doesn't matter if it's night. I don't need eyes as long as I can count and touch the road. One night I walked into New Galilee; know how many steps that was?"

"No," I said.

"Well let's see, it's 1050 over the hill and down to the road; then I turn right and go 703 paces to the intersection of 351 and the old road to New Galilee; from there it's 2,786 steps to the railroad crossing in town. If I walk back down the tracks to the first crossroad, it's 2,060 steps; then I hang a left and go 899 steps, and I'm back at the first crossroads again. It's a little shorter, but it's tricky along the railroad tracks. I almost got hit by the train a couple of times because I can't always tell which direction a sound is coming from. That's why I prefer the road. It's easier for me to get to safety if I need to."

"Don't you ever get lost?" I asked, still unsure if I believed all this counting business.

"Of course I get lost sometimes. But you do too, I bet. Having eyes isn't a guarantee you won't get lost. Even I know that. Anybody, no matter if they can see or not, can get lost along the way if they don't pay attention. If they don't keep their bearings. For me, that means counting. I count, and I follow my nose, and I get where I want to go. Everyone's got to find their own way to feel the road in front of them. Once you can do that, you'll be fine."

I just about broke my nose the next day trying out Charlie's philosophy of counting. I closed my eyes when I sat up in bed; then I stood up and walked to the door, counting all the way. Four steps and one stubbed toe. Then I opened the door: stubbed toe number two. I stepped out into the hallway, turned and started walking, this time with my toes curled, touching the wall as I groped my way to the bathroom: six steps. I opened the bathroom door, and it wasn't all that hard to find the toilet. My peeing accuracy with my eyes closed left a little to be desired, but I figured this must be a commonplace occurrence for Charlie and nothing to worry about, although I did promise myself to go back later and clean it up before Aunt Dee found out. I found the faucets on the sink easy enough and turned them on, splashed some water on my face, and when I couldn't find a towel, I wiped my face on my t-shirt.

I turned for the door, getting ready for my six-step trip back down the hall, when suddenly I found myself on the floor, blood oozing from my nose. Hadn't anticipated the door drifting shut all by itself and me smashing into it. At first I thought, My God, is this how Charlie's face got so horribly mangled? Did he smash his face over and over again until there wasn't a face to smash anymore? Would I end up just like Charlie if I continued this silly experiment? I decided there had to be other ways to get to wherever I was going without quite so much danger, so I opened my eyes, and there stood Aunt Dee, looking all puzzled and just about to laugh.

"You okay, Jack?"

"Got a handkerchief?" I asked.

Aunt Dee pulled one out of her apron and suggested I just keep it. "What were you doing?" she asked.

I didn't know what she'd think about me imitating Charlie—I mean, Henry—so I wasn't sure what to say. "I guess I wasn't paying attention where I was going," I answered unconvincingly.

"Put your head back," she said. "Pinch just between your eyes and hold it like that for a minute." She took the handkerchief from my hand, ran cold water on it, rolled it up into a tight wad, and tucked it into my left nostril. I wasn't sure if she was helping me or just trying to make me feel silly.

Whichever it was, my nose stopped bleeding pronto.

"Thanks," I said.

"You're welcome, Jack. Now, what were you doing walking up and down the hall with your eyes closed?"

I couldn't believe she had been watching me the whole time. I felt like such a doofus.

"Well," I started, "I was, well, I guess I was trying to see what it would be like to be blind. Like Ch...Henry." Aunt Dee looked at me long and hard, like she was quickly going through all the possible things she could say. I looked her straight in the eye myself and never blinked. I knew I wasn't doing nothing wrong no matter what she thought. The right corner of her mouth went up a little, just like it did when she seemed satisfied with what she put on the dinner table or how a pair of pants looked after she'd finished darning them.

20

Charlie and I spent more and more time together, mostly in the evenings because the sun wasn't good for his skin. He slept a lot during the day and stayed in his room. Sometimes he'd go to the barn, but he rarely, actually never, went out in the daylight. Around dusk, though, he'd come out on the porch and pull up a chair and sit with Abigail and me, while Aunt Dee red up the kitchen and did the dishes. He'd pull out his pocketknife and a stick and whittle away at it, a little bit at a time, turning the stick slowly so the point was always perfectly centered. He'd stop occasionally and touch the tip with his thumb and then smile and keep going, his head bent over like he was praying.

He gave me one of his old pocketknives. It had a rough handle that looked like the bark of a tree. There was a little silver plate on it that said Winchester. Charlie told me that was the best kind. It had three blades: a short one that could be used like a screwdriver, a middle-sized blade with a snub nose that was for chopping, and finally a long sleek blade that looked like a barracuda. That's the one you used for whittling. It felt good in my hand, and I kept it with me all the time.

"A pocketknife sure comes in handy," said Charlie.

So I took up whittling too, although I wasn't nearly as good. His fingers were all gnarled like the roots of a tree, but his hand and wrist were thick, and when he ran the knife along the stick, it looked effortless. He could make a stick into something the stick never imagined it could be. My poor sticks must have felt I was torturing them with my gouges and nicks and broken points. And I had two hands! "Steady as she goes," was all Charlie would say when he'd hear another stick break. "Steady as she goes."

Once the sun went down and the moon came up, me, Charlie, and Abigail would take a walk up the hill or sometimes down to the road. One night, we walked the whole way to Charlie's house, although it didn't look much like a house to me; it was more like something that Abraham Lincoln might have been born in.

When we got to the top of the hill, we didn't go down the other side. Instead, we turned left and walked along the ridge. There was an old path that was easy to follow even when the moon wasn't full.

"Indians made it, and deer and other critters have kept it clear," said Charlie. That seemed awful unlikely to me, but he insisted. "Who knows," he went on, "maybe even George Washington himself walked on this path."

With that, I laughed. "Was that old George's wig I saw in the barn today?"

"I'm not kidding," said Charlie. "Don't they teach you anything in school? George was a surveyor back in the frontier days in western Pennsylvania; who knows, maybe he surveyed this land and divided it right on this path." I just looked at Charlie, puzzled.

Sometimes he had these unusual ideas, the kind that I might have had when I was a little younger, but not anymore. Ideas about things that couldn't be possible, but if you talked about them just the right way, they seemed very possible.

In a way, that's what I had done with Charlie. Me and everyone else, that is. Me, Brian, Tommy, Kelso, and most of the adults in Ellwood City and all the other nearby towns. We all had come up with the same kind of idea and we had called it Charlie No Face, and it didn't matter what the facts were because the idea was so much more lively and entertaining. So we had stuck to it, and we had added things along the way, and pretty soon it was truer than true.

I watched him walking along the path, his head down, stick going back and forth, quiet now, probably counting. How did things ever get like this for him? I wanted to ask but was afraid to. In the old days I would have been afraid that he would have killed me, but now I was afraid I'd hurt his feelings. You know what I mean? Like when something is real obvious about someone, but no one ever says it out loud because it would hurt the person too much. For instance, Olivia Otto, a girl in my class who had a harelip. Well, everyone knew it, but no one said so until this new kid, Herman, came to class, and on the very first day he asked her what was wrong with her mouth. Olivia didn't come back to school for a week. And even after she came back, she didn't look anyone in the eye for a month or more.

We continued walking along the ridge, the sun warming our faces, the cool breeze comforting our shoulders. Charlie was breathing easy now. Abigail was running around in circles, biting at the wind and any bug that came near her. I felt a smile on my face even though I didn't remember putting it there. Through the summer music of birds chattering, leaves rustling, cicadas humming, and trees creaking as they bended into the wind, I heard a low rumble in the distance.

"What's that?" I asked.

Charlie stood still as could be and leaned his head toward the west.

"Must be the three o'clock crossing the Ohio line. B&O's always on time."

In just a few minutes, the B&O came chugging by on the tracks below us, smoke billowing from its stack and steam spewing out in every direction. Boxcar after boxcar clickety-clacked along, each screeching so loudly when it reached a bend in the track that you nearly had to squint your eyes and cover your ears.

"Something, isn't it?" said Charlie, listening close.

"Yeah, neat," I said.

"Now listen; it's coming," said Charlie.

"What's that?" I asked.

"They're almost to the crossing, aren't they?" he said.

"Don't know," I said, wondering what he was talking about.

"Must be by now," said Charlie. "Here it comes."

The engineer took a long drag on his line and the whistle blew—whoooooooo whoo!—that deep warm sound that vibrates in your stomach. Whooooooooo whoo! again, and with that Abigail's head went back, and she started howling such a low mournful howl that we both laughed.

"Abigail better get back to choir practice." said Charlie. "She couldn't carry a tune in a bucket." Whooooooo whoo! cried the train again, and Abigail with it. I threw my head back this time and started howling as well, and soon enough Charlie did too, only his howl was all wheezy. There we stood, the three of us howling like maniacs. Abigail was the first to stop. She scratched my leg and whimpered like she was worried that we'd lost our minds. And maybe we had. Charlie stopped last, but I could still hear his laugh. "If Abigail goes back to choir practice," I said, "maybe she could take us along." Charlie was still trying to catch his breath, but he reached out with his arm and found my shoulder. He pulled me to his side and patted my back several times. I could have sworn there were tears in his eyes, although they could have been wet from laughing. I guess it didn't matter what the reason was.

Charlie caught his breath finally, patted me one more time, and said, "Better get going or we'll never get back."

Charlie's house sat down at the bottom of a hollow. There were grassy hills on two sides and woods on another. There was a stream nearby and pine trees all around. There was shale and coal on the ground in places. I noticed right off that there wasn't a driveway, and the main road was out of sight.

"How did you ever find this place?"

"Belonged to a miner," he said. "They did a lot of strip mining along the ridge, and when the mine went bust, they just left. This place was abandoned for years until I fell upon it once. And I *do* mean fell. So I kinda moved in. Didn't tell anyone 'cept Dee. I stay here when the weather is acceptable. Can't get in here in the winter much at all. But the rest of the time, it suits me well enough." Abigail ran up onto the small front porch and started scratching at the door.

Charlie paused and took a deep breath. "Y'know, Jack, I never brought anyone here before. You know what it means when someone says, 'Loose lips sink ships', don't you?"

"Yeah, it's from the war."

"Uh huh," said Charlie. "It refers to cabins hidden in hollows as well."

"Don't worry; I won't tell a soul."

I helped Charlie gather some dry twigs from the corners of the cabin. We put them in a tiny stone fireplace and then added a few logs that were leaning against the hearth. Charlie handed me the matches, and after a couple of tries, I lit one and tossed it into the fireplace. It took a few minutes of watching and blowing, but pretty soon the twigs started crackling and the logs began to sizzle. It reminded me of when my dad and I burned trash in our backyard.

Charlie and I pulled up two chairs and sat in front of the fire, me staring as the flames danced, and Charlie enjoying the heat on his face. I looked around, amazed that I was sitting in Charlie's house, if you could call it a house. He had some old *Life* magazine covers tacked on the walls, mostly

Norman Rockwell scenes; there was a lantern on a table in the corner and a bed—actually a bunk—in the other corner, a thin mattress covered with a plaid blanket; no pillow. He had a sink with pipes exposed and a hotplate where he could cook some food. There was a variety of knives on the table and a stack of kindling and longer limbs beside the fireplace. A single light bulb hung from the rafter, but with the fire going, we didn't need it. It wasn't much, but it felt good being there with him, being there in his home.

Abigail curled up near the fire until it really started to roar; then she got up and circled around and around until she found the right spot near my chair. Soon she was snoring, completely dead to the world.

"She sure got the life," I said.

"Yes, she does," said Charlie.

Both of us arranged our chairs until they were just right, the heat lapping at our faces and the cool evening air massaging our backs. Everything felt good. So why did I have to ruin it by opening my big mouth: "Does it bother you what everyone calls you?"

"Well, it depends on what they call me," said Charlie. "If it's something good, then I don't mind at all."

"Well, I mean the thing they call you mostly?"

"You mean Charlie?" he said.

"Well, yeah, that's part of it," I said.

"What do you and your friends call me?" he asked.

My face turned red as a beet, and it wasn't because of the fire. I didn't know what to say. I mean, I didn't want to admit that I called him Charlie No Face, but like I said, that's what I did call him, and I didn't want to lie because Charlie was the kind of person you couldn't lie to. He was honest in a way that was more than not lying. Around him, I felt like I should try a little harder to be someone good. But did he really want me to tell him?

"Are you sure you want to know?" I asked.

"If you want to tell me," he answered. Well, of course, I didn't want to tell him, but I knew that I should.

"Well, I didn't make it up myself. Everyone calls you this when they talk about you. I think it's been around for an awful long time. My dad knows it, even though he doesn't like me to use it. All my friends' parents know it, but they don't seem to care if we say it. I don't know if people are being mean when they call you this; it's just what they call you. I always thought it was really your name, even though that sounds stupid now."

"So, what do they call me, Jack?"

"Charlie No Face," I said, regretting the words as they came out of my mouth. It never seemed wrong to use it before, but here in front of Charlie, it seemed like I was calling him a bad name, something I wouldn't say to someone's face.

"Yes, that's what I've heard." Charlie reached for another log, shuffled to the fireplace and tossed it in kind of sideways. He settled back into his chair and sighed. He didn't say a word.

Finally he spoke. "Is that why you don't call me by name?" He was right. I had never called him anything to his face.

"I guess so. I guess I didn't want to call you that, because I didn't know what you'd think of it. I didn't want to say something that would make you feel bad."

"Do you know what my name is?"

"Well, yes, I do."

"What is it?"

"It's Henry."

"Henry what?"

"Henry Hopewell."

"Then that's what you should call me. Not Mr. Hopewell, but Henry, or if you'd like, you can call me Hank."

"Okay."

"Okay, what?"

"Okay, Hank."

"That's the ticket," he said. And that was the last time I ever called him Charlie. Hank was funny that way. He didn't dwell much at all on the bad stuff, and yet you could see the hurt all over him; not just how his face and body were mangled but how he was mangled inside, too, like someone took a fork to his heart.

The fire was roaring good now. It filled the room with dancing shadows and made the ceiling crawl. It was the spookiest place I'd ever been, the kind of place that would have made me think of Charlie No Face when I was back home. It would have been the perfect place for tons of stories about Charlie's exploits. Now I realized that we mostly made those stories up as we went along, just like Brian made up good breast stories because we wanted to keep the idea in our heads. I guess we wanted to keep Charlie in our heads, too, even though we acted so scared of him all the time. Hard as I thought about it, I couldn't come up with a real good explanation for why it was so important to keep the stories going. I hated to say it, but it was fun to talk about him and to scare each other and to wonder what he was like or what he'd do to us if he ever captured us. It wasn't really about him, in a way; it was about us trying to have a good time. I never really thought much about there being a real, actual person on the other end of our good time.

Even worse, I'd gone hunting for Hank with Kelso and the guys, like he was an animal or something. That's exactly the way we had treated him, now that I thought about it. I mean, Kelso was the worst, poking him and making fun of him, but I was right there, and I never lifted a finger to stop him. I never said a word. I mean, yeah, I was scared. I'd never seen someone who looked like that, and I probably never will again, so I was in a kind of shock, but even that didn't really get me off the hook. Me being scared didn't make it okay to treat him like that.

Hank was leaning on the back legs of his chair looking very relaxed. The fire was calming down. "Whadaya say I toss another one on her before she goes out all together," I said.

"Mmhmm," was all Hank said. I took the log with both my hands and waddled over to the fireplace. I leaned in and could feel the heat heavy on my forehead. I dropped the log as close to the fire as I could and then pushed it with a stick until it sat across the other one, looking like a Civil War canon.

"Pack it loose," said Hank. "Just like everything else, fire needs air to breathe."

"Okay," I said and sat in my chair again, trying to balance on the back legs, too.

It was quiet for a time.

"Henry."

"What is it, Jack?"

I wasn't sure if I should say something or not. "Oh, nothin'," I said. We fell silent again, except for the fire and Hank's troubled breathing. But the thought of what I had done with Kelso and the guys kept tugging on my mind and wouldn't let me go. I felt like I had to tell him or I might just explode.

"What is it?" said Hank. "What's on your mind?"

Geez, I thought, this honesty business sure ties a boy up in knots.

"Well, it's this way, Hank. You remember a while back when those kids were in the car, and they was bothering you, and then I came out of the woods and tried to scare them away?"

"Yeah, I remember that. And I thank you for it."

"Well, maybe you shouldn't thank me so quick until I tell you the rest. Do you remember a time a little while farther back, maybe six weeks ago? You were out on the road, and you had fallen down or something and you were just sittin' there along the road? Do you remember?"

Hank considered what I was saying for a moment, and I realized that maybe this happened to him so often that it was hard to separate one time from another. "Yes, I do remember it," he said finally.

"And then a car come up near you with a bunch of kids in it? And the car stopped, and one of the kids got out, the oldest one?" I took a breath and gulped, my Adam's apple sinking into my stomach.

"I remember it because I had tripped and fallen along the road, and I couldn't find my walking stick, and I got all turned around." He laughed to himself.

"And then the one kid, the oldest one again, he started poking at you with your walking stick, only he didn't know it was a walking stick."

"Uh huh, I remember," he said calmly.

"Well. Henry. I wasn't the kid poking at you, but I was there. I was one of the ones in the car. I was there when it all happened. The whole thing scared me half to death, and I thought about it afterwards, and I couldn't get you out of my mind."

Hank tipped his chair again and then leaned his head back, too, like he was looking around for a thought that got lost. "Let me see, oh yeah, Kelso; that was his name, wasn't it?"

My eyes almost bugged out of my head. "How did you know his name?" I asked.

"Easy enough, I heard someone call his name—'Kelso'!" I didn't say another word. Just looked at him. How in the world, was all I thought. As if that wasn't enough, Hank went on, "It took me considerable time to figure this out, but that was you, wasn't it? That was you yelling at Kelso to stop. At first I couldn't put it together. I'd hear you talking out in the yard or down in the kitchen and I'd think I must have met you before because your voice had a faint familiarity to it. But I couldn't place it, so I figured I was mistaken.

But the feeling didn't go away, and that night, when you came hollering out of the woods, I knew where I had heard your voice before. Kelso!" he called, trying to imitate me. "I agree," he went on. "You did sound scared."

"Yes, that was me. I'm sorry."

"No need to apologize."

"But I feel bad."

"Well, then, I accept your apology," said Hank.

I looked real hard at him, but I couldn't see anything that looked like anger on his face. I mean, if it were me, I would have been furious; I'd have told me to get out and never come back, but not Hank. "How come you never told me you knew?" I asked.

Hank shrugged. "Water under the bridge. I guess if I was a kid, I'd probably want to go huntin' Charlie No Face, too. Besides, if your friend Kelso hadn't picked up my walking stick and poked me with it, I might never have found it. I might still be crawling around out there, no idea what I was doing or where I was going. You never can tell what the outcome of meanness is gonna be."

Hank had the oddest way of thinking about things. Most people would have gotten swallowed up in a whirlpool of anger and frustration if the same thing had happened to them, but he just called it "water under the bridge." I didn't know exactly what to make of it. Maybe he was missing that thing inside that gets you riled up when people do mean and stupid things to you. Whatever the reason, he always looked at things kind of tilted, like he was turning a dirty old lump of coal around and around until he found a flat shiny surface, and that's what he'd notice most. Was that a blind thing? Or a Hank thing? It sure wasn't a Jackie thing, at least not yet. If I were Hank, I would have wanted to punch Kelso's lights out—my lights, too. That would have made me feel a heck of a lot better. But that sort of thing seemed useless to Hank, like he didn't have time for it, like there was something more important to do, even if it was only carving another walking stick. He sure was put together different than anybody I had ever met. Made me think about all those times my dad got upset with me for talking about Charlie No Face. He knew, but like a lot of things, he never told me.

Must have been after eleven o'clock when we started back to Aunt Dee's, Hank leading the way and me following. I couldn't see Abigail at all, but I could hear her shuffling through the dried leaves and sneezing every once in a while when she sniffed something that surprised her nose. She loved the woods. I could hear her happy panting all around us. I knew that by the time we got home her ears would be full of burrs and Aunt Dee would be upset because she usually had to clean old Abigail up, but since Abigail was having so much fun, I didn't want to stop her.

We were an odd threesome, Hank, Abigail, and me. Wasn't sure if we were the Three Stooges or the Three Musketeers, but we were definitely connected in a way I would never have expected. My summer sure had taken a strange turn.

I wished Dad would come back soon, though, because school was just around the bend and, even though I loved being here, it made me nervous that nothing was settled. Usually I liked things to march along in a straight line, if possible, and this summer, well, the line had been completely erased. Instead, here I was following a one-armed blind man!

"Still back there?" called Hank.

"Yes, sir. I'm back here, sir," I said, like he was Sergeant Bilko or something. "You still countin' up there?"

"Always," said Hank, "always counting." My God, I thought, I couldn't live like Hank. It would have driven me nuts if I couldn't see nothin' and everyone was afraid of me and everyone made up stories about me all the time. Even worse, he didn't have any friends. I mean, there was Aunt Dee and me and Abigail, but that wasn't the same thing. He didn't have a buddy to sit down with and just talk about the day. I mean, he didn't even have a regular day like everyone else. He didn't do any of the things that make for a regular day. I mean, he didn't work and he didn't drive a car and he didn't go to the store and he didn't stop by Pee Wee's for a dog. I mean, he had to count his steps every minute of every day just to know where he'd been and where he was going. Who had to do that? Nobody! Nobody had to think about that stuff at all. They just did what they needed to do like it was nothing, when actually it was a miracle, if you looked at it Hank-like. Come to think of it, most everything was a miracle when you thought about it Hank-like. Seeing, breathing, walking around—never gave any of that stuff a thought, really, until you thought of it from inside Hank's world. Then it was all amazing. I didn't know what I'd have done if there wasn't anyone else in the world who was like me, even a little. I didn't think I could be Hank.

Abigail got to the front porch before either of us. Her thumb was going a mile a minute, like she was ready for another adventure. Then she just collapsed, rolled over on her side, and fell fast asleep. I decided to leave her there. "Hey there, young fella," called Hank once we got in the house, "thanks for coming with me."

"It was an honor, Mr. Hopewell," I said with a royal flare. He took a deep breath as he started up the stairs and followed with a laugh. He waved his hand, tilting it back and forth like he was the Queen of England in the newsreels. I laughed and headed down the hall.

Charlie No Face

21

When I woke up, Aunt Dee was standing in my doorway, her arms folded, her chin jutting out, and her lips pursed. "Imagine my surprise when I woke up out of a sound sleep to something screaming like a banshee at the front door. Then imagine my surprise when I open the door and in runs what looks like a little black porcupine. Looked a whole lot like our Abigail, but I thought, Couldn't be. No one would leave poor old Abigail out all night where she could run herself into a mess of burrs and leaves and God knows what. Must be a porcupine, but it didn't look like any porcupine I'd ever seen before, and it didn't act like one either. This porcupine jumped up on my leg and panted like a puppy. Gracious sakes, it was Abigail," she said, deadpanned. "Then I wondered how this could have happened and who could explain it." Her voice got low and gravelly. "That's when I thought—Jack."

I yawned. "You thought right, I'm afraid. Me and Abigail and Hank went out last night." Aunt Dee was upset about our outings at first, but lately she hadn't minded much, although she still acted all serious about it.

"Where did you go this time?"

"Hank took me and Abigail to his cabin."

"He did what?" said Aunt Dee, truly surprised.

"He took us down to the hollow where the old miner's cabin is. We made a fire and sat for a long time, just talking, and then we came back, pretty late, I guess."

"Huh, he took you to his cabin." She said this in a whisper, like she didn't mean to say it out loud at all. "You know, Jack, he's never done that before, never in his life."

"That's what he told me. He told me to keep it quiet, because loose lips sink ships, but of course you know where his cabin is, so I figured it's okay to tell you."

"Yes, it's fine, but, you know, I've never been there myself. I've taken him down the road and dropped him off. I've watched him disappear into the woods, but I never been there myself." She smiled at me. "He must like you, like you a lot to do that." I smiled back, not knowing what to say. I never thought that, well, that we might be friends.

"And neither one of you had the good sense to keep Abigail out of the bushes? And neither one of you had the common decency to clean her up, now, did you?" Her words were sharp, but her face was light.

"Once I get dressed, I'd be glad to help you, Aunt Dee."

"Well, if it happens again, I'll take you up on the offer, but not today. There's someone here to see you."

When I went outside, there was Brian standing on the front porch, looking around, his big old face hanging out. "Hey, man!" I called.

He turned and chuckled; his face was brown, and his freckles were in full bloom. "How you doin', muttonhead?" he said. I was so happy to see Brian that I almost hugged him, but instead I smacked him good on the back and slugged his arm. "Ow!" he said. "What was that for?" And then he punched me back. We went back and forth like this until we were both in hysterics.

"Boy," said Brian, "how in the heck did you end up out here? I mean, does your aunt have a toilet, or do you go out back and pee in the woods?"

"Don't be ridiculous; if I gotta pee, I just go out my bedroom window." With that we started laughing all over again.

Aunt Dee was at the door by then. "I see you two are catching up. Are you hungry?"

We both said, "Yeah."

"Why don't you stay out here while I put something together?"

"Seriously, Brian, how'd you get here?"

"My dad's car," he said. I looked at Brian, assuming he would crack a smile, but he didn't. He was serious. Good ol' Brian.

"Okay," I said, "let's try this again. How did you know where to find me?"

"Your dad called my dad and asked if I could come out to see you once we got back from the lake. Hey, man, do I have stories to tell you. You wouldn't believe what I saw on the beach! It was amazing!"

"My dad called your dad? When did he do that?"

"About a week ago."

I had talked to my dad just a few days ago, and he never mentioned it, but that was okay; he was so excited about his new job that maybe it had slipped his mind.

"Yeah, so your dad gave my dad your aunt's phone number and he called her last night, but you weren't around; she didn't seem to know where you were." He squinted at me, like he wondered if I was really here when his dad called and just didn't want to talk to him.

"I was probably out in the woods with Abigail."

"Oh, yeah," said Brian. "I met Abigail already; thought she was going to bite my leg off."

"She's fine, just a little nervous is all."

"So your aunt told me to come as soon as I could," said Brian. "So here I am."

"Breakfast is ready, boys, wash up!"

I knew I had missed Brian, but having him there made me realize how much. I mean, Brian and I were the best of best friends. We loved all the same things, and we could talk for hours about breasts and baseball and stuff, and even when we got into a fight we knew it wouldn't last more than a day. That's a friend for sure. I was so glad to see him.

But I also felt a little uncomfortable. I wondered about Hank upstairs and what would happen if Brian found out. I figured I'd better keep the whole thing quiet. Brian was a blabbermouth anyway, and in about ten seconds everyone would know that Charlie wasn't dead and that Charlie wasn't really Charlie. But geez-o-man, I was itching like crazy to tell him. I decided I would try my best to keep my piehole shut.

We had a great day. Brian brought his baseball mitt, and we played catch for the first time in weeks. I got to tell him blow-by-blow about the championship game, and Brian reacted like it had just happened yesterday —"Oh, man, no!" It made me feel good. He understood what it meant more than anybody else. We did a little gardening for Aunt Dee, although Brian wasn't much for that kind of stuff.

"You did this everyday, Farmer Brown?"

"Yeah," I said, a little sheepish, since we had always made fun of farmers for some reason, like they weren't as good as people who lived in town.

I showed him around the pond and reenacted my tumble into the water, without telling him about the walking stick, of course. He thought this was hilarious. He howled and howled and almost fell off the board into the water himself, which, I think, was exactly what he wanted to do. "You're a total dink," he said.

Later, after lunch, Aunt Dee made us chocolate milkshakes, and we took them up on the hillside and drank them under the shade of an old sycamore, Abigail whimpering and begging beside us.

"Look at that!" said Brian when Abigail sat up.

"Yeah, she's a genius; been doing that since she was a pup." Aunt Dee made the thickest shakes this side of J&T's. We sucked our paper straws flat as pancakes and then tossed them aside. We held our glasses up and coaxed the shakes down the side, slow as icebergs. Man, was that good.

Brian looked all around to make sure nobody could hear him.

"Okay," he started. "I can make it happen whenever I want."

"Make what happen?"

"Whadaya mean, make what happen?" he said, looking at me all puzzled. "C'mon, son, you know what I'm talkin' about: *Operation Petticoat* all the time. Mrs. Musselman anytime I want."

"Oh!" I said, smiling.

"I met this kid, Jesse, at the lake, and I mean the kid was something; he was thirteen and he knew everything you'd ever want to know about, you know. He had a sixteen-year-old sister who brought some friends along for their vacation and, I mean to tell you, I'd never seen anything like it. We'd sit on the beach with our sunglasses on so nobody could tell what we were really looking at, and he'd call to one of his sister's friends—'Hey, Suzanne!'—and she'd come over to the towel and talk to us, and she'd be leaning over the whole time, the front of her bathing suit completely open and there they were. I mean, I coulda reached out and held them in my hands, they were so close. I'm telling you, she never knew what we were doing.

"Jesse knew everything there was to know about girls. Did you know there's a name for what happens when you get all hard? It's called a boner. That's, like, the official name to use if you ever talk to other guys about it. Like, 'Hey, I really had a boner last night,' or, 'Wow, that girl gave me the biggest boner ever,' stuff like that. I mean it; the guy was amazing."

"Boner, huh? I guess that's as good a word as any," I said. Then I told

Brian about the Penney's catalogue and how I could put Mrs. Mussellman on every page, wearing bras and underpants and even girdles, although that one didn't quite get the job done. He laughed like crazy at this.

"Guess what?" Brian said.

"What?"

"You'll love this. I told Jesse about what you and I do to make ourselves, you know, at night when we think about Bunny and Sandy and all that."

"Uh huh."

"Well, get this, he just laughed at me like I was some kind of moron. He said, 'Are you guys crazy? Why make it so difficult. Just take the boner in your hand and start pumpin'.'

"At first I thought Jesse was makin' this stuff up. I told him I couldn't just do it on purpose like that. What would people think if they found out? What would my mother say? My God! But he says, 'You kiddin' me? Everyone does it.' He said, 'Even your old lady knows everyone does it,' which almost made me sick to my stomach. I told him I didn't believe him, but he told me that he knew for a fact that his father did it and that his older brother did it, and he thought even his uncle may have done it once or twice. He said his friend, Mark, who was fifteen, told him it was normal. I guess he does it every time he gets the chance, even in school in the boys' lav."

He looked at me and smiled. "I couldn't wait to tell you about this, Jackie. This is perfect for you. I mean, you got nothin' to do out here. It must be driving you batty. This will give you somethin' to look forward to all the time. You can make some real use out of that catalogue of yours. I'm tellin' you, it's changed my life. It's better than birthdays; it's even better than Christmas! I mean to tell you, you'll thank me."

"That's great," I said. "Very cool."

I picked some bark off the sycamore tree beside us and threw it at Brian's head. He took a pebble and tossed it back, nailing me in the cheek.

"Hey, watch that," I said, laughing. We both lay back on the grassy hillside, our hands clasped behind our heads. White clouds drifted by on parade.

I wanted to tell him about Charlie in the worst way. I felt like I would burst. But I wasn't sure. I never felt stuck like this with Brian before. Even when we made fun of each other, like when Brian told me he was trying to break the habit of eating his boogers, we always knew it was okay to talk about anything. There weren't any secrets between us, none. And here he was telling me all this important stuff about boners and what to do with them, and I had this gigantic thing I wanted to tell him, and yet I couldn't. I mean, I didn't think I could. All I knew was that for the first time, I wasn't sure I could tell him a secret of mine, and not just any secret; this was the biggest and most important secret in the history of secrets.

I looked at Brian. "I want to tell you something, Brian, but you got to promise me you won't tell anyone."

"What is it?" asked Brian.

My piehole was about to open so wide that a truck could have driven through it.

"No, I'm telling you; you gotta promise first."

"Okay, I promise." He said the words, but they didn't sound right.

"No, really, Brian; if you tell anyone I may have to break your neck."

"C'mon, Jackie, don't be crazy."

I grabbed his arm and looked him in the eyes. "I mean it! Promise!"

He crossed his heart and promised. "Okay?" he said. "Okay, geez-o-man."

I sat up, pulled my knees to my chest, picked a handful of grass, and took a deep breath. "A lot has happened since the last time I saw you."

"You better believe it," said Brian, laughing again. He rolled over on his side and propped himself up on one elbow.

"Can you just forget about your thing for a minute?" I didn't know where to begin. I felt like I needed to protect Hank, but if I didn't tell someone about him, I'd explode into so many pieces that they'd find parts of me over in Ohio. "Look, remember when we went hunting for Charlie?"

"Do I remember? Geez, we may have been the last to see him."

"Remember how Kelso kept jabbing him with that stick, and I was right there, and how we all got scared to death when he turned around?"

"Uh huh."

"And remember that time when Kelso came back into Pee Wee's and told us Charlie was dead because no one had seen him in weeks?"

Brian sat up and crossed his legs in front of him. He looked at me, squinting into the sun. "Jackie, this is old news. Why are you asking me if I remember? It just happened last month! I ain't been gone a year, y'know. Yes,

I remember when we went with Kelso, the punk, and yes, I remember the stick, and yes, I remember what he looked like. How in the heck could I forget? It kept me awake for days. And yes, I remember Kelso telling us Charlie was deader than a doornail.

"I remember all of that stuff, Jackie, who doesn't? I mean, we kinda made history, being the last ones and all. In the future little kids will look up to us because in the summer of '59 we were the last ones to see Charlie alive. And we were pretty doggone lucky, too. Remember when he stood up and turned around and told us he was gonna get us, that he wouldn't forget what we did?"

My arms fell to my side. I stood up. "What are you talking about, Brian? He didn't say a thing. He could barely stand."

"That's not how I remember it, and that's not how Kelso's been tellin' it either." Brian stood up, too. He picked up a stone and threw it as far as he could. It landed beside the pond and skipped in, kerplop. I tapped Brian's shoulder before he had a chance to throw another stone.

"What are you talkin' about?"

"Kelso's been telling everyone that he saved our lives, that Charlie tricked us by lying on the ground, and when we got close, he jumped up and lunged at us, and if it wasn't for Kelso beating him with a club, we'd all be goners."

"But that's a lie!" I said.

Brian took a step back and looked at me. He shrugged. "Yeah, so what? I mean, Charlie's dead; why do you care what anyone says about him? We're all heroes now! Kelso's even tellin' everyone that you tossed the club to him. I knew he always liked you best." He threw another stone. This time it reached the pond on the fly.

I didn't say a thing. I could feel my face turning red.

"What's the matter, Jackie? You look volcanic."

"Nothin'," was all I said. My mouth was tight as a drum, just like my dad's when he was about to explode.

"What do you mean, nothing; I can tell there's something. What is it? What's the big deal?"

I kicked at the soft dirt under the sycamore. "Look, Brian, it's all wrong. All of it. I'm tellin' you."

"What are you tellin' me? You're not making any sense, Jackie." Brain dropped the stone and wiped his hand on his pants pocket.

"Look Brian, trust me on this, what Kelso and everyone else has been saying is all lies. All of it. None of it is true!"

"What do you mean—all of it?"

"All of it, that's what I mean. Everything they've said about Charlie is a lie. He never did none of that stuff. People have been lying about him for years." I looked Brian in the eyes.

He stared back, trying to tell if I was kidding or not. "C'mon, Jackie, you gone nuts or something? Everyone knows that the stories about Charlie are true, or at least mostly true. Why else would they have lasted so long? I mean, wasn't it you who said that?"

"I don't know why they've lasted so long. I just know they're not true." I was beet red and sweating like crazy now.

"Look, Jackie, okay, so Kelso stretched the truth and maybe some of the other stories were made up, too, but basically, the truth is still the truth. We seen him, we seen Charlie No Face with our own eyes, and we know that even if only one out of ten stories was true, he'd still be the meanest, most dangerous person to ever walk the face of western Pennsylvania!"

"No, man, I'm tellin' you; it's not the truth and it never was."

"C'mon, Jackie, what are you—"

"What would you say if I told you he was still alive?" There, I said it.

Brian squinted at me like I was from a different planet. "What? Aw, c'mon, Jackie, livin' out here has made you a little wacky. I know there've been rumors; a few people say they seen him, but nobody believes them. Kelso heard that they found part of Charlie stuck to the front of a B&O freight train. No way he's alive!" Brian's voice was creeping higher and higher. He took a breath, looked at the ground, and then back at me. "C'mon, bud," he said, patting my shoulder. "You know it's not true."

Brian waited for me to say something. I didn't move. I barely breathed. Abigail came bounding back down the hill and lay on the ground beside us, panting. I reached down to scratch her ears but didn't. There was no way to convince Brian, and I knew it; there was no way to get around all the stories we'd heard and believed. They were like this big mountain that I was picking away at with a little spoon.

"I mean, he's just some guy who never..." I didn't know what else to say. Brian looked at me like he was being patient with somebody that wasn't making any sense. I felt like I was lying on the centerfield grass again, looking at the ball on the other side of the fence.

"Look, Jackie, he never was 'just some guy'. I mean, you remember what he looked like. Nobody who's 'just some guy' looks like that."

I realized I had spent so much time with Hank that I didn't even notice how awful he looked anymore. To me, he just looked like himself. How do you explain a face?

I wanted to tell Brian the rest of the story: that Charlie was missing an arm but he could still carve the neatest walking sticks ever, and that he grew up in a home for kids that nobody wanted, and that he took me on long walks in the woods and even showed me where his cabin was, and that he looked after me and I looked after him. I wanted to tell him that Charlie wasn't really Charlie at all; he was Henry Hopewell, but I called him Hank. And he was alive as could be, and he was my friend. And I was his.

Suddenly, Abigail's ears perked up again; she stared into the woods, her tiny tail wagging, then off she ran.

Brian looked at me, kinda worried. "Look, Jackie, if you want to believe all this stuff about Charlie, that's fine, man. It doesn't matter to me, okay?"

Both of us jumped when we heard the car horn blaring in the driveway. It was Brian's mother, come to pick him up. It was time for him to go. There wasn't much point in trying to explain things now.

"Hey, seriously, man; it doesn't matter to me at all," said Brian. "You're my best friend, and if you're just a little loony, that's okay." He smiled at me.

"Look, Brian, thanks for coming out here today. And thanks for all the inside dope on boners. I'm sure it will come in handy."

"I'm tellin' you, man; your life will change forever," he said, laughing. He gave me a good hard push but held onto my arm so I wouldn't fall.

"Go on, get out of here; your mommy's waiting," I said.

"See you when you get back," he called over his shoulder. He ran down the hill towards his car, where his mom stood talking to Aunt Dee. I waved to Brian's mom and then watched as they backed down the driveway. Brian rolled down his window, leaned out, and waved.

It was quiet again, except for the whoosh of the wind through the trees and the busy chatter of birds. I sat down in the dirt and leaves, knees up to my chin again. I picked up a piece of bark and tossed it at nothing. "Hey, girl, there you are." Abigail came running through the leaves and jumped on my back; then she ran around in a tight circle, stopped suddenly, then ran around again. "What's got into you, girl?"

"Hey, Jack."

The sound of his voice startled me. I had never seen Hank outside in daylight before. "Geez, you scared me half to death."

Hank steadied himself with his walking stick as he ambled down the hillside. "How are you doin' today?" he asked.

"Pretty good, I guess."

He picked up a piece of bark from the sycamore and gave it a toss. "Did you have a good visit with your friend? Brian, that's his name, right?"

I felt uncomfortable, like I had done something wrong.

"Thanks for not saying too much," he said.

"I'm sorry. I just had to tell someone, but I didn't..."

"I understand. You had this secret and it was just gnawing at your insides trying to get out."

"Yeah. But he just thought I was crazy." Hank put his stick on the ground and eased himself down beside me, heaving a sigh. I grabbed a twig and fiddled with it. Hank sat perfectly still as he caught his breath.

Once his breathing was in rhythm, he cleared his throat. "Crazy? That's not so bad. People have thought worse things about me all my life. I guess you get used to it after a while. I knew I was different and would always be different. Because of that, my life would be different, and people would be people. My world got small, you might say, after the accident. I wasn't ever going to do what everyone else did. You know, grow up, go to school, work at a job, marry, buy a house and have kids. It just wasn't in the cards for me. So my world got small. After some time, I realized small wasn't so bad.

"When I step out the back door at night and take a deep breath, the damp air fills my nose with the smell of fresh-turned dirt. Then I start up this hill, the crunch of twigs and leaves under my feet, and stop for a moment along the way to take the world in. I hear a critter skittering through the brush. I hear the distant whistle of the B&O, the clackety-clack of the trestle, and I lean against the solidness of a tree, its rough bark feeling like old skin, and I have to smile. It's like there's just so much. You know, my little world, all of a sudden, feels very big."

We were quiet then. I looked at him, his swollen head, his cratered face, and the dark sockets that had come to look like eyes to me.

"Hank, what happened to you?"

He didn't answer at first. He picked up another sliver of bark, turned it in his hand, fit it between his forefinger and thumb, and then flung it. Then he bowed his head, considering things, I guess. But he stayed like that for such a long time that I worried something was wrong, that my question had hit a spot that wasn't ever supposed to be touched. Maybe I should have kept my mouth shut. I hoped I hadn't hurt his feelings. I was just about to change the subject when Hank started talking.

"When I was a boy, Jack, a couple years younger than you are now, I used to play in these very woods with my friends. We'd play hide-and-seek and tag and cowboys-and-Indians, and we'd spend our days exploring this very hill, probably even the spot where we're sitting right now. That was before everything changed, back when there wasn't a worry in the world, as best I could tell."

He bowed his head again. "Let's see, there was Zachary and Milt and Ricky and another boy whose name escapes me." He paused. "Doggone it, what was his name?" He couldn't recollect it, so he kept on. "And there was a girl who lived down the way who could play ball as good as any of us and who would punch you right in your face if she thought you were treating her like a girl. They were my friends, the ones I played with and shared stories with and made adventures with.

"Well, one day Ricky and the doggone boy I can't recall and the girl who acted just like a boy, we all went down to the Beaver River to see the trees and other junk that were passing by after a big storm. We were having a high time watching that angry river and all the trees and tree stumps and even a doggone car tossin' and turnin' in the current. We kept getting closer, trying to grab whatever floated by, when all of a sudden Ricky slipped and fell in. Scared us half to death. Me and the other kid pulled on him like crazy while the river pulled back. Then the girl jumped in up to her hips and started pullin', too. I thought for sure the river was gonna have all of us for supper, but together we were strong enough, and soon Ricky was layin' on the riverbank, huffing and puffing like he was 'bout to die. He was scared and wanted to get on home after that, and the other kid said he'd go back with him to make sure nothin' else happened along the way. Together they would make up a story that suited Ricky's mother's curiosity without getting them in trouble.

"Me and the neighbor girl stayed on for a while, though, walking along the riverside and then back up on the trail until we come to the railroad bridge across the river. It hung over us like some prehistoric dinosaur. Soon enough, a Pittsburgh-Harmony-Butler and New Castle train come barrelin' across, the trestles shuttering like the whole thing might fly apart. We stood under the bridge, lookin' at the bottom of the train and listening to the fury of the tracks. My friend spied a redheaded woodpecker that was startled out of its hole on the wooden support beams under the bridge. My God, she was beautiful with her brilliant red bonnet and black and white wings and that long beak piercing the air."

Hank sort of smiled as he thought about this; he waved his hand slowly out in front of himself, like he was tracing the flight of that bird.

"Then she nudged me again and pointed at the hole in the bridge support, and she says, 'I think I seen somethin' peeking out of that hole.' And we both figured the momma was looking after her babies. I said, 'I wonder how many there are.' And that's when I got the idea."

Hank bowed his head, trying to hide a laugh, like you do in church when something funny strikes you at the wrong time.

"There was a big old maple under the bridge that reached up to the bottom of the trestle. It looked like an easy climb, so I decided I'd go up and take a look inside that hole. My friend wasn't sure it was the best idea, but I told her not to worry; I'd done this kind of thing many times before. She still tried to talk me out of it, but I was settled on making the climb.

"Finally she said, 'Wait a minute,' and she reached into her pocket and pulled something out. I couldn't tell at first what it was, but then I could see. It was a buckeye. It was her lucky buckeye, the one that she carried with her all the time. She said, 'Here, take this with you.'

"I didn't think nothin' of it, but I said, 'Okay,' and put the buckeye in my pants pocket." Hank put his hand in his pocket like he was reaching in for that old memory.

"The climb was slow but easy enough. She called to me from time to time, 'Are you alright? You're gettin' awful high up there, Henry Hopewell, you think you better come back down?' Of course, now I wanted to impress her with my braveness. Finally I reached the underbelly of the bridge and crawled onto one of the beams. I saw a little head pop out of the hole and then another.

"I called back to my friend, 'There's at least two!'

"All she said was, 'Be careful up there!'

"Well, I was determined to get a good look, since I had come this far, but the hole was at an odd angle, and I had to lean out from the bridge to see in just right. So I reached up under the trestle to take hold of anything I could get my hands on." He took his hand out of his pocket and wiped his face. He pulled his legs up close and leaned on them with his elbows.

"The next thing I remember is waking up in a hospital, feeling like my skin was on fire. I couldn't see a thing, and I could barely take a breath, but I could hear the doctors and nurses and my mother and father talkin' about me like I wasn't there. 'Is he gonna make it?' was the question on everyone's mind, and for days, I didn't for the life of me understand what they were talking about until I realized I couldn't move and I couldn't talk and I couldn't see and I couldn't eat nothing. But I could hear my mother cryin' day in and day out, and I could smell the tobacco on my father's clothes. And I figured I was gonna die, or maybe I was already hovering between life and death, halfway gone. But each day I woke up, and soon weeks passed, and I wasn't as dead as I was in the beginning, and before I knew it they were talkin' all different about me. They were talking about me living, and my mom continued to cry, but her crying was different, too. It was a happy kind of crying, and she'd reach out to me and pat my head and ask the nurse if it was okay and the nurse would say it didn't much matter because I wasn't all that aware of anything, but she was wrong 'cause I could feel it all." A single drop of sweat slid down the side of Hank's face.

"Soon my throat started healing up good, and I could eat ice cream and tapioca pudding, other soft things, and I could talk just a little, but my voice sounded like sandpaper, and my mother kept crying, but the crying was different again. It was the crying of someone who's lost and doesn't know where to turn. I could hear her and my father, and they'd ask the doctor 'What will his life be like?' and 'What will we need to do?'

"And late at night I heard a nurse say, 'I think that little boy would have been better off never waking up. My God, look at him,' she said, her voice all twisted in despair. 'Whatever will he do?'" Hank straightened his back and then stretched out his legs. He leaned over to one side.

"Well, I'll tell you what I did. I came home. I came home and I talked again and I walked and I ate and I learned how to tie a shoe with one hand and how to get around by counting and how to tell where I was by the feel of the sun on my face and, with that, life went on. I made it, but everyone else wasn't quite so lucky, I guess. My mother kept crying, and after a while it wasn't just about me. She cried when my father left, and she cried when the doctor told her I'd be better off living with 'my kind,' and I'm sure she kept crying long after she stopped coming to see me or writing to me. As for me, I couldn't cry. Long after the pain went away, though, I ached inside. But in time, that went away, too."

I wiped my eyes as I listened to Hank. I tried not to sniffle because I didn't think he wanted anyone else to cry for him.

"My God, Hank," was all I could think to say.

It was quiet again between us. I didn't know what to make of the whole thing; it was so awful, and yet Hank didn't say it with any complaint in his voice. He wasn't matter of fact, though, either. It was more like he was saying it because it needed to be said, like he wanted to have someone hear it, not to feel sad for him, but just so someone else would know, would know it from his own mouth. Kind of like, "Everyone has a story. This is mine."

I looked over at him, his face folded in upon itself, his skin raw and coarse-looking, his hair like thin weeds that never drank a drop of water, his eyes that hadn't been eyes for so long.

"Hank, what happened up there on the trestle?"

Hank took a deep breath and let out a familiar-sounding sigh, like a wagon wheel creaking. He took a second breath, this one to get him started. "Yes, I guess I didn't tell you that part." He shifted his weight until he was comfortable on his other hip. "It wasn't until I was home from the hospital that I pieced together what had happened. I told you I was reaching around to grab hold of something so I could lean out from the bridge. Well, I found something. It was a coil of wire that had 11,000 volts of electricity running through it—11,000 volts of electricity that shot through me like a lightning bolt. I guess there was a blinding flash followed by a crackling sound and then the smell, well, the smell of me burning. I fell from the bridge support and, lucky for me, I guess, some small branches broke my fall so I wasn't killed."

I shuddered. My body tightened up, and for a moment nothing inside moved; I couldn't find my breath.

"Geez, Hank." I reached out and put my hand on his foot. He took another deep breath and waggled his foot in response.

"So, I mean, what, what happened when you fell?" I asked.

"The girl, my neighbor friend, I guess she stayed right there and began to scream for help. Turns out a couple of gandy dancers were working on the tracks and heard her. You know, Jack, I was a mighty awful sight, I suspect. My face all burned, my skin smoking, my eyes gone, my arm cut right off. I was just about the scariest thing in the world, plenty scary enough that most kids would have run for their lives. But she didn't. She stayed and she wailed and wailed until help came. That's all she could do for me, but it was enough. If it wasn't for that girl, I don't think I'd be here talkin' to you today."

I didn't know what to say. "Man, it's hard to think of you as being lucky, but I guess you were. I guess you were lucky to have a friend like that."

"Sure was," he said. "Sure was."

"Do you remember her name?"

Hank shifted his position again and scratched his chin. "Yes, I do remember her name, Jack."

"What was it?"

"Gretchen, her name was Gretchen."

"Gretchen?"

"Yeah."

"That's pretty amazing," I said. "That was my mother's name."

Hank picked up another piece of sycamore bark and tossed it. He took a deep breath and pulled his legs up to his chest so he could rest his arm on them. "I know your mother's name was Gretchen."

At first I didn't understand, but then the wheels started turning faster and faster as my mind caught up with what he was trying to tell me. "You mean, wait a minute, are you trying to say that, well, hold on a second. Are you telling me that your friend, that girl who screamed and screamed until someone came, are you telling me that was my mother?"

"Yes," was all Hank said. I stood up, my mouth open, not knowing what to say. I was quiet for so long that Hank finally asked if I was still there. I said I was, but in a sense I wasn't there at all. I didn't know where I was. I had heard my father's stories and the ones Aunt Dee had told me recently, but Hank's story was so different. He knew my mother as a friend; he knew her when she was nothing more than a kid like me, before my father, before anything, back when she had no idea what was to come. There was a time when she walked these woods with Hank much as I was walking them now.

"What did she look like, Hank?"

"What did she look like? Well, as I remember, your mother was kind of a skinny kid with brownish, reddish hair that she tucked behind her ears. She always wore a blue hairband because it matched her eyes. In the summertime her face broke out with freckles, and she dared any of us to say anything about it. And she was strong; I remember that. Ricky learned that the hard way when she challenged him to a wrestling match and then promptly beat him. And she was funny. Know what the first thing was that she said to me when she came to the hospital?"

"What was that?"

"She came to the side of my bed and she said, 'I guess that buckeye wasn't so lucky after all.' And I laughed right out loud. Then, of course, I cried because it hurt so bad. But to laugh out loud—it felt good."

That night I lay on my back, eyes wide open, unable to sleep, unwilling to sleep. I replayed Hank's story over and over again in my head, trying to make sense of it all. Every once in a while I would close my eyes tight and try to imagine a girl with reddish hair and blue eyes and a blue hairband. I'd try hard not only to see her but to make her move and smile and talk, make her as alive as I could, and I imagined that I was one of the kids who lived in the neighborhood and that I knew her, and not only did I know her but I knew what was going to happen to her. I knew that she would die too young to really get to know me at all, and I'd look at her and she wouldn't have any idea who I really was, but I would know.

Hank said she came at least once a week to see him in the hospital, and she came to visit him at home, too. He said she would read comic books to him and she would tell him about school and what his old friends were doing and she would try to keep him a part of things, even though he wasn't and never would be again. Hank said she never talked about the way he looked. At first when she came to visit him, her voice sounded hesitant, and he figured it was his face that frightened her. But that didn't last long, and after a while, she talked like she always did, a mile a minute.

Hank said that once he asked her what he looked like. And without skipping a beat she said, "Why, Hank, you look like you, of course." She said it with such a matter-of-fact air that it made Hank feel normal somehow.

I grabbed hold of Abigail and pulled her to my side. She snorted and sniffed and wagged her little tail hard and licked my cheek and then promptly fell back to sleep. I scratched her ears and rubbed her belly and was glad I had something to hold.

Then from out of the darkness came a knock at my door. "Jack, are you still awake?" It was Aunt Dee. But for some reason I didn't answer. She came in anyway. I closed my eyes tight and let my mouth fall open a little like I was sleeping. And she sat down on the bed beside me and ran her fingers through my hair. She smelled like the kitchen with a dash of cinnamon.

"Sleep well, Jack, sleep well," she said in a whisper. "'Cause today you've come face-to-face with real honest-to-goodness truth. Sometimes the truth comes wrapped up in bad stuff, Jack. So bad that we can barely recognize it. And if we're not careful, we may settle on the notion that life is just made up of bad things. That it's all about children falling from trees and mothers dying before their time. But it's not so at all. Bad things are just bad things. It's what you see inside them that matters."

Abigail startled and just about jumped out of her skin. Aunt Dee said, "Hush, old dog," patted her, and then pressed Abigail back down on the bed until she was settled again. "Shhh," she said, as if Abigail understood, and maybe she did, because she went all quiet. I turned my face to the pillow a little, wiping my eyes. Aunt Dee didn't say anything, but she kept scratching my head until I fell asleep for real.

Charlie No Face

22

I woke up late the next morning to the sound of woodpeckers and the smell of hot sun. I threw on my jeans and sneakers and a t-shirt and staggered down to the kitchen where Aunt Dee had kept a pot of oatmeal steaming, now so thick that we could have plastered the walls with it. I scooped a glop into a bowl, drowned it in some milk, and then covered it with brown sugar.

Aunt Dee came down the steps and said, "Good morning, sleepyhead. How are you doing?"

At first, I didn't know how I was doing, but after considering it for a minute, I realized I was doing okay—okay enough, anyway. "Okay, I guess," I said.

"That will have to do for now, won't it?" she said with a slight smile. "Anyway, there's someone on the porch who's been waiting all morning."

When I went outside, Hank was rocking in Aunt Dee's old bentwood in the bright morning sun, his walking stick across his lap, Abigail lying beside him. In the sunlight, his greenish skin was the texture of leather. He had a red flannel shirt on with one sleeve sewn shut, overalls, and work boots. I thought he'd die of the heat, but it didn't seem to bother him at all.

"C'mon," he said and stood up, ready to go. I looked at his face, swollen and pocked.

"Where to?"

"You'll see," he said, stepping down off the porch and heading across the lawn towards the pond. I caught up to him, Abigail panting at my heels.

I was puzzled when he didn't turn onto the usual path. At first I thought he'd made a mistake. "Hey!" I called.

"Just follow me," was all he said, so I did. We walked along the base of the hill behind several farms, around fence posts and barbed wire, never going into the woods, but never getting close enough to any houses or roads that we might be seen. He was concentrating hard, probably counting. His pace was fast at first, but then we slowed, and finally he had to stop, his breathing all heavy and rapid. We sat on the ground in the shade of a pine tree.

Hank always had trouble breathing. His lungs were burned and scarred from the accident, and the doctors doubted that they'd ever heal proper. They worried this might be his downfall in the long run. But Hank told me that after the accident, he practiced breathing every day, slow and deep, stretching his lungs and getting them in working order again. He said some days that was all he did. He'd lie in bed counting each breath, going as deep as he could, until he'd start coughing, and then he'd try again. As the days and weeks wore on, he went deeper and deeper, stretching his lungs back into shape enough to go on with life.

I looked at him and could see that his chest was moving in and out easily, so I knew he was getting his wind back.

"Are you okay?"

"Never better," he said. "How about you?"

"I'm fine if you're fine."

He stood up slowly. "Then let's keep moving," he said, and away we went.

After about an hour, we came to a path that veered off to the left and wound steadily up the hill, at times so steep that I had to grab hold of saplings and anything else within my reach just to hold my ground. Abigail was panting like crazy now, and she barked several times as if to say, "What the heck!" This time, *I* ran out of steam and called ahead to Hank, "Hey, can we take a break?"

And so we sat again amidst pine needles and dry leaves and cool dirt.

"Are we lost?"

Hank laughed. "Why do you ask?"

"Because we're going somewhere but getting nowhere." He laughed again. "How in the heck do you know where you're going?" I asked. "I mean, I know you do all this counting and stuff, but still, I don't get it."

"You know," said Hank, "I'm not sure I get it either. When I first started going out on my own, I didn't go far at all, maybe twenty steps, then fifty, then more, and each time I had to remember what I'd done and where it had gotten me. I had to remember all the little details, like, 'If I walk a hundred steps in this direction, I'll trip on a tree stump' or 'If I walk this far from the house into the wind, I'll find an opening to the woods.' So I kept trying. And I kept remembering. Sometimes I'd go in a direction that didn't get me anywhere, and I'd have to go back, step by step, until I reached where I had been. Then I'd erase that path from my mind and start on a new one. There are so many paths out there if you keep looking.

"After a while, I got so used to the woods that I noticed everything about it, like how it smelled different or felt different depending on where I was. For instance, there are mock orange bushes on the path to my cabin, and in the late spring and early summer I can smell them from far away. They're so sweet. So I tell myself the mock orange are at such and such a number. Next I keep track of my steps until I can hear the stream. And finally I count until I reach the slope that runs down to my cabin. Over time, I stored all of this in my head so that, eventually, I knew where I was, even if the flowers weren't in bloom or the stream had run dry. I knew because I marked it all with numbers—3,563 smells sweet, and 4,288 babbles, and I'd better watch my step at 5,347. I carry all the smells and sounds and even the feel of the ground with me. The paths are written on my mind. So I don't need anything else to get around. I can follow my insides and get wherever I need to go."

"That is either the craziest thing I've ever heard or the most amazing," I said.

"Probably both," said Hank. "You ready to go? We're almost there."

That's when I noticed the sound of a train whistle calling in the distance, groaning but steady. I looked up but couldn't see anything. "Where are we going?" But Hank had already taken to the path and didn't hear me. As we balanced on the downward slope, I could see the river below. Muddy brown, the water ignored everything in its path and just kept pushing, insistent on its right of way. The sound of it built with every nearing step, and soon the hum turned into a roar, and the swells looked like fists clenching and unclenching over and over again. I picked up a stone and tossed it into the raging foam. The river swallowed it without so much as a ripple of recognition. I had never been that close to anything so powerful, so uncaring.

I turned again to call for Hank just as he disappeared around the next bend, a little black shadow trailing behind him. I ran to catch up, and when I rounded the next bend I stopped dead in my tracks. There it was, no more than a hundred yards away. A brave-looking stretch of track, a shadow against the blue sky, balanced on a lattice of wood and steel.

I walked up to Hank and stood beside him. "Is this it?"

"Yes, I believe this is it. I can smell it. I can feel it. This is where it all happened."

"My God," I said, "it's beautiful."

"I know," said Hank. He took a couple of deep breaths, as if he were considering something. He even turned his head slowly from side to side, as if he were surveying the scene. Then he spoke.

"There should be violets in the grass along the riverbank, maybe daisies, too. And if the water's not too rough you should see a handful of giant boulders, like a small school of baby whales." He stopped, thinking for a moment. "Is the willow tree still tiptoeing on the surface of the river?"

I looked around, and there it was, bent over, its long curved limbs skimming the water.

"Yes," I said, "how'd you—"

But he kept talking. "There should be a grove of white ash to our right that reaches almost to the bottom of the train tracks. And if you listen to them when the wind blows, they sound like someone just turned on the shower. And with the sun out, there should be a wide black shadow, like a giant barber's strap, across the river right under that old train track. The underbelly of the train trestle should look like a great arch from one side to the other, with stern-looking beams and metal arms criss-crossing its length."

"Yes," was all I said.

"Now," he said, pointing straight ahead, "there is a tree on this side of the river. It's nestled under the right shoulder of the arch. It is a silver maple, maybe one hundred feet tall by now, a great silver maple with jagged leaves. They're light green on the sunward side, but when the wind blows and the leaves turn over, they look like little flashes of white lightning." Hank was right. As the wind swirled and the sun hit the white underside of the maple's leaves, they looked like hundreds of flashbulbs going off at once.

"We used to stand under that tree and watch for the seeds to drop. They twirled round and round like helicopters, and we'd try to catch 'em if we could. Some took off and were never seen again. Some landed in the river and were swept away. And some fell right into our hands." He smiled at this thought. "Oh, my," he said, "such a wonderful place."

I looked at him, not knowing what to say. His face looked peaceful, if that's possible; his shoulders were relaxed, and his breathing was even and steady.

"This is a special place," I said. He didn't answer me. "I mean, well, special is the only word that comes to mind even though this is where, well, this is where it all happened."

"Yes, it is," he said, his voice faint as a whisper. "This is where everything happened."

We stood for a long moment, listening to the river and the birds and feeling the cool breeze on our faces in the shade of the ash trees.

"How did you know everything?"

"What do you mean?" said Hank.

"Well, you described everything exactly the way it is: the boulders and the shadows and the trees and even the flowers. How did you know?"

"Simple enough," he said. "Those were the last things I ever saw in my life. Haven't seen another thing since. At least not with my eyes. This was it. Believe me, I traced and re-traced every detail on my mind until it couldn't be erased. That way I'd always have this place, even after the darkness came."

He turned his head in my direction. "And, of course, Jack, the last person I ever saw was your mother, back when she was just a little girl, my good friend. You know, she woulda laughed and laughed at the idea of being someone's momma. In fact, she might have punched me for even suggesting such a thing. She wasn't much like a girl in those days. But even then, there was something about her, something I didn't understand until later."

"What's that?"

"She had an impossible kind of love," said Hank. "A love so wide open and unafraid and so full of acceptance that it didn't even care how foolish it might have seemed. That's what she gave me on that day so long ago. And you know, Jack, that's what she gave you, too."

I didn't know what to say. I didn't want to cry, but I had to.

"I don't know why I'm crying," I said.

"Yes, you do," said Hank, and he put his arm around me. He was right. All of a sudden I knew my mother. I knew her and I missed her like I'd never missed her before.

"Here," he said, handing me a wad of Kleenex.

He kept his arm around me as we walked closer to the silver maple.

"Do you see any birds up under that old trestle?" he asked.

"Yes, there're barn swallows everywhere, swooping like planes in a dogfight."

"Nothing with a red head?" he asked.

"No, nothing with a red head."

"All the descendents must have moved on," he said.

I stood under that old tree, looking up through its core, its great limbs shooting skyward, swaying back and forth with such ease that if I hadn't known better, I'd have thought the tree was waving on purpose. The lower limbs leaned down to us, inviting us, it seemed, to reach up, much as they must have invited Hank when he was a boy. I leaned against the tree, its bark all reddish-brown and flaky like old skin. It made my head spin to think that Hank had stood here with my mother, and now I was standing here with him.

"The workers up there on the track told the newspaper they had never heard a sound quite like it," said Hank. "They had been startled by the flash and then smelled the smoke, but what came next gave them gooseflesh. At first they didn't think a human being could make such a sound. They looked over the side of the trestle, and there was this little girl far below, standing straight and still, her mouth wide open, and even with that, they couldn't believe the sound was coming from her. And yet it was." Hank squeezed my shoulder. "Little girl, big lungs," he said with a laugh. "Lucky for me," he said, "or I wouldn't be standin' here with you today."

We stood quiet as could be, listening and just feeling the place, then and now.

"I wanted you to see this place, Jack. Thought it was important." Hank patted my shoulder and, walking stick in hand, turned to go back up the path.

I stood for another moment, alone under the tree, thinking about Hank high up on that trestle, thinking about my mom, young as could be, standing where I was standing now, watching her friend, just two kids. Then without thinking, I leaned my head back, cupped both my hands over my mouth and wailed—"OOOOOWWWWWWWWWoooooooooooooo!" I stopped and listened, the echo pulsing through the trestle and down the river canyon and away to wherever echoes go. Then it was quiet again and together we turned to the path and headed home, Abigail, Hank, and me.

23

If I thought things had changed fast since Memorial Day, I had no idea that Dad and I would be breaking the sound barrier over the next few weeks. Kaboom!

The phone rang and rang and rang the morning after Hank had taken me to the bridge.

I was still in bed thinking about my mother and everything I had learned about her. Thinking about her red hair and freckles and her courage and how I looked like her and how Aunt Dee could see her in me and how her voice might have sounded on that day she screamed her life-saving scream. I was also thinking about the ghost of Charlie No Face and how it had evaporated like a fog on a hot summer morning, and how Hank had taken his place, and how right my mother was when she told him he looked like himself, as if he couldn't look like anyone or anything better, and how it was fine to be yourself no matter the craters or the green skin or the one arm or the missed fly ball, and how he was my friend.

The phone rang and rang and rang the morning after Hank had taken me to the bridge.

As I lay in bed, I thought about our walk back home from the creek. We were quiet mostly. We had walked slowly, like the whole thing had tired us out, but not worn-out tired, more the satisfied tired you get after you try real hard at something and are surprised it came out good. We walked near enough to New Galilee that I went to the A&P and bought two Verner's and even got a paper bowl of water for Abigail. Hank seemed more comfortable in the light than usual, although we didn't take chances. We hugged the train tracks mostly, and several times we ducked behind trees when cars drew near.

One thing was still on my mind. Hank had told me that my mother had given him a buckeye before he climbed the tree, before he was electrocuted.

She had given it to him for good luck, hoping he would make it up and down without any trouble. She was his friend and she was worried and the only thing she could think to do was give him a buckeye from her pocket. So, what the heck was a buckeye, and why was she carrying one with her? And what happened to it? I felt a little stupid about this because Hank had mentioned it so matter-of-factly that I didn't want to say, "What are you talking about?" It would have been rude to ask "What's a buckeye?" right in the middle of his awful story. The only buckeye I'd ever heard of was the football team, and that didn't tie in at all with Hank's story. So on the way home, I asked him.

"Well, a buckeye is a nut that grows on a tree, like a horse chestnut. There're a lot of them over the state line and some around here, too. The outside shell is a nasty-looking thing with prickly spines like a porcupine. Inside, though, is the smoothest nut you ever felt. It's all brown and awkward-shaped, like soft clay that suddenly turned hard as a rock. And at the base is a whitish scar. It's comfortable in your hand. It's also big enough to carve out the inside, thumb in some tobacco, and use as the head of a pipe. Not what your mother was doin' with it, though. But, that's a buckeye. Ain't you ever seen one?"

"Maybe I have, but I can't recall." We walked a little further. "So why was she carrying this buckeye with her?"

"I don't know exactly, but she always had it in her pocket. If we were sitting by the river just talking nonsense, she'd take it out and rub it between her fingers and sort of cradle it in her palm. I guess it was comforting somehow; something to hold onto. God knows your momma didn't have much to hold onto, that's for sure. I mean, do you know about her dad and mother?"

"Yes," I said.

"Then you know what I mean. Yes, I think it gave her comfort," he said. "A little, anyway."

The phone rang and rang and rang the morning after Hank had taken me to the bridge. It rang so long that I thought I'd have to get up and answer it. But then it stopped mid-ring, and I heard Aunt Dee's voice all surprised and happy and then low and murmuring.

I lay back on my bed and thought some more about the buckeye and Hank and my mother. I wished I had a buckeye of my own so I could roll it on my fingers and carry it in my palm, a little part of something much bigger. Who knows, maybe if I took special care of it, it would sprout right there in my hand, sprout into a tree with long thin branches and pale buds that would burst into young leaves, and then longer, thicker branches and broader leaves. And birds would come make nests, and the sun would caress it and the rain would shower it, and up, up it would go, and at the very top of the tree a little boy and a little girl would sway in the breeze, unaware of anything. And they'd laugh and wave down at me, and they'd be safe, and they'd never worry, and they'd never hurt, and they'd never be lost. They would live there forever, there in the palm of my hand where I could look after them.

Aunt Dee called to me, "Jack!"

"Yep!"

"Come here!" So I ran down the hall to the kitchen, where Aunt Dee was holding the phone and smiling wide.

I looked at her and said, "Who is it?"

And she just handed me the receiver and said, "Here, you'll see."

"Hello," I said, and the voice on the other end said, "Hi, J, how you doin'?"

"Dad!" I cried, almost bustin' his eardrum.

"So, what happened to it?" I asked Hank.

"What happened to what?"

"The buckeye; what happened to the buckeye? I know she gave it to you, and you climbed up the tree, and you touched the electric cables, and then the world came crashing down. But I was wondering, what about the buckeye? Do you still have it?"

Hank stopped on the hillside to catch his breath. He was wheezing something terrible today. I waited a long moment or two.

"Well," he said, still a breath or two short of normal. "Well, I guess the answer is yes and no."

"Yes and no, what?" I asked. Hank always answered questions this way. Things were never just yes or just no, they were always yes-and-no. It was like he didn't see anything straightforward; everything was kind of mixed together, like a tossed salad, when he looked at it. Good could be just a little bad, and bad could be just a little good. When I told him about how we lost the championship on Richie's homerun, and how Richie was the last one cut when I made the Kiwanis, and how it really hurt that I didn't make the catch, he said, "Looks like it was Richie's turn; your turn will come again, you'll see." What do you say to an answer like that? I mean, it made sense, but still, it wasn't the answer I expected. Hank was like that.

"Well," he said, the crease on his face widening into a smile, "yes, in that your momma's buckeye has never left me. And, no, in that it's nowhere to be found." I frowned at this and he squealed. "Let me tell you what I mean," he said, his smile passing and his voice thin and serious. "When the electricity went through me, it not only burned me up bad, but it burned everything I was wearing and everything I was carrying, including the buckeye. When I hit the ground, I guess I was naked as a newborn; everything else was gone. So the buckeye that your mother gave me, the buckeye she took from her pocket and I put in mine, disintegrated."

"So it's gone," I said.

"Not exactly," said Hank.

My father was very excited. He loved the training he got from the Kodak people, and he loved everything about the company. He said, "I've never worked for a company like this. They are committed to their employees. They want you to stay with them for a lifetime. And the opportunities are endless. I mean, we'll always need film."

"That's great," I said, glad to hear my dad sounding so happy. "So when are you coming home?"

"Tomorrow," he said, and I dropped the phone right on the floor and yelped as loud as I could. You'd have thought I'd won the playoffs with a homerun in the bottom of the sixth. "That's fantastic!" I yelled and then realized I didn't have the phone in my hand. Aunt Dee watched and laughed. Abigail growled and wagged her thumb and ran around in circles.

When I put the phone back to my ear, I could hear my dad laughing like crazy, laughing like he had when the summer was young. He calmed down quickly, though. "Listen, J, there's more."

"What do you mean, not exactly?" I asked Hank.

"Well, I didn't notice this until weeks after the accident. There was a spot on my hip near where my pants pocket had been. It was raw, and it hurt like crazy, and even though the nurses told me not to touch it, I couldn't help myself. It oozed like everything else, and after a time it started to scab, and finally the scab fell off but a scar was left behind. I felt it for a long time tryin' to figure out what it was and then it dawned on me. My God, I thought, could it be? And I answered myself, Yes, it could. It was a scar from the buckeye your mother gave me for luck, the buckeye I stuffed in my pocket before I started climbing that old tree."

I looked at Hank, my mouth half-open, not knowing what to say.

"So, you see, Jack, the buckeye is all gone, but it's never left me."

"Yes," I said, trying to take in his meaning.

"Think about it, Jack. It's sorta like your mom."

"Whadaya mean?"

"Well, the awful truth is that she is as gone as gone can be, but it's just as true that she has never really left you."

I just looked at Hank. He was right. She was gone, but I had never lived a day for as long as I could remember without her being some part of it. Even if she was just a tiny thought way back in the corner of my mind, she was there.

"You know, Jack, that buckeye scar is the most beautiful scar I got, because it's the only one that came from something good. Sometimes even the very best things leave a scar."

"What else?" I asked Dad. "Are they giving you a car, too?"

He laughed again and said, "Matter of fact, they are, but that's not the biggest news." I couldn't imagine what news could be bigger than this. I mean, my dad had been unhappy for weeks and now he had a new job, and he was coming home, and everything was gonna be the same again.

"So what's the biggest news, Dad?"

He was silent for a moment and then cleared his throat. "Well, my bosses were so impressed by how quickly I learned everything during the training that they offered me an even better job."

"Wow, Dad, that's fantastic!"

"Thanks, J," he said, but not with the same excitement. "There's a bit of a catch, though. You see, this new job would mean that we'd have to move."

"Move," I said. "Move where?"

"Well, up here to Rochester," said Dad.

"What?" was all I said, and so he told me again—"We're going to move"—and this time I heard the words clear, but they still didn't register, like they were just some words thrown together that didn't add up to anything, and he said, "J?" and I said, "What?" and he said, "Did you hear me?" and I said, "I think so," and he asked what I thought about it, and I said I didn't know, which wasn't true because I knew exactly what I thought; I just didn't want to say it—"Dad, that's awful news, that's about the awfulest news I've ever heard!" I didn't say it on the phone, though, because he sounded so excited, like he had done all of this for me, like he was giving me some kind of gift, like he had finally made everything better. How was he to know how much I had changed since he was gone? And I sure couldn't explain it in a three-minute long distance call.

So all I said was, "Gee!" which was pretty dumb, but he took it to mean I was excited, and before I knew it, I said goodbye and he said goodbye and we both hung up, and there I stood in Aunt Dee's kitchen wondering if anybody got the license plate of the truck that had just run me over.

Aunt Dee understood because even though she said, "Isn't that exciting!" she was sniffling and wiping her eyes and blowing her nose and carrying on so much that even Abigail stared at her, as if to say, "What's got into you?"

I tried to smile, I did, but my face wouldn't have it. I went to the bottom of the stairs, and I could see Hank's shadow in the hallway, but then it just slipped away.

24

In almost no time at all, we left. I mean we up and left our home in Ellwood City and we left Nick and the Snack Bar and Brian and Tommy and Mrs. Sanders and the busted-up patio in the backyard and the trash barrel where we cooked our hot dogs and the baseball field and the swimming pool and the park and everything.

We left Aunt Dee. We left Hank.

Dad said he was sorry that we had to leave so quickly, but he thought it would be best if we got to Spencerport, a town near Rochester, in time for the first day of school. He had stopped by my new school and told them we were coming. They were all friendly. I'd love the school, he assured me. We'd live in an apartment for a while, but he had his eye on a house that was right across from the fire station. On and on he went, using his best sales voice.

But I was still back in Ellwood thinking through those final days.

I had known from the first time I met Brian way back in kindergarten that he was a crier, but I hadn't expected the flood of tears that came when I told him we were moving. I mean, his face got all red and his eyes got all pinchy and the corners of his mouth fell down below his chin and then the tears came and came. I mean, he couldn't say anything. Of course, this made me cry, too, so there we were like two kindergartners on the first day of school. His parents had me over for dinner and a drive-in movie at Spotlight 88 and we tried to have fun, but mostly we just felt sad and uncomfortable, and after a while I think both of us wished we could just say goodbye. Boy, was that hard. I mean, Brian was the very best friend I'd ever had in my whole life. We played ball together and traded cards together and swam together and slept out together and hung out at Nick's together and discovered breasts together and hunted for Charlie No Face together.

When we got down to our goodbyes, I slipped a card from my pocket into his hand. "Here, knucklehead, this is for you." It was my last Mantle card.

He smiled and pulled something from his pocket. "Here," he said. "I know how much you love him."

"Willie Mays. Thanks, man," I said. Then we actually hugged.

I ran for my car before the waterworks started again.

Nick came by the house one night with a sheet pizza full of pepperoni, sausage, hamburger, and chopped-up hot dogs: the works. He and Dad cracked open a couple of beers and stood on the back patio talking. Nick congratulated my dad and wished him luck. He told Dad how much his support had meant when Nick was going through his "troubles", and Dad said the same. Nick made me promise to keep playing baseball so he could watch me on TV when I made the Majors. I promised. I told him that I'd keep my head down and my eye on the ball. Nick said, "That's the ticket."

Geez, I didn't even get to say goodbye to Tommy. Things had exploded between his mom and dad. He and his mom were living in Beaver Falls with Tommy's grandmother. I hoped they had pinball down in the valley.

I remembered the first time I had met Aunt Dee and how she seemed so, well, odd, with her sneakers and black socks and cackling laugh and the way she just said whatever came into her mind. I ate an awful lot of oatmeal at her house. Probably wouldn't have to eat oatmeal again for about ten years, although maybe I'd have some once in a while, just for old time's sake.

"Jack," she had said with tears in her eyes, "I don't know what to say." She took me in her long, lean arms and squeezed hard, and I didn't mind it at all. It wasn't until that very moment that I realized how much she had been my mother during those long weeks while Dad was away. She let go and held me at arm's length and looked at me like she did that very first time.

"I was right all along; you have your mother's heart and a pair of good eyes," she said. "I won't have to worry at all about you. Just make me one promise."

"What's that?" I said.

"That you'll come back and visit this old woman when you get the chance."

I told her I would, and then I grabbed hold of her waist. "I love you, Aunt Dee," I said.

"And I love you, too, my Jack."

I snorted and wiped my eyes and walked to the car where Abigail sat in the back seat, wagging her little bum thumb. Yes, Aunt Dee gave me Abigail. I was shocked, but I didn't hesitate when she asked if I would like to take Abigail along to my new life. Abigail stood on my lap and hung out the window for almost an hour on Route 19 as we headed for Erie and then Buffalo and finally someplace called Spencerport. Eventually, she curled up on my lap and fell asleep, snoring like she did on my bed every night at Aunt Dee's.

It was a long ride. I had a lot of time to think. Hank didn't come out to say goodbye with Aunt Dee. I knew he wouldn't. He came to my room the night before we left. He told me he planned on going to the cabin the next day and would probably leave a little before dawn. He asked me if I'd packed the walking stick, and I said, "Yes."

He smiled, cleared his throat, and took a deep breath. "I am not here to say goodbye. I am here to thank you, Jack."

This confused me. Why in the world would he be thanking me? I racked my brain trying to remember something I might have done, but for the life of me, I couldn't think of a thing. "Thank me? For what?"

"When I had that awful accident, I was just a boy. Just a boy out with his friends, one of those friends being your mother. Isn't that something? We were kids, and we didn't know there was real danger in the world. But there was. Everything in my life changed forever. I got over most things. I got over not seeing. I got over not looking like anyone else. I got over not being able to do some things and not being able to get about the way others do. Like I said, I got over most things." Hank paused and then cleared his throat again. "'Cept one. In all these years, I'd never been back there," he said.

"What do you mean?" I asked.

"In all these years, I'd never been back to the bridge. I wanted to go, but I couldn't. But then you came to me. It's as if that little girl…it's as if she sent you to me." Hank laughed a bit when he said this. "So thank you, Jack; thank you very much."

I thought Brian had cried a lot when he heard I was moving. That was nothing compared to this. I didn't know what to say, so I took hold of Hank and hugged him as hard as I could, and I buried my head in his old flannel shirt.

Charlie No Face

Epilogue

It would be several weeks before I'd know how to tell my father about everything that had happened while he was away. The feelings were there, but I couldn't attach the right words to them. In a way, I hadn't wanted to. Instead, I liked having that deep-down feeling, that feeling that was pure and simple as rain, that feeling that warmed you right down to the bone. Maybe it was the same feeling my mother had when she decided that keeping life wasn't as important as giving life. Maybe the word for it was love.

Abigail woke up, stood on my lap, looked into my eyes, and licked my face. Then she made a few circles on the seat beside Dad and me and laid down again, fast asleep in no time.

Dad looked at her and laughed. "Looks like she's feeling at home already."

"Yes, I think you're right," I said.

"How are you doing, J?"

Without giving it a thought I said, "Actually, okay; I'm doin' okay."

Yes, it was a long ride. Grapevines hung on lines, fruit bulging; Lake Erie twinkled in the western sun; smoke stacks near Buffalo reminded me of Pittsburgh. We took 33 east through places like Corfu and Pembroke and Batavia and North Chili, where we turned north again for a few miles. Spencerport looked sleepy and much smaller than Ellwood, but otherwise friendly enough.

"Here we are!" announced Dad as we pulled into the parking lot beside the apartment building. A couple of boys were playing catch outside, and they looked like they knew what they were doing. A good sign.

"That's it," said Dad, "number eight." We took the tarp off the trailer we were pulling and looked at all our stuff. It seemed like an impossible job.

"Let's take a look inside before we unpack; whadaya say?"

"That's fine with me."

There was new carpeting inside that went wall to wall, something I'd never seen before. Our voices echoed through the empty rooms. Dad showed me my bedroom which, like everything else, was painted white. It was actually bigger than my bedroom in Ellwood. We tried the toilet and all the faucets, and they worked.

There was a knock at the door. "Hello! Anyone home?" It was a tall gentleman with a brush-like mustache and big ears.

"Hi folks. I'm Mr. Genovese."

"Oh, yes," said Dad. "We talked on the phone."

They shook hands, then Mr. Genovese turned to me and extended his hand. "Welcome! You must be Jackie, and that must be Abigail." I reached out and shook his thin, bony, warm hand.

"I have something for you," he said. "It came in the mail today."

I looked at my dad and shrugged my shoulders. "Wow," said Dad, "you must be pretty popular. Maybe Brian sent you a housewarming gift."

"Yeah, maybe," I said, not really convinced that Brian would do such a thing.

"Here you go," said Mr. Genovese, handing me a square box wrapped in shopping bag paper.

"I'm gonna bring in the first load, J," said Dad. "I'll be back in a minute."

"Okay," I said, staring at the box and turning it over in my hands. What could it be? I wondered. Abigail tilted her head to one side as if she wondered as well. I sat down on the floor and tore through the brown paper. There was a thin cardboard box inside. I opened it and found a crumpled-up wad of the *Ellwood City Ledger*. When I took the paper out, I discovered another box inside. I placed the inner box on the floor. It looked like the kind of box you'd find at Kimpel's Jeweler's, but I couldn't imagine anyone sending me jewelry.

I picked it up and placed the box in the palm of my hand, then lifted the lid. When I saw what was inside, I smiled. Then I laughed. Then I cried and smiled again. It was a buckeye. I held it in my hand and examined its smooth, curved surface. I rubbed it against my cheek and tossed it in the air, catching it with my left hand. "Thanks," I said under my breath. I put it deep in my pocket and then ran to the front door. "Hey, Dad, guess what?"

Charlie No Face

About the Author

David B. Seaburn is the author of two previous novels, *Darkness is as Light* and *Pumpkin Hill*. He is also a psychologist, marriage and family therapist as well as an ordained minister. Seaburn and his wife live in Spencerport, New York.

See more at http://www.davidbseaburn.com

If you enjoyed *Charlie No Face* consider these other fine books from Savant Books and Publications:

A Whale's Tale by Daniel S. Janik
Tropic of California by R. Page Kaufman
The Village Curtain by Tony Tame
Dare to Love in Oz by William Maltese
The Interzone by Tatsuyuki Kobayashi
Today I am a Man by Larry Rodness
The Bahrain Conspiracy by Bentley Gates
Called Home by Gloria Schumann
Kanaka Blues by Mike Farris
First Breath edited by Z. M. Oliver
Poor Rich by Jean Blasiar
The Jumper Chronicles by W. C. Peever
William Maltese's Flicker by William Maltese
My Unborn Child by Orest Stocco
Last Song of the Whales by Four Arrows
Perilous Panacea by Ronald Klueh
Falling but Fulfilled by Zachary M. Oliver
Mythical Voyage by Robin Ymer
Hello, Norma Jean by Sue Dolleris
Still Life with Cat and Mouse by Sheila McGraw
Richer by Jean Blasiar

Soon to be Released:

Ammon's Horn by G. Amati
In Dire Straits by Jim Currie
In the Himalayan Nights by Anoop Chandola
Number One Bestseller by Brian Morley
Manifest Intent by Mike Farris
Blood Money by Scott Mastro
The Treasure of La Escondida by Carolyn Kingson
Wretched Land by Mila Komarnisky
My Two Wives and Three Husbands by S. Stanley Gordon
Chan Kim by Ilan Herman

http://www.savantbooksandpublications.com

12251563R00144

Made in the USA
Charleston, SC
22 April 2012